Castle Bookshop, Ludlow, 14/10/2n

CW00546972

THE MORTIME

THE MORTIMER AFFAIR
Joan de Joinville's Story

Alice Mitchell

YouCaxton Publications
Oxford & Shrewsbury

Copyright © Alice Mitchell 2020
The Author asserts the moral right to
be identified as the author of this work.

ISBN 978-1-913425-24-1

Published by YouCaxton Publications 2020

YCBN: 01

All rights reserved. No part of this publication may be reproduced, stored in a retrieval system, or transmitted in any form or by any means, electronic, mechanical, photocopying, recording or otherwise, without the prior permission of the author.

This book is sold subject to the condition that it shall not, by way of trade or otherwise, be lent, resold, hired out or otherwise circulated without the author's prior consent in any form of binding or cover other than that in which it is published and without a similar condition including this condition being imposed on the subsequent purchaser.

YouCaxton Publications

enquiries@youcaxton.co.uk

For my own Roger,
(1946-2019)
who enjoyed this story

Contents

The Mortimers of Wigmore

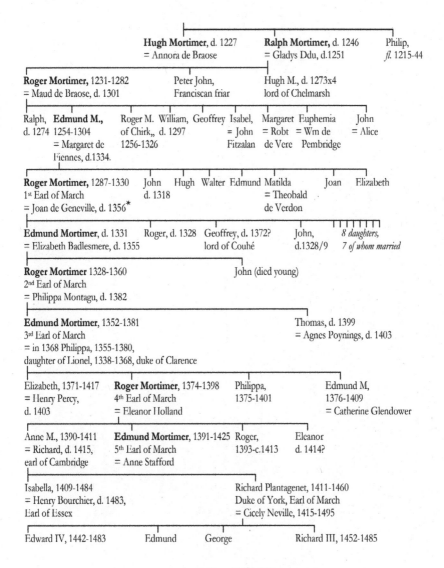

Hugh Mortimer, d. 1227
= Annora de Braose

Ralph Mortimer, d. 1246
= Gladys Ddu, d.1251

Philip,
fl. 1215-44

Roger Mortimer, 1231-1282
= Maud de Braose, d. 1301

Peter John,
Franciscan friar

Hugh M., d. 1273x4
lord of Chelmarsh

Ralph, d. 1274   **Edmund M.,** 1254-1304 = Margaret de Fiennes, d.1334.

Roger M. of Chirk,, 1256-1326   William, d. 1297   Geoffrey   Isabel, = John Fitzalan   Margaret = Robt de Vere   Euphemia = Wm de Pembridge   John = Alice

---

Roger Mortimer, 1287-1330
1st Earl of March
= Joan de Geneville, d. 1356*

John d. 1318   Hugh   Walter   Edmund   Matilda = Theobald de Verdon   Joan   Elizabeth

---

Edmund Mortimer, d. 1331
= Elizabeth Badlesmere, d. 1355

Roger, d. 1328   Geoffrey, d. 1372? lord of Couhé   John, d.1328/9   *8 daughters, 7 of whom married*

Roger Mortimer 1328-1360
2nd Earl of March
= Philippa Montagu, d. 1382

John (died young)

Edmund Mortimer, 1352-1381
3rd Earl of March
= in 1368 Philippa, 1355-1380,
daughter of Lionel, 1338-1368, duke of Clarence

Thomas, d. 1399
= Agnes Poynings, d. 1403

Elizabeth, 1371-1417
= Henry Percy,
d. 1403

Roger Mortimer, 1374-1398
4th Earl of March
= Eleanor Holland

Philippa,
1375-1401

Edmund M,
1376-1409
= Catherine Glendower

Anne M., 1390-1411
= Richard, d. 1415,
earl of Cambridge

Edmund Mortimer, 1391-1425
5th Earl of March
= Anne Stafford

Roger,
1393-c.1413

Eleanor
d. 1414?

Isabella, 1409-1484
= Henry Bourchier, d. 1483,
Earl of Essex

Richard Plantagenet, 1411-1460
Duke of York, Earl of March
= Cicely Neville, 1415-1495

Edward IV, 1442-1483   Edmund   George   Richard III, 1452-1485

Ian Mortimer, 23 May 2019

***Geneville is an alternative spelling of Joinville**

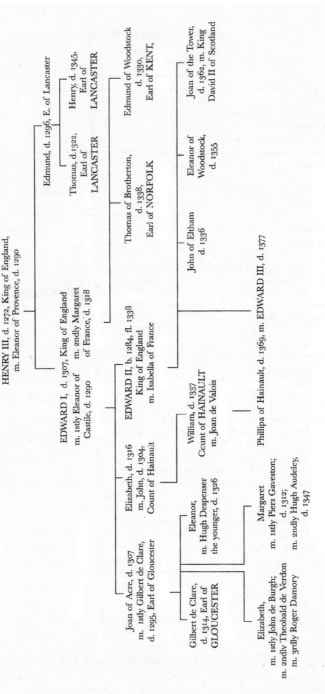

THE ENGLISH ROYAL FAMILY

HENRY III, d. 1272, King of England,
m. Eleanor of Provence, d. 1290

Edmund, d. 1296, E. of Lancaster

Thomas, d. 1322, Earl of LANCASTER

Henry, d. 1345, Earl of LANCASTER

EDWARD I, d. 1307, King of England
m. 1stly Eleanor of Castile, d. 1290

EDWARD II, b. 1284, fl. 1338 King of England
m. Isabella of France

Edmund of Woodstock d. 1330, Earl of KENT,

Thomas of Brotherton, d. 1338, Earl of NORFOLK

Eleanor of Woodstock, d. 1355

John of Eltham d. 1336

Joan of the Tower, d. 1362, m. King David II of Scotland

Phillipa of Hainault, d. 1369, m. EDWARD III, d. 1377

Elizabeth, d. 1316 m. John, d. 1304, Count of Hainault

William, d. 1337, Ccunt of HAINAULT m. Joan de Valois

Joan of Acre, d. 1307 m. 1stly Gilbert de Clare, d. 1295, Earl of Gloucester

Eleanor, m. Hugh Despenser the younger, d. 1326

Margaret m. 1stly Piers Gaveston; d. 1312; m. 2ndly Hugh Audeley, d. 1347

Gilbert de Clare, d. 1314, Earl of GLOUCESTER

Elizabeth, m. 1stly John de Burgh; m. 2ndly Theobald de Verdon m. 3rdly Roger Damory

Diagram from Ian Mortimer's 'The Greatest Traitor'

THE BARONS AND EARLS

Geoffrey de Joinville
(Joan's grandfather)

Roger Mortimer of Wigmore
(Joan's husband) - referred to as Roger of W in this list.

Roger Mortimer of Chirk
(Roger of W's uncle)

Edmund Mortimer of Wigmore
(Joan's father in law)

Piers Gaveston
(Edward II's favourite who becomes Earl of Cornwall)

Roger Damory and Hugh Audley
(both passing favourites of Edward II)

Hugh Despenser the Elder
(who becomes Earl of Winchester)

Hugh Despenser the Younger
(his son who becomes Edward II's final favourite)

Bartholomew of Badlesmere
(father in law to Joan's eldest son, Edmund)

Thomas, Earl of Lancaster
(first cousin of Edward II)

Henry of Lancaster
(Thomas' younger brother who inherits the title)

Guy de Beauchamp, Earl of Warwick
(an enemy of Gaveston and indeed the King)

Aymer de Valence, Earl of Pembroke
(a trusted adviser to King Edward II)

Humphrey de Bohun, Earl of Hereford
(Constable of England)

Gilbert de Clare (the young) Earl of Gloucester

John de Warenne, Earl of Surrey
(whose father was a cousin of Roger of W)

Edmund Fitzalan, Earl of Arundel
(the grandson of Isabella, one of Roger of W's aunts)

Robert Clifford, First Lord of the Honour of Skipton,
and Marshal of England, and his son Roger who both
supported the Mortimers

Robert Bruce, Earl of Carrick
(subsequently King of Scotland)

Edward Bruce
(his younger brother and self -styled King of Ireland)

The Earls of Moray and Douglas
(the Bruces' commanders)

The Earl of Ulster
(Robert Bruce's father in law)

Theobald de Verdon
(married to Roger of W's sister, Matilda)

Hugh and Walter Lacy
(kinsfolk of Joan's grandmother)

John Gifford,
Lord of Brimpsfield in Gloucestershire

Edmund of Woodstock, Earl of Kent
(half-brother to Edward II)

Thomas of Brotherton,
Earl of Norfolk (also half-brother to Edward II)

Thomas of Berkeley
(son in law of Joan on marriage to their daughter,
Margaret)

The Earl of Lincoln
The Earl was alive at the time of Edward II's coronation
but the title was not used after his death

PROLOGUE

TRUTH COMES OUT by candlelight. Eventually. For the darkness, even in a monastery, is full of susurration: the rise and fall of rumour, murmur and gossip flapping like the wings of a bat. Can it be true that the old King, buried in Gloucester these five years gone, is alive and well? And what, if anything, does the Dowager Lady Mortimer know of this?

Young Brother Jerome watches her rise slowly from her knees, for she has been praying by the altar. A small woman, though her waist and hips are thickened by many years of childbearing. Dressed in black, for it is barely a year since the death of her beloved elder son. The colour of her hair is hidden, as it is drawn back and hidden beneath her white wimple. Nun-like, yet not a nun. Her gaze is firm and steadfast, her deep-set grey eyes serious, and the strong lines of her forehead, nose and chin resolute.

"Will he see me now?" she asks.

The young brother inclines his head.

"He will, though he sends apologies for not leaving his humble cell and having nowhere better to receive you. He is frail and feels the cold keenly."

"No apology is needed. I have been used to quarters no less bare."

He leads her through the listening cloisters and out beneath ragged, wind-blown clouds punctured by stars, to the monks' dormitory adjacent to the abbey church. An owl, watching for prey, hoots in the distance.

The room is overheated from the glow of a brazier in the corner. The old canon is propped up with cushions in a chair next to his bed, and there is a desk before him supporting a quill pen and the large volume of work she seeks.

He makes a feeble effort to rise but she stalls him and takes a lowly stool next to his chair, scooping his parchment-thin hands into hers.

"My Lady," he says, with moist eyes. "My dear Lady Joan. How good it is to see you! But how very sorry we are for your loss, so soon after his father. Poor Edmund! And what of Geoffrey?"

"Geoffrey is in France. Of course he cannot return. Though he is far from having a hard time of it. But we have Edmund's boy still. He's fine and strong though he is only three years old. Another Roger. We have great hopes of him."

"Come closer, my dear. I do not see as well these days." Brother Benedict peers at her through milky eyes.

"Great hopes of him?" he repeats.

"That he will fully restore our fortunes and reputation. In time."

"And what of the Lord's body, my lady? Have you come to tell me it has arrived back at Wigmore at last?"

She shakes her head.

"I am afraid not. It is still in the Greyfriars' church in Coventry. The King has decided he should not be disturbed again. He must rest in peace there."

The canon presses her hands against his in the silence which follows.

"You have suffered much."

But Lady Joan is unwilling to dwell on this.

"You know that Edmund was pardoned before his untimely death, and we will have Ludlow restored to us, along with my lands in Meath, though we are still waiting on the King's goodwill."

She might have added that this would be mainly due to her own strenuous and protracted efforts in the courts if it happens, but does not. Instead, she hesitates and glances at the vellum bound book on the desk.

"I have come to make a request of you, Brother Benedict."

"Anything, dear lady."

"I want the Chronicle."

Brother Jerome gasps in the background.

"But, forgive me Madame, it is his life's work!"

"Not all of it. Of course not. I would not take that away from you. Only some of the relevant passages pertaining to our dear late Earl of March. Shall we say between the dates of 1320 and 1330?"

"But the book is already bound, my lady!"

"Naturally I would bear the cost of its repair."

Jerome cannot resist a further interruption.

"It would be a total desecration of history!"

Lady Joan turns sharply towards him.

"History is written by men. It does not necessarily reflect the truth. There are plenty of others who are paid to blacken my husband's name. I do not want these outrageous stories to stain the pages of the Wigmore Chronicle."

Benedict gazes at her with sadness.

"I understand, my lady," he says. "You may have these pages; only let me send them to you in an organised fashion. There is to be no tearing out."

She raises his blue-veined hand and kisses it.

"Thank you, and I plead with you to continue to pray for Roger's immortal soul, as I have begged you before, for he does have great need of it."

Brother Jerome is quietly seething when he puts the old canon to bed later.

"How could you agree?" he asks. "How could you relinquish your principles to cover up the truth so easily?"

But Benedict is calm with the wisdom of old age as he meekly accepts the small services Jerome offers him.

"The truth," he says, "but what is the truth? The lady is right. If we are to believe the rumour that the old King lives in a monastery in Italy, then our former lord cannot possibly have murdered him."

He suffers himself to be helped into a nightshirt and nightcap.

"Tittle-tattle," says Jerome, contemptuously.

"I could not deny the poor lady her wish. She has endured so much."

"On account of *him*! Why is she so anxious to excuse him?"

"You are young, Jerome. We cannot fully understand what is in another's mind, especially where love is concerned."

Jerome helps him into bed and smooths down the covers. The fire has died down to embers now. He places one candlestick by the bed and blows out the others. Immediately, the dark shadows leap up again.

"Shall I read to you a little?"

"Not tonight. I feel too tired from the Lady Joan's visit, though it was so good to see her… and looking well again."

He closes his eyes and sighs at his memories.

"It was a dreadful day when they took her and the children. Dreadful. She was so brave."

Jerome sits with him a while, waiting for his breathing to settle into the rhythm of sleep. He thinks it is almost there, when Benedict opens his eyes again and smiles at him.

"Stop fretting, boy," he says. "It is of no concern. The Lady Joan must have the pages and may burn them if she likes. See you obey now!"

"Ten years!" Jerome says in exasperation. "Ten whole years. And such terrible, startling years at that. Erased. Just like that."

Benedict closes his eyes once more, though the ghost of a smile still plays round his lips.

"Tut now!" he says. "Naturally I made a copy."

PART ONE
THE WHEEL TURNS

PART ONE

THE WHEEL TURNS

Chapter 1

MY HANDS STILL shake as I read his letter again:

Beloved wife and dearest lady of my heart, may God commend and keep you this day.

I can no longer deny the extremity we face. Uncle and I are holed up in Shrewsbury Castle. I went out over the black river tonight to speak with the men in the encampment. They are a goodly number but nothing against the might of the Royal Army a few miles away.

It was snowing a little – white flakes stinging our faces as we rode across the bridge – but not enough to settle, though the wind flapping the tents had a keen edge to it. I would not have chosen to campaign this time of year, even though our men are used to the cold and wet after the exigencies of Ireland. Neither will I let them be butchered on my account because of this sorry state of affairs. They trust me implicitly, and I them.

My poor Uncle Roger cannot rely on such. We have heard the Welsh are attacking his castle at Chirk as we speak, and he has had many deserters. By God's wounds! They would not have dared to do so in the past! But mine uncle ages visibly now. I hear him creaking as he walks and I know his old war wounds trouble him more each winter. He is not accustomed to this position of open rebellion against the Crown; I have brought him to it, but we will not fight against impossible odds.

Our only chance is if Lancaster joins us with his army, as he promised to do. But we have waited too many days and nights for him already. The Earl of Pembroke, meanwhile, tries to steer a diplomatic course with the King.

How I wish Piers Gaveston were here now! If he had been allowed to remain the King's favourite, we would never have been brought to this pretty pass, nor suffered the Despensers' control over the King. For all his faults, Piers was a fine fighter and true to his word. And what

1

harm did he ever really do? You remember how good he was to us, Joan? Poor Piers. He did not deserve his fate.

If we fail now, as it seems we must, young Hugh Despenser will be recalled from exile and be stronger and more malicious than ever.

So I fear for us all in the Marches – for you, dear Joan, and our family especially.

I fear Lancaster will not come because of his petty quarrel with Badlesmere, whom I naturally supported. How could I not, when our son has married into the family? But, because of this, Thomas of Lancaster will not leave Pontefract, even though he agrees with our cause. What a puffed-up peacock he has become! No, not a peacock. I will not dignify him with the name of our beautiful Wigmore birds. A surly toad more like, belching in and out from the safety of his lily pad, making a great deal of noise but moving nowhere. Well did Piers nickname him 'The Fiddler'!

But enough! Whatever the Earl of Lancaster may be: he has not come, is not coming, and will not come. So tomorrow I shall ride to the manor of Betton Strange, where the King has taken lodgings. He has promised me safe conduct and I may take twenty companions. The Earls of Pembroke, Arundel and Surrey have all pressed him to negotiate with us. I have no doubt it will be for our lives. They tell me the King is mighty sore and enraged. At best, we face imprisonment. But surely he cannot discount past services and will be merciful in the end, providing Despenser is not with him already? Pembroke has assured me it is likely he will relent, and Arundel has promised it will be so. However, the Earl of Hereford, who has been with us till lately, suspects this will not be the case, and is marching north to muster more support.

I am so sorry, my dear and gentle wife! But you, above anyone, know how loyal I have been to the King: supporting him all through the Gaveston years, restoring his law and order in Ireland, standing with him at Bannockburn, and keeping our own Welsh Marches under control. It is our liege Edward who has been faithless to the Crown. Our loyalty remains to the Crown, if not the King, because he rules so unwisely, and I have had to agree, in the end, because of Hugh Despenser.

Our wheel of fortune is bound to turn downward. Let us pray it may rise once more. Be brave, dearest heart, hold fast and true, whatever they may throw at you, none of which you will have ever deserved. Young Edmund and Roger are with me and are well. Comfort my mother, if you are able, as you always have, and be strong for our little brood left at home. I shall write again as soon as I am able.

Finally, I urge you to repair to the Abbey where you will be safe under the protection of the Church. May God grant we meet again soon, under happier circumstances.

Your most true and loving, loyal Lord,
Roger Mortimer of Wigmore, Ludlow and Trim.

The letter is dated the 20th of January, in the fifteenth year of the reign of our Gracious King, Edward the Second, and sealed with Roger's personal seal. Two days ago. By now, negotiations with the King must be well under way. I have heard nothing since, but have given orders to the household to make ready to move to the abbey.

But now I hear a shriek from the Great Hall below. This is followed by the laboured breath of my good servant, Avice, who carries excess flesh, lumbering up the steps to my solar.

"Madame!" she cries, bursting into the room. "There are hundreds of men at arms approaching, and Hywel says our lord is not amongst them. They wear the King's livery! He has ridden hard up from the town to warn us."

"Dear God save us! So soon?" I rise and cross to the window.

The castle stands high on a ridge so I have a good view. The men at arms have already left the town and are winding their way up the hill. I estimate they are merely between fifty and one hundred, but that is daunting enough. Their pikes glint in the sunlight and their horses' breath steams in the cold air. It is too late to seek the sanctuary of the abbey.

My lord must be in custody, but the King's response is far quicker than expected, and this does not bode well. There is nothing we can do other than face the men and submit to the King's will. For I know it is likely their leader will bear letters of appointment from the King, to present to Roger's castellan for admittance.

"What shall we do, Madame? Whatever can we do?" wails Avice.

"Calm yourself, Avice," I beg, with a composure I do not feel. "Bring young John and the girls to me, and we will gather together in the Hall to greet our illustrious visitors. Send for my knight and men at arms too, if you can, though they are likely to be detained in the bailey."

When I descend the steps to the Great Hall, I find only my two clerks and my chaplain, Richard Judas, there beside John. John will be a tall boy soon, with the darkly handsome looks of his father. He stands worried and frowning now, trying his utmost to look more than his thirteen years. I want to hug him to me but let him stand proudly by my side, clenching his fists. With the elder sons away with their father, and the next born, Geoffrey, in his grandmother's house in France, I know he is conscious of being the only male representative of his family present and wants to protect his mother and remaining six sisters, who join us in the hall. Little Joan comes first with Isabella, and then Catherine, holding the hands of Agnes and Beatrice, followed by Blanche toddling along behind with Avice.

It is one Alan de Charlton who strides into the Great Hall as if he owns it and makes a cursory bow, failing to be charmed by the scene before his eyes. Sir Richard de Burgh, my own faithful knight, and Ockley and Bullesdon, our men at arms, are with him, but are flanked by Charlton's guards.

"My lady, I bid you good day."

I reply with deliberate coolness and an eye on his sword.

"Your manners, sir, are sadly lacking. You have entered the castle of our most respected Lord Mortimer wearing a weapon at your side. How dare you not surrender it to our gatekeeper?"

"Madame, I beg your humble pardon, but this is not so."

"Do my eyes deceive me then?"

"I fear not, my lady. But I am ordered to inform you this castle is no longer in the ownership of the said Lord Mortimer, and is in forfeit to the King, by reason of Mortimer's rebellion and great treachery."

"You are mistaken, sir. My husband is no traitor."

Charlton passes over the letters of appointment from the King, as I expected.

"As you will see, Madame, these letters bear the Royal seal and fully authorise my actions."

The notice regarding the forfeiture of the castle and our lands is only to be expected. But I am also informed that my husband, Lord Roger Mortimer of Wigmore, and his uncle, Lord Roger Mortimer of Chirk, are on their way to the Tower of London, there to await trial for treason at the King's pleasure. My heart beats a little faster.

"Well, all seems to be in order," I say, "though I repeat: my lord is no traitor, as he has fought for the honour of the Crown, and I suspect you understand that perfectly well!"

Alan de Charlton inclines his head with a show of meekness.

"Nevertheless, I needs must carry out the King's orders."

"Then we shall retire to our abbey in the meantime, and leave you free to do what you will."

"I am afraid not, my lady."

I tilt my chin.

"May we join the Dowager Lady Mortimer at Radnor then – in order to break this sad news to her gently?"

In truth, I believe Alan de Charlton feels some compassion, but it only serves to limit his patience.

"No, you may not. The castle of Radnor is also in forfeiture to the King. However, your younger children will be escorted to the Dowager Lady there and remain in her care."

He consults his papers.

"John, Joan and Isabella are of an age to accompany yourself into captivity."

A cold chill steals over me.

"May I not take all of my family to Ludlow, which is my own rightful inheritance?"

"No, my lady. It is no longer yours since you married Mortimer, as you well know. You are most likely to have been complicit in his perfidy and must come with us."

This was appalling. How could the King stoop so low?

"You cannot imprison my mother, nor me. We have done nothing wrong!" yells John, red in the face but struggling with tears.

Thank God he is too young to wear a sword. I lay a firm hand on his shoulder.

"Hush, John! I am sure our appeal to the King, which I shall make through our gracious Queen, who has ever been a good friend to me, will not fall on deaf ears. All will be straightened out in time. It is not like our dear King to cause unnecessary suffering to womenfolk. It is not in his nature. But for now we must obey his messenger."

"Prudently said, my lady," says Charlton, with considerable relief.

"So where are you taking us?"

"To Hampshire, my Lady."

I gasp.

"So far? In the middle of winter? With the children? You must allow us to take warm clothing and provisions for the journey, at the very least!"

"You are to take as little as possible, but warm clothing will certainly be needed in the waggon."

I put Avice in charge of the other women packing for the children, and dispatch John to his brothers' rooms with Richard Judas, who will see he gathers up warm clothing and a few possessions. John asks if he can take his pet kestrel and it hurts to say "no", seeing his face fall, and his ongoing struggle to hold back tears. An armed guard accompanies each one of us to our rooms.

The fellow guarding me stands outside the door to the solar when I say I must change my robes, but he leaves the door open all the same and turns his back briefly.

My mind is reeling…what to take? Certainly warm gowns and furs. Some towels and linen, combs and hairpins. I feel a rising tide of panic, looking round my bedchamber with its beautiful green bedcover embroidered with owls, its fine Flemish hanging tapestries and the yellow curtains embroidered with red roses. No doubt I will see none of these again, and the realisation brings a sharp pang of regret. But what am I thinking of, indulging in sorrow over such trappings? I was happy here, lying beside my lord, and now he is shut up in the Tower, with his life in danger.

He said I must hold fast and so I must – for the sake of the children – even though my heart beats with dread and fear.

I must be practical: a psalter for comfort, my embroidery, a much-loved ivory carving of the Virgin? No, no, pens and parchment will be more use, along with my personal seal. I shall take my books for solace. But the guard has turned now and is hovering behind me, so close I can smell his foul breath.

"Just clothes," he says. "No luxuries. No writing materials. And you won't be needing these," abruptly taking my four books away.

Dear God, what are they intending to do with me? Surely not to expose me in a cage as the barbarous old King did with Robert Bruce's sister and mistress? I cannot believe our young King Edward would be so cruel, and must try to hold on to that.

I have to bite my lip when we are all marched out to the two waggons drawn up in the inner bailey. Catherine, Agnes and Beatrice are taken away into the first carriage, along with some of my maidservants. Blanche is roughly taken from my arms to join them. I am not even allowed to say goodbye properly, and my heart is breaking for the children, even though they do not fully understand what is happening. At least the little ones know their servants and their grandmother. It is still exceedingly hard, and I struggle with tears now.

Six men of my household are to be allowed to ride beside my waggon, including my chaplain and knight, which is a comfort. The Lady de Burgh, wife of my knight, Sir Richard, will accompany me inside, along with Avice and John, Joan and Isabella. Both women are weeping.

The peacocks shriek as we move off past the barns, the granaries, cow byres, pig sties and haylofts in the outer ward, watched by the gawping, frightened eyes of remaining servants. The birds have never sounded so mournful. I fix my eyes on the whitewashed walls of our castle and chapel. What will happen to Wigmore now? My much-loved comfortable home. Will I ever see it again?

I hold on tightly to my lord's letter, which I have stuffed into the bosom of my warmest rich-velvet and brocade gown. Everyone is tired and Isabella is sobbing bitterly. Of an age indeed! She is barely ten and has always been a sensitive child.

I help Avice and Lady de Burgh bed the children down and wrap them in miniver furs against the cold, uttering as many comforting words as I can.

"Hush now! It will only be for a little while we are apart." I wish I had more confidence in that.

The waggon jolts along uncomfortably, despite our cushions, reacting to every bump and rut upon the bad road. Hampshire is such a long way away.

Chapter 2

I AM AWARE you do not know who I am. Few people do. You may or may not be familiar with some of the earls' names. You will certainly have heard of my beloved but infamous husband, and may well consider him a traitor, though he was not always so...

Yet now, my lord is told the King has spared their lives. Only a week before, he and his uncle were dragged from their cells to Westminster Hall for trial. The verdict was not a surprise for any Contrariant, as they now call them. Both men to be hung for treason – for the taking and plundering of Gloucester and burning Bridgnorth, as if in war. Displaying the Mortimer banner against the King, as if in war. Well, of course they were in war – civil war – as many barons had been before them. The Earl of Pembroke appeared grievously mistaken in his prediction of mercy.

The rest of the news is equally dire. Humphrey de Bohun, the Earl of Hereford – who left them in Shrewsbury to gather more support, hoping to meet up with Lancaster in the north – is dead. The Constable of all England, no less. A noble man in every sense, and former brother-in-law to the King. Killed excruciatingly and not at all fairly in battle. A pike man below the Borough Bridge skewered his anus by thrusting upwards between the planks in cowardly fashion. That was not right for such a man. Sir Roger Damory also died of his battle wounds. So much for the love of a King towards a former favourite.

The King's own first cousin, the Earl of Lancaster, was captured and beheaded. He was not allowed to speak at his makeshift trial, conducted by the Despensers on behalf of the King. That was shocking. It was the first time an English Earl had been executed by the King for well over two hundred years. It has not stopped there either: my son Edmund's father-in-law, Baron Badlesmere, is also beheaded, after being dragged through the streets of Canterbury.

Several others, including Sir John Gifford and the very young Roger Clifford, barely into his twenties, have all met the same fate. These are men who risked their lives for the King at Bannockburn, but supported my lord. Many, many others are imprisoned or heavily fined, with lands taken away from them and their wives and children incarcerated for good measure, as am I.

King Edward has ordered a complete review of my lord's government in Ireland, out of spite. The only result of that will be for the land to go backwards. Yet Roger's life is suddenly spared. It seems the King may have listened to what Pembroke said after all, and had a change of heart – possibly from the memory of past loyal services. But I wonder how long it will be before he changes his mind again. For all of England is in the Despensers' hands now, and they will restrict everyone else's access to Edward, that is for certain.

The two Roger Mortimers, uncle and nephew, are only spared for life imprisonment.

I know that part of my lord would prefer the block; for what sort of life can it be, locked up in a barren, high cell in the White Tower on 3d a day for everyone? Miserable rations and nothing to his name, except the shirt he stands up in, which must stink. There is only Richard of Monmouth, his faithful squire, to share his moods and gloom. His uncle is kept separately with no communication allowed between them.

Everything my Lord Mortimer of Wigmore owned is forfeited for the King: all of the horses, dogs and birds, as well as every last cow and sheep. Meanwhile, I am imprisoned with John, Joan and Isabella in Hampshire – no-one knew where then – but in extremely poor conditions. Our sons Edmund and Roger are prisoners in Windsor. Geoffrey has the sense not to return from France. My elder daughters, Maud and Margaret, remain under the protection of their husbands, whilst the four youngest are with Roger's mother. Even she was set to lose her rightful inheritance of Radnor until the King relented, no doubt put to shame by the spirited protests of a feisty old lady.

I am told Wigmore is a shell of its former self. The King has no need of a castle there and could have left it with me. But no – it has to be a nominally royal farmhouse. Naturally they have taken all the armour, the mangonels and weaponry. The abbey has been stripped of all the belongings hidden there; I can visualise the bodies in the crypt turning in their graves and Brother Benedict, the scribe, wondering how best to phrase the account of these calamitous events in his chronicle. All opposition to the Despensers is crushed. The Mortimers were the last of it and might as well be gone also.

Even now, Roger must feel his muscles wasting and know his skin has grown pale. He will try to exercise in his cell but it must be hard going. How he will miss his horses and his Irish wolfhounds, the exhilaration of being in the field and the adrenalin of battle. Us, too, of course: the children, the comfort of his own fire, food and faithful servants and myself.

He will be driven mad by not having any fresh air in his lungs and the wind on his face. When he sleeps, I wonder if he will dream of his grandmother and her wonderful tales? Lady Maud was the granddaughter of the renowned Crusader knight, William Marshall, who acted as Regent when the young Henry III came to the throne. She was the widow of Roger's grandfather, whom he had been named for, the first Baron of Wigmore, and scourge of the Welsh. He supported King Henry against Simon Montfort and was instrumental in the death of that rebel at the Battle of Evesham. Because of this, he was allowed to send the head of Montfort home to Maud as a trophy and was much rewarded by the King.

My Roger had seen the skull as a child – Maud showed it to him before he left home at seven to train as a knight with his uncle – and he had been much impressed by the story. No doubt at that time, he imagined he would always be loyal to the King.

Chapter 3

I REALISED LATER, even though I was never to meet her, that Maud's childhood stories had been a seminal influence on Roger. My grandfather, Sir Geoffrey de Joinville, a considerable Crusader knight in his own right, sowed the seeds of the course of my own life more directly. Two summers before Roger was shown Montfort's skull and was sent to his uncle, Piers de Joinville, my father, died leaving no male heir.

Or at least I was told he was "commanded to God", as they say. Being a child of six, I assumed he had gone away to fight an important battle for God and would hopefully return unscathed. After all, he often did go away to fight and at this moment was in France, as was my mother. It was Avice who had to disabuse me of this notion.

My dear Avice, the nursemaid who was closer to me than my mother, and me to her. She was childless, with her first and only baby stillborn six years ago, yet still able to supply me with maternal milk at that time. Avice, who was so much younger then, even though she had been old to bear a child at thirty. She was slimmer then, too, and even pretty with her long dark hair yet to go grey. She had the gentlest of smiles and warmest of cuddles. It was she who had to tell me that Father was dead.

What did this mean?

"Well," said Avice seriously, "everyone must die when God chooses them. With God's grace, this will not be until our fifties."

I knew already this was far from true.

"No, they do not, cannot, ever come back. It is like Bella, the lovely old wolfhound that used to grace our hearth, patient and sleeping, even when you pulled her tail – though you were warned not to. Dogs become older more quickly than we do, and die sooner as a result."

"But where do they all go?"

"To God and to Heaven," said Avice, "although they may have to spend some time in a place called Purrga-tory to repent of their sins, which is why we pray for their souls."

"Bella didn't have any sins," I complained indignantly, and Avice agreed that Bella would have gone straight to heaven. She seemed less certain about my father, though added he was no doubt a very good man. Anyway, whether in the P place or Heaven or worse, he was not coming back.

"Would mama marry again?" I wondered. Avice rather hoped not, but said, even if she did, there was still the question of Sir Geoffrey's inheritance to be sorted and it would not go to her. I was the eldest of three girls. Although it would have been customary to divide the land and the monies between us equally, my grandfather had decided to settle all of it on me and pay for my two younger sisters to embrace the religious life in a nunnery. This would mean I was very well endowed to make a good marriage in time.

Consequently, we were summoned to Ireland by my grandfather, who wished to take my education in hand. This was an enormous decision for him to put his trust in being able to educate a little girl, but of course I had no idea of its revolutionary thinking at the time. The summons sounded almost as bad as being commanded by God. Avice was instructed to ready me and herself, and my mother would join us there shortly, after the funeral in France.

So off we went to Meath in Ireland, where Baron Joinville was Lord of Trim. I think Avice was secretly as frightened as I was, having never set sail across any sea, not to mention going to such a wild, inhospitable land into the bargain.

We sailed from Bristol in a sturdy vessel which I believe was called a cog, and were fortunate with the voyage as it was midsummer and not too rough. I was not ill, though Avice was, dreadfully, even though she desperately tried to suppress it and clutched at her St Christopher medal throughout. I was tired when we arrived in the port of Dublin, as we had set sail at dawn and it was now pitch dark. I believe we were met by a party of the Baron's men at arms, and put straight into the small but richly cushioned waggon, which was to take us to Trim, rumbling over rough roads through the night; but I was already half asleep in Avice's arms and remember little of that.

What I do recall is being woken in the morning and poking my tousled head out of the curtains to see I had slept within the most massive, white-towered castle in the world, or so it seemed to me then. I was not sure how many towers there were, as my counting was poor, but they were bigger and taller than those at Ludlow and the crows circling above them looked like tiny black specks, though I was not so naïve as to be unaware they were in fact big birds.

Inside the castle everything was steps: steps, dark corridors and yet more winding steps. Outside, there were insistent bells ringing from the Augustinian abbey over the river, marking out the hours and the days with their regular tolling.

Grandfather soon took care of the counting, and I quickly learnt to read under his tutelage. Of course, he employed a diligent tutor as well: a young monk from the Black Friary on the edge of the town, but Grandfather himself would test me every week when he was resident in the castle, and always on his return. I soon began to ride well and he would take me on horseback through the town so the people could see his young heiress. He also told me about the world, the Crusades and the many wonders he had seen on his travels.

When first I saw him I was a little afraid, for he was a big, solidly built man with a somewhat brooding look and an outright manner of speech. With me, he was nothing other than kindly, however, and my progress pleased him so much it made him smile broadly and praise me warmly. He told me I was a clever little person and I was relieved not to disappoint him.

He had wolfhounds too – great Irish ones with long, grey bodies and black noses – who slept before the fire, and he was delighted I was not at all frightened of them but liked to sit amongst them and nuzzle their grizzled beards.

Grandmother Matilda – a Lacy rather than a Mortimer – drilled me in needlework skills, which I did not in any way find as entertaining as riding, though I recognised their worth and in later years, especially in my confinement, I find surprising comfort in the mindlessness and patience required. Grandmother was rather a strict old lady, less indulgent toward me than Grandfather, and she used to make me take out the stitches and rework them if they were not neat enough. I remember that still!

What else do I remember? Mother visiting from time to time in her widow's weeds. Mother with her sadness, sweetness, and elegant French. Avice and I were relieved to hear she had no wish to remarry, at least not straightaway. Avice remained with me. Her French was not as elegant as Mama's by any means, and she could not get her head around what I was learning, but she was warm and tender and constant. Mama suggested I have a change of maidservant, but I would not hear of it and went into a huge tantrum at the suggestion, so the idea was dropped.

My younger sisters remained back home in Ludlow. At first I missed them; then they faded into little girls no longer known or remembered clearly. I was in Trim for over two years, and it was a formative period for a six- to nine-year-old-girl. By the time I returned to Ludlow, I was confident, highly educated for a girl, a little too sharp, and thought I knew absolutely everything. My mother was of the opinion my manners needed a great deal more refinement.

I missed Grandpa and the wolfhounds. But Avice was still with me, adoring me unconditionally, as always, and she stayed with me long after I had achieved my excellent marriage.

Chapter 4

THE SUN HAD barely risen but the manor house was already bustling. Servants hastily kicked new life into fires, brought basins of water for washing, and laid out riding robes and cloaks. There was bread and cheese to fortify them for the journey, and their swords to guard them on the road. In the stable, grooms were saddling their palfreys and strapping bundles on a packhorse. When young Roger Mortimer came out of the dim hall into the morning light, he took a deep breath of the fresh and mild air. It bode well to be a fine day.

"Nervous, lad?" grinned his uncle, who was also called Roger.

"A little," he admitted.

"Don't worry if her face looks like the arse-end of a mule! It's a damned fine match…you can always blow the candles out. Let's just hope she has a sound constitution, good child-bearing hips and isn't averse to a laugh or two!"

Young Richard of Monmouth was leading their horses out and overheard them.

"I've heard tell she's passing comely," he said, "and a lively, merry, strong wench."

"That may be. We'll see."

Uncle Roger mounted up and waved Richard away impatiently, bending over to tighten his own girth with one leg confidently cocked up on the saddle. At forty-four, he was a big black bear of a man with strong, war-scarred features and a tough, muscular frame – the kind of man anyone would feel safe with on the road, sword or no sword. The servant saddling up behind him was only needed to lead the packhorse. His nephew mounted, too, smiling ruefully.

At thirteen, it was high time for him to be betrothed and he knew it would make little difference what he thought of his bride to be. His parents, who would meet them at Ludlow today, had laboured hard on his behalf for this match. At fourteen, I was the sole heiress of my rich grandfather, and Roger's father, Edmund Mortimer, was in need of money. Wigmore and Ludlow united into one would cement the Mortimers' power base in the Marches, and came with lands in Ireland too. Roger laughed as Richard made a lewd sign.

"You can come to the wedding," he said, "and bow down before us!"

"Except today," his uncle interrupted them. "He has to stay here and get that young boy of mine back on a horse. Mind you knock some sense into him or I'll want to know why."

Richard made an even ruder sign behind Uncle Roger's back, but was grinning ear to ear at his friend as they clattered out of the courtyard through the stone gatehouse and over the drawbridge, scattering squawking hens and startling a couple of crows from the timbers of the manor roof.

"You're a touch hard on him, Uncle. He's only seven."

"What, young Monmouth? Acts like it sometimes! You know I've got eyes in the back of my head."

But he spoke in a jovial manner as he rose up and down in his saddle.

"You know I mean your little son, Roger."

"You were only seven when you came to me, lad."

"And I've learnt a lot since then."

"Aye. Do you remember that first day when I asked if you could ride? You were so damned insulted. 'Course I can,' says you! Then I took the reins out of your hands and told you to ride with your legs and not hold the pommel. You made a decent shot at it but fell off the first time the pony swerved."

"I remember. You roared with laughter but then you came and caught me up in your arms, asking if anything was hurt apart from my pride."

His uncle nodded.

"You certainly didn't weep and wail. In fact you kicked your legs in fury to be set down and your fists were clenched tight. You got straight back on and swore it wouldn't happen again, and you know what?"

"No?"

"Well, of course it did, but not that many times. You were a quick learner."

"You told me I had to do it – to learn to ride with my legs – if I ever wanted to carry a lance and a shield as well as handle the reins."

"Your little face was very determined. Set lips and a frown. Still is, come to that, when you're concentrating and have forgotten your sense of humour."

There was a short silence as they picked their way uphill on the rutted track. The trees were coming into new leaf with that fresh shade of green that is never repeated, and the only sounds to be heard apart from the creaking of the saddles were birdsong and the running of a small brook close by. Uncle Roger's dark eyes had lost some of their joviality.

"My boy's not like that," he said at last. "Always running off to hide in his mother's skirts like a milksop. Always afraid of me. Will hardly say 'boo' to a goose! Maybe we had him too late in life. Sometimes I even wonder if he's really mine, though he has the Mortimer looks. He would have been better suited as Edmund's Roger, and you mine. You always think your children will be just like you, but they rarely are. Strange but true. You only have to look at the royal houses for that."

Roger was uncertain how to reply. His uncle was not usually in such a reflective mood. He was spared by him gathering up his reins at the top of the rise.

"Ground's a touch smoother here. Race you to the pond by the pine!"

Then he was off. Roger followed him and despite the lack of notice soon gained on him. The wind rushed past his ears, the short sword in its scabbard banged his legs and his cloak billowed behind him like a red flag. He loved riding and he knew and trusted his mount well. She was surefooted, even when given her head and throwing up clods of earth. By the time they pulled up at the Scots pine, he had overtaken his uncle and was a good four horses' lengths ahead.

"You didn't let me win, did you?" he accused him.

"Never!" His uncle was breathing hard. "This grey nag is feeling her age, though she rides comfortably enough. And so am I. Well done, lad."

They let their horses drink from the fresh water of the pond and crop a little grass before urging them forward at a gentler pace, once the manservant had caught up, with the packhorse.

"I want you to be my squire, lad, now you've come into your fourteenth year. It's not too young when you have aptitude and application like yours. And I've a mind to take you and Richard Monmouth up to Scotland with me next month to see a bit of action – from the sidelines, mind."

"I would be honoured, sir."

"Manners too, eh?" he roared with laughter. "Not like me. The chaplain tells me you excel at reading and Latin. Also not like me. There must be a streak of Edmund in you after all. All very necessary and proper, mind. I see you at court with the King's son, and that not too far off."

Roger's cheeks burnt with pride. What was more, he knew his uncle had the means to bring this about. He was rough and ready, and often uncouth, but he did have the esteem of the King. He was the third son of Maud and the old Roger Mortimer; Edmund was the second and was studious. He was educated at Oxford and bound for the Church. But when the eldest son died, he had to assume the baronetcy and return to Wigmore.

Despite their father's reputation – and *his* father's marriage to the Welsh princess, Gwladys Ddu – the Welsh princes remained pugnacious and troublesome so that the cantrefs of Maelienydd and Elfael in the centre of the Marches were continually changing hands. One prince in particular, Llewellyn ap Gruffyd, was more successful than most in the co-ordination of his fighting men and attacks. The Mortimer brothers led him to his death by tricking him into a parley. The parley did take place but Llewellyn was ambushed by Mortimer men at arms whilst returning to his troops. Edmund had his body laid reverently to rest in the Abbey of Cwmhir, but Uncle Roger sent his head to the King, who was now Edward the First.

After this, Roger was granted the lordship of Chirk and was building a great castle there, under the supervision of the King's master mason himself. The modest, fortified manor at Tedstone Wafre had been brought by his wife Lucy and was only a temporary accommodation until Chirk was ready. He had also been made governor of Bourg and Blaye in Gascony, and was one of the guardians of Prince Edward, the present King's son and heir.

His nephew had enjoyed his training at Tedstone. It was good to have Richard from Monmouth sent there, too, instead of the company of his younger sisters. They wrestled and hawked and went cockfighting together all the time.

Whilst Roger loved his father, Edmund, he had never felt sure how to talk to him, whereas his uncle was bluff but companionable and open to any questions, especially when in his cups before the fire. It was true he could be a hard taskmaster, but he was quick to praise them when it was deserved, and the worse you could get was a cuff round the ear or a bit of a beating. Edmund would not dream of doing that, yet somehow Roger always felt his pained look at any bad behaviour was far worse. You knew where you were with Uncle Roger, fair and square.

Not that Uncle Roger did not have a dark side, hinted at by the black ermine on his coat of arms. After an earlier and equally troublesome Llywellyn's death, he was given wardship of the two sons and heirs – who were later found drowned in the River Dee. Edmund and his wife Margaret preferred to draw a veil over this as being an unfortunate accident. But Uncle Roger told them it was true – he had given the orders for their death – had to, in the same way he had to fight, supplying troops for the King, and put an end to the Welsh wars that beset the Marches.

Your first duty, he told the young Roger and Richard, is to protect and advance your family, and then support your King. It is not necessary to be liked, but very necessary to be feared, because through fear comes respect.

Uncle Roger was going to Scotland next month to assist Prince Edward, who was in his seventeenth year, in his first campaign alongside the King against the Scots. So his boast about seeing his nephew at court before long was not an idle one. Roger thrilled to the idea of going with him, even if it were only to clean mail and armour, and put up tents. I am sure he hoped his betrothal would not get in the way.

By the time the sun was overhead, they met the banks of the Teme at Tenbury, where they stopped for refreshment at an inn, and to rest the horses before crossing the river and following the bank of the river westwards. The weather remained fair and a few hours later they were on their final approach to the town of Ludlow, which lies in a loop of the river below the Clee and Titterstone hills. The approach road is better maintained now, with evidence of tree felling on either side of the high common, but it is likely to be more crowded, too, with ponies and packhorses travelling to and from market, farmers driving noisy sheep, and itinerant friars, peddlers and merchants.

Roger liked Ludlow. It was only a couple of hours' ride from Wigmore and set in the same rolling hills that meant home to him. Its liveliness was refreshing for him after the rural backwater of Tedstone, and no doubt it was very satisfying to think that one day it would be his. He was told he had met me once before and we had played together as children, though he really could not remember it, try as he might, and neither could I.

At last, they crossed the Ludford Bridge and entered the town through the drawbridge at the Broad Gate, walking their horses up Broad Street to the market cross. Roger's senses were hit by a melee of sounds and smells from the traders' stalls. There is wool, leather, and fine cloth on sale as well as tallow, milled corn, butter and cheese, herbs, and eggs. Plenty of hens, goats, pigs and farming tools. There is even a wonderful stall with fine spices and salt, and the shopkeepers put their boards down to sell meat and fish.

But they ignored the general hubbub, the cries of the pie vendors, and the picking hands of the dirty urchins who fell back behind them as they held up their heads high, turned right, crossed the square and rode up to the whitewashed walls of the castle, through the gatehouse, and across the busy outer bailey to the high-towered keep. There the door was opened to admit them into our inner castle's stone womb of safety and privilege.

I had bathed that morning and dressed carefully, choosing my favourite over-mantle of deep green brocade, wearing it over the new, cream, silk gown that Mama had sent for from France. I knew the colour suited my brown wavy hair, which was brushed until it shone, and I felt beautiful, whether I was considered so or not. Now it was all about waiting, and the hours dragged. I scarcely ate any food, though Mama did not object in view of the feast planned for tonight. I kept on pricking my finger over the tiresome embroidery I was given to occupy my hands, if not my mind.

I knew I was the most fortunate of daughters, not only because I was my grandfather's sole heiress, but because he had agreed to betroth me to a young boy of my own age, rather than some bad-tempered, old, widowed knight. Grandfather chose thoughtfully and wisely because we needed to raise a new line of male heirs. The Mortimers were strong and powerful and lived in the bordering county. It was the very best I could have hoped for, and at fourteen it was certainly time to be married. I was told the young Mortimer heir was healthy and strong, handsome even. Yet suddenly, all my new-found confidence – nay, self-importance, to be honest – vanished into mid air.

For I had also heard tales of how young Roger Mortimer's namesake and uncle was a ruthless womaniser and a cruel man, not above murderous acts; although the young Mortimer's parents seemed courteous and civilised enough. Lord Edmund in particular was serious and kindly, and clearly nothing like his notorious younger brother. They were already staying in the castle but Roger's uncle was bringing him today. I feared young Roger might be a younger version of his uncle, having trained with him since the age of seven, though desperately hoped he would be like his father. The whole course of my life would depend upon it.

Mama knew this and understood, so she did not blame me too harshly for being up and down to the window which overlooked the outer bailey, as if I had the fever of St Vitus's dance burning within me.

It was the middle of the afternoon when I saw them ride in. He was not, after all, as big and tall as his uncle. How could he be, at thirteen? But the view of the top of his head told me little about his features, though I noticed he had a good seat and rode well.

"Mama, they are here, they are here! When can we meet?"

"Calm yourself, child!" she laughed at me. "You must let him rest after his ride and greet his parents first, not to mention your Grandfather and myself. Then we might arrange a short meeting for you before the feast."

Our first meeting took place about two hours later on the sward of the inner bailey, close to the gardens where our physician grew his medicinal and culinary herbs. It was quiet and peaceful there, and, suddenly, everyone had been told to leave us alone. We went for a walk with Avice following a respectful distance behind, though I knew her ears would be pricked up and she would be inspecting his every move.

My first impression was that Roger Mortimer was in fact tall for his age and rather thin, but very solemn for a thirteen-year-old, though his manners were surprisingly good considering he had spent several years under his uncle's tuition in a rough manor house. As he began to relax and smile, his face changed and the frowning brows became less prominent. He was good-looking and would grow to be manly enough, though I could still see the boy underneath, which touched me. His eyes were extremely dark like large, brown pools – large enough for me to drown in. Would I sink or swim? I asked Mama and Avice afterwards, would all be well? Neither of them could answer me definitively.

"Are you in agreement with our betrothal?" he asked stiffly.

It was a kindly enough question, for I was supposed to give my consent, however difficult it would be to question my grandfather and mother.

"Why, yes – that is, if you are."

"Most assuredly."

How formal we were!

He meant it, though. I knew I was not a classic beauty, with my high forehead and straight but prominent nose. However, he thought me comely enough, as Richard had said, with the bloom of youth on my skin and my long, brown hair glowing chestnut in the early evening sun. My figure already had soft, womanly curves. Best of all, Roger could see I was not frightened of him. He would not have liked that. He told me later he believed I would not be frightened of anybody. My eyes had the light of humour in them and my jaw a determined set to it. He fancied I would not be what his uncle called "a moaning wench". He would not have liked that. No, I was a healthy, bonny girl and maybe we could be good friends. I felt that, too.

"I think we could get on well," he said, suddenly awkward again with the gaucheness of youth.

We sat on the grass for a while in compliant silence, and I know he was pleased to see that I did not fuss over whether it would stain my fine new robes.

By the time we had ridden and hunted with the new kestrel his father had given us, played chess and draughts together, danced to minstrels, and shared intimate bowls of food at the raised dais with both our families in the Great Hall, I felt much easier with Roger. We found we could talk naturally to one another without restraint. When we said goodbye it was with genuine regret, at least on my part. He kissed me on the hand and embraced me, and I was able to return his warmth and ask his uncle – who did not seem that frightening, after all – to promise to look after him, as he was going to Scotland as a squire soon. Uncle Roger was at his heartiest and best, and told me quite coarsely he would be well out of the line of any bowmen, with the parts that mattered most being well protected. Then he gave me a lewd wink which made me blush with embarrassment.

After they had gone, I lost all my decorum and ran up the steps of the keep to the very top, panting and breathless so I could see them make their way down the broad streets of the town to cross the river, and have a last glimpse of him. There were more in the party now, for Roger's parents were also on their way back to Wigmore with their entourage, and the azure and gold livery of their retinue could be picked out at some distance as they wound their way over the bridge like a bright, undulating caterpillar. I felt relieved, even happy. And so our fate was sealed.

Chapter 5

SIX MEN OUT of the sixty-strong garrison were hung from the battlements before they struck camp that morning. Roger stared as they twitched convulsively like marionettes before their bodies fell still. Their faces turned a livid purplish blue and their swollen tongues protruded out of their mouths. He had imagined it would be instantaneous but this was not the case with some of them. He heard gasping and choking, and saw their hands involuntarily clutch at the ropes. He swallowed hard and thought it was far worse than being run through by a sword; after all, they did this to common criminals. It did not seem fitting for fighting men and did not fit into the tales of chivalry he had been told. Now they swung, turning slightly in the breeze, on creaking ropes.

"How were they chosen?" he asked his uncle, who shrugged.

"Who cares? That's war. You have to make an example of some of those left alive. To show your strength and determination."

The young Lord Edward was standing nearby, and Roger saw he paled for a moment, too. But then Edward's friend, Piers Gaveston, who was a little older, slapped him on the back and said they should celebrate the outcome.

The walls of the castle lay in ruins, whilst fires raged inside and its Constable was led away in chains. Their very first barrier to the western entry of Scotland was no more.

It had taken four days for the castle to fall. By the end of June, Lord Edward, son and heir to the King, had joined the Royal Army at Carlisle, and on the 4th of July they had advanced into Galloway to besiege Caerlaverock. This was Roger's first taste of a campaign and he told me he loved it. He had never travelled so far north before. He found the journey in the company of his uncle, his best friend Richard, and a large body of armed men exhilarating, despite some unseasonable driving rain.

He was learning the logistics of keeping such an army reasonably content on the road: when to pitch camp and keep the ale flowing, when to withhold it and urge marching forward, the importance of digging the latrines as soon as possible, and the necessary raiding of nearby villages and homesteads for fresh supplies of grain and meat, whilst needing to keep the men under some control to avoid gratuitous carnage and atrocities, without denying them the sense of a just reward. They encountered little resistance on the way and left a trail of smoking barns and empty homesteads behind them.

Caerlaverock, on the north side of the Solway Firth, was different from any castle Roger had seen before. Wigmore stood high on a hilltop with an irregular curtain wall, the chapel higher than the gatehouse, the living quarters higher still due to the increasing gradient, and the great keep dominant, visible for miles below. Ludlow's whitewashed walls were part of the town, though raised above it, with a massive outer bailey and towers overlooking the river on the western side. His uncle had taken him to see the advancing building work at Chirk, which sat grey, grim and solid atop a hill, looking down steep, wooded valleys into Wales. But Caerlaverock only had two tall towers on either side of its gatehouse, with curtain walls spreading out to complete a triangle in the middle of a moat, surrounded by deep earthworks and marshy ground. The gatehouse resembled the prow of a ship afloat on its moat and there was no prospect of riding up to the walls without drawing a hail of arrows down on them. So the siege engines were brought in and they settled down to wait.

If truth be told, the young men found this part boring. Those older and wiser were content enough to wait for the engineers to work their inexorable assault. They rolled the lumbering engines into position at first light. Then it was a case of winching up the weighted basket, loading the slings with the biggest boulders available, and releasing the opposing winch and weight. The sling arms shot up like the thin necks of startled, ancient monsters through the morning mist, and the boulders flew on a well calculated trajectory. The air was full of the crack of stone on stone as dust and mortar spilled from the sandstone towers into the waters of the moat. It was hard, back-breaking work for the sweating men who laboured on the wooden engines. But there was little to do for the knights and the squires.

Their encampment lay at a suitable distance across the marsh, well out of reach of the keenest arrow shot. The outbuildings around the castle had been taken with little trouble, as most of the inhabitants had fled to avoid being cut down. They dug their latrines and pitched their canvas tents, stabled their horses and lit their fires. Animal dung and the smell from boiling stew pots mingled with wood smoke and the rotten smell of the marsh. There was ample time for the young men to roam about and meet each other.

That was how Roger met the King's heir, and Piers Gaveston, a Gascon knight. Edward was now in his seventeenth year, three years older than Roger, who accorded him suitable respect. He was already as tall as his father, whose nickname was 'Longshanks', but without the drooping left eye. His hair fell in long and wavy golden locks. This was also inherited from the King, though his hair was now iron-grey. Young Edward's frame was strong and muscular – they said he was not averse to digging the odd ditch or thatching, and loved rowing a boat and swimming. The aptitude for such common physical effort showed in his fine, rippling muscles.

He wore a surcoat with the Kings' Arms – the three golden leopard-like lions passant of England on scarlet cloth – over his chain mail and a blue band on his arm to distinguish him from his father in battle. Roger did not see how anyone could make that mistake. He was upright and strong, his father's spine bowing a little more every day. Young Edward was handsome and laughing with good humour, his father eaten up with unfulfilled ambition and permanent bad temper.

Naturally, Roger was awed by the prince. But Edward seemed to set great store by Piers Gaveston, and it was easy to make friends with Piers. His prowess at tourney was second to none. He was also appealing in his looks, though not as handsome as the prince, confident with a wicked humour, warm and convivial, with natural charm. He seemed keenly interested in youngsters like Roger, rather than ignoring them as he could so easily have done. He called Roger 'Childe Mortimer', even though he was only a few years older himself, but softened the nickname with a friendly cuff on the cheek, which told Roger it was not meant unkindly. He had far worse names for the older members of the court and kept them all rolling about with laughter, for he was an accomplished mimic.

It was Piers who organised a tournament on the firmer ground outside the encampment and thereby gave the young squires much-needed relief from their boredom, with the spectacle of men on horseback and on foot, in teams of two, crashing and laying into each other. Fighting – as good as. The Lord Edward was not allowed to take part, in view of his sole heritage to the Crown, but he applauded the others, especially Piers, who shone and appeared indestructible.

The younger squires were not yet ready to take part in this, but rode with blunted lances against the quintain mounted on a pole. If you aimed at the right spot, you could carry off a ring. If you failed, it would spin round like a mad thing and sandbag you. Roger was especially good at the quintain and drew fulsome praise. Afterwards, they all repaired to the Prince's tent for a skin of wine.

It was pitch black, apart from a few glowing fires, when Roger made his way back to his own tent, which he shared with his uncle in the camp. He felt happy and supremely confident. He certainly did not feel in any danger. The siege engines had ceased their noisy bombardment long ago, and the distant castle was quiet. No bowman could take aim in the dark. The wine and the fresh air hit his head after the warmth of the tents and he stumbled over what he thought was a branch in the dark.

Then a dark shape suddenly leapt on him from behind and took his legs from underneath, so he ended up winded on the wet ground, with his arms pinioned behind him and his face screwed viciously into the mud. He came up gasping for air and choking.

"Got you – 'Childe Mortimer'!"

His tormentor let his arms go and lit a rush candle, showing brown hair and a coarse-featured face puckered up in ugly hatred.

"Think you were the best squire then today, do you?"

Roger continued to spit mud and blood from his mouth where he had bitten his tongue.

"What is it to you?"

"Don't you know my name?"

"No. You didn't compete today."

"Boy's stuff. I'm waiting for the real thing."

"But it's best to practise. It was good enough for Piers Gaveston and he's the best at tourney."

They both sat back on their haunches and Roger saw his assailant was about the same age as himself. He remembered having seen him sitting at the back of the tent earlier, looking sullen and envious.

"Who are you then, fellow?"

"Hugh – Hugh Despenser. I'm here with my father."

Roger began to understand.

"And you've been waiting for me all this time coming back from the royal tents?"

"Your grandfather killed my grandfather!" and the boy spat in his face. Roger calmly wiped it away and got to his feet. He drew his short sword from its scabbard and raised it in a grand gesture.

"Get back to your father's skirts and leave me alone!"

The boy, wary now as he was unarmed, backed away.

"I'm not afraid to fight you face-to-face. But if you want to be a real knight instead of a common thief and vagabond, you never, ever strike a man from behind. Don't you even know that? Begone!" Roger continued.

Hugh obeyed but flung a bitter retort over his retreating shoulder.

"Will always hate you, Mortimer. Always! Will get you one day! See if I don't."

Roger knew he had made his first mortal enemy and, when he told me about this later, I knew it was true.

The plan now was to push further north into Carrick, the lands of the Bruce, before working their way up to Stirling, that great castle which guarded the gateway to the Highlands. The old King was determined to subdue the Scots now the Welsh had been conquered, even if it bankrupted the Crown after his additional campaigns in Gascony. He was fortunate there were three contenders for the Scottish throne without any one clear line of succession, and even managed to get himself proclaimed 'Overlord' as a result. He chose John Balliol as the Scottish King, under his protection, rather than the Bruces or Comyns. But Balliol did not prove to be a satisfactory puppet and was now imprisoned in France, though the Pope was making urgent noises for his release.

In the meantime, the fiery William Wallace stirred the Scots to outright rebellion, and demanded independence. Edward Longshanks would not rest until he saw him captured and executed, and all the Scots bow their head to Edward Plantagenet alone.

Except that it was not easy to bring the Scots to battle in their large, wild land of mountains and glens. In the same way the Welsh princes had retreated into Snowdonia, they could retreat into the Highlands beyond Stirling and wage sporadic attacks, waiting until the English had retired before swarming back down into the Borders to raid and burn at will. Wales was small in comparison, with half of its southern lands well under English rule already, and the borders held in control most of the time by the strong Marcher Barons. There was an easy road to be forged along the North Coast to Anglesey, where ships could land with supplies for the armies. The final coup had been marked by an iron ring of intimidating new castles, built by Edward.

Scotland was an entirely different proposition. The King himself would have pushed on until death, no matter how far forward his aging body bowed on his war horse against the rain and the wind. Already supplies were running out and men deserting in consequence, and it was barely autumn. In the end, to the King's fury, there was nothing for it but to retreat to Carlisle and make for winter quarters.

Caerlaverock had fallen, but that was all. Wallace was still at large and rumoured to be in France, seeking support for his cause. The campaign had been desultory and completely unsatisfactory compared with Edward's triumph at Falkirk four years before.

In addition, the Pope was pressing the King to relinquish his support for the Flemish and make peace with France, even though the French still held Aquitaine, which was Edward's birthright. The King was far from happy. But it was never going to be possible to fight the French and the Scots simultaneously; there was no money for extra arms and men, and the spectre of France coming to Scotland's aid was a nightmare to contemplate. No, if the Pope insisted, it had to be peace with France, and he would betroth his son to the French King's daughter to cement the pact.

Then he could turn his attention back to the Scots. He swore he would hammer every last Goddamn one of them into this earth before he left it.

Chapter 6

THEIR HORSES CHURNED up sand and mud, enjoying the cool water as they forded the brightly shining shallows of the estuary. Ahead, the whitewashed walls and round towers of Conwy Castle reared proudly up against a backdrop of mountains. This was the beginning of Snowdonia, a land of mist, legends and Welsh princes. Seagulls wheeled over town, quay and castle, squealing their joy at the clear daylight and blue sky.

It was nine years since the King first arrived here, bringing his Army up the western bank from the valley. Even now, the rubble of Llywellyn's castle was just visible in the distance, on two stumpy hills of the eastern bank. Edward ignored its ruins and built a new castle on the rocky outcrop of the western shore, creating a whole new town within its walled embrace. He moved the Cistercian monks of Aberconwy unceremoniously down the valley to Maenan, to make way for it.

After Llywellyn's death near Builth, engineered by the Mortimer brothers, a group of Welshman presented King Edward with the Croes Naid, a fragmentary relic of the True Cross. It was a token of his absolute victory and brought good fortune with it as, not long after, Llywellyn's remaining brother, Dafydd, was captured, and hung, drawn and quartered at Shrewsbury. So two heads were impaled on London Bridge as a gruesome reminder of the finality of Edward's conquest.

And now he had made his son Edward, who was entering his eighteenth year, Prince of Wales; and today the new prince was holding court inside the castle, to receive homage and fealty. Roger and his uncle had set out early from the half-built Chirk this morning to pledge their loyalty and now, with the forded river behind them, they rode up the ramp from the town side, across the lowered drawbridge into the Western Barbican, and through the main gate. The inner ward was alive with excited activity. The new Prince's retainers relieved them of mounts and weapons before they were allowed to pass through the Inner Gate to join the queue of noblemen waiting to be admitted into the Royal Chamber.

"It cannot be long now before he sits on the throne in his own right," said Roger.

"Nay, lad," his uncle disagreed. "Aging his father may be, but he's a stubborn old warrior, much like me. He won't loosen his grip on life or his throne without a battle, nor rest happy till the Scots have been thoroughly beaten."

For they had been called up again to join the armies in Scotland next month, with Edmund Mortimer also requested to supply men and arms at his own expense. Edmund was fast running out of money and anxious to hasten Roger's marriage for his dowry. But, once again, Scotland must come first. The Mortimers would be part of the new Prince's household and battalions, for he was being given more responsibility this time, albeit under the sharp eyes of older knights like Uncle Roger.

When their turn came and they were ushered in, the new Prince looked like a young man anyone would be proud to follow, in his scarlet robes, emblazoned with the golden lions of England. He sat erect on his father's throne – tall, handsome, broad shouldered and muscular. He remained clean shaven, though his golden locks were grown long. On his head he wore the crown of Arthur, wrested from the last Llywellyn after the last battle.

The legendary crown of Arthur! For an instant, Roger imagined himself wearing that golden coronet set with heavy jewels; after all, his line of descent from his great-grandmother, the Welsh Gwladys Ddu, must surely come down from Arthur himself and even Brutus, the first British King. He remembered once, as a child, asking his grandmother Maud, who had passed away peacefully this year, if it were possible for him to become a King. Her measured reply was ambiguous: "Not us from Kings, my dear. But Kings from us may come."

He banished such seditious thoughts as he knelt before his Prince with hands clasped, as if in prayer, and then turned palm up, outstretched towards his liege lord. The oath was very solemn and the heartfelt words seemed to hang heavy in the air.

"I promise on my faith in God that I will in the future be faithful to my lord, never cause him harm, and will observe my homage to him completely, against all persons, in good faith and without deceit."

Then Edward rose to enclose Roger's hands in his own and raise him up so their eyes met.

"Well said, young Mortimer, and gladly accepted. We look forward to your expected long service when you come of age."

Then he turned to receive the older man, as Roger meekly stepped aside to allow his uncle to bend his knee and make his oath.

"We have been well trained by this most loyal servant and bravest of barons and so we are in no doubt of his fealty," he declared, with the due respect owed to the older man.

Allowing his attention to wander during the prince's subsequent conversation with his uncle, Roger became aware of the fetching Piers Gaveston, richly attired in velvet and furs, standing directly behind the Prince. He caught his eye and Piers gave him a broad wink, showing he had not been forgotten. Roger smiled back. Piers, disrespectful as always, seemed to be implying there would be good feasting, entertainment and dicing in the Great Hall tonight, after this tedious business was over, and "Childe Mortimer" would be welcome. When his uncle stepped back, they were shown to comfortable quarters for lodging.

"Don't be up too late carousing now, young man," his uncle warned him. Roger was surprised, for his uncle was not usually averse to feasting and enjoyment.

"Now this is done, we ride for London at dawn tomorrow."

"But why, uncle?"

"To buy new armour and weapons, of course, for the campaign. But also to give you a merry time in a different way, and finish off your education!"

For the second time that day, Roger was the recipient of a knowing wink.

"I promise you will enjoy London, even if the pigs run riot and the red kites feed off the garbage. "

"And then straight to Carlisle again?"

"Aye, needs must. But your father is anxious to return to the March before September is out, for I am told the Mortimers have an important wedding to attend!"

Chapter 7

I WAS MORE than a little nervous and I am sorry to say it made me truculent.

"Mama, I wish you had let me wear green! He likes me in green and it is my best colour!"

"Nonsense, ma chère. Green is not a noble colour, and you must wear blue to signal your purity. Remember, you were born on the Feast of the Purification. See now how pretty it looks, with the pearls and amethysts worked into the cloth around the neck!"

I was being sewn into the tight sleeves of my wedding gown, a deep and vibrant blue damask brocade laced tightly at the bodice and deeply slit at the front to show an ivory under-gown with its train.

"Does it look well on me?"

"Wait until you have your over-mantle on," Avice begged me, finishing with the needle and thread, but still with a stack of pins in her mouth. "It's such a lovely pale lilac and so expensive, with all that beautiful, gold braid trimming."

With Avice's help, my mother draped it around my young shoulders and I pushed my deep-blue arms in and out through its long, hanging sleeves.

"Perfect," breathed Avice, "and now for the garland."

My long, brown hair was left loose in shining waves for the wedding – the last time it would be on public show, for a married woman's hair is only shown to her husband and her most intimate maidservant. That was a sobering thought. Avice set a blue cloth band, embroidered with pearls and interwoven with gold leaf and white flowers, in a low coronet around my brow, and they gave me a little blue purse of rosemary to hold.

Both of them stood back and sighed with deep satisfaction at the result.

"Ma chère!" Jeanne said tenderly, with a catch in her voice, whilst Avice wiped flowing tears from her homely face with the back of her hand, "You are a woman!"

"Such a picture," came proudly from Avice.

"You think my Roger will be pleased with me?" I asked.

"How could he not?" asked Avice, wiping her hands on her apron. "How could he not?"

It was a quiet, golden day with the leaves still to turn and the afternoon air pleasantly warm. The de Joinvilles had arrived from Ludlow yesterday and were settled in lodgings opposite the Hall at Pembridge Manor, which belonged to the Mortimers. The buildings stood on a raised mound and across the ditch-bridge stood the stone church of Saint Mary the Virgin, with its separate wooden bell tower. It was here the Holy Sacrament would take place to bind us together, and the Bishop of Hereford himself, a family friend of the Mortimers, had come to officiate.

Jeanne led me down the stairs to meet my beloved grandfather. I noticed he was looking older and greyer.

"It is, I believe and hope, a happy day, Jeanne?" he asked my mother.

"Indeed, sir. You have made good provision for the family by settling all on Joan, instead of any division amongst the daughters. This is a good marriage for her. With God's blessing, Roger and Joan will be fruitful and form a new dynasty."

Roger was dressed in azure velvet stitched with gold, and standing beside the old knight, but now stepped forward to take my hand, trying to look capable of his new relative's trust.

"Allow me to escort you to the church, Madame, as my wife is already there," said Sir Geoffrey to my mother. Jeanne put her hand gratefully in his, as she had been feeling her husband's absence more keenly this morning.

"Let us follow the young ones in all their glory."

"How goes it with you, my lady?" whispered Roger taking my hand, which trembled a little, despite myself.

"It goes well, my lord."

"Then let us go together, for now and always."

The Bishop of Hereford met us at the entrance to the church door and asked for our consent to be man and wife, so that our individual inheritances of land could be jointly bestowed to each other, the notices having already been read unopposed. Then he blessed us and passed the ring to Roger to place on the fourth finger of my right hand, after passing over all the other preceding fingers. As this was done, he intoned solemnly:

"In nomine Patris, et Filiis, et in Spiritus Sancti, et Amen."

The ring finally rested on my marriage finger, feeling cold and solid.

Then the Bishop led us into the church and down the nave to announce our conjugation before the attendant families, whilst we had to prostrate ourselves under the veil before the high altar.

The subsequent feast in the Great Hall was as merry as the ceremony had been solemn. No expense had been spared, and the table was sumptuous with many dishes of fish and pheasant, venison and boar, nuts, dates and fruits, whilst the wine flowed freely and the minstrels played. There were many cousins and noblemen with their families from the Marches present as guests: the de Bohuns, de Warennes, the Clares, the de Veres, Fitzalans, Cliffords, Giffords, and the Lacys from Ireland.

Beatrice and Maud, my sisters who were bound for the Priory at Aconbury, were there, and I was acutely conscious of them eyeing Roger, looking envious. I vowed to visit them often, to take them gifts, and make sure they wanted for nothing, feeling a twinge of guilt.

If Uncle Roger got a little too inebriated and started slapping the serving maids' neat behinds, no-one seemed to mind too much, with the possible exception of his wife, Lucy, but she was used to holding her tongue. Sir Geoffrey and my grandmother Matilda kept their own counsel, though I could sense Grandfather's disapproval. Jeanne, Edmund Mortimer and Margaret seemed particularly relaxed and happy. Richard of Monmouth made a great display of ostentatious bowing before us, which Roger seemed to find very amusing.

It was late when we retired to the bedchamber. But there was the Bishop, present to bless the marriage bed, with everyone gathered around to witness us get in, according to custom. I wore my beautiful ivory silk chemise and Roger a fine linen shirt and braies. We both wriggled down with embarrassment as far as we could, on the freshly filled mattress under its magnificently embroidered coverlet.

Then at last everyone was gone, and we were left alone in the candlelight.

"May God be praised for that!" said Roger, and we both started giggling and could not stop. It was an auspicious beginning.

At fourteen and fifteen, we were old enough to live as man and wife, though hardly experienced. Uncle Roger had made sure his nephew was well prepared, however. After Conwy, they travelled to London together as promised, and amongst all its rough clamour, stinking smells and vibrancy, they took a boat to the Southwark Stews. Here, his uncle personally chose a prostitute for the young lad and instructed her to verse him well in what was expected of him, and in the arts of pleasuring a woman. She was an expert at her trade. Of course, I did not know this at the time, but guessed later.

So Roger was not at all nervous, though he understood that as a virgin I might be, and took his time, kissing me tenderly and stroking me gently. The silk of my chemise seemed to increase his desire, but he was pleased when I had the courage to take it off and we could lay with bare skin against bare skin. His hands worked their way down from my breasts, across my flat stomach, into the insides of my soft thighs and the parts my brown bush protected. I clung to him hard when he finally entered me, gasping and crying out, in pain, as well as pleasure.

In the morning there was blood on the sheets, our union consummated, and we lay intimate and warm in each other's arms. When Avice eventually arrived, in a lather of anxiety to help me dress, Roger got up to bathe and I announced to Avice that I would like to do so, too.

"So, was it...acceptable?'

"No, it was not!" I teased, and then burst out laughing when I saw Avice's crestfallen face.

"It was far better than that. I am a little tired and sore inside, and need my bath. But, oh Avice, I am wondrous happy, and believe I am in love with him already."

"Blessed be to God, this is good news indeed, my lady!"

"Why did my mother never tell me how good this could feel?"

"I daresay she didn't want to risk your disappointment, my lady. Many young women are not so fortunate."

Avice filled the bath tub with hot water and herbs, and helped me step in.

"He was so kind and gentle. He said my inner parts were like a rose!"

"Indeed, my lady. That is pretty manners."

"Of course, he was strong and thrusting at times, as well as courteous. And it did hurt a little, for he has a large member."

"I was not aware of it, my lady."

We both broke off in peals of laughter.

"Forgive me, Avice, I cannot talk like this to Mama."

"I know, my lady. But this is good news to share. And I am so pleased for my darling girl!"

I emerged dripping from the bathwater and gave Avice a hug.

"You must come with us to Wigmore. For I cannot manage without you."

"Of course! I see plenty of work with little ones there, God willing."

I saw Avice's eyes were moist with tears and hugged her again.

"I promise you will always be well treated in all our houses."

"I have no doubt of it, my lady, and thank God for it daily."

It was a fine day and a comfortable ride to Wigmore, where I was welcomed right royally by all the Mortimer retainers, with yet more feasting on roast boar, and many sweetmeats and delicacies to follow. When it was completely dark, we all left the great Hall, with its roaring fire, to climb up to the battlements, for there was a wondrous sight in the heavens above: a comet with a blazing tail, streaking across the night sky.

"An illustrious sign indeed," Roger's mother, Margaret, cried.

"Of fame and fortune?" Roger asked eagerly.

"Perhaps," his father smiled, but remained thoughtful. "Whatever it may portend, we can be sure that Brother Benedict will record it as such in his chronicles. Alhough it was scarcely a good omen for the old Saxon King Harald when the same event occurred before the Battle of Hastings."

"But it was a good omen for our Norman King, William, who won the battle," Roger pointed out gleefully.

"True. So perhaps we make our own fortunes before God?" Margaret was a little impatient with him.

"But it may prove a good sign for our son, as he says."

"We ought not to forget he was born on the Feast of St Mark," Edmund chided her, gently, "the twenty-fifth of April."

"So was Prince Edward," countered Roger.

"Yes, and I am sure it disturbs him that the people dress in black and veil their crosses as they pray to avert famine and disaster in the year ahead, for it is not known as a good day."

I was silent, knowing only too well what they spoke of. My great-uncle, Jean de Joinville, had done much to validate this superstition by foretelling that hundreds would die in the Seventh Crusade, led by King Louis IX of France, because he, too, was born on this date. My great uncle was proven correct when the campaign was disastrous, as he chronicled. Not only did they fail to retake Jerusalem from the Saracens, but the Grand Master of the Knights of the Temple was amongst many others who died, whilst the French King himself suffered imprisonment for a while. I shivered in the night air, which had grown cold.

"But Roger is not a king," Margaret protested, unwilling to let the evening end in such melancholy, "so the portents may be more favourable for him. Anyway, is it not our dear, newly wedded Joan's comet too?"

Edmund smiled more warmly now, for I am glad to tell you he already seemed to have grown fond of me, as his new daughter-in-law.

"Indeed it is! Perhaps it speaks of their fortunes together. Mark that, Roger and treat her well. And now we must go back to the fire, for your new bride is cold and we must see no harm comes to her."

Chapter 8

AND, AT FIRST, it seemed as if nothing ever would, nor could be, of harm. Scotland meant only the temporary absence of my new young Lord then, and Ireland was merely the place where I had received an education from my earnest grandfather.

I found Margaret de Fiennes a little opinionated but intelligent, welcoming, and of good support to me at Wigmore when I missed my own mother. Margaret schooled me in the niceties of running the household. She was French, like Jeanne, and, slowly, I began to feel more comfortable with her and learnt to hold my tongue on occasion.

Edmund and Roger were home not only for the winter, with its festival of Christmas, but for the rest of the New Year. For it seemed as if the wars with Scotland were over, for the present at least.

I am sure I was not alone in being confused about Scottish politics, but Lord Edmund took the time to explain them to me. Last year's Scottish campaign had achieved little, although the Prince's Army took Bruce's seat, the castle of Turnberry, by siege, razed it to the ground and sacked Ayr; except Robert Bruce was not there, had not been for some time it appeared, and William Wallace was still at the French court. Even worse, John Comyn had routed an English party at Lochmaben in Annandale, and John Balliol was released from papal custody in France.

King Philippe of France was now demanding an English truce with Scotland prior to Balliol's return, on the understanding that the English claim to Gascony would not be upheld if Edward disobeyed and continued to support insurrection against the French in Flanders. The King had no intention of returning Balliol or anyone else to the Scottish throne, but was loathe to lose Gascony or disobey the Pope, who seemed to be on France's side.

So he grudgingly accepted a temporary truce. Shortly afterwards, amazingly, and with considered pragmatism, Robert Bruce gave himself up into the custody of the King. So now there was peace in Scotland and the Mortimers could return home to look after their own lands.

Very soon, I was with child. Looking back, this was an idyllic time: newly married, in love and expecting our first child. As I grew bigger, I was not able to go out riding or hawking with Roger, but he read to me in French from the Roman de Brut, about King Arthur and Guinevere, and their court, and we played chess together most of every day. Of course, Roger wished for a son, though in truth I did not mind so much. If I had managed to conceive so quickly, I was sure there would be others.

As time wore on, I grew anxious that Roger may be getting a little bored. Although his father was involving him in the day-to-day running of the estates, I knew he missed army life and companionship. He spent a lot of time riding and wrestling with his younger brother John, newly returned from his own schooling as a squire, but it was not like sharing life with Richard of Monmouth in the Army. So it was my idea he bring Richard into our household for company, if he would come and Uncle Roger would let him go. Richard was a congenial young man with a genuine devotion to Roger, and they had sworn to be blood brothers. Richard duly came to Wigmore shortly before Easter, and I could see Roger was glad of it, though he did not neglect to see me at least once every day, and to read to me from the tales of romance and chivalry we both loved.

Richard would be a welcome distraction for Roger whilst I was confined. He had grown too, in the meantime of course, but he retained a boyish look with his clear face, slightly flattened nose, and honest grey eyes under a light brown mop of hair. He seemed in no hurry to marry, and was perfectly content to act as Roger's squire in the future.

By the end of June, my time was growing close and there came an end to this close companionship, for I was required to retire into female company, attended only by maid servants and Margaret. I missed Roger, and it was hard to be kept indoors in midsummer, away from sunlight and fresh air.

They made my solar chamber womb-like, with layers of carpet on the floor and hanging tapestries of pleasant rural scenes, with nothing to alarm a young mother-to-be within its embroidered pictures. It was overly warm, especially at night. For two weeks, I languished in boredom with nothing to do but sew and read, and visit the chapel daily with the women to pray. Just like a nun in Aconbury Priory, I thought, except that all my meals were brought to me. I begged Avice to tell me stories of ordinary folk and how they lived, but Avice was keener to pray to St Margaret of Antioch for a safe outcome.

When I think of it now, it reminds me of the precursor of the confinement to come. But I was delivered of a healthy son.

It was some hours later when they let Roger into the room to see his son. He held the bundle cautiously in his arms, hardly knowing what to say, and kept repeating: "A son, I have a son! A son and heir."

"We are blessed! Are we not?" I said happily.

"A Mortimer heir! Yes, we are indeed blessed." Roger sat on the bed beside me, not taking his eyes off the reddened lids and puckered face of his child. Then he glanced at me, at last. I probably looked flushed, as my brown curls were lying damply against my brow.

"We may call him Edmund, as we should?" Roger asked.

"Of course… I hope he may take after your father, too."

"I am not so sure of that! But are you well, Joan? Will you stay well? You are not flushed with fever?" he asked anxiously.

"Not at all! Only this room is so very hot!"

Roger looked around at all the carpets and tapestries, with the candles still lit though dawn had broken long ago.

"Indeed it is! However do you women bear it? You are weaker than us men and yet I should not like to be in your place. My mother said you were brave, but that all women must suffer hard in atonement for Eve's sin."

"So I have done, but now it is all forgotten!"

I will not bore or shock you with the details; they were burnt into my mind, though…the lengthy time before labour truly started, the vellum prayer roll Avice placed around my middle, the magical jet bowl from which I must drink, and most especially the midwife lathering her arms with butter.

"See how tightly he clasps my finger, even in sleep!"

I nodded.

"Avice says they all do that to start with."

"You are very fond of her, are you not?"

"I trust her with my life."

"Then she shall always stay with us. How good she is not to hurry me off yet!"

"But you should leave soon, young master, and let her rest," came her voice from the shadows.

Roger laughed.

"I spoke too soon. But it's true I should go down to the abbey and ask them to say Mass for us all in Thanksgiving. I should make a pilgrimage, too."

"Not yet, my love. Let us all go when I am recovered and Baby Edmund is a little older."

"You do not think he will fall sick?" Roger examined his son earnestly. "He is very small."

"No, my dear lord. All my womenfolk say he is very big and Avice says she never saw such a fine, lusty baby!"

"Then I must obey Avice and give him back to you."

I took the soft bundle from him and Roger stayed awhile still, stroking my hair gently and kissing my forehead before leaving.

"You will make the perfect mother," he said. "So calm and kind, yet so brave and full of laughter, too."

My cup of happiness was then complete.

Chapter 9

JULY 1304 – DEATH AT WIGMORE

MY SECOND CHILD, born only eighteen months later, was a daughter and we named her Margaret. Roger was not there this time. He had been in Stirling since April, where the castle lay under a lengthy siege. Their attack was formidable upon a garrison of only thirty men commanded by William Oliphant in the castle, but he was holding out obstinately. The King was promising the imminent arrival of a new Saracen weapon, which could cause explosions of fire to break the deadlock.

Peace with Scotland had not lasted, despite the surrender of Robert Bruce, and John Balliol continuing to be rendered ineffective in France. William Wallace, the hero of the Scots, was newly returned from France and continued to fight on alongside John Comyn, the remaining contender for the throne.

Lord Edmund was not required to muster arms on this occasion. I believe he was glad of it. Uncle Roger was there in full force, along with my lord and Richard of Monmouth, as his squires. The campaign did not sound dangerous, although if Stirling were breached it would open up a path into the Highlands and that might be a different matter. I had begun to feel more anxious over these perpetual Scottish wars and wished the King might leave the Scots alone to choose their own ruler, though I knew Roger did not agree.

In contrast, I had no fears about my father-in-law travelling to Builth Wells to attend an entirely routine court session to settle a number of disputes. How wrong I was! I had been fortunate in my upbringing, despite the death of my own father whom I scarcely remembered. But death is a constant stalker of life and comes in different shapes and guises, often unexpectedly. Then it changes everything.

It was Hywel, one of our older and most trusted Welsh servants, who alerted us that evening. He rode hard from Radnor Forest and threw himself out of the saddle, covered in a lather of his own sweat and horse spittle. There had been a skirmish on the outskirts of the woods. It sounded more like an ambush, in truth: the men were off-guard, returning home, when arrows flew out of the trees.

There were barely half-a-dozen men with Lord Edmund. The Lord had drawn a little ahead to discuss some matters with one of his retainers. He remarked on the beauty of the day and the excellent weather. Their guard was down as all seemed well, until the volley of arrows came. One of them pierced Lord Edmund's left thigh. He wheeled his horse round. Another struck him in the ribs on his right-hand side and a third arrow went into his belly. The horse bolted as he fell.

His foremost retainer dismounted at once to attend to him. The other four plunged into the forest, hacking at the trees with their swords, but the attackers were on horse and already away. The men were sorely ashamed they had lost them. Now they were bearing poor Lord Edmund home on a litter, jolting over the rough tracks through Radnor Forest towards Wigmore. Every step of the way must be causing him unbearable pain.

Margaret turned white but composed herself and sent another servant off to Ludlow to fetch the barber surgeon, Gilbert. I suggested we send a messenger to Roger, too. It was at least six days' ride, even with fresh horses on the way. But my lord must know what had happened, especially if the wounds proved to be mortal.

When my father-in-law arrived at last, I was shocked to see him looking so clammy and gray, and knew I had been right to send for his son. In the meantime, Lady Margaret and I got him to bed, cut off his tunic and cleaned away the dirt and grit. There was not much blood, so we were hopeful at first. We dared not disturb the cloth around the wounds until Gilbert of Ludlow arrived with his instruments. We gave our lord draughts of wine with herbs for the pain, and wiped his face and limbs with cold water, as Avice advised, for he already had a fever on him. We both sat up and watched him by candlelight all night, with Lady Margaret tenderly wiping the sweat from his face.

Gilbert arrived the very next morning. He brought a friend with him, another surgeon from London, who was staying with him in Ludlow. This man had studied in Italy, at the University of Bologna, so we felt most fortunate to have his services as well.

They dealt with the arrow in the thigh first, pushing it through, for the head was barbed and they said it would do more harm than good to pull it straight out.

Margaret and I held Edmund's hand on either side, so he could grip us tightly whilst he screamed, trying to stay still for them. Gilbert had brought myrrh to put in the wine but it only seemed to help the pain a little. There was blood then, but they managed to staunch it with a firm bandage above the wound, and applied a salve of honey, rosewater and wine.

The arrow in the chest was next – not embedded in that far. Praise be! They said it was unlikely to have pierced any vital organs, being stuck in the lower ribs, and prised it out gently with pliers. Neither arrow had carried poison, as far as they could tell. Now, only the third arrow remained in the abdomen.

That was the worst: they discussed between themselves what to do, warning us it would be a miracle if it had not pierced the bowels. They probed the wound very carefully and tried to get a purchase on the head of the arrow, with forceps to crush the barbs. Everything they did was done with great care. But when they withdrew the shaft, a dirty, brown liquid followed it. That was when they told us nothing more could be done, and the wound would be fatal within a few days. We took it in turn to sit with Edmund then, though I had to reassure Margaret I would fetch her immediately if there were any change. She was extremely brave but still seemed to entertain some hope, despite what she had been told. I had none, but I prayed for Lord Edmund desperately, in the sickly sweet foetor of the sickroom. I felt I had grown up overnight.

The following morning, he asked to see our children and seemed to brighten at their smiling faces; but it did not last long once they had gone. Brother Benedict came to shrive him of his sins. There was only one real sin to my mind, listening to his faltering and tremulous confession, and that had not been intended. Yet he had agreed to send the severed head of the Welsh prince to the King, urged on by his brother.

By the time the Abbot came to administer the Last Rites, Edmund had sunk into unconsciousness, his face gaunt and already corpse-like, his breathing laboured. In the quiet, dark hours of the night, he passed peacefully with Margaret alone by his side.

It was six days since the messenger set out from Wigmore. Another six days of hard riding followed, which reminded Roger and Richard how idle they had been, in truth, since pitching at Stirling, despite daily practice at combat.

They mounted promptly at dawn and pushed on hard every day until dusk, which was thankfully late in July, sleeping at inns or friaries, even rough lodgings if none better could be found. Once over the border, it was hard to find good horses, even with generous payment, for the land had been stripped bare of livestock on the Army's march north.

In Cumbria, the weather turned bad, with downpours of rain swelling the rivers and turning the roads into muddy quagmires, so they had to go miles out of their way to find a safe crossing, and the horses tired more quickly and slowed down.

At night, Richard slept the sleep of the untroubled, in his exhaustion. Roger's body was aching, too, but his mind continued to turn over all the possibilities pondered during the day.

Supposing his father died? He felt a small pit open up somewhere in his innards. It was not that he felt any strong emotion, as yet; at fifty-two, his father was no longer a young man, and inevitably fathers had to die and hopefully leave sons to inherit. Roger had not the least doubt he could fulfil that role. But not yet! Even though he was married with two children, he was still only seventeen, and would be considered a minor. That meant he would have to become a ward of someone outside the family, at the King's choosing, with the Mortimer lands held by his guardian. Everything would be turned on its head – I understood that.

Perhaps his father would recover? He was a strong man, physically, possibly not as fit as Uncle Roger but strong nevertheless, and very pious. Roger told me of the silent prayers he mouthed for him in the night.

"You know my father is a good man, Lord. Can you not let him recover and live just a few more years? That would be so much for the better!"

It sounds heartless, but there was another reason Roger wanted his father to live, above mere convenience: he wanted Edmund to be proud of him. Edmund's pleasure in his marriage to me and the arrival of grandchildren was obvious enough, but there could be so much more to come. True, Roger was becoming accomplished at tourney and the Lord Edmund knew about that. But his father never praised him for it. Of course, Roger wanted his father to see him victorious in battle too, but he knew he would have to do more than that to earn his respect: to gain further land and wealth, and protect the family, yes, of course, but also to become something of a diplomat and statesman.

Because Roger knew, deep down, that his father did not entirely approve of military prowess and thought his own brother boorish. What is more, he often compared the younger Roger to the elder, just as the uncle did. But I am not boorish, insisted Roger, "I am not crude like my uncle. I am educated and literate just as you are, father, and I shall very much appreciate the finer things in life. I shall gain honour and respect, and there is no shame in outshining you on the field. You only have to think of William Marshall. You will see I am the best of sons and a worthy successor!"

By the time they got to Chester the wet weather eased off, bar an occasional shower, and at last they could get good horses. It seemed no time then before they crossed the Severn at Shrewsbury and turned westward toward the dying light and the rising hills of Shropshire, with the sun dipping below them. With the sun gone, they were weary and sought shelter at Stokesay Manor for the night, even though they were now close to Mortimer lands, with the Long Mynd behind them to their righthand.

It was there they learnt from William of Ludlow, the owner of Stokesay and a wealthy wool merchant well known to the Mortimers, that the Lord Edmund had entered the afterlife three nights ago.

Next morning, as Roger rode along winding tracks through the green forest, his emotions were mixed. They let their horses amble now, for there was no further need of hurry. William of Ludlow had provided them with two men at arms to ride with them, in view of the uncertainty of the times.

Roger remembered his father taking him hunting, giving him his first bird of prey and his first puppy, lifting him gently into the saddle, and being, it must be said, an unfailingly kind father. He thought about Maud, too, the grandmother he had respected, who had always been there in his childhood. Stiff, stern Maud in her white wimple, sewing away despite swollen knuckles and telling such wonderful tales and stories. Maud favoured Roger, but he suspected she was disappointed in her second son, Edmund, who was never meant to inherit the title but to take holy orders. Roger saw now it must have been so: Uncle Roger earned more respect in her eyes, and that was why she had insisted Edmund send his son to him. Poor Edmund! It was a sad thing not to turn out as expected, Roger reckoned. But then, if Edmund's elder brother had survived, Roger himself would not have been born at all! Life is not so easily relied upon – so he could not feel that sorry for his father's destiny.

Richard rode beside him, attentive as ever, but silent, for once, out of respect for his friend's loss and thoughts. They emerged out of the forest, from a canopy of trailing boughs and green leaves, into the open air and, unbidden, both drew rein at the same moment to look ahead. The towers of Wigmore rose impressively out of the hillside before them, like spear-like fists thrust up towards the sky.

"Look!" said Richard. "Wigmore at last. And it's all yours, my Lord Roger Mortimer!"

Chapter 10

JULY 1304 – THE AFTERMATH

BY THE TIME Roger arrived with Richard, I had been in mourning for three days.

"You're here! Oh my dear lord, you're here at last! Now all can begin to be well again," I cried.

Roger hugged me close in his arms, despite his damp and stiff, mud-spattered clothing. It felt good to breathe in his warm body.

"You must be so tired – Richard too!"

"Not so bad, my Lady. We were able to rest up at Stokesay last night, though we would rather have reached Wigmore. So it has not been so very far to come this morning."

Hearing Richard address me as *my Lady*, when he had always called me Lady Joan before gave me a start. But it was true. I was now the Lady of Wigmore, and Roger's mother the Dowager Lady.

"Mother?" Roger asked of me.

"Resting. She sat up with him almost all the time and is still worn out."

I led them into the Great Hall and ordered servants to bring them wine. I was glad Margaret was not there, for now I had to tell the story all over again.

"He died three nights ago, on the seventeenth. It was a good death. He has been laid in his shroud to await burial in the Abbey."

"Do we know who killed him?"

I shook my head.

"But tightly organised with a good fletcher of Welsh arrows and bows, I'll be bound," and Roger's face darkened with anger. "Couldn't they catch any of them? By God, we'd have strung them up, if they had."

"The main concern was for your father, seeing as they were not pursued."

Roger's face stayed dark.

"It was intended for Mortimer. That much is clear. Maybe an old compatriot of Llywellyn ap Gruffuyd."

"So long afterwards?" Richard asked.

"The Welsh have long memories."

I fell silent, remembering Edmund's deathbed confession.

"No-one from this family must ever ride abroad again without a fully armed guard. And I mean *no-one*. If only I had been there!"

"Under the circumstances, it would have made no difference, like as not," Richard interrupted, with a hand on his shoulder, "except to get yourself killed too."

"He died well shriven?" Roger asked.

"Oh yes. And there were not so many sins! He did say he never intended for Llywellyn to die that way and regretted it. It was… someone else's idea…to let their men at arms kill him on the way back. Edmund paid for Masses to be said for him in the Abbey at Cwmhir because he felt the guilt so keenly."

"I know. That someone was Uncle Roger, who was less sentimental about it all."

I winced at his reaction.

"Brother Benedict was here day and night too, and we all prayed together. And the Abbot came at the end."

There was a knock at the door and Roger looked up to see Avice there, with a bundle in her arms, and little Edmund peeping from behind her skirts. Edmund shrieked with joy and ran headlong across the floor to his father, who caught him just in time and swung him into his arms.

"My, he's grown! What a big, strong boy you are!"

"That's what they do, master!" smiled Avice.

I rose and took the bundle from her.

"And here is your new daughter, already beginning her third month of life. Isn't she pretty?"

Roger took her carefully and looked down at the soft, pink, sleeping face.

"Margaret," he said. "Nothing but the best husband for her!"

"A long way off," I chided him gently.

"Yes, but time passes quickly. Here we are, Joan, as Lord and Lady of Wigmore, already. One has passed from life and one entered in – a new generation is coming."

"Your father asked to see them both in his last lucid moments, and was very comforted when they were brought to him. He asked Benedict to bless them. Then he turned away to gaze on the Cross, muttering prayers, until he passed into unconsciousness."

"You were better comfort to him than I would have been," Roger acknowledged. "Thank you, dear heart."

"He did ask for you. We told him you were with the King and the Prince in Scotland, with Uncle Roger; and he understood that."

"And he couldn't wait."

"No," I put a tender hand up to his cheek. "God bless him! He couldn't wait any longer."

By the time the funeral was over, and Lord Edmund Mortimer's body laid to rest in Wigmore Abbey, Roger had become accustomed to everyone in the castle and its environs calling him 'my Lord', even though I was not accustomed to my new title. But we knew it could not last and, when his mother called us into her private rooms, he was due for a rude awakening. Uncle Roger was there too, having come down for the funeral, bearing the news that Stirling had finally surrendered. Roger was sorry not to have seen the 'Greek fire' his uncle spoke of, which had eventually blasted the gate apart.

"We must discuss your future," Margaret began.

"My future is with the family, mother. As the Baron of Wigmore. Ludlow too, in time."

"I know that, Roger. But your uncle has been told you must enter wardship first."

"Can the King not make an exception for a married man in his eighteenth year, and an active one in his campaigns?"

His uncle chuckled. "Good try, Roger, but you know he will not. He insists you must be a ward until you reach twenty-one. Still, it's only temporary."

"'Temporary' – at the King's pleasure!"

"Actually it's at his son's pleasure. It means you will automatically enter his household."

Roger stared in disbelief.

"Not as his ward, surely?"

"As good as. Can't you guess? As Piers Gaveston's. Gaveston has been offered custody of your lands at the Lord Edward's express wish, and of course he has accepted them."

"He's barely older than I am!"

"Do you object to him?"

"No, I like him well enough, and can learn much about jousting from him."

"Then count yourself lucky. It could be worse."

Roger was thoughtful.

"What about Joan?

"The Prince is set to marry soon, and Joan will be offered a role as lady-in-waiting. So she can go too. The children will remain in good hands with your mother."

All this without me being consulted, I thought, wryly but stoically.

"And what of mother herself? Her wishes should be considered too."

"I am content to live quietly at Radnor in the meantime, with the Prince's blessing."

"Not to remarry?" Roger was wary. I knew he would have no mind to share his inheritance with another.

"I think not. At thirty-five years of age, I feel my childbearing years can be put behind me. I was fortunate enough to be married to a kind and gentle man; I doubt I would find his like again.

"Though Matilda and yourself are well married, and John wishes only to emulate his big brother, I am still needed to nurture my younger ones, as well as your two, for the time being. My Joan, unlike yours, is a shy and timid girl who wishes to enter the nunnery at Lyngbroke and I rather think Elizabeth will take after her. I would prefer to remain a widow and bring up the three smallest boys on my own in a studious fashion, and I know my lord would have approved of that. I have no desire to sully his name with another's, and I am determined to protect my own interests and that of the family."

Roger bowed. "That makes me very happy, Mother. So we will thank Piers for his largesse until I can return. I would like to look into buying my freedom a little sooner than the three allotted years, however, so I can be back in charge as soon as possible."

Margaret sighed.

"Always so impatient to grow faster! Well, I cannot blame you. Though something in you tells me you will never return for long. You are bound for active life. May God watch over you."

"Don't fret, mother. It will not be long. I think Piers will be amenable to letting me go sooner if we can only raise the money."

Margaret inclined her head, and smiled at her son.

"You know him better than us."

Chapter 11

MY LORD SAT well back against the cantle of his saddle. His gloved left hand held the Mortimer shield, with its azure and gold cross bands and white centre. It also held his looped reins. Holding his grey mare back with a light touch, he snapped his visor shut and took up a lance with his right hand. He knew he was perfectly balanced and it gave him supreme confidence.

I was watching from the viewing stand for ladies in Prince Edward's household, and thought my lord looked very fine in his rich, golden-brown quilted gambeson over chain mail, with plate armour over his elbows and knees, and the magnificent plume of gold and blue feathers atop his iron helm. The lists were well advanced and already Gaveston had knocked our kinsman, John de Warenne, to the ground.

It was a warm summer's day with a light wind fluttering all the colourful pennants. A similar frisson of excitement ran through the stand. Only Piers Gaveston was left to meet my Lord Mortimer's challenge. Everyone held their breath.

Roger certainly looked the part of a worthy challenger to Gaveston. He was tall, upright and muscular for a young man, with an easy seat in the saddle. But looks are far from everything in the lists. Marcher, his favourite mare of the moment, was pawing the ground in that showy way she had, champing at the bit and fidgeting her hindquarters. It looked intimidating, but I knew Roger remained in full control as he lowered his lance. Across the meadow, Gaveston, dressed strikingly in black and white, and mounted on a beautiful black steed, did the same. I felt sick with nerves as they dug in their spurs and took off at a gallop, with thundering hooves.

Through the slits in his visor, Roger could see Piers veering across to him. Too close! Too close by far! Roger's tactic was to hold on unnerved, and force a swerve off course, at the last moment. Both held their ground. A collective cry of horror rode up from the crowd. Surely they must clash head-on! Then a gap opened up, in the last few seconds, but their knees glanced off each other on the first pass. There was no room for effective lance work and so these flailed wildly in the air. Both men were flung back in their saddles and did well to remain seated, though they had dropped their lances.

It was Roger who turned first, pulling up and turning more quickly. Marcher span round in a prancing pirouette and a shower of saliva. He deftly caught a second lance from Richard of Monmouth, a fraction of a second before Piers was ready for his turn.

Once more they hurtled together. Roger's lance was steady but Piers had grabbed his in haste and it was subject to an infinitesimal wobble. They clashed again and this time Roger's lance struck the very centre of the black-and-white shield, and threw up a shower of wooden shards. One of them caught Piers with a crack under his jaw and he toppled sideways, stunned. His own lance landed wide on the Mortimer shield and was easily deflected.

When Roger turned again, he saw Piers had hit the ground heavily and lay still. The black horse careered off wildly, pursued by varlets. He raised his lance to the heavens in triumph.

The Prince screamed. He rose from his seat trembling. We spectators drew our breath in sharply as Edward rushed down onto the field to sob and cradle Piers' head in his hands.

"Perrot! My beloved brother!"

But Piers was only winded and rolled over, feigning laziness. Then he sat up and removed his helm to shake out his straight, brown hair, still somewhat dazed from the tumble.

The crowd cheered and Edward fell around his neck and embraced him with a tender kiss.

"I am perfectly unharmed, my Lord," Piers laughed ruefully. "Childe Mortimer did well to unseat me, but it takes more than that to keep me out of the saddle. Bring my horse and I shall re-mount!"

Only the Prince would not hear of it: he bade his 'Perrot' retire, to sit next to him the rest of the tournament, if he loved his sire in return. Roger, who had been sitting quietly in the saddle after his first involuntary expression of triumph, rode slowly back without a weapon, dismounted gracefully and bowed, removing his own helm and plumage. Piers was still seated on the ground, with Edward in an undignified posture on his knees next to him. Roger extended his gloved hand to Piers, and Piers took it, allowing himself to be helped up. He clapped Roger on the back.

"Well done!" he said. "I suppose that means I have to stop calling you a childe! Will young Mortimer do instead?"

Roger nodded and smiled, and they embraced to show there was no rancour between them. The crowd cheered again to see it. The Prince, after scrambling to his own feet, frowned, but Piers was quick to mollify him.

"He was as straight as a die and deserves his victor's purse. None of us are invincible, my Lord. We should be proud of him."

At last, the Prince smiled, the crowd applauded again and the awkward moment passed. Edward took both of them by hand, one on either side, and led them up to the gallery, insisting Roger sit on his left hand with me beside him, and Gaveston on his right. As I raised my skirts to move obediently up the stand, I breathed more slowly now, with some relief.

I presented my husband with his purse from the Prince, and gave him a kiss on the cheek.

"Was that wise?" I whispered under my breath as Roger took his seat next to me again.

"What would you have me do?" he replied, in the same cautious tone, under cover of bending to remove his armour plates. "Piers will respect me the more for it and I must make my reputation."

Edward had recovered his equilibrium and his manners now but clearly lost all interest in the joust, which now concerned battles between the mere runners-up. So he invited us to accompany himself and Piers to view the latest addition to his animal menagerie.

We made our way back towards the manor house and its outbuildings with a handful of retainers. It was here that the Prince kept his caged lion. It was very different to its depiction on the royal coat of arms, for this was a sturdy beast with a great head and mane, and massive paws – not at all like the sleeker, more elongated version, which Roger told me was really a leopard or panther. But we had seen the lion before and I disliked watching it pace up and down in its cage.

However, the new creature captivated me. It was large and sand-coloured; sitting down, chewing its food with slightly hairy, rubbery lips, watching our every move with long-lashed eyes. Then slowly it rose onto its knees and got up, making me squeal with delight.

"Look at its hump! And such a haughty look. What is it?"

Prince Edward was gratified by my response.

"It's a camel," he said. "They say they store water in their humps. The infidels ride them like horses over the desert. They can do this because camel toes splay out on the sand and get a firmer grip. They can run very quickly and their temperament is more biddable than the lion – much like our own horses."

"But not a very comfortable ride for the ladies. And too slow for the joust, I fancy!" quipped Piers.

We all laughed and the mood was lightened again.

Later on came the feasting, with dancers, minstrels, jugglers and tumblers aplenty. Prince Edward knew how to provide good entertainment: and there was much wine. It was already late when we ladies retired to bed.

But, after yet more wine, Roger found himself in the Prince's solar with Piers, de Clare, Warenne, Robert Clifford, Fitzalan, Badlesmere and Damory. All of them noblemen in Edward's inner circle. Now he was included too, and this was worth staying up for!

It was a sweaty night and the candles blazing in the sconces burnt hot as hell, so the Prince allowed them all to strip to their braies. More wine was consumed. It seemed it had turned into who could drink whom under the table the quickest. The Prince was not ready for bed yet. He must dice, even though the numbers blurred into each other in the heat and the wine and candle fumes. Someone called for ale to quench their thirst. Gilbert de Clare, still too young to hold much drink, lay slumped unconscious in his seat. John de Warenne was prattling on unintelligibly about Langton the Treasurer's meanness and the King's lack of reason in banishing the Prince and his entourage from court (which explained why they had all come to Langley) after a row between father and son.

"Completely uncalled for!" Roger agreed, as this was always Edward's opinion. Then the Prince started wrestling amicably with Piers in a brotherly fashion, but broke off to embrace him and kiss him, with his mouth over his companion's, in a far from brotherly way, as they both collapsed onto his bed.

Roger began to feel giddy and uncertain about what he was seeing, but Edward remained expansive towards them all and insisted Roger sit on his left as Victor Ludorum, with Piers on his right. He put his arms around them both.

"What a boon it is to have such faithful friends!" Edward cried. The candles seemed to grow ever more luminous and the shapes in the room more indistinct.

Then Roger suddenly found himself on the floor wrestling with the Prince. He had demurred a challenge, as far as he was aware, but it was still happening. They rolled like young bear cubs, but some of Edward's fumbling felt wrong and was more intimate. They both had slowed reactions and although the prince was strong, he was not alert enough to come out on top. Except Roger was not so far gone he did not know he needed to let this happen. So he soon lay spread-eagled on his back in a hard hold and banged his arm on the floor for submission. Edward whooped with delight.

"I have won, have I not, Piers?"

"You have, sire!"

"And now we need to piss."

They all staggered off to the garderobe and held a contest to see who could piss the furthest.

Back in the bedchamber, with a stiff erection and his braies around his ankles, Edward lost interest in everyone else but Piers.

"Come to bed, my beloved," he implored, lasciviously, "and let us close the curtains!"

Roger, John, Clifford and Fitzalan stood transfixed and looked askance at Piers. The others had staggered off some time ago, either to vomit or to sleep.

"Leave us now," said Piers quietly, with a grin.

Snatching up their clothes, they left and did not stop to put them on till some way down the corridor.

"Well!" said John de Warenne, suddenly sober. "What are we to make of that?"

"Horseplay?" from Roger, though he knew it was not.

Warenne shook his head.

"I don't think so."

"But we know the Prince loves Piers as his brother, like David loved Jonathan," from Robert Clifford.

"Yes, but David didn't bugger Jonathan!"

"Maybe he was confused and over-amorous in his cups? And Piers will calm him down and look after him," Roger could imagine that.

"Maybe."

They all looked at each other but still felt uneasy.

"The King mustn't get to hear about it, for sure," said Robert.

"By God, no!" Roger swore. "Mark that, Fitzalan! He's already sore with Edward about hunting stags in Langton's land without permission."

So they parted drunkenly with an agreement to say nothing to anyone.

Feeling the need for normality, Roger slipped quietly into bed and I stirred sleepily.

"What's wrong?" I mumbled.

"Nothing. It's very late. Go back to sleep."

But I was awake now and it felt good to be held.

"Where have you been?"

"With the Prince and Piers."

"All this time?"

"There was a lot of drunkenness and… horseplay."

"Were they angry with you?"

"No, not at all."

"Then what?"

"We left him going to bed with Piers."

"Oh, that? So it's true then."

"What do you mean?"

"There have been rumours – from the ladies married to the chamberlain and valets to the Prince."

"You never told me! Joan, you are astonishing."

"Well, I thought it was just malicious gossip."

"He does love Piers immoderately."

"Richard of Monmouth loves you."

"Yes, I guess he does, but I don't take him to bed with us, Joan!"

"Nor at any other time?" I teased.

"Of course not! The very idea turns my stomach."

"Well, we don't actually know, do we? About Piers and the Prince, I mean?"

"No – no, we don't. But what I saw tonight was…well, it was pretty damning."

"Does it change your regard for Piers?"

Roger considered this. "I don't know! We're told it's a mortal sin. I'd like to think he was in more control of himself, but then how could he be when royalty is concerned? Edward will be King one day, and soon. Piers certainly takes all the advantages he can from him and he is a bit of a rogue, though a likeable one. He doesn't have much respect for anything or anyone." He thought some more. "And our good fortune is tied in with Piers. So we must turn a blind eye to it."

"Hmmm," I murmured. "Perhaps they both just need to be married and then there would be an end to it."

Chapter 12

MY LORD WENT to kneel at the tomb of William Marshall, the Greatest Knight, his great-great-grandfather on Maud's side. He had told me her stories about him many times. It was thirteen years since he told his grandmother he wanted to come here, to the Temple Church. Now, at the age of nineteen, he was here and his heart was singing.

In April, he had been endowed with the full possession of his father's estates and become Lord Mortimer, Baron of Wigmore. Two thousand, five-hundred marks were duly paid to Gaveston for his early release from wardship. He was known at Court, respected for his excellent fighting and jousting skills, married with two children, and another on the way. It felt like the best day of our lives, with more to come.

We were now living back in Wigmore with the children, but had returned to London for Roger to be knighted on Whitsunday, prior to another Scottish campaign. A rare honour to receive at such a young age! The old King held on, despite poor health, but there was the sense of a new guard of young men champing at the bit, in the wings. My lord made a solemn vow to William in his grave to do him proud in this new Round Table, before crossing himself and leaving the round nave for the bright sunlight outside.

A huge camp had been set up in the Temple gardens and the orchards of the Priory of St John. These fields were packed with canvas pavilions, bathing and robing chambers, and noisy, excited people throbbing with colour and life, for the prospective knights had all brought their families to the celebrations. There were so many of us that the fruit trees in the garden had to be chopped down to make room. The fallen blossom made a pretty white and pink carpet for the ladies to parade on, trying to outdo each other in their finery. I had been much concerned about my attire for weeks but Roger said I looked beautiful. There was a positive buzz of excitement from everyone. Never before had so many men been knighted at once.

Everything had been provided for by the Prince of Wales. He was to be knighted first by the King in the Palace of Westminster, his quarrel with his father forgotten, and would then proceed to the Abbey to knight over two hundred more in a mass ceremony.

Roger went to rejoin his uncle and comrades by their horses. Many of them were cousins, like Lord Berkeley and his son, Hereford's nephew, and Fitzalan, soon to be the Earl of Arundel. The very young de Clare of Gloucester was there, too, with Clifford. There was much jovial clapping of backs and mutual congratulation, during which Roger and the young Hugh Despenser greeted each other, firstly by accident, and then through gritted teeth.

Richard was there, of course, to help him mount and hand Roger his sword. Then they were off in a great procession through the streets of Clerkenwell, past Smithfield where the unfortunate William Wallace had been executed, with his guts torn out, the previous year. The cheers of the crowd rang in their ears, and children ran behind them, throwing their caps in the air, so they felt like Kings themselves. They entered the City through the New Gate, turned down the Lud and bore right along the Strand, past all the fine houses of bishops and the richest of merchants, all the way to Charing Cross, and finally down to Westminster. We ladies preceded them, in plushly furnished waggons.

The din of excitement made us all heady – there was nothing the London populace liked better than a spectacle and this was certainly that, with all the jewel-encrusted velvet and rich brocades worn by the future knights. They held glittering swords at their sides and rode astride magnificently groomed horses, in their own colours.

The din was scarcely less in the Abbey Church, with spectators crammed into every nook and cranny, even shinning up the columns to get a better view. There was a great cacophony of shouting, scarcely suitable for a consecrated place. Warhorses had to be brought in to clear a path for all the dismounted knights and the Abbey monks had to plead for silence repeatedly, so the Mass could be sung with a little more sobriety.

After Mass, Roger and his uncle waited their turn for their names to be called in Latin. My heart was swelling with pride as I watched Roger wash his hands in the silver bowl proffered by the priest, who sprinkled him with holy water. Then he was before Prince Edward, making his vows to uphold Church and Crown and the order of the knighthood: to be merciful to his enemies, to respect women, and to live in moderation and chastity. The touch of Edward's sword on his shoulder must have felt as if a tightly wound spring had been released inside him. He took a deep breath of uncoiled pleasure as he held out his hands to receive his belt and sword and spurs. Gaveston, knighted earlier, standing at the right hand of the Prince as usual, gave him a knowing smile. When the ceremony was done, the knights processed solemnly to the Great Hall in Westminster Palace and there the noisy congratulations began again.

We had attended a good many banquets by now, but none as fine as this, with so many courses and so many minstrels and players. The highlight was the bringing in and parading of a gigantic silver salver, with two swans appearing to swim in a net of gold. Then the King rose to speak. He was stooped now, from his former great height, and his beard and hair were white, but his voice still rang out firmly.

At first, he spoke of the virtues of knighthood and his hopes for those before him. Then, inevitably, he turned to the state of Scotland. Although William Wallace was gone at last, that foul traitor, Robert Bruce, had absconded from Court and stepped up to claim the throne of Scotland, after killing his rival claimant John Comyn, murdering him before the altar of the Church of the Greyfriars in Dumfries.

The uproar over this reached all the way up to the timber of the rafters in the Great Hall. Nothing as shocking and abhorrent had occurred since the murder of the blessed Thomas à Becket in his own cathedral, over a hundred years ago. It was not that the two victims were comparable, but the sacrilegious deed and subsequent self-crowning of the criminal, Bruce, was outrageous. Furthermore, Bruce had declared his independence from England! Scotland as an independent country – it was not to be brooked!

The King took a few steps forward and held up his hand for quiet, though the outraged reaction had pleased him greatly.

"By the God of Heaven and these swans," he roared, indicating the silver salver bearing the regal birds, "I will avenge the death of John Comyn and wreak vengeance on the perfidious Scots."

He turned to his son and chief nobles at the high table.

"As soon as I have accomplished this task, avenging the injuries done to God and to the Church, I will go to the Holy Land and end my days fighting the infidel. Only swear to me this: that if I die before the task be finished, you will carry my bones with the Army and not bury them until you have brought full vengeance to the Scots!"

An answering roar of assent echoed round the rafters again. Cheering knights rose to their feet or bent their knee, trying to outdo each other in their oaths of acquiescence, with Roger amongst them, to my dismay. Prince Edward swore he would not sleep two nights under the same roof until he reached Scotland to help his father finish the job.

Under the tide of general enthusiasm, Roger leant across me to drop some quiet words into his uncle's ear.

"If the old man dies before it's done, it will go hard for young Edward."

"It is our task to see they do not fail, man or boy. Young Edward has a strong and manly bearing now."

"Aye, before others. But I have seen a different side to him, Uncle. His nature is not warlike."

"Then we must stand by him and make it so. You especially Roger, for you seem to have Piers' ear."

"See how he brings in the minstrels, tumblers and clowns again."

His uncle shrugged.

"Today we celebrate well. I see no harm in that. Tomorrow we fight. You know that Aymer de Valence has already secured the border?"

"No, I had not heard the latest."

"You must remember to keep your ear to the ground! We stand by to follow, of course, and must achieve more this time."

Roger was certainly itching to honour his new spurs and I would now inevitably follow his encampments.

The omens were good to begin with. As the army marched north in June, we heard that de Valence, soon to succeed as Earl of Pembroke, had defeated the Scots resoundingly at Methven and was pushing on towards Perth to establish his headquarters there. The Prince's Army, under Hereford and the Mortimers, advanced to Lochmaben, which surrendered without a struggle. But the King was lagging behind; because he became too ill to ride, he was forced to travel by litter and had only reached Nottingham. The important prisoners from Methven were sent to him there, in irons.

Bruce sent his womenfolk to the castle of Kildrummy, but Pembroke followed them and laid siege. They managed to get a castle blacksmith to set fire to the granary, forcing the women to flee. They were soon captured and sent south to the King, too. Roger was hardened by now to seeing harsh treatment but what happened next, he said, made him uneasy, and I was appalled.

King Edward insisted that Bruce's sister and his mistress were incarcerated publicly, like animals in wooden cages, hanging outside Roxburgh and Berwick castles respectively. The only woman he spared this indignity was Bruce's wife, Elizabeth, who was the daughter of the Earl of Ulster. Twelve knights were hung at Berwick and two sent to London for a public execution to rival the horror of Wallace's death. Well, that was vengeance, we supposed, but what of the women? How could the vows of chivalry be taken so lightly? Even Uncle Roger admitted it was a bad move.

By September, the King had made his painful progress up to Carlisle, feeling every bump and stone on the road in his swollen belly, just as Lord Edmund had. There, the campaign was temporarily halted.

Robert Bruce had not been brought to justice, but many had, and his women were there to be bargained with. The whole Army was recalled to Carlisle to loiter there, in view of the King's health, with the young knights kicking their heels again after their first taste and scent of blood.

"It's too much to expect us to stay," Piers complained, lounging back on a couch in the Prince's pavilion. "Our combat skills are growing rusty again. What we need is a good tournament."

Roger agreed. Far from being a barrier to friendship, his amicable emergence from Piers' wardship, admittedly with the payment of 2,500 marks over three years, seemed to have bound them together more closely. I was not always happy about this. Nevertheless, Piers no longer called him anything but Mortimer, or even Roger, and seemed proud of his emergence as a hard, toned and courageous knight.

"The King won't let anyone go," Roger pointed out. "Especially us."

His uncle had confirmed the King was growing more suspicious of Piers' influence on his son.

"Be surprised if he missed us, he's certainly too frail to follow," replied Piers.

"But, as we know, he'll send us others to bring us back."

"Not if we're quick about it. Come on, Roger! Don't you fancy a proper tournament in Gascony where the sun still shines and the whores are pretty?"

Roger admitted he was tempted, I hoped more so by the tournament than the whores, though I was pregnant yet again and about to go home.

"Ned is in agreement, though he feels constrained to stay. In case, well, you know what…"

Ned seemed to be in agreement with everything Piers said these days. For he had recently sworn that Gaveston and himself should be as brothers-in-arms, standing and fighting against all men, if necessary, and sharing their possessions. Roger thought this was a noble and courtly thing to do as the Prince clearly loved Piers so much. He blocked the memory of that appalling night when the

Prince had wrestled him. It was only a jape, after all, a bit of fun, and Piers was certainly full of fun and excellent company.

Privately, he doubted whether Piers returned Edward's love in the same way, suspecting he was merely using the Prince for his own betterment. But Roger respected Piers' fighting skills and looked to him to give good counsel in military matters after a succession. Now he had time on his hands, and so did Roger, not even able to return to his own lands.

"Are we agreed then?"

Roger stretched out his long legs and smiled, both hands behind his dark head of hair.

"Agreed. Anything's better than dying of boredom."

They took off that night with a handful of others and all their retainers and men at arms.

However, they had scarcely left when 'Ned' sent messages for them to return post haste and make for Wetheral Priory, close to Carlisle, where he had persuaded Queen Margaret to intercede with the King. He said his father was more than furious, stamping his feet in a torrent of wrath, positively foaming at the mouth in his rage against 'the deserters'. They must all be arrested, no less, and have their lands forfeited to the Crown. Despite his illness, the old man still had plenty of Plantagenet temper left in him.

Roger was lucky, for the Queen was as good as her word in appealing for Edward's mercy to be shown to the younger knights. Not so Piers. This was entirely the Prince's fault because he unwisely sent the Treasurer, Langton, to the King, to request that Gaveston should be elevated to the rank of Count of Ponthieu, now that he was young Edward's 'brother in arms'.

The old King could scarcely believe it and sent for his son, immediately. Unfortunately, the Prince entered the pavilion with an insensitive nonchalance.

"Did you send Langton to me?" thundered the King, gripping the arms of his throne so tightly that his clenched fists showed white around the knuckles.

"I did," Edmund faltered slightly now.

"And did you instruct him – nay, *order*, him – to plead with me because you believe Gaveston should be elevated to the rank of Count? Of Ponthieu?"

"Indeed I did. We are brothers in arms."

"God's wounds! What in hellfire does that mean? All knights are your brothers in arms. You do not pick Gaveston out to be a brother! You already have two half-brothers, Thomas and Edmund, thanks to fair Marguerite. Do they count for nothing?"

"Yes, sire, but Piers is my true soul's brother."

At this, the King flew into an even greater rage and it was a wonder he did not suffer an apoplectic fit then and there, so red grew his face.

"You wretched son of a whore!" he cried, temporarily forgetting his own great love for the deceased Eleanor of Castile, his former Queen, and this son's mother. "Damn you for being the only son of my first marriage to survive!"

Edward opened his mouth to protest but the King shouted him down.

"Do you want to give away your lands? You! You, who have never gained any! As God lives, if it were not for fear of breaking up the Kingdom, I would never let you enjoy your inheritance."

When the Prince made as if to speak again in defence of Piers, his father lunged at him, grabbing his long hair with such force, he tore out handfuls from his scalp. The Prince dare not retaliate and allowed himself to be thrown to the floor despite his superior strength, where the King kicked and kicked him in front of the shocked courtiers, until he fell back exhausted on his throne.

There was an awful silence as the bruised Prince pulled himself into a kneeling position, hands clutching his burning scalp. The King was taking great gasps of air and called for wine. It was brought by a frightened courtier who passed him the goblet with shaking hands. Slowly, he rallied and bent his hard gaze upon his errant son.

"You must swear to me," he croaked, "on your immortal soul, that you will never see Gaveston again without my permission."

Prince Edward bent his head and wept.

"For the sake of your Kingdom and the country!"

The oath was taken through stammering lips.

"And to make doubly sure, I pronounce Piers Gaveston banished from our realm."

"No!"

"Yes! Leave me now! You have worn me out!"

The Prince was inconsolable in his own tent. His knights and men at arms reassured him the King's wrath would not last forever, but to no avail. In the meantime, Piers had been called for his own audience with the King.

The next day "Ned" showered him with expensive presents and rode with him to Dover to bid farewell in tears. But then Piers was gone, no doubt to make a great deal of money from the tourneys in France, and the whole court heaved a sigh of relief, including myself.

Chapter 13

I WAS BACK in Wigmore now, but Roger told me what happened next. It was another year, with plans for yet another Scottish campaign. The old King held on and resolutely headed north. My lord and his uncle were summoned again to attend with the rest of the Army. Bruce was stronger than ever, despite his setbacks last year and the capture of his women. It seemed this made him only more determined. In May, he defeated Pembroke and drove him back to Ayr Castle, where he awaited the King and his reinforcements.

Prince Edward stayed behind for the present at Lambeth Palace. Roger was aware he was sulking — there was no other word for it — due to Piers' banishment. The last time he saw the Prince it was all he could talk about. Did Roger think his father might allow Piers to go to Ireland on service? Would Roger visit his prospective estates in Meath and invite Piers so that Edward could meet him secretly there? This worried me. In vain, Roger tried to focus his Prince's mind on the coming campaign in Scotland. He was dismayed to see that Edward had no interest in this whatsoever.

"Sire," Roger said, "you must be patient. The King is sixty-eight and a sick man. Already he has stopped appearing in public. Once you are King, all of this will be forgotten and Piers may rejoin us. Until then, you need to show your father some prowess in warfare at the head of his army. That way, he will be quicker to forgive, and the people will welcome you as King."

"Do you think so, Roger?" Edward said, stroking his fair beard, "Yes, you are right. Of course you are right. You have wisdom beyond your years, Mortimer, I know you do. I promise I will follow you to Scotland as soon as I may."

But already, Roger knew that the Prince would speak to someone else more engaging the next day and change his mind again, always

75

believing the last person he spoke to was in the right. This did not bode well for the future. My lord said it might be better if Piers were to come back – the Prince was so lost and indecisive without him. His own course was clear enough, at any rate . Now he was a knight of some standing, he needed to follow his uncle and the King, however familiar the road to Carlisle had become.

It was true the old King no longer appeared in public. By the time the Army was gathering towards Carlisle, there were even rumours he may already be dead, rumours which reached the ear of the King. When he heard them, he struggled out of his bed and took horse again, in front of the thousands of men who had obeyed his call. Onwards to Scotland to face the Bruce.

He managed two miles each of the next two days but refused to take to his litter, merely requesting a day of rest. A strange air of foreboding hung over the camp that night. Everyone was quietly employed cleaning their armour and tending to their horses, but secretly wondering if they would ever manage to relieve Pembroke at Ayr, even though they were now close to the Solway Firth. It was light almost till midnight, being so far north, with no need for torches to burn earlier. But the mood was sombre and the day dawned wet and windy.

Despite the advice of his retainers, the King rose from his bed with dogged determination and insisted on his horse. Everyone expected him to call a halt again after two miles, but this time he carried on. The wet was miserable, as it often is in July, somehow made worse by dripping greenery. It was not truly cold but the damp created a chill nevertheless. The King must be soaked to his very bones. The further they went, the more his lean body sagged and bent in the saddle, head down against the driving rain and capricious wind.

It was four in the afternoon and the Mortimer retinue had long since caught up with the advance guard, in which the King insisted on riding.

"Should we not stop him, Uncle?" Roger asked. "I am afraid he will fall from his horse."

The older man shook his head.

"You cannot stop a King, Roger. Let him be."

"Even for his own good?"

"Especially for his own good."

Another two agonising miles. Then, at last, they saw the waves in the Firth and made their way down to the green, marshy plain of Burgh le Sands, as flat as a piece of unleavened bread. The King stopped his horse and did in fact fall from his saddle. But he brushed aside those who rushed to help him, Roger amongst them. Instead of accepting their arm, Edward drew himself up to his full height, which was still considerably more than most men, and drew his sword from its sheath with a shaking hand.

Raising it in the air, he uttered a strangled cry like some wild animal.

"Scotland!" he yelled, "Scotland! Scotland in sight!"

Then he crumpled like a lanky puppet suddenly released from its strings and fell to his knees.

My lord was the first to raise him this time. The King was still conscious and his clouded blue eyes, or rather one of them, for the drooping lid on the other was now so weak it had closed, looked into Roger's deep-brown ones.

"Who are you?" he demanded.

"Mortimer of Wigmore, sire."

"Ah yes. I know your uncle of Chirk well."

"Yes, sire."

"You are one of my son's followers, are you not?"

"Yes, sire."

The King grabbed his gambeson and croaked at him hoarsely.

"He must not, I repeat not, have anything to do with Gaveston again. Do you hear me?"

Roger swallowed hard.

"I don't think Gaveston has committed any wrong, sire. As far as I know."

"I know that, fool! Why do you think I gave him a King's pension when he left us? It's not Gaveston to blame for taking advantage. It's my son!"

Roger bowed his head in silent acquiescence.

"You have some sense about you. Swear to me, young Mortimer, you will endeavour to guide my son…for the sake of the realm. He would do well to listen to your like. Swear!"

"I swear, sire."

Then his chamberlain came up to bear him away and the order was given to make camp.

The King was taken to Lanercost Priory nearby to have his soul shriven and be put to bed. The following day dawned as fine as the last day had been dreary, but the mood of the camp remained subdued. There was talk that the King's chaplain had been with him most of the day at the Priory.

At half past three, Roger Mortimer of Chirk came looking for his nephew.

"It's over," he said in answer to Roger's uplifted, questioning face. "About half an hour ago. He asked for a drink, though he had been barely lucid all day, and fell back on the pillows. The King is dead. The campaign over." He seemed genuinely upset, and certainly perturbed. The old order had passed away at last, and he was part of that. "King Edward is dead!" he sighed, regretfully.

My Lord Roger Mortimer of Wigmore rose to his feet.

"Long live King Edward!" he said, quietly, and the two men clasped hands.

And so the new order began.

PART TWO
THE NEW KING

Chapter 14

1323 — SOUTHAMPTON CASTLE

WHEN THEY FIRST brought me to Hampshire, we reached Southampton after a long and difficult journey and entered the town through the Bargate. The castle contains Royal apartments, but they put us in the Arundel Tower. This is a circular, limestone drum tower on the northwest walls. It looks towards the quay in one direction and a Franciscan friary in the other. Although it is named after the present Governor of the castle, the locals call it 'Windwhistle Tower' because of its exposed and draughty position.

It is noisy because barrels of wine from Gascony are unloaded off the ships most days, and roll thunderously into the castle vaults. The tower itself is little better than a storage vault and considerably smaller, being cramped, gloomy, cold and damp. Its walls are scantily whitewashed and bereft of any hangings or tapestries. So the wind does indeed whistle through the unglazed window slits and threatens to put out the miserable fire. The garderobe is so cold the children refuse to use it, so of course I let them use chamber pots.

Sir John Arundel is the Governor and comes from wealthy West Country farming stock, with a ruddy complexion and sturdy frame to match. He has never seen the Marches, though he has of course heard of them. He is not impressed by the Marcher Barons nor their ladies. I do not think he is entirely stony hearted but he has his orders from the Sheriff and the King, and this includes no comforts. Although he did seem embarrassed at the cold when he saw young Joan and Isabella, and brought extra blankets for their pallet beds. I am afraid John took them in a surly fashion, so I had to reprimand him for forgetting his manners. We must at the very least remain dignified, no matter how we are treated. But we are not treated well.

All that winter, I was expected to keep my household on a penny a day. Of course, it was impossible, even though Ockley and Bullesdon were promptly taken elsewhere as 'I have no need for men at arms'. The de Burghs were also excused my plight, with further copious weeping from Lady de Burgh on her departure. I am left with the three children and only Avice to attend to our needs, plus one clerk, Walter of Evesham, as I may now write letters – though I am perfectly capable of doing this myself - and my Augustinian confessor and chaplain from Wigmore, Richard Judas. Walter and Judas sleep below with the guards.

If it were not for Judas, I do not think we would have survived that first winter, for he is allowed more freedom of movement as a cleric and can visit the Franciscan friars outside the walls. Here, he gains information about the outside world, and usually returns with some of the friars' welcome produce to keep us going. He also brings in wood for the fire as well as spiritual comfort, and vital paper and ink! I have therefore been able to keep a journal, which I have found helpful. So far, I have written all about our youthful days and auspicious beginnings, as you know. Now I must turn to darker days and the reasons for our downfall.

Through Judas, I learn that my sons, Edmund and Roger, are kept prisoners at Windsor whilst Geoffrey is still marooned at his grandmother's house in France, but Margaret and Maud are still allowed to live with their respective husbands. Roger remains under sentence of life imprisonment in the Tower with his uncle. My little ones were indeed taken to my mother-in-law, thank the Lord, and I have no doubt she is doing her best to bring them up as good Christians, though I miss them sorely.

Spring seemed to come very late to us this year, and drags itself reluctantly toward summer. Gradually, the children's colds have eased, though Isabella seems to have a permanent cough, which worries me. She has never been a strong child. Nevertheless, I worry most about John, who is old enough and man enough to miss his older brothers and the outdoor life. He is bitterly resentful of being cooped up with womenfolk and his moody silences grow worse.

Unfortunately, he does not show Judas or Walter any respect, though both do their best to tutor him. He mimics Father Judas rudely, behind his back. It is true that Richard Judas' appearance is not prepossessing – he is a small, though lithe figure, very dark, and fully bearded with a prominent, hooked nose, all of which bestows upon him a sinister look, and he speaks with a low and thickened lisp. Yet he has the mildest of demeanours, the best of hearts, and does not deserve to be ridiculed.

We have long suspected he has Jewish origins, though never openly mention it, since Edward I banished all the Jews from England as long ago as 1290, when I was four. Even my confessor's name has awkward connotations, though he has taken holy orders. His devotion and loyalty to me is staunch, however, and I genuinely trust him with our lives.

If it were not for him, I may never have seen the light of day, apart from a brief and guarded daily walk along the quayside, shivering against a biting offshore wind, watching bales of wool replace the wine barrels on the ships, and wondering if any of it were Mortimer wool.

However, in the summer, Judas gains permission to take us to Mass in St Julien's Chapel by the Maison Dieu, at the south-eastern side of the town, next to the marshes. The Maison is a hospice for pilgrims from France on their way to Becket's shrine at Canterbury, and the Chapel is intended to serve their needs. Judas stressed my own devotion to St Thomas à Becket and a hunger to hear my native language again, and Arundel eventually agreed. It is so wonderful to be able to walk through the town, even though we are still heavily guarded. It makes me feel more alive again. Under any other circumstances, Southampton would be an interesting place with the sound of several foreign tongues on the streets, including the rough Basque of Lower Gascony.

The first time we attend Mass at St Julien's is the 7th of July, which is the anniversary of the old King's death. I try hard to pray for his soul as I am sure he has need of it. There is no doubt he was a cruel man. At least I am not imprisoned in a public cage like the Bruce's women were. My prayers inevitably lack enthusiasm, however, and my thoughts turn to our new King, the second Edward.

I remember how Roger wrote to me in great excitement from Carlisle to tell of the death of the old King. His excitement was infectious. Although the country mourned for the passing of the only monarch most of us had ever known, they also rejoiced at the succession of his handsome and strapping son. How, then, did it all go so wrong?

The first year of the new reign was heady and optimistic. Edward's immediate action was to recall Piers, of course. He was reunited with him at Dumfries, having been forced to go to Scotland to collect his father's body. Then he made Piers Earl of Cornwall. By rights, this should have gone to his half-brother, Thomas Brotherton of Norfolk.

"So much for oaths given," Roger said to me wryly. "All this barely a month after the accession, with the funeral cortege still on its way back to Westminster. But we should fare well enough as Piers' friends… "

The second thing the new King did was imprison the Treasurer, Archbishop Langton, on a charge of alleged mismanagement of the accounts. I have no idea if that was true, but I do know Langton had long been disapproving of the heir, and a thorn in his side. Edward wrote to the Pope asking for his old friend, Robert Winchelsea, to be made Archbishop of Canterbury instead.

Finally, he made a half-hearted attempt to pursue Robert Bruce in Scotland but this was soon abandoned. Roger said it would never have worked under Edward's command, with such lack of planning, and he was right. So they all retreated to Piers' castle in Knaresborough for much feasting and celebration. Eventually, they made it to Northampton where Edward held his first Parliament. This mainly agreed expenses for the funeral, the coronation, and Edward's proposed marriage to the daughter of the King of France. An inordinate amount of falcons and hunting dogs were ordered, but then everyone expected the new monarch to come in with style.

At the end of October, I joined Roger for the old King's funeral at Westminster Abbey, and then we went to Berkhamsted to attend Piers' wedding. This was a surprise to me, but Roger said Edward had planned it for some time, the idea being to bring Gaveston into the Royal family through marriage. The bride, Margaret de Clare, was the King's niece by his sister, Joan of Acre. Margaret was thirteen. Her brother Gilbert was sixteen, and still in wardship after his father's death. Normally that would have been the case until he was twenty-one, but Edward released him and granted his inheritance of the earldom of Gloucester exceptionally early. So Gilbert was not one to complain about his sister's marriage.

There were plenty who did, though. I did not think it such a bad match for Margaret; after all, Piers was only in his mid-twenties. He was good looking, very witty and full of fun, and seemed likely to retain the King's favour. She would lack for nothing with his new-found riches, and in time it would likely lead to children, maybe even love – and hopefully put an end to that other business. Still, we overheard Lancaster and de Warenne speaking of Piers as "a peasant knight and ne'er do well". Roger says this is completely untrue as his father was one of the foremost barons in Gascony, and they are only jealous of his influence on the King.

It was certainly a beautiful wedding, though the celebration afterwards became a touch riotous at the end for my liking. The King, as usual, was overly lavish with his presents and Piers paid more attention to him than his young bride.

In the meantime, Edward had been betrothed to the twelve-year-old Princess Isabella of France for four years. His father, on his deathbed, had urged the marriage should take place as soon as possible. For once, Edward was listening, and the plans did advance. He intended to sail for France in December to pay homage to King Philip and finalise the agreement. The alliance was generally popular in the country; it was bound to hold the French back from coming to the aid of Scotland in their ongoing war against the English. Everyone said Isabella was exceptionally beautiful, and this was encouraging. If Edward could fall in love with her, then surely it would temper his other relationships? But then the year ended on a sour note with the fiasco at Wallingford and, although the barons were unhappy before, this cemented their hatred of Piers. I think that was the turning point.

I have plenty of time to think over these events now. Excepting the presence of three of my children and Avice, I could be an anchoress locked away in her cell and I dread the return of another winter. Now that my gaolers know I can read and write, Walter has been cursorily dismissed. I am sure he is relieved and I do not blame him, though it puts more pressure on Judas to school an unruly John. I continue to write letters to my lord, to my mother-in-law, and to the Queen, though I never know if they are delivered, as I have none by return. It is especially cruel that Margaret's letters do not come through to me, as I have no knowledge of my youngest girls and how they are faring. Yet I am sure Lady Margaret would have her clerks write back to me about them. I have to avoid thinking about our abrupt leave-taking, otherwise I break down, and I do not want Joan and Isabella to see my tears. I am not always successful.

Nothing can hold the winter back and I begin to feel old and stiff and aching before my time, in its chill grip. Another new year, but with no relief in sight. Isabella has been very poorly again with her chest, and I fear for her future resilience. Joan is more robust, more like me I suppose, but I confess I love Isabella's gentleness a little more, despite, or because of, her frailty.

Then, just a week ago, Sir John announces to me, on his weekly visit, that the Queen has pleaded most strenuously with the King on my behalf, reasoning with him that the conditions we endure are far too harsh for a noblewoman and her children. We are to be moved out of this horrible tower into a more congenial Norman house within the castle, adjacent to the Royal quarters, and our daily allowance is to be raised with a grant to cover new clothes annually. I am even to have a groom for a horse I may ride out on occasionally – under strict supervision. God Bless Queen Isabella for answering my letters and prayers in such positive fashion.

Of course, there will be no release. But I must remain thankful for small mercies, and I am. What is more, John is to be sent to join his brothers at Windsor. I shall miss him, of course, and continue to worry over his attitude, but Edmund and Roger will be far better company for him, and this may relieve some of his premature bitterness and anger. Judas will stay with us, and I am sure he will find the education of Joan and Isabella more congenial and less taxing.

The bad news is that Judas has picked up talk of the King being considered unwise to let the Mortimers of Chirk and Wigmore live. This will be the Despensers' doing, no doubt. So my heart aches sorely at what may happen, and I wonder if I will ever see my beloved lord again.

Chapter 15

1308 – WALLINGFORD

BEFORE THE KING left for France, he gave Wallingford Castle to Piers Gaveston. It was previously a Royal residence, so what could be more fitting for one recently married into the Royal family? Piers decided to hold a grand tournament there to celebrate, and every earl and newly made knight was required to attend, as if by Royal command. The earls were furious at such a summons.

Wallingford is south-west of Oxford, pleasantly situated on the banks of the Thames, with extensive meadows very suitable for a major tournament. Only maybe *not* at the beginning of December, when the ground is saturated after rain. The horses would make it a mud bath and the fighting - for that is what it was, with a very fine line drawn between contest and battle - was likely to be concluded on foot with sword, battle axe and mace. Excellent training for combat no doubt, but not particularly enjoyable, and potentially humbling for the cream of England's nobles.

Piers' proposition was to field two teams made up of the newly knighted against the earls. We foresaw a problem: with the exception of Arundel, Surrey and young Gloucester, most of the earls were older men like Hereford, Pembroke and Warwick. They were certainly experienced, but the younger men were likely to be more agile with greater stamina. However, Piers was adamant on the composition of the teams and determined to field two hundred knights, with himself at the head, and Roger as his right-hand man. We later found the agreement had been for sixty men on each side.

The King was intending to be there to cheer on his favourite but in the event stayed behind at King's Langley, writing letters to the Kings of Castile, Aragon and Portugal in support of the Knight Templars, thereby challenging his prospective father-in-law,

Philip the Fair of France. Philip was demanding Edward arrest all the Templars in England, as he had done in France.

For a great scandal was afoot: apparently, the imprisoned men had confessed to a multitude of crimes including sodomy, heresy, idolatry and corruption. Edward could see, or at least suspect, that Philip would have tortured the Knights to obtain these confessions. He knew that Philip was likely to be short of money after his father's war against Aragon, and in debt to the Templars, who were extremely wealthy, having involved themselves in banking and commerce for many years, since support for the Crusades had waned.

After the Jewish merchants that Philip, like Edward's own father, had expelled, the Templar Knights were easy and rich pickings for the French King. He could now seize their assets. Our Edward applied himself with diligence and wrote a firm but balanced letter on the subject to his royal cousins, demanding proof of the allegations before any actions were taken. This was admirable, but did not endear him to Philip.

Back at Wallingford, the day dawned gloomy with a persistent drizzle of rain. A mist of low cloud hung over the river and it was damp and cold. The armoury tents had been put up the day before, so they could all be on the field early to make the most of the short daylight hours.

I was one of the few ladies prepared to be out in such weather, well-wrapped up in furs, but there was a good crowd of local spectators, keen to see how the high and mighty fared. The smell of horses, smoking fires, and the ringing of blacksmiths on anvils was everywhere, whilst town peddlers were doing a good trade with hot pies and spiced wine.

"Don't give them any quarter," Piers told Roger, as they were being dressed in their armour. "The greater the earl, the more need to bring him to his knees…literally!"

I saw Roger hesitate and frown.

"That won't go down well, Piers."

Piers winked.

"That's the general idea."

Roger sighed. There were times when Piers seemed to go out of his way to stubbornly court dislike.

"Don't you think it would be wise not to insist on too much humiliation? They need to enjoy the sport too. Some of the earls are still sore at your rapid advancement as it is."

"They cannot question the King's decision."

"Not in public maybe, but behind his back, they'll seethe with unrest."

"Don't be so prim! Let's have some fun!"

"They'd love to knock you down."

"Some chance! You're the only one who's ever managed that."

My lord had not meant this literally. But there was no stopping Piers today. He considered himself impregnable, and certainly seemed to be so on the field, once I had taken my seat under a dismally leaky canopy to watch. They had worked out tactics for the team together and they worked well.

Despite his protestations, I know that Roger enjoyed seeing his kinsmen, the arrogant Fitzalan with the dark, Italian looks of his mother, and the burly John de Warenne, Earls of Arundel and Surrey respectively, brought down unceremoniously by Piers, though surely he found the display of making them stay on their knees, faced with a battle axe, gratuitous?

When it came to his turn and he found himself up against his mother's second cousin, Hereford, he unseated him easily enough and none too gently, for that was unavoidable. But I was glad to see he immediately dismounted, holding up his gauntletted hand to rein back any other followers from pitching in, and extended an arm to help Hereford up from the mud.

"Thank you, Roger," Humphrey grunted breathlessly. "What a swinish feeding trough this has become!"

"I advise you to retire, cousin," said Roger quietly, "but I do not expect the Constable of England to kneel and plead."

"Then I yield you my ransom money willingly."

When Roger re-grouped with Piers, he found him in fits of laughter, having just run rings round the Earl of Warwick. He had taken to calling Warwick 'The Black Hound of Arden', explaining he was black because he was covered with mud and worse, from head to toe, from the remains of the cattle previously grazed on this meadow. All his young adherents were laughing, too, and it was infectious, so Roger could not help joining in.

Tellingly, the only earls to attend the feast at Wallingford that night were Arundel, Pembroke and Hereford. 'The Black Hound' had already left for Arden and John de Warenne had gone with him. Many others joined them, and all harboured bitterness in their hearts.

The King eventually set off for France in the New Year. He had to cave in to Philip's pressure over the Templars because of a Papal Bull instructing all monarchs to comply, and it was high time for his visit to pay homage. He left Piers Gaveston in charge of the country as Regent.

It was a relief to go back to Wigmore for Christmas after all the backbiting and tension at court; not that any of it was directed against the Mortimers. Roger and his uncle of Chirk were favoured for their loyalty, without any baronial opposition. Chirk was made Justiciar of Wales and my grandfather, Geoffrey de Joinville, was given permission to pass on his lands in Ireland to Roger and myself, along with all of Roger's own, fully restored Irish lands from his grandmother.

I desperately wanted to go to Ireland to see my grandfather, who was now a very old man and had not been well, but that was not going to be possible for some time. The King desired Roger to accompany him to France for the Royal Wedding, whilst I was required to assist in making Westminster Palace ready for his Queen. This would be followed almost immediately by the coronation. The best Roger could manage was leave to return and see to his affairs in the Marches briefly, over the festive period.

Ludlow was undergoing some restoration and re-decoration of the Great Hall, but I preferred Wigmore at Christmas anyway.

Smaller than Ludlow, it seemed more homely to me now, snug and commanding on its hilltop, secluded amongst green pastures, rolling hills and old forests.

Rather to our surprise, we were joined over Christmas by Roger's kinsman and erstwhile friend, John de Warenne, Earl of Surrey. 'Kinsman' because Roger's aunt had married Robert de Vere, the Earl of Oxford, who was John's grandfather, and friend because they had seen much of each other in the Prince's household as wards. Such links through intermarriage and wardship were common, and Warenne had been our guest before. Roger had not seen him since the tournament at Wallingford. He had assumed their relations would cool, due to some offence being taken.

Furthermore, Warenne had married young Joan of Bar, one of the many royal nieces, last year, and might have been expected to stay at court for Christmas. She was not, alas, with him.

I divined the true state of affairs instinctively, greeting Warenne with sympathy and respect, welcoming him to stay, whilst Roger received him courteously enough.

I felt proud that Wigmore was at its best, lit up by a multitude of torches and warm with roaring fires and braziers, the floors spread with clean and fragrant rushes, and the Great Hall decked with evergreens. Wild boar were being roasted over the fire and the air was full of the smell of exotic spices: oranges from Portugal and good Gascon wine. Warenne was warmly appreciative of our hospitality. Outside, there was a sprinkling of snow on the border hills, but none underfoot, and the twinkling of candle lights from the town below mirrored the stars, with the bells of the abbey ringing to welcome the birth of Christ.

Before the fire, after supper, Warenne relaxed and admitted the truth to my concerned questioning. His new marriage was not going well...in fact, it could hardly be worse.

"I am afraid we are estranged, Madame," he admitted.

"But she's only a child."

"Aye, and a spoilt and petulant brat at that!"

"She will grow and mature in time."

Warenne shook his big head and shrugged his thickset, brawny shoulders.

"I'm afraid once a King's niece has learnt to stamp her little foot in rage, there is not much hope of going back. Anyway, she detests me."

"She may not always."

However, I knew that Warenne had never been a favourite with the ladies. In looks, he was indeed the nephew of Mortimer of Chirk, rather than a cousin of my own fine-looking lord, and he made no concession to airs and graces to soften his appearance.

"No, Madame, the marriage will never be consummated in a hundred years – which suits me very well as I intend to divorce her."

Roger raised an eyebrow.

"The King will take that badly."

Warenne threw back his head and laughed without any mirth.

"Then I shall go to the Pope. She shall not cling on to my earldom!"

He took another mouthful of wine.

"I have a more pleasing mistress in Matilda of Nerford, whom I would like to marry."

"Oh dear," I could not help saying, "then the rumours about that are true."

"I hesitate to give you any advice," Roger said quietly, "but that's hardly an advantageous match for one in your position."

Warenne smiled.

"Look at you. Look at you both!" he said, wistfully.

We were sitting close to each other by the fireside, with Roger's long legs stretched out at ease before him, one hand holding his goblet and the other arm casually thrown around my shoulders in the relaxed way he had with me in private.

"You are so fortunate, Roger. There sits your handsome lady, rosy-cheeked and obviously with child again – begging your pardon, my dear – and she, the most intelligent, capable and kindhearted of young women who obviously adores you. You already have three happy and healthy children and maintain such loving companionship between yourselves!"

He choked a little, but then went on. "It shines out of you and I envy you both, keenly. You cannot understand my situation."

I leant forward and placed a tender hand on his knee.

"No, you are right. We cannot," I said gently.

"And of course we wish you to find happiness," Roger added, giving my shoulders a squeeze as I settled back. For there was no doubt that Warenne's unfortunate marriage had soured him. All good humour seemed to have gone out of the man.

"Now I must give you some advice," said Warenne, waving away the serving girl proffering nuts and exotic dates.

"Indeed?" said Roger, suspecting what was coming.

"Piers Gaveston."

"The King's favourite and a generous friend to us."

"It will not end well, Roger. You would do well not to become too entangled with him."

Roger sighed. I knew he could see there was a risk, but could not begin to imagine how he could possibly withdraw his support from either friend or King, and he said as much.

"He stops the King from consulting with anyone else, and you know he is to be left in charge of the Kingdom whilst Edward is in France?" Warenne pressed.

Roger nodded. "To be fair, I doubt Piers wanted that."

"I'm not surprised. He will be out of his depth."

"It's only for a few weeks. Lancaster would hardly have been more capable."

Lancaster was the King's cousin. There were also Edward's half-brothers, but they were too young to be left in charge.

"Pembroke would have been a better choice."

"True. Pembroke is always a good choice. But what harm can he really do in such a short time? I doubt he'll do anything much."

"Precisely like the King!"

Roger fell silent. I knew he did not feel comfortable agreeing to this, even though it remained his deepest fear.

"It may be true he will do nothing," Warenne continued, "but the principle is wrong. You know a man by the company he keeps. If the King carries on in this fashion, we will have to take measures. To protect the Crown."

"We?"

"Lancaster, Warwick and myself. Maybe Arundel and Pembroke, too. Some of the Bishops."

"What measures?"

"To get Gaveston banished again."

"At least wait until after the marriage and the coronation!"

"Queen Isabella may change everything," I pointed out, anxiously.

"She is only twelve, Madame, and may turn out to be another Joan of Bar."

"Not from what we have heard."

"Joan is right. It is too early to judge, either the King or his wife."

"You're not with us then, Roger?"

Roger slowly shook his head.

"I cannot be. Not against the King."

"Then I advise you to stay out of the way. Go to Ireland as soon as you can!"

There was a further awkward silence, broken only by the crackling of the fire and a falling log.

"We intend to," I said, with forced brightness.

Warenne realised he had overstepped the bounds of expected manners and changed the subject.

"How's the hunting hereabouts?"

"Excellent," said Roger, absently. "We shall try it out tomorrow."

"Tomorrow is Christmas Day!" I reminded him sternly. "Starting with Mass bright and early. How can you forget?"

"Of course it is. I meant the following day, of course."

The breach seemed to be reconciled with Warenne's eager acceptance. Hunting in the Mortimer Forest was bound to live up to his expectations, accompanied by Roger's fine horses and hounds.

My lord was aware his kinsman had stature and a sound heart underneath his brusque exterior. He knew too that Warenne's advice was given out of concern for us and that the breach between Gaveston and the Earls was unlikely to be healed. It was Piers he needed to advise, keeping his oath to the old King. But unfortunately that seemed less possible with each passing day.

Chapter 16

THE BRIGHT BLUE sky was full of seagulls racketing up the chalk-white cliffs. Down below, the quayside buzzed with anticipation and excitement. The Narrow Sea to France looked unusually calm and untroubled by waves, as if it were aware it transported a precious cargo. I shivered slightly and drew my fur-lined blue cloak closer round me, for there was still a chill in the air, despite the hint of an early spring to come. I was looking forward to seeing the Queen, as well as welcoming my lord back home. For Edward of England had finally married Isabella of France in Boulogne Cathedral, two weeks ago.

In the meantime, Piers Gaveston had been in control of the country without any actual calamity befalling the nation. No doubt all the intrigue was going on in France, as the majority of the earls were gathered there to attend the marriage ceremony. Piers arranged for all the chief ladies of the new Queen's household to be of French origin and to greet her at Dover. I, for one, approved and applauded his consideration and sensitivity. Foremost amongst the ladies was the King's sister of course, Elizabeth, now Countess of Hereford. But they included myself.

When Edward appeared on deck, there was spontaneous cheering from the crowd. Isabella was disembarking from the next boat. Edward's eyes darted around anxiously, but not in search of his bride. As soon as they alighted on Piers, he gave a whoop of delight. He positively ran down the gangplank to embrace and kiss him repeatedly, rudely ignoring Lancaster and everyone else who stood at his side. Queen Isabella was being helped off her own hulk by her French uncles, and the crowd fell silent.

Elizabeth of Hereford was the first to step forward, followed by the other ladies, all of us flushed with embarrassment. We made our curtseys as deep as possible and our words of welcome as warm as we could. Instinctively, we enfolded her so she should not see the King with Piers. We fluttered with concern, like butterflies, full of questions about the voyage. How fortunate it had been so calm! We continued to enfold her in our protective wings, expressing hope she would find the royal apartments in Dover Castle to her liking, and gushed fondly over her little person.

I thought she looked totally bewildered. We took the unprecedented step of escorting Isabella, on her own, to her coaching waggon, bound for the castle, leaving the King to follow behind. It was more of a group strategy than a conscious decision. I caught my lord's eye briefly as we moved off, and we exchanged a smile, although he raised an eyebrow. I was anxious to hear his account of the wedding, but he lingered with Piers and the King, who scarcely seemed to notice the ladies depart.

The Queen was undoubtedly pretty, with long, fair ringlets and large, prominent blue eyes. I did not think her so very beautiful then, but could see she might mature into a beauty. She had a pert, upturned nose, which men seem to favour, and small, bow-shaped lips, one corner of which could raise itself sharply when displeased. But she did not stamp her foot like Joan of Bar. On the contrary, her manners were impeccable and her expression bright, intelligent and enquiring. I found myself warming to her as she chattered away in French.

Despite being the tender age of twelve, she showed a concerned interest in my pregnancy whilst being dressed for the feast to be held in Arthur's Hall in the castle. Had my lady felt her quickening yet? I had. How many children would this be? Four. Would I be going home to give birth? Yes, to a place called Wigmore in the Marches of Wales – all being well.

At the feast, her younger brother Charles sat on her right hand, next to their two uncles. Edward sat on her left hand but spent most of his time talking to Piers on his left. Isabella wore her wedding gown to display it to the English nobles and ladies who had not been in Boulogne. The gown and tunic were a sumptuous blue and gold, and her mantle a vibrant red lined with yellow sindon. Edward wore an ivory satin surcoat and golden cloak embroidered with many jewels, yet Piers was almost equally well dressed. It was not a relaxed occasion for anyone other than him and his friend, the King, though the wine flowed freely and the food was appropriately rich and satisfying. Isabella looked dismayed and I felt sorry for her.

"Oo is this man?" she had asked me quietly, on entering the Hall to find Piers already installed next to her husband. Poor little girl! All her life, she had been waiting to marry this handsome English prince and, now he had brought her home, he was hardly taking any notice of her. There would be no time for any intimate conversation later, as naturally she was not expected to share his accommodation yet, because of her tender years. Whereas I, once my duties were over, was able to join Roger in our bedchamber for an affectionate reunion. We did not join together, as my pregnancy was well advanced, but pleasured each other nevertheless.

"Well?" I asked, lying in his arms afterwards, warm and contented.

"Well what?" he teased.

I gave him a playful jab in the ribs.

"What was it like? In Boulogne."

"The wedding itself went well. Both of them looked splendid together, as you saw tonight."

"Who was there for her?"

"All the French Royal family including the Dowager Queen, of course. Our Dowager Queen, Marguerite. The King of Navarre, King of Sicily, the King of the Romans and his Austrian Queen... oh, I forget now..." he yawned, but I jabbed him a bit harder.

"...The Archduke of Austria and the Duke of Brabant. A string of nobles and princes from all over the place! It was a truly grand affair, glittering with jewels and crowns."

"And the festivities?"

"All eight days of them?"

"Yes."

"Let's just say, they could have ended sooner. There was some strain between our Ned and King Philip."

"Oh dear."

"Nothing terribly serious. The usual list of grievances from the Gascons, along with dire warnings not to dare annul this marriage under any circumstances. Philip did provide a dowry in the end, courtesy of the Knight Templars, no doubt. But the Duchy of Aquitaine is assured. And the wedding presents were generous enough – exquisite jewellery for them both and some splendid warhorses for Edward. You were too hasty in leaving the quayside to see them."

"You can hardly blame us when Edward took so little notice of his bride."

Roger brooded, silently.

"What else?"

"Oh, nothing."

"I know you too well not to know when you are worried."

"True. Well, our earls were not exactly inactive."

"Which ones?"

"Lincoln, Pembroke, and our cousins, Surrey and Hereford. Along with the Bishop of Durham and five others."

"Including Warenne, then?"

For he was the Earl of Surrey, of course.

"Oh yes. I imagine he knew this was being planned at Christmas."

"What have they done?"

"They drew up a declaration saying they would always act to protect the honour of the King and the rights of the Crown."

"There doesn't sound anything wrong with that."

"Note the careful wording. The King may dishonour himself. Ergo, he would then be disloyal to the Crown. In which case, the oath of fealty could be read as meaning loyalty to the Crown, not the King wearing it. Not if that King does not act in the best interests of the nation."

I took a sharp breath in.

"That's clever," I said, "and maybe not unreasonable."

"No. But it was being passed around to collect signatures – literally during the festivities. I didn't like that."

"It's mainly about Gaveston."

"Of course. They hate his arrogance, which Piers does nothing to control. It is true no-one can get to see the King without him now, so his influence is paramount."

"Did you sign?"

"No, I did not. How can I when the King and Piers are my friends and have shown me nothing but favour?"

"I'm glad you didn't. Things may improve as the Queen grows up. And they deserve a chance."

I was quiet for a moment or two, remembering something that Bess of Hereford had told me that morning.

"Did you know there are underground tunnels beneath this castle?"

"Can't say I did. But it doesn't surprise me. It's not that uncommon."

"You don't think the earls would use them to arrest the King?"

Roger laughed.

"Now you're letting your imagination run wild. That isn't what the earls want. They would have to replace him with Thomas of Lancaster, and he isn't popular either. No, I don't think it will come to that. They just want to control the King, not depose him. There's no need to worry."

"But it is worrying. I think it would be good for us to go to Ireland as soon as we can."

"I know." Roger stroked my loose brown hair gently. "What did you think of the new Queen?"

"I liked her. She has sweetness and manners. Very conscious of her position of course, but that's only natural. I think she could grow up very determined."

"Well, let's hope she does. And becomes popular with the people. That might rein our Ned in a bit."

"Yes, and she is pretty. He ought to find her beautiful enough to love. Don't you think?"

"There's more to love than prettiness. She's not as handsome nor, I should think, as strong-minded as you are. That would be like comparing a silly young filly with a beautiful mare – one

101

with steel and courage. It remains to be seen whether Isabella can manage that."

"Oh, I think you'll find she's no fool. Tomorrow we have to get her ready to go to Eltham and it's barely three weeks to the Coronation. Then she really will be Queen of England. We're going to be kept very busy."

"Speaking of which, there is one more thing to tell you. A tiny matter. But I gave you the bad news first." He was in teasing mode.

"What is it?"

"Your husband and Lord will be one of the four noblemen carrying the cloth bearing the royal robes for Edward."

"That's wonderful! Such an honour. Oh, I wish I could be there to see it!"

"Ah, but you will. The wives of all the peers and nobles are invited to attend, for the first time!"

I was thrilled but had also become more knowledgeable and cynical about the Court.

"If you're carrying the robes, what's Piers' role?"

"I'm afraid he's carrying the crown."

"And the earls are letting him?"

"They have agreed – providing the King will sanction all policies introduced by the next Parliament."

"But then they might insist Piers is banished again."

"Correct, and highly likely! But Edward gives his promises so lightly he doesn't care about going back on them. He's generous to a fault, yet duplicity is his most unappealing trait."

"Oh dear," I repeated.

"What now?"

"I wish we were in Ireland already."

"And miss me carrying the royal robes?"

"No," I admitted, nestling comfortably into the crook of his shoulder. "I wouldn't miss that for the world."

A coronation is a grand and special occasion, rarely witnessed more than once or twice by the populace. So many of them lined the streets for this one that a wall collapsed and crushed an unfortunate knight to death in the crowd. But I, as Lady Mortimer, was seated safely inside the Abbey, waiting for the procession and knew nothing of this till afterwards.

The gilded spurs were carried in first and the Earl of Hereford followed, bearing the heavy jewel-encrusted sceptre, with Henry of Lancaster, Thomas's brother, holding the Royal Staff. Then came the Earls of Lancaster, Lincoln and Warwick with the three great Swords of State for Temporal Justice, Spiritual Justice and Mercy. My lord followed on with his cousins de Vere and Fitzalan, and, less fortuitously, Hugh Despenser, each carrying a corner of the cloth on which the Royal Robes were spread out. I thought my heart would burst with pride. The Treasurer and Chancellor of the Kingdom walked behind. Finally, Piers brought up the rear, bearing the crown of Edward the Confessor as Edward had wished.

Gaveston had the right to wear cloth of gold in the King's presence, like all the other earls, now he had Cornwall. But, to everyone's dismay, he was dressed in imperial purple trimmed with pearls. The earls universally gritted their teeth when they saw it. Still, the ceremony proceeded undisturbed, with the Bishop of Winchester crowning Edward after anointing him with holy oil from the gold Coronation spoon.

At the banquet which followed, the newly crowned King sat next to Piers, instead of his Queen, laughing and joking with him as if no-one else were there, and Piers naturally rose to the occasion by showing off hugely. The Queen's French uncles left early in disgust.

So it was not a surprise to anyone that, despite the grandeur and pleasure of the coronation, tension grew in advance of the next Parliament. For the King and Gaveston had precious little support other than from the Mortimers. By Easter, castles were fortified throughout the land and retinues fully armed. Conspiracy was everywhere. Even Philip of France was said to have secretly sent money to rid the land of Gaveston.

When Parliament did convene at Westminster at the end of April, the rebellious lords attended with armed men, and were in no mood to be ignored. They insisted Gaveston must be banished for treasonable acts to the Crown because he had appropriated Crown lands to himself, and brought the Crown into disrepute. So had the King. If Edward did not agree to the banishment, he would also stand accused. There was no other choice for him, so he had to agree – though he made Piers Lord Lieutenant of Ireland to soften the exile.

By now, I was ready for my confinement and we left for Wigmore as soon as Parliament was over, both of us escaping cleanly away from the brewing disorder left behind and to the gracious gift of another child, born safely into this chaotic world without any problems. Thanks be to God!

Chapter 17

AUTUMN 1308 – IRELAND

I WAS A mere child the previous time I had been at Trim, but the castle and its massive keep made a lasting impression on me. I was a little afraid it may have shrunk in the meantime, as childhood places often do when revisited by an adult. This was not the case. It really was a colossus, with its five storeys and four towers joined by a tiled roof, timber bratices, and sturdy curtain walls. It was built to put the fear of God into all who came across it, and it did exactly that. So I was pleased to see my lord looking impressed as we approached on horseback, surrounded by our retainers and men at arms.

It was four days since we had landed in Ireland, having set sail from the port of Conwy. My mind was exercised by what to take for the family, for we had the new babe, Maud, who was barely five months old, in addition to six-year-old Edmund, four-year-old Margaret, and a two-year-old Roger now. I was adamant they should all come with us so my grandfather could see them. It would probably be for the last time, as he had reached the astonishingly venerable age of eighty-two, outliving his younger wife by six years.

At least I knew the cellars in Trim would be well stocked with food and drink, and that grain and vegetables would be widely available if the harvest had been good. Although Trim was a small town, it was an industrious one with bakers and butchers, tanners, hornmakers, and potters aplenty to supply the castle.

I regretted leaving my beautiful white gyrhawk behind, though it would be well trained and exercised by a servant. This was Roger's most expensive gift to me yet, after the safe delivery of Maud. It was a highly prized bird, being the largest and loveliest of all the falcons, with its grey arrowhead plumage. Yet I did not need to be told I was unlikely to be able to go out hawking in

Ireland. For it was a wild, unruly country, only nominally under Norman control, and only that in Meath, Leinster and Ulster. Scarcely a day went by without the burning of a homestead, or even a whole village somewhere, with cattle stolen and wayfarers being molested or murdered. My lord was taking a string of good Welsh cobs, but they were to be used for more practical purposes like the serious hunting of stag and boar.

We sailed from Conwy because we had stayed at Uncle Roger's newly finished Chirk Castle on our way, whilst the boats were being readied. We found him revelling in his new role as Justiciar of Wales and pursuing it with characteristic ruthlessness. He was still a hard and uncompromising man to my mind, but my husband warned me the same would be needed in Ireland, as it sounded like the Welsh Marches a hundred years ago – except that some of the English lords had been there so long and become so isolated, they had adopted Irish ways and alliances. Well, could you not say the same about us and the Welsh, I wondered?

We now knew that Maud Mortimer's father had dallied and slept with Llewellyn's wife and paid for it with his life, though she never told Roger that particular story. Her husband, my lord's illustrious grandfather, was, of course, himself the offspring of a Welsh noblewoman, Gwladys Ddu, from the very same Llewellyn stock. I did not see anything wrong in this, but had learnt to hold my tongue when politics took over the domestic.

Richard of Monmouth was coming with us, and two of Roger's other friends, Walter de Thornbury and John de Hothum, as they were to take up the positions of Chancellor and Treasurer of the Exchequer at Piers Gaveston's request. Mind you, I gathered it was doubtful there was any money to be had in the impoverished Irish coffers.

So it was seven cogs in all that finally left the quayside at Conwy, fully laden and lifted by the incoming high tide. It was a fine, clear day, the sky merely pockmarked with a few puffy, white clouds, and the sun shining brightly on the water as we left the whitewashed towers of castle and town walls behind. We sailed out into the open sea under the watchful eye of the majestic mountains of

Snowdonia. It seemed calm enough to begin with, and the waves were gentle. Even so, after steering a wide berth round the island the Welsh call Ynys Mon – to avoid its treacherous rocks – we were met with the full, slapping swell of the Irish Sea, and the boats began to roll.

I remembered that motion only too well and was pleased to find the children coping, for it was their first sea voyage; the Irish Sea could be much worse than the Narrow Sea. Thankfully, the children squealed and giggled in delight, until Edmund went quiet and fell sick. Avice, on the other hand, was not at all happy, and sat with her apron over her mouth the whole time. Poor Avice! She detested a sea voyage, but would never have agreed to being left behind, regarding that as a dereliction of duty.

It was dawn next morning when we reached Dublin and offered up grateful prayers for an uneventful and speedy passage. We were reunited with Piers in the safety and hospitality of Dublin Castle and, oh my, was he thrilled to see us, for he claimed to be living in terminal boredom away from court! He welcomed Thornbury and Hothum, both of whom came recommended by Roger, for offering their services in his administration. But it was Roger himself who really lit up his face as they embraced warmly.

Now he had his young Mortimer with him, he said, they could set to and beat the place into some shape and order. Roger laughed and protested he was only here on family business, but Piers would have none of it and kept him up half the night, discussing potential military strategies long after I retired to bed. Not that my lord seemed to mind. He told me he could smell opportunity in this land.

On the third day, we managed to disentangle ourselves from Piers' hospitality and set off early, keen to push on to Trim. The children and women servants travelled by waggon, guarded by men at arms. I was with them most of the way, but joined Roger on horseback for the last few miles, eager to catch the first glimpse of my grandfather's bastion and caput town once again.

And now here it was, with its whitewashed towers thrusting up from the green land into a fading afternoon sun. We drew rein and took stock before riding on. Piers said it had become a frontier castle again, for the Irish clans had driven a wedge between Meath and Ulster, and all the lands to the north and west were "beyond the pale" as a result. Still, it looked fit enough for any task on its shoulders, and Roger smiled at me.

"Ours," he said, triumphantly.

"Don't forget the Lacys *entirely*," I chided him. "You must be careful."

"They lost it to us fairly and squarely in law."

"I mean, you must be mindful of it. I imagine they are still sore and it may not be possible or even wise to count on their support."

It was true, and I think Roger knew I was canny to remind him of it. Not for the first time, I punctured some of his pride and tempered it with a more cautious reaction, to bring him back to reality. I am glad to say, he was intelligent enough to know it was good for him then, and to value it. With a brief "Tsk!", he urged his horse on.

For the fact remained it was Hugh Lacy who had built the castle of Trim and held the Lordship of Meath, granted to him by Henry II way back. Hugh's son Walter had died without a male heir so the inheritance was passed down the female line to Matilda Lacy, my grandfather's second wife, and now through the female line once more, to myself. Or rather to my lord, through our marriage.

Walter had brothers with sons however, another Hugh and another Walter, both of whom were now vassals of the Joinvilles. They might be expected to resent this and chafe against the yoke. Roger's lands in Leinster also came down the female line from his grandmother Maud. The truth of it was that the law was not always clear and much depended on the King's patronage.

We approached Trim from its safer south-eastern side in coming from Dublin, and saw to our left a cluster of burbages outside the walls. These were the workshops of the bonecarvers, the hornmakers and the tanners with their lime kilns. We turned to the right before reaching them, away from their rancid smell, and crossed fertile pastureland where fine cattle grazed, before entering the heavily guarded Barbican gate of the castle. Dusk was gathering, for the days were already growing shorter.

Once inside, it was apparent that all of the D-shaped flanking towers, of which there were many in the strong, curtain walls, were open-backed to make them more difficult to undermine. They could be filled quickly with bands of armed men to resist battery. The tops of the walls supported fighting platforms and there were sally ports at strategic points at the base of the walls, to access the moat. Roger took all of this in with approval.

Our entourage clattered and rumbled its way around the colossal keep to its westward side. Crossing the inner causeway over the filled-in ditch, we pulled up at the reception hall and were greeted by the Steward.

The main hall was on the second floor of the South Tower above the cellars, to which it had access. It was more conventionally approached by two wide staircases, the one to the rear being straight and leading to a corridor towards the main bedchamber. It was just as I remembered it. Roger considered the Hall itself to be a little cramped after the new hall rebuilt at Ludlow, and told me later he was already thinking of re-designing and extending it in his mind's eye. However, he liked the nicely pitched ceiling with its supporting cross beams, and was later to find it led to a more private chamber at the back of the corridor, which he would often use.

The hall was lit by four torches in braziers at its corners. At the far end was a short dais with a trestle table backed by a fine tapestry in blue, yellow and red thread depicting the Annunciation. Flemish and good quality, too. At the opposite end was a great, open fireplace set into a hole in the walls, so it did not smoke into the room. Two equally great Irish wolfhounds slumbered beside it, but raised their noble heads and grey beards at the approach of strangers, getting up and barking gruffly so that the children following behind were startled, and little Maud began to cry.

My grandfather, Geoffrey, sat by the fire and seemed to have been dozing too, but struggled up to greet us and hush the dogs.

Neither of us had seen him since our wedding, and the intervening seven years had not been kind to him. I uttered a cry of joy and embraced him gently, fearing for his obvious frailty. He followed on by holding me at arm's length to peer closely into my happy face, and seemed to liked what he saw. His own face was craggily lined now and he had lost most of his hair, save for a few strands of grey that straggled down the back of his neck.

He was dressed very plainly in a loose, white hooded robe – as if he were a lay brother of the Black Friars. Gone were the rich-velvet brocades and the furs appropriate to his status. Crinkly flesh hung loose from his arms, and his fingers were bony and devoid of rings. It seemed he was preparing for a more ascetic life.

Overcome with emotion, I kissed his hands. Then the children were presented in turn and he blessed them all. Maud stopped crying to stare wide-eyed at her great grandfather, with a finger in her mouth. None of the children had ever seen such an old man before.

When Avice took them off to their quarters to ready them for bed, we ate a supper of mutton pies, washed down with wine. Grandfather confirmed he would retire very soon to the Dominican Friary he had founded to the north of the town, on the road to Kells.

The monks were a preaching order known as the Black Friars because they wore black cloaks over their white robes. They were totally dependent on alms, though my grandfather had endowed this particular Irish order richly. So much so that the interior of the Friars' church at Trim was built from Purbeck marble. He assured me it was not as uncomfortable to live in the Friary grounds as might be expected. Nevertheless, it was his intention to live simply as a lay brother, to read and study and pray for God's mercy and forgiveness, for he had killed many men in the Crusades in the past.

He had never thought to live so long, and it was fitting he made this recompense now, in what must be his final years – though he thanked God for his good health. He promised to take me to meet the Friars and see his quarters, and would arrange for the steward to show Roger every inch of the castle tomorrow.

Roger had considerable respect for my grandfather. After all, he had been a Crusader, accompanying the old King Edward to the Holy Land. He had also been Marshal of the Welsh and Flanders Armies, the Keeper and Custodian of several castles, and a consummate diplomat and envoy at the highest levels. Not to mention being a former Justiciar of Ireland. His mind was still sharp enough, and Roger anticipated many useful conversations with him in the days to come. He was keen to engage in one now, and listened attentively to his brief explanation of Irish history and the nature of warfare here. But Grandfather was easily tired now and said it was his habit to retire early after supper, though he apologised for cutting the discussion short.

I was woken next morning by the sound of bells transporting me back to my childhood. They came from the Augustinian Abbey of St Mary, across the river. I recognised and remembered their tones from all those years spent with grandfather, who taught me so much, and became closer to me than my father had. At the time, I had not really understood fully he was grooming me to be his successor. But now I did.

Roger was already up and about, eager for his tour of the castle with the steward, and left me to drowse on. I threw back the green covers and the curtains round the bed eventually, and pushed my bare feet down to the floor, crossing to the window of the solar in my chemise. It was a perfect autumn morning, cool and clear and bright. I could not quite see the Abbey, as we were lodging in the south tower and it was further round to the west, but the bells insistently announced its presence. Instead, I saw the grey stone quadrangle of the Franciscan friary, with its gardens and orchard across the outer moat. Trim was well blessed with religious houses. I called for my chambermaid to help me dress and then Avice brought in the younger children to see me, and the day had begun.

Roger rejoined us at eleven in the hall, ready for the main meal of the day. Grandfather seemed anxious to know what Roger thought of the castle.

"It's generally well maintained, sir, and a splendid edifice, of course. I would only say the walls are in need of some repair behind the piggeries." Geoffrey nodded over his pottage.

"You are right. We have a murage grant for that. What did you think of the Riverside Gate by the Boyne?"

"It seems strong enough. I watched the fishing boats from Drogheda unloading their catch. It could be a weak point, but we can see them coming from a fair way off, round the bend of the river. I would only say that more men need to be stationed at the Gate on a permanent basis. Though you say you always have lookouts up on the main towers?"

"Constantly, since the Earl of Ulster lost his grip on his southern borders. The O'Neills and the O'Hanlons have made significant incursions. It is to the north and the west you must expect trouble. Though the O'Reillys and O'Connors are less favourable towards us than they were. I regret to say it is also necessary to keep the peace amongst our own fifty knights of Meath, too."

"And may we count on our Lacy cousins or not?"

"They need careful handling. But at present they are more inclined to war with their neighbour, John FitzThomas."

They went on to discuss the various loyalties of the clans.

After the meal, I asked to ascend the South Tower to see the view and Roger accompanied me up the stone steps: past our private chambers above the hall, past the upper chambers presently occupied by Geoffrey, through the gallery next to the retainers' lodgings, through the guardroom and eventually onto the timber-edged battlements themselves, at the very top of the castle. It was a stiff climb, but the stairs were mainly wide and well built. I emerged breathless, letting go of my skirts at last. The soldier on lookout bowed to us both and Roger asked him questions about his hours of guard duty, his replacements and the last time he had seen anything to cause alarm.

Meanwhile, I leant on the open sill facing the town and took it all in, from the Town Gate, with its drawbridge over the moat, to the Franciscan friary on the right of the bridge, the stables and smallholdings on the left, and up the wide cobbled street, which was the Market Street, with its patchwork of tiled roofs and timber frames. I went round each window in turn, to see the abbey and the Sheep Gate across the river, with the streets leading up to the Church and the Black Friary in the distance. The river itself was bordered by elder and alder trees, and wound its way to a new settlement with new churches out of town, and finally there were the green pastures and marshy lands we had ridden through. Roger finished his conversation and came to my side, laying a cautionary hand on my shoulder as I leaned out, taking in the views.

"What do you make of it all, Joan? he asked. "Your grandfather seems to think we can expect troubles. But you seem very calm."

I smiled at him.

"I feel safe here. Maybe my trust in Trim is misplaced, but I do. I always have, right from being a little girl. I expect that has something to do with it. It's just too large and too much of a labyrinth inside to be blown away."

"Will you feel safe when I am not here?"

I nodded.

"Yes, my dear lord, I think I will."

The next day, when Grandfather took me through the town to visit the Black Friars as promised, I felt even more assured. He was well respected in the town, and it seemed that most of the townsfolk stopped what they were doing and came out to see us pass by. Many of them said they remembered me as a little girl, and were obviously curious to see what had become of me now I was a grand lady, and seemed genuinely pleased to have me back.

I stopped at one of the potteries to order some new green, glazed jugs, for I could tell Grandfather had not paid as much attention as he ought to his tableware in the last few years. Another halt was necessary at a hornmaker's to ask for more lanterns to be made to better light the children's rooms. Both visits led to great delight in seeing that the new Lady of Trim was keen to buy their wares, as I hoped it would. The message spread quickly to convert those who feared I might bring everything with me from England. So much so, that on my return journey, I was greeted with cheers and waves, and many 'God bless Lady Joans!' to my gratification.

In the meantime, we crossed the river on the low, timber bridge by the ford and rode on up the High Street, turning onto Haggard Street to go past St Patrick's Church and climb up to the North Gate to reach the Friary.

The Black Friars professed themselves honoured to receive me and showed me their house and their church, which was dedicated to St Mary of the Assumption. The church was indeed very fine, with its Purbeck marble and the cloisters pleasant and peaceful. They led to the kitchen, the refectory and the living quarters. Outside were three houses with gardens, and it was to one of these that Sir Geoffrey would retire and be served by some of the Friars. I was relieved to hear this. He would not be in a cell. There was also a well on site, a four-acre orchard, a vegetable and herb garden, a cemetery and a three-acre pasture, with more fine agricultural land beyond.

"So this is where I shall end my days," Grandfather said, taking my hand. "Can you imagine anywhere better?"

I had to agree I could not.

"I shall enter at the end of the week."

"So soon?"

"My dear, it is not as if I am far away. And as you can see, I am not enclosed in any way. It has been wonderful to see you again and meet your children. But I have grown tired in these last few years since Matilda died. Very tired indeed of all the steps in the castle! And, as you probably notice, I eat little and sleep more now."

That was self evident. He had only eaten from two out of the five courses of our last meal and excused himself early.

"I shall be here whenever Roger wants my advice. I forget so many things now, but not the old things. It is time to hand over the castle and the lands to a younger man, and you will get on better there without me. I can see Roger's plans are sound, and he is not one to brook any delay or nonsense. Come now…let's sit awhile in the garden and listen to the birds before the sun goes cold."

I sat quietly with him as bidden. The afternoon was still and warm, but would end soon and grow colder. Meanwhile, the air was so hushed that the fall of a leaf and the flutter of a sparrow's wing could be heard. It was hard to believe so much bloodshed had taken place in this land, and indeed continued to do so. Hard, too, to remember that perpetual winter rain and gales would arrive only too soon.

It was me who broke the silence first.

"The Friary is beautiful, Grandfather, but I wish it had been built inside the town walls for your greater protection."

"The Dominicans would not have wanted that. Their mission is to reach out to all to preach and give succour, and that is not best served by hiding themselves away in a fortification."

"I know, but it faces northwards towards Kells and Athboy. The very direction where we now expect to encounter troubles. What if there is an attack on the town?"

Grandfather took my hand and patted it.

"I am not afraid of that, little one. Do you mind if I call you that? In my mind's eye, you are still that bright young girl, though you have grown up a good wife and mother, strong and brave and kind. I do not believe the good friars would be harmed, and I need to be here to pray and repent. In my day, I have killed many men…it is high time to look to my soul."

The very next week I found myself alone in the castle – as far as anyone can be said to be alone in any noble household, with all the servants and retainers always around. In charge is probably the better term. Grandfather departed for the Black Friary, true to his word, and Roger, having made the acquaintance of the local Anglo-Irish nobles such as John de Cusack of Killeen, whom he thought a good man likely to prove useful, returned to Dublin. He needed to attend the Courts over a dispute regarding the tolls collected, on our behalf, by one of his Irish manor houses. He also wanted to fulfil his promise to Piers Gaveston in helping his military strategy, and was relieved to find Piers in a good frame of mind and constructive mood.

Something had to be done about the lands to the south. The Wicklow Mountains were notorious as a hideout for raiding parties and robbers; the road to Leinster must be improved and made safe. To achieve this, it would be necessary to fortify the castles of Kevin and Newcastle McKynegan.

Roger now knew my grandfather had been defeated at Castle Kevin forty years earlier and understood the reasons why. The fighting had amounted to guerilla warfare, and he was able to share that with Piers. It was vital the road to Leinster be made safe because it was the route to Youghal, which provided a shorter sea crossing to the South West of Wales, to Bristol and to Cornwall.

My lord encouraged Piers to attack the project with vigour and promised to back him with men in the spring. He was pleased when Piers agreed they needed to make a rapid impact, though less delighted on finding out the reason for it.

Optimistic as ever, Piers was convinced Edward would be able to recall him next year, and of course there was no doubt he would obey. The King was doing his utmost to pacify the barons by offering them large grants of land so they would return to his fold, but all to this end. In addition, he had made a large grant to Isabella to regain her father's favour, and was busy bribing the Pope. Roger was disturbed when Piers told him all of this with great glee. The worst of it was, to his mind at least, that the King wrote to Gaveston every day. This did not bode well.

My week passed quickly enough. I was able to rearrange all of the quarters to my satisfaction, and give tactful advice to the kitchen over our meals. I also sat down with the castle accounts, the clerks, and the steward, and ordered provisions for the winter to come. The heads of the Potters' and Hornmakers' Guilds visited, as promised, caps in hand, and I requested fresh linen from the Trim mills as well. There was no doubt Grandfather had become lax about some matters in his old age, though this was only to be expected without a wifely hand for so long. Fresh rushes were certainly long overdue.

I also made friends with the young wolfhound Sir Geoffrey left behind, taking only the older one as his companion to the Friary. He had long favoured these Irish dogs, and of course I remembered Bella well, a particularly gentle and faithful one, left in Ludlow by him in my childhood. I was pleased to see this one had the same nature and introduced the children to her, cautiously but successfully. They all agreed to call her Bella the Second, and she became a great favourite.

I was happy to see my lord back, as ever, to tell him about my doings, and with yet more good news, for I was with child again, though it was a little early to say. But by now I knew the earliest signs so well I was not in any doubt, and felt confident I was not prone to miscarriage. If this one was a boy, we would call him Geoffrey, after Grandfather.

Chapter 18

1309 — BACK TO PARLIAMENT

AT CHRISTMAS, PIERS and his wife Margaret joined us at Trim. Piers proved himself a charming guest, more than willing to party and entertain the children and Margaret was a pleasant though shy companion. He spoke warmly of fathering his own children. It would not be too long now she was entering her fifteenth year, though perhaps they should wait until their return to England in the new year. The possibility he might not be able to return clearly never entered his head. The one thing Piers never lacked was confidence.

My lord managed to distract him long enough to draw up a plan of action for a spring campaign, and within six months they were seeing the fruits of their armed forays into Leinster, which was secure again, with the rebellious Irish lords and clans defeated. Furthermore, a road was built from Castle Kevin through the mountains to the coast. It was a job well done and both men were pleased with their success. Piers was insisting he could now return to England with his head held high.

He let Roger know his intentions a month earlier, though he had not been formally summoned. Apparently, Edward told him that the barons would agree, providing he accepted all of their other demands regarding taxes. My lord felt uneasy, but his own presence at Court had been formally requested and Piers begged to travel in his retinue. They would be able to try out the new sea route from Youghal.

Margaret and I were to stay behind for the moment. Roger was not willing to risk my safety, especially when I was pregnant again, nor that of Pier's wife, on the new and untried crossing. So he arranged for the children and myself, and young Margaret de Clare, to return from Dublin to Wales, there to be met by Chirk's men, who would escort us safely back to Ludlow where we would stay with my mother Jeanne for a while. Piers could collect Margaret from there later.

The two men made landfall secretly in Cornwall and now had several days of riding before them for London. They travelled up the north coast and stopped to see Tintagel, where legend has it King Arthur was born. It was sadly in disrepair but Piers vowed to rebuild it when his earldom was re-instated, as he was confident it would be.

What then fell out , I learnt from Roger later. He assured me he had taken the opportunity to try and make his friend see it would be good policy, on his return, if he were to endeavour to stay in the background and not antagonise the nobility of England any further, nor over-influence the King.

"You will still have a great deal of power," he told Piers. "We know you will have the King's ear, and no doubt his affection toward you remains the same. But you must be more careful not to make such a show of it and not to openly insult the earls. They are dangerous men."

Piers pulled a face and said he would behave, if they would. Roger suspected his words fell on stony ground. At the inns and houses where they stayed on their journey, Piers made no attempt to conceal his identity, though it was true the folk here would not recognise him anyway. Nevertheless, Roger remembered his cousin Warenne's warning and resolved to try and withdraw somewhat from his friend on their arrival in London.

Once reaching Westminster, Roger found he was in the favour of the King, who issued a mandate to restore to him all the rights of his predecessors in Ireland, particularly in Trim. Therefore it proved impossible not to remain at Court at the King's request and keep his company. He was even asked to join Edward on an expedition with some of his more common friends, rowing up the Thames to a house they were thatching, and had to admit the excursion was enjoyable, if not a noble occupation. The banter and bawdy drunkenness in the inn afterwards did not please him however, as he saw the King openly called Ned by these friends, and considered they were given far too much money in appreciation of the day's activities. At least Edward, although delighted at Piers' return, was proving cautious in keeping him in the background at King's Langley, well away from the Court itself. Or so Roger believed.

Then Parliament met at Stamford and Piers made an unexpected appearance at the King's side. So the secret was out. Edward granted Piers the Earldom of Cornwall again and by Christmas, everything was as before, including Piers' animated disrespect of the earls. He was reunited with Margaret by then, and was hoping for a child, but still frequented the King's bed when they were together. Was this the example of courtly love and chivalry then, which they had spoken of so warmly whilst taking the opportunity to visit the ruined Tintagel in Cornwall?

My lord managed to excuse himself for a short stay in Wigmore in July, on account of the birth of our third son, Geoffrey, who had a cheeky little nature from the start and a winning smile within a few weeks. Back to us and the sanity of his family, Roger said – including an emotional reunion with his younger brother, John, who was growing up fast, and whom he promised to take to Ireland with him on his next trip.

On his return to court, he found that Lancaster, Warwick and Arundel were pushing for another banishment of Gaveston, infuriated once again by his insolent behaviour. Warenne seemed to be remaining loyal to the King this time, but Roger knew he secretly wanted rid of Piers as much as the rest of them. Edward's response was to send Piers north as a concession and a precautionary measure, far out of reach of the court. He was also forced to accept the founding of a committee of twenty-one 'Lord Ordainers', drawn up specifically to limit the Royal power.

My lord assumed it was because of this he was summoned to the King's private chambers shortly after returning to Westminster. He found he was alone with Edward, who was not at all discomfited, but welcoming and expansive, plying him with good red claret and seemingly anxious to ask for advice.

"Our earls," said the King, "are too much concerned with our mutual friend."

Roger sighed. It was warm and comfortable before the fire, with the wine slipping down pleasantly, but he knew he must not relax his guard.

"Sire," he said, "I have spoken to Piers, who is indeed a good friend to me, as is my noble liege, who has been so generous in granting in me so many favours."

He had recently been granted the constableship of Builth Castle, in addition to having his lands restored in Ireland, and was indeed grateful for this, as a fitting tribute to his father.

"I have recommended that Piers mind his manners on meeting with the earls and to proceed more cautiously with them, but...," Roger began saying.

Edward laughed and waved away his concerns.

"Our Perrot is not one to rein in his humour."

"No, you are right. I fear he is not."

"And why should he? It is merely his bon ésprit!"

My lord remained silent.

"I have sent him North."

Roger bowed his head.

"I commend your prudence and wisdom for this."

"What the earls need now is a distraction."

"A distraction, Sire?"

"Yes, of course. And you are the man to arrange it for me!"

My lord was wary now.

"May I ask in what manner?"

"What did my father want the most? And which the earls cannot deny?

Scotland!" Edward answered his own question with deep satisfaction, and Roger's heart sank.

"We have been tardy in seeing to this matter, I confess. I shall announce a campaign for the coming summer. And we will move the whole of the government to York."

"Your intention is sound, Sire," Roger said, carefully. "But it will take a deal of planning. The Scots are not an easy target."

Edward brushed away his concerns with another desultory wave of the hand.

"Don't trouble yourself over that. I have no real intention of engaging with Scotland, my dear Mortimer! Only to show the will to do so and distract the barons. Meanwhile, I shall be in York with my dear Perrot."

Roger was appalled, but cleared his throat and chose his next words carefully.

"It is an honourable intention to engage Scotland in battle, Sire," he said. "But it is not a matter to be undertaken lightly nor to be treated as a distraction. We know from experience they are a considerable foe. It needs much forward planning. Otherwise it would be wrong to call so many men to muster from their homesteads at harvest time and risk their lives. Also, with the greatest of respect, the Royal person himself should lead the Army to encourage those men."

Now it was Edward's turn to sigh.

"Always so serious, Mortimer! Perrot has said as much to me. You are growing to be no fun at all."

"I am sorry, my liege. It is a serious matter."

"You will not deny me some men?"

"No, but I urge you to use them well."

Edward threw him a haughty glance.

"Of course. And I need you to be at the head of them."

"Sire, I beg leave to return to Ireland instead. You may have the men but I request leave for Ireland. There is still much to do there."

The King rearranged his robe, fussily.

"You may be right," he said. "Don't think I cannot manage without you, Wigmore! You get above yourself."

"I am sorry, Sire. But Ireland is still in a state of disarray. We do not want the Scots to find natural allies there."

"True, true," Edward mused, still in a huff. "Don't think I have not considered well on that too. Very well – you have my leave to go. But I want three hundred men from your Welsh lordships, mind."

"You shall have them, Sire," Roger said with some foreboding, resisting the temptation to repeat the King should use them well.

"I must also have leave to return to Wigmore to raise these men. And, if Piers is not to return to Ireland, I shall need more men there, too. The attacks on our lands there increase daily."

Edward feigned knowledge of this.

"You want men?"

"A few, my Lord – men like Hugh Turpington, who is worth his weight in gold. The rest can come from Mortimer manors."

He saw with relief that the King was somewhat appeased.

"Very well, you may have them. I do need a strong man in Ireland. Piers has said so."

"Yes, sire. Thank you, sire."

He understood instinctively that the audience was at an end and that he had emerged relatively unscathed, although it was the closest he had ever come to arguing with his liege, and the King was now angry with him.

Edward was not entirely true to his word. He issued a writ for the Army to muster at Berwick in August, but indecisive and contrary as always, also demanded, nay begged, that Roger be there too. Only by then, we were back in Ireland, safely and firmly ensconced in Trim once again.

Roger knew Gaveston remained unrepentant about his behaviour, and that even the elegant and diplomatic Pembroke had broken with the King over it, a man whose wisdom and loyalty had never been questioned before. For the first time ever, my lord also ignored the request from the King, after what amounted to a quarrel between them. He supplied the men asked for but would not go himself. He was not the only one to do so. The other earls were also disgusted and found Edward's ploy transparent.

Little wonder then the campaign went badly and Bruce did not engage, knowing the English Army would soon retire. Instead, the Scots launched sporadic ambushes, which proved more effective.

So 1310 passed away into another new year, with nothing achieved and an ineffective government continuing under Edward and Gaveston. The earls began to fear they would lose Gascony as well as Scotland, with nothing being done about the warring between lords there. Only Wales, and to a lesser extent Ireland – for Roger had been successful in repelling attacks and putting down Irish rebellions – remained more secure. Both were due to the strong control of my Mortimer family.

We were told the Lord Ordainers grew more restless and began to increase their demands on the King, including the banishing of Gaveston once more. The King ordered a short exile for Piers to mollify them, but he was back within the year, irrepressible as ever.

Chapter 19

BY THE TIME the messenger rode his horse hard across the pastureland up to the great, white towers of the castle, it was very late, and the light faded enough to warrant the lighting of candles, that is, if Roger was to continue reading the documents strewn over his table in the private room behind the Hall. My lord always wished to do so these days, for he was nothing if not conscientious, and not one to tolerate slack administration.

He had learnt much about such matters in these years in Ireland, becoming more competent, but also a harder man by putting down several riots and rebellions. This country was still not a safe place, but we both felt optimistic for its future. Richard of Monmouth and Hugh Turpington were both serving loyally and my lord had kept his promise to bring his younger brother John to Ireland to train as a squire. John was full of the fire and rashness of youth. Probably much as Roger was at the same age, though I fancied my lord was a tad more cautious. He was not one to act on any stray impulse.

John and his sister Matilda, married to one Theobald de Verdon, who also had land in Ireland, were the closest of Roger's siblings. He privately thought of the younger ones, schooled by his mother, as 'the pious ones', no doubt destined to become canonesses and rectors, which would please his father. Roger had his eyes set on more temporal rewards and for the moment, I have to admit, I was completely swept along with him.

But now there was a commotion in the inner bailey outside, and I put down my embroidery work to wonder what could be happening. Hugh Turpington soon came into the Hall.

"What is it, Hugh?"

"We have a messenger, my lady, from England. Wearing the Earl of Pembroke's livery."

"Well, it's late, but it must be of some importance. Bring him up and we will take him to Roger in his private room."

Pembroke had been diligent in keeping Roger informed on court matters in general, and the doings of Piers Gaveston in particular, whilst we had been away. He had warned Roger not to return on any account, "lest he be dragged down with Gaveston".

The messenger almost fell into the hall, exhausted, dirty and sweaty after his headlong ride. I offered him some wine but he declined, insisting on seeing my lord straightaway. So Hugh and I took him back to Roger's inner sanctum where my lord looked up in surprise.

"Sire," the messenger croaked, with a throat full of dust, and then broke down in a fit of coughing.

"Spit it out, man! I trust this is urgent, judging by your state?"

"It's the Earl of Cornwall, my lord."

"Yes? What of him now? What has he done?"

"He has been commanded to God."

My lord stared and I gasped.

"Speak plainly. You are telling me he is dead?"

The man jerked his head in assent. Roger took a swig of wine from the goblet before him and swallowed hard. It was barely four months since Piers had written in pride and joy with the news of the birth of a daughter.

"Did he fall into an ague?"

It was hard to believe in one so lively, but Piers could have become sickly, like any man.

"No, sire. He is murdered. Brutally murdered, and sadly whilst under the protection of my lord, the Earl of Pembroke."

Hugh Turpington exclaimed in the background and Roger sat down in shock. I was struck dumb.

"May God have mercy on him! Murdered? But surely not by Pembroke, of all men? How did it come about?"

The messenger passed him a letter, wordlessly, and Roger weighed it in his hand. It was thick.

"Thank you for bearing this news, bad though it is," he said, more kindly. "Hugh, see this fellow fed and watered, and paid well for his trouble."

When we were alone, my lord broke Pembroke's seal on the letter and read it out loud to me, slowly. The Earl wrote in a highly emotional state, constantly berating himself, aghast at the thought of what the King might do. We pieced the sorry tale together with some difficulty, as a result.

It seemed Piers had returned from yet another exile in the early months of this year, and immediately attracted the Earl of Lancaster's wrath. Lancaster had asked Pembroke and Surrey to raise armies against the King's favourite. In addition, Piers had been excommunicated by the Pope at the barons' request. Not that he seemed at all concerned by either action, as he was in York again with Edward and Isabella. After the birth of his daughter, they all moved further north to Newcastle for greater safety. However, Pembroke now told how the barons' army surprised them there, so they had to take flight. On the fourth of May, they took sail for Scarborough, in such a hurry they left their riches behind, and these were taken by Lancaster.

The King was sufficiently alarmed to return south to raise his own army. Lancaster moved his men between them and laid siege to Scarborough Castle. Piers, now lodged alone in Scarborough, was totally unprepared, and bereft of any men at arms, so had to give himself up. Of course, he expected lenient treatment and so did Pembroke, who had sworn an oath to the King to protect Gaveston's life, and have him returned safely. So Pembroke took Gaveston into his custody, intending no harm to come to him. Except that Warwick, the 'Black Hound of Arden', would have none of this, and kidnapped the prisoner during their return journey back through the Midlands, taking him to his own castle.

Even so, Pembroke insisted he could not possibly have foreseen what happened next. At this point he sounded distraught again. Lancaster and Arundel now caught up with them, and Warwick was persuaded to surrender Piers, which he did with some relish. Pembroke was away that night, visiting his wife, believing his charge to be safely in Warwick's care, and having exacted a promise from him that no harm should come to Piers. But Lancaster took Gaveston to Blacklow Hill, on his land nearby, and paid two Welshmen to behead him. He did not even attempt to deny it.

There was no trial. No opportunity for Piers to plead for his life. He was put in rags and led to the hill in the darkness, barefoot and bareheaded, on a mangy horse. The only concession was execution by decapitation, rather than hanging, as befitted his quasi-noble status. But they made sure they ran him through with a sword first, and left his body on the road where it was found by local monks.

More self recrimination flowed through the ink of Pembroke's pen. If he had only thought...but he had never imagined...God knows, he never liked the man, but did not want this to happen! It was an outrage against any earl, however spurious. An abominable act.

The country was in turmoil and uproar, the King in a coldly furious state of shock. Civil War was most likely between Lancaster and the King, who must take arms, in Pembroke's opinion. He begged Roger to return. At any moment, the King might lapse into the torpor of grief and his resolve would need stiffening by loyal and firm men such as the Mortimers. My lord must make all reasonable speed!

Roger did what he always did when troubled. Calling for his favourite wolfhound, he turned on his heel, leaving the room and went out into the night to walk the battlements. Checking that men were at post and on guard where they ought to be, looking out into the distance, past the subdued lights and fires of the town. He had no need of a cloak, for the air was soft and gentle, the night tranquil and still after the long, midsummer day, disturbed only by the flutter of moth wings toward candlelight.

Quietly, I joined him, placing my hand on his arm. Somewhere out there, Pier's soul might be fluttering with these moths, lost and alone. He had died excommunicate and so his soul would be condemned to wander forever. He did not deserve that. We began to speak to each other, at last, in low tones.

Roger fancied Piers would be surprised at finding himself slain. Kidnapped by the 'Black Hound of Arden' and beheaded by 'The Fiddler', of all people! It was indeed monstrous. Pembroke was right. It was an outrage not to allow him the judgement of his peers, not that there would have been many to defend him. It gave Roger no pleasure to know he had warned him, time after time. Piers had thought he was untouchable under the King's protection.

And what of the King? He was certain to be paralysed by sorrow, as Pembroke suggested. His anguish would be unbearable. The Mortimers would be needed, along with as many men as they could raise. Lancaster could not be allowed to take the throne. We took a few more breaths of the sweet, night air before descending into the depths of the castle, and made our plans to return to England.

Chapter 20

SEPTEMBER 1312 – GASCONY

ALTHOUGH CIVIL WAR was not as imminent as Pembroke feared, Edward was determined to exact revenge on his rebellious barons but was biding his time. My lord was surprised to find his mind focussed and his vision clearer than before in grief. He shut the gates of London and defended the lands around it so the rebels slunk back to their own lairs.

But then, with Gaveston dead, there seemed little else they could gain. Faithful nobles were sympathetic towards the King, and even the Pope was appeased. Pembroke urged negotiation with the earls, but this was a royal step too far. Edward was determined there should be no forgiveness, especially for Lancaster. The only good piece of news was that Queen Isabella was expecting a child in November.

In the meantime, Robert Bruce was continuing to harry the north, no doubt encouraged by Edward's troubles. To make matters worse, there was trouble in Gascony again, and it was my lord who was dispatched to deal with it because Edward did not feel he could spare Pembroke.

Roger   found the King in a strange mood where he was concerned. On the one hand, he would beg for advice and support, and on the other, behave as if he could hardly bear to see him. My lord wondered if it was because of his close association with Piers over the years, and the memories it brought back, whilst I thought it more likely to be their quarrel over the desultory Scottish campaign.

Roger took me with him to Gascony. We sailed from Bristol to Bordeaux and stayed at Blaye Castle within Bourg-en-Blaye, which remained in Roger of Chirk's ownership. My kinsmen through my mother were directly involved in the local disarray, for Sir John Ferrers, the English Seneschal, had abused his position by attacking one Amanieu d'Albret and it was now suggested that another Frenchman – Amaury de Craon – should become Seneschal instead. Both Albret and Craon were related to my mother.

The situation was even more delicate, as Amanieu had gone to the French King for support, and Philip was demanding compensation for his insult. Once again, Philip could exert pressure over the English King, theoretically a royal equal, but merely a duke in this colony of Aquitaine. Philip wanted reparation as well as homage, and it was an opportunity to rub Edward's nose in the dirt. Oil therefore must be poured on troubled waters.

My lord was also tasked with paying his respects to Piers' old family household, to offer condolences, and convey Edward's promise that he would seek revenge on the murderers before his friend was laid to rest. In truth, the King could not bear to contemplate a funeral as yet.

Pembroke, only just emerging from his own state of shock, had given Roger various errands, too. So my lord was extremely busy and preoccupied, travelling all over the colony. Meanwhile, I had time on my hands and rested in the Citadel of Blaye, being heavy with child again.

I no longer wept over Piers, even though I was very sorry and sad for his little wife, Margaret, with her baby daughter – another Joan, named after her grandmother Joan of Acre, though Piers, with his typical insincere charm, had insinuated she was named after me. Mindful of Warenne's warnings, I am sorry to say I felt secretly relieved that Piers was gone. For we might have been brought down, too, had it not been for Ireland; and now, surely, Edward could give his queen his undivided attention.

It was pleasant in Gascony in September with the fiercest heat of the summer gone. The forests around the citadel of Blaye were green and shady, but completely different from the mild, wet green of Ireland. The air was warm and somnolent with the sound of the vast waters of the Dordonne flowing fast down below, on their way to join the Gironde estuary. The abundant vines were almost ready to be harvested outside the sun-bleached town with its red tiled roofs.

I was feeling more tired with this lying-in, for some reason, and hoped it was not a bad omen. Only yesterday we had learned, amongst other despatches from home, that Roger's sister, Matilda, married to Theobald de Verdon, had died in childbirth. This had shaken me to the core. It was Matilda's fourth child, so she was not untried, and she was a few years younger than me, seemingly healthy, without any earlier misfortunes.

This was my eighth pregnancy, at the age of twenty-six; a little John and a little Joan had joined the others since I bore Geoffrey. Following Roger around, as he wished, exacted a high price. I now had seven children already and was about to have my eighth. Each of them I loved the instant they arrived, and looked forward to seeing them grow. But I sometimes wondered if being with child would ever end. It seemed not.

I wondered if Roger would become tired of this, too, but he greeted each new arrival with pleasure, and told me they would all extend the family's influence in time. He was proud of my strength in childbearing, and if he visited the occasional prostitute or serving wench when I was large, I did not mind, as long as I did not know about it. It was only to be expected in a man.

Nevertheless, although I put it down to the heat, I was fatigued most of the time now, and my body had grown slacker after each delivery. I was grateful for this rest away from the children in Gascony, and that was not like me, for I usually missed them so. I did not feel like doing anything much, and sat with my puffy ankles raised on a footstool in the castle garden, listening to the birds under the shade of the fruit trees.

I wondered how the Queen was faring with her lying-in, and prayed for a good outcome for her. Dozing, inevitably, I also wondered if Roger might secure an appointment in Gascony. I might like that – away from the cares of England and Ireland – providing Avice could face the long journey to bring the children over with her. Currently, she was in Ludlow with my mother, and I missed her, as well as the children. But Roger said the

Gascon nobles were so changeable in their allegiances that any appointment here would be worse than home. So it was all just a foolish dream and wishful thinking – not at all practical in reality, however attractive this land seemed.

My lord also said a full and real campaign against Scotland would be necessary soon: more warfare, and he would be at the forefront once again. Would that never end?

I woke with a start to hear his firm and confident tread approaching. He flung himself down in the seat next to me, calling for wine and peeling off his riding gloves, dusty from the road.

"How goes it?" I asked.

"Frustrating!"

"Will Ferrers not go?"

"Oh yes – he knows he must. And de Craon will take his place. But d'Albret is still moaning. I am afraid Edward will have to swallow his pride and visit Paris to conclude negotiations and grant him a great deal of money. There are several other appeals gone to the French King as well, and it would be good for Edward to smooth his way with some concessions. His father-in-law needs careful handling."

"Perhaps he will be softened by them taking a new grandson to visit?"

"Yes, that would be a fine thing, wouldn't it? A future Edward the Third, no doubt. Let's hope so!"

He swatted a fly away from his goblet of wine with one of the leather gloves.

I studied my husband with solicitude. He seemed tired of Gascony already. Naturally, he was sad to hear about Matilda, but it was more than that. At twenty-five, and tall and dark, he would have been very handsome if it were not for eyebrows which were a little too thick, and eyes which were a little too penetrating. He did not smile a great deal either, though the aspect of his face was much improved when he did. A frown tended to knit his forehead most days now. His body remained lean, toned, muscular and fit. A soldier's body, tight and hard. I sighed without meaning to.

"What is it?"

"Oh, nothing. Just what you said about Scotland."

"We can't let the Bruce carry on as he is doing, though it will have to wait till after the Royal Birth, and now this trip to France."

But then he did smile, and leaning over, took my hand.

"This time we must beat them, and we will!" His large hand squeezed mine hard.

On the 13th of November, the feast day of St. Brice, Queen Isabella gave birth to a son at Windsor, who was indeed named Edward, as expected for a royal heir. A few days later, I gave birth to Isabella, named after Roger's aunt rather than the Queen. She was a sickly child to begin with, and I feared she might be my only newborn to die, but she managed to thrive somehow, despite an early chronic cough, which never completely left her. As you know, she is now subject to much frailty. Perhaps my feelings during that lying-in had been intuitive after all; she has always needed the greatest of care.

The following May, Edward and his Queen left on their long-promised visit to France. Edward ignored the Ordinances from his barons, which required consent to leave the Kingdom. Instead, he loudly proclaimed he was going but would be back in time for a July Parliament. In fact, he was not. The social side of their visit proceeded in great style and was extended for a leisurely trip through France, via Pontoise, Poissy, Montreuil de Mer and finally Boulogne. The King and Queen seemed especially close, however, and she was able to comfort him on the anniversary of Piers' death.

In Pontoise, a tragedy was narrowly averted when Edward rescued Isabella from a fire, which broke out in the wardrobe of their silken pavilion at night. He carried her to safety in his strong arms. Understandably, she needed time to recover after this, as her arms had been burnt rather badly, and furthermore, the ladies' waggon broke down on the way back, requiring repair, causing another delay. They finally arrived back at Dover five days after the planned Parliament, but were forgiven, under the circumstances.

The news was grim however. Robert Bruce was fighting the English in the Isle of Man whilst his brother Edward, Earl of

Carrick, had laid siege to Stirling Castle. Sir Philip Mowbray, in charge of the castle, had held out for three months but then broke the siege by parleying with Edward Bruce. He promised him that, if the siege were lifted, the castle would be Bruce's – providing Mowbray had not been sent a relieving army by the English King within one year. Edward Bruce, equally anxious to get away with his men, agreed.

Messengers were sent to inform King Robert and King Edward of England of the understanding. Neither were best pleased. A showdown with the whole English Army was not something Robert Bruce desired; meanwhile, our King was placed in an irrevocable position. Neither monarchs could ignore this challenge. The die was cast for serious warfare, and my heart duly sank.

Chapter 21

June 1314 – Bannockburn

AT LAST THEY were on the road. It was six months since they had been summoned to assemble with their men at Berwick. Six months in which to prepare a huge army of twenty thousand. Ninety-five earls and barons obeyed. They did not include Thomas of Lancaster, nor the Earl of Warwick. The King intended to deal with their insurrection on the way back. The thought of that gave him more satisfaction than this long-overdue Scottish campaign, even though Robert Bruce had systematically taken all the English fortresses on his side of the border, except for Stirling. Now time was running out for Stirling. But it was about to see the biggest English Army ever encountered in the north come to relieve it. At the very last moment.

I was no longer on the road with them. On the seventeenth of June, the men left their ladies in Berwick, including myself, Lady Clifford, and the Countess of Hereford, all of us in attendance on the Queen. Each lady watched the squires help their lord get ready, handed them their swords and spears, and sent them off with heartfelt prayers but huge optimism in their hearts, and confident expectations of glory to come.

Our only recourse then was to wait anxiously for their return, though we heard every detail about it from our lords thereafter, and that was not commonplace for a battle. But this was no ordinary battle.

It was in Berwick I became closer to Maud, born a de Clare, but now Lady Clifford, married to Robert, who was Marshal of England and regarded as the chief guardian against Scotland with his lands in the north. She was first cousin of Gilbert, the young Earl of Gloucester, also riding to Bannockburn with Robert, and to his sister Margaret de Clare, Piers' widow. I began our discourse by asking her about Margaret's health and happiness.

"Well, of course her dower as Countess of Cornwall was disputed," Maud said, "on account of Piers Gaveston. The King has seen fit to grant her Oakham Castle and other lands in Rutland as partial recompense. I gather she is very happy there with her own small household and her little daughter."

"I am glad of it," I said, sincerely. "She must have had a difficult time these past two years."

"Maybe not as difficult as before," and Maud raised one eyebrow. "Unfortunately, it won't last. She is considered too marriageable to stay single for long. No doubt to one of the King's new favourites."

Maud's candour was refreshing. I soon found I could speak very freely with her and she was not in the least surprised or offended. Whilst Bess of Hereford kept herself somewhat aloof, as befitted a Countess and sister to the King, Maud and myself were more equal. She was born in Ireland and brought up in the Marches. The Cliffords used to be a Marcher family until Robert Clifford's father married into the rich Vipont family of Westmorland, and Robert subsequently exchanged his Monmouth lands for Craven, taking up residence at Skipton Castle. Maud was also in the Prince's household along with Robert when we were there. So we had much in common, even though she was ten years my senior. I liked her immensely and I think she liked me too. She cheered me so many times in those endless days at Berwick. All of which made what happened to her family more devastating.

The men marched along the Roman road to Edinburgh from Berwick, and their leaders reached the city two days later. Here they rested, but had to wait for the others to catch up. For the army was so massive, and required so many baggage trains, it stretched out for twenty leagues. There was precious little rest for those bringing up the rear, as they needed to push on to reach Stirling by Midsummer's Day to keep the agreement made between Sir Philip Mowbray and Edward Bruce.

By the twenty-second, they were at Falkirk. Yet again, there was little sleep to be had, for they must press on at dawn to have any chance of getting within a league of Stirling. Despite the strength of the Army, Roger told me he felt uneasy from this point on. It was a hot midsummer, and barely grew dark at all in Scotland. This meant more light for advancing, but the men were growing ever more tired. Tomorrow was the eve of St John the Baptist, so they would have to march on empty stomachs to keep the customary fast. Roger was a soldier through and through, and knew this was not how to keep an army going. They would not fight well hungry. By late dusk, they would be a league's distance from Stirling, but their bellies would remain empty and growling until the next day.

The Earl of Pembroke had managed the difficult advance so far, keeping to time. He was now relieved of command, as was expected. The King ordered the twenty-two-year-old Earl of Gloucester to take over, which was far from expected. Everyone had assumed the Earl of Hereford would be chosen, as he was Constable of England, and had far greater experience. Roger had nothing against Gilbert de Clare himself, but surely Edward knew he was still wet behind the ears where military experience was concerned?

It smacked of spite against the older Earl, who had been outspoken against Gaveston. Hereford himself was outraged. Had he not been with his own father, also Constable of England, and Edward I, at the glorious success of Falkirk sixteen years earlier? He said Gilbert was barely out of swaddling clothes then, which was only a slight exaggeration. The other barons also muttered their dissent, agreeing wholeheartedly with Hereford. But the King was not to be swayed.

Dawn broke after a bare few hours, with the promise of a fine day to come. At early light the powerful destriers, unridden till now to save their strength, were groomed and harnessed, the men fully armoured, and a host of brightly embroidered standards and banners taken out from iron bound chests. The air was full of nervous tension with the sure and certain knowledge of an encounter to come. Grooms whistled as they worked and men spoke to each other heartily. But their jollity was forced.

Their spies reported that Bruce's army had withdrawn from the Torwood, where they had been training, but only to more open ground, and they were at least making a show of being ready for battle.

Impatient now, young Gloucester rode off with a vanguard to the Bannock Burn, leaving the main body of the army still preparing to set off. Hereford and his nephew, Henry, went with him – the elder de Bohun gritting his teeth at Gloucester's premature initiative. Roger stayed behind with Pembroke and the King. Almost as soon as the vanguard set off, Sir Philip Mowbray arrived from the castle and was admitted into Edward's silken pavilion, where the King was dressing. Mowbray was ecstatic. Now the English Army was so close, his honour had been saved, and he said he would be able to reprovision his garrison and welcome the King right royally within the castle. Come now! There was hardly any need for immediate battle!

Outside the pavilion, holding the reins of the azure and gold-caparisoned Marcher, waiting for the order to mount, Roger grimaced at the raised voices from inside. Now that Gloucester had hurtled off with the vanguard, it was rather late to avoid battle. Edward emerged, seemingly unconcerned but indecisive. He called Robert Clifford to him and ordered him to take his brigade of three hundred men forward on horseback. They should reconnoitre a route through to the castle.

Roger inwardly groaned. To do this, they would have to strike an arc eastwards, crossing the Bannock Burn higher, and that meant entering the mudflats. He made so bold as to interrupt the King.

"Sire," he said, "we must bring the infantry and the archers up immediately to support Hereford, and indeed Clifford."

Edward wagged his head dismissively at the mention of Hereford.

"They can follow our route but camp south of the cavalry, and make two parallel flanks to support the main army and our royal person."

"They will not be able to do that well from the distance involved," Pembroke said, echoing Roger's own thoughts.

"Aymer, you must trust Gloucester now! Let us wait to hear a happy result from him."

Edward's tone was sharp, and he glared at them both. He would plainly brook no opposition. Mortimer and Pembroke avoided each other's eyes as they were dismissed. They were told to make ready for movement, but not to depart.

The day dragged heavily for them, as it did for all the other subordinate commanders, all banned from any movement until Clifford should return.

Hereford was the first to get back, early in the afternoon. Roger could tell by the slump of the earl's broad shoulders that something was wrong. He was riding slowly with a mere handful of men behind him. At first Roger thought his nephew was not with them. Then he saw the armoured body in blue and white colours, hanging limply over its horse's saddle. Closer at hand, he saw the helmet cleft in two. No-one could have survived such an axe blow.

Men ran out with cries to help Hereford dismount and discharge his heavy cargo. Smiths were sent for, to remove Henry de Bohun's damaged helmet. The Earl himself made his way wearily to the knot of waiting nobles. It was a sorry tale he had to tell. Once the vanguard had reached the Bannock Burn, they spied a small band of Scotsmen hastily withdrawing. Amongst them, they spotted Robert Bruce himself, recognisable by the glint of the golden crown atop his chainmail. So they all galloped across the burn and up the hill in hot pursuit. Only Henry de Bohun outdid Gloucester in his youthful ardour to get there first. He rode straight at the Scottish King with his lance at full tilt. Bruce swerved expertly to avoid him, and then stood in the stirrups of the grey mare to bring the axe down with an almighty clang.

The rest of them were involved in an embarrassing and fruitless skirmish until more Scots appeared out of the trees to rally round Bruce. Gloucester was unhorsed, but not harmed, and the retreat was sounded by Hereford. The remainder of the vanguard were now following on behind.

"I blame myself," Humphrey told Roger quietly, his face grey with grief, "for filling him full of tales of the glory of Falkirk and firing such impetuosity."

Roger shook his head.

"No need for blame, cousin. He was blind with the heat of the moment and the rashness of youth."

"Aye, but how do I tell his mother that? When she expected me to keep a watchful eye on her beloved son? Your mother would have expected the same at one time, but thankfully you have a sound head on your shoulders, and more experience."

There was worse news to come when Clifford's detachment came limping back shortly before dusk. They had succeeded in skirting the park on the way to the castle, unseen to begin with. But when they drew closer to the castle, they were suddenly faced by a brigade under the command of Thomas Randolph, the Earl of Moray. Instead of encountering a disorganised rabble, they found themselves up against compact circles of footsoldiers armed with long pikes. Each circle was made up of thick concentric rings of these men. When one man fell from it, another immediately took his place from within.

"It was like trying to do battle with a wheeling hedgehog," Clifford said. "The horses were no use at all. They just ended up with a spear through their chest. At first, we expected the circles to break into panic and run, but they were either remarkably brave or extremely well trained and disciplined. Possibly both. I've never seen any Scots band work like this. If only we'd had the archers! We lost too many good men and horses."

Robert Clifford knew what he was talking about, after years of rebuffing border raids in the North. But now they must camp for the night and, given the need of fresh water for the horses, would have to move eastwards and upwards to the Burn. The only available ground which could accommodate all the horses was just to the north of the Bannock Burn, close to where it met the Pelstream, another tributary of the river forming the mudflats. But the infantry and baggage train would have to remain to the south.

Edward did not seem at all dismayed by this, especially as it meant the flower of the cavalry was closer to the castle. Gloucester also remained undeterred, though he bore the brunt of the King's harsh words for his perceived failure in letting Bruce escape. Hereford and Clifford were full of foreboding, having witnessed the Scots firsthand, and their mood quickly transferred itself to others, my lord included. Unless the Scottish army melted away in the night, as it had done so many times before, they knew they were in for a hard fight.

That night, no-one slept well. In the morning, they woke to find Seton gone. Sir Alexander Seton was a Scottish knight who had joined Edward some years ago. Now he had turned coat again, and could tell tales of dissension and disorganisation in the English ranks. He would convince Robert Bruce it was time to stand and fight, if anyone could.

The second day began with Mass said well before dawn, and thankfully followed by breakfast. Daylight showed the disadvantage of their position, hemmed in by the marshy ground between two burns, with the infantry still well off to the south. Yet they still had two-and-a-half thousand mounted knights, with fifteen thousand footsoldiers behind, and did not imagine the Scots would dare attack with their paltry eight or nine thousand. If they did, the commanders expected to ride in pursuit up to the park, and force the outnumbered enemy to retreat before their onslaught.

Edward favoured a march northward, however, across drier land up to the castle, leaving the infantry even further behind, and he determined to lead the head of this battalion himself. Next to him rode the Earl of Pembroke, and one Sir Giles d'Argentan with their men. The Mortimers followed on behind. A messenger was dispatched south to command the archers to move forward. On the left flank rode Hereford and Gloucester, out between the King and the park. They were the first to see Edward Bruce's men advance out of the trees. He was flanked by the battalions of the Earl of Moray and the Earl of Douglas.

Edward caught sight of them, too.

"What!" he shouted, in genuine surprise. "Do they mean to fight then, after all?"

The next instant, the whole of the Scottish army went down on one knee and clasped their hands in prayer.

Edward laughed out loud.

"Look at them! They beg for mercy."

"Yes, but not from you," muttered Roger. "They are asking God to forgive their trespasses, for they intend to win – or die."

Hereford and Gloucester were seen to hesitate at the fore of their men.

"What are you waiting for, Gloucester?" yelled the King. "Are you now guilty of treachery and deceit as well as tardiness?"

"Today, it will be clear that I am neither!" Gilbert hurled back in anger. He dug in his spurs and led his five hundred men straight for the ranks of the Black Douglas. Roger saw he was riding without his surcoat and heraldic colours; he could not have been entirely ready on setting off. This was mad. For Douglas would not recognise him, and only see Hereford in his blue colours behind as the commander. Other men followed Gloucester, but Hereford held his back for the moment.

They looked on in horror as the Scots advanced in their schiltron formations just as Clifford had described, with only a few on horseback. Gloucester did not stop or even swerve. He plunged straight into them, as if intent on suicide. There came the clash of iron on iron. Gloucester's horse screamed, skewered through the chest. Gilbert de Clare was down and the Scots were on him. He was hacked to death before anyone else could catch up, and the air was filled with unearthly war cries from jubilant throats, as if wild animals were howling.

"They don't know who he is!" Roger shouted to his uncle, who nodded gravely. But now the charge was sounded for all, and the time for rational thinking was over.

Except that it was clear the space they rode from was far too narrow. The men behind had to wait at the back, with the screams of horses and men ringing in their ears. When their turn came to charge, the churned up mud was already stained with blood and their horse's hooves trampled on freshly dead corpses. Riderless horses got in the way. Pike shafts and lances splintered. Armour was rent by axes, and shields quickly splattered with blood so that colours could hardly be seen.

At last the archers were catching up and unleashed a hailstorm of arrows. But they were still too far back, and many fell short, slicing into Englishmen instead of Scots. The next moment, Robert Bruce attacked the archers from the side with his battalion. There was no chance of the cavalry wheeling round to protect them, and no infantry yet in sight. The archers threw down their bows and ran.

By now, King Edward was in the thick of the battle. He rode forward bravely enough, but his horse was felled underneath him. He was unseated and a cry rose up from both sides at seeing the Crown fall. Sir Giles and Roger rode in to save him from an answering swarm of Scottish warriors.

Roger bashed his way through with a mace, but his faithful Marcher took a spear in the neck. He leapt out of the saddle as soon as he saw the red blood spurt and felt the mare's legs buckling. He bludgeoned the man who had done it, smashing his face in fury. Dodging the swing of axes and the thrust of spears, he drew his sword. But Sir Giles had already reached Edward and was dragging him away from the scene.

Another yell rose from the Scots.

"On them! They fail, they fail! On them!"

It came from the throats of the camp followers on the ridge, rushing up to see the slaughter below. But it seemed like yet another wild army from below, and many Englishmen fled.

Pembroke brought up another horse for Edward, who was stumbling but unharmed, under Sir Giles' protection. Out of the corner of his eye, Roger saw them get him on to it and Pembroke lead him away. Sir Giles remounted to ride back into the fray, axe aloft to clear space for the King's retreat. He levelled his lance and Roger saw him ride on to his inevitable death. It was hand-to-hand combat now for all who remained.

Roger lost his sword from the sideways swipe of a pike. Reaching for his axe, he felt a sharp stinging in his left shoulder, but there was too much adrenaline for any real pain. He was on the pikemen in a second with his axe, severing his jugular. Wheeling round, he hacked at another coming for him, and caught him sideways through the tendons at the back of the knee. The next one had the wrist of his sword hand chopped into pieces. Roger's shield dripped blood as he raised it to deflect another spear. If Sir Giles refused to leave the field, then so would he. It would gain time for Pembroke and the King to make their escape.

After a short while, he was dimly aware of being back amongst Pembroke's men. Many of his own had been lost or fled. Grabbing the reins of a riderless horse trying to push through in a panic, he threw himself into the saddle. He intended to retreat at last, fighting with the undrawn sword he found next the pommel.

But the Scots were on them again in a moment. Within the space of five minutes, he was totally surrounded by a ring of spears. There was nothing else to do but surrender. So he threw down the sword and slowly raised his shield – in his right arm, for he found he could no longer raise his left – as a sign of submission. He had lost most of his colours with Marcher, and his shield was red, but there was still some blue and azure visible on his bloodstained surcoat enough for his captors to realise he might warrant a ransom. So the rough hands which dragged him from the stranger's horse did not kill him, but took him away with them to Bruce's camp.

Chapter 22

HE WAS TAKEN to the Scottish King's headquarters above the Bannockburn. Barely recognisable, being drenched in blood, sweat and mud. But Robert Bruce knew who he was. They had met before, in the King of England's court during Bruce's period of acceptance of the truce. Mortimer had been a mere adolescent then, but Bruce knew of his successful career in Ireland since. After all, Roger was an ally of the Earl of Ulster, Bruce's own estranged father-in-law.

For Roger's part, he remembered a quiet man of thirty years or thereabouts, soon to vanish and be utterly condemned by the English, after his murder of Comyn and assumption of the Scottish throne. The intervening years, spent in almost constant warfare, had been hard on him, and he seemed older than forty now, whilst Roger was still in his prime, at twenty-seven. There was something more prominent and rugged about Bruce's face, and Roger briefly remembered the rumour he may have leprosy. Could a King have leprosy and conceal it? He also remembered Bruce's careful deliberation and the calmness of his determination, now given gravitas by wearing a crown. So different from King Edward!

"Mortimer?" he was asked, and Roger nodded. He was not going to bend his knee, though briefly he felt he should.

"You fought bravely," and King Robert smiled beneath the crowned helmet, with its chainmail still hanging around his face like the ears of a lugubrious bloodhound. "Like a demon, in fact, and all to protect your poor King!"

He turned to his men and camp followers.

"Treat him well, as with all our captured nobles."

Bruce's servants took him to a treatment tent, where he was painfully stripped of his armour and bloodstained clothes, his wounds and bruises swabbed with witch-hazel, and was given fresh linen. An overworked barber surgeon arrived to inspect his shoulder, which had dropped down below its socket. Without any warning, he put his foot in Roger's armpit and yanked it up back into place, which was excruciating but nevertheless done well. The actual wound was pronounced well clotted, though this maneouvre had opened it afresh, so egg white was applied, to cleanse and seal it. Then he gave Roger a heady draught of herbs, wine and hemlock for the pain. He soon lapsed into a deep and welcome sleep.

At first, he dreamt of the metallic smell of blood filling his nostrils, and the clash and clang of iron ringing in his ears, accompanied by hellish screaming, but then he slipped further down into the arms of a deeper, darker place and slept undisturbed.

When he awoke, the camp had long since moved and he found himself in a simple but comfortable room, attended by a Scottish servant with flaming red hair. The man was attentive, despite his fiery appearance, and brought him food and drink. He said his name was Rory and that he had strict orders to ensure his prisoner's needs were met.

Rory told him he was in Stirling Castle and that he had been brought here on a stretcher two days ago, in a comatose state. There was some anxiety that the barber surgeon may have over-estimated the amount of hemlock in his sleeping draught; so it was a relief for Rory to see him alive and well, as the servant may have been held to account for any other outcome.

Roger felt as stiff and sore as an old man but the throbbing pain had gone, as long as he remembered not to move his left arm too quickly. He ate and drank with gratitude. Stirling Castle! How often he had been encamped below, part of some interminable siege. Now he was within its walls, but not as a conqueror. Clearly Mowbray had been forced to cede the castle, with the English Army so utterly and completely routed, and its King fled. Now Roger must wait in captivity until a ransom was paid for him and the rest of the surviving barons and earls, including his uncle and the Earl of Hereford, so he was told. Well, Edward might be persuaded to pay up for Hereford, who was his brother-in-law, but Roger suspected he would have to rely on his own family to find money for the Mortimers. Then Rory told him the Scottish King wanted to see him as soon as he was rested enough.

"I am rested now," Roger said, "and not used to being treated with kid gloves. I'll hear what he has to say without delay."

In due course, Rory ushered him into the Great Hall of the castle. They had lost no time in erecting a throne at the high end, and King Robert was sitting there, with a long, trestle table before him, and his younger brother, Edward Bruce, Earl of Carrick, standing behind him. In the light of morning, Roger saw the King's bearded face was lined and he had a rash on his bare forearms. However, he wore a fine scarlet robe which covered his elbows, and the crown on his head completed the picture of a noble King. His voice was strong and measured.

"Ah, Mortimer the younger. No need for ceremony. Come closer."

As Roger did so, he spotted a Seal and a shield lying on the table before the Bruce. They belonged to the English Edward, and the sight of them jolted his nerves.

"Fear not," said Robert Bruce. "He got away – thanks to your admirable Earl of Pembroke and Sir Giles d'Argentan. But he did leave these behind on the battlefield."

Roger bowed his head in humiliation.

"You asked to see me, sire. I can hardly imagine my ransom has been paid already."

"No. But I do not require a ransom in your case, cousin."

It was a shock to hear the Scottish King refer to their distant kinship. For they were third cousins, albeit somewhat removed, through the same lineage of the de Clares of Gloucester.

"I have a task for you, instead. A request, Lord Mortimer of Wigmore, if you will: to carry the Privy Seal and the Royal Shield back to its rightful owner. Our spies tell us he has gone back to Berwick, to join the ladies. Tell him his belongings are restored from one true and royal monarch to another."

Roger nodded with no thought of demurring. It was, after all, a chivalrous act.

"You may also take two bodies, which we have had embalmed. The very young Earl of Gloucester – and Sir Robert Clifford."

Roger felt a keen pang of sorrow. Gloucester he knew about, having witnessed his recklessness, but not Clifford, a lifelong friend since they had been in the royal household together. Robert Bruce saw the shadow pass over his face.

"Many of your best men died that day."

It was simply said without any malice or crowing.

This was a man you could negotiate with, Roger thought, a wise and reasonable man. He was only fighting for his own birthright and his own lands and country. Was it really beyond the realms of possibility to recognise him as a King, even if not *the* King? Why, the man could even be an ally, if respected.

Then he caught sight of the brother, equally capable though hot-headed and ambitious, standing behind him, smirking in triumph. No, it had to be war. Bannockburn was a disaster which should never have happened. But its finality could not be allowed.

"I will, of course, do as you wish," Roger said stiffly, adding more respectfully, "your Grace."

"I do not require you to set off straightaway. You should rest until you are strong enough. Your arm…"

"Is healing well, I think. Your surgeon was helpful, if somewhat brutal. Besides, I have been used to riding with no arms – I will have no problem riding with one."

The boast was irresistible, to recover some dignity."

"As you please. I daresay you are keen to be free. We will supply you with fresh horses and some of our retainers for safe passage."

It was a miserable journey, with their precious cargo and heavier burden of bodies, even though the days were light and long, warm, and pleasantly full of birdsong. A light rain began to fall as they approached Berwick, and this seemed more fitting.

We ladies, left at court in Berwick, had been shocked to the core by the return of Pembroke with the King. Edward had little to say, but the Earl told us the dire news of total and utter defeat, though not in such detail as Roger recounted to me afterwards.

It was Pembroke who broke the news of Clifford's death to the Lady Maud. He had seen him fall with a blow that was surely mortal, and trampled underfoot, unable to get up. The Countess of Hereford paled at this news, as well as Maud. We had never imagined the nobility would be in such danger. Pembroke assured Elizabeth the Earl must have been taken prisoner – he could not begin to imagine anything else for the Constable of England. Of Roger, he had no idea, though he had seen him last in the thick of the fighting. So I was left with a sickening uncertainty, whilst doing my best to comfort Maud.

Because I had prepared myself for the worst, I was overjoyed to see my lord's party ride in, a few days later. This was tempered by the knowledge he bore the bodies of Maud's husband and cousin. There was little time to greet each other properly, however, as Roger was immediately ordered to attend an audience with the Queen.

Isabella had grown into a beauty at eighteen, and one with some spirit as well as professed piety. She looked splendid in a gown of rich purple trimmed with the finest cream lace, but Roger was wearied at the prospect of further explanations, though he bowed low to her.

"Madame? You wished to see me?"

"'Ee is devastated. The King!" She still had trouble with her English pronunciation, though her words were sharp enough. Roger felt irritated. He felt he did not need the Queen's opinion on the matter when she had not been there.

"We all are, Madame," he said, failing to keep a note of bitterness out of his voice. "I have ridden back with the bodies of two of my closest friends – Gloucester and Clifford."

"Ah, yes, and Gloucester leaves only sisters. That will create a problem."

"Indeed it will. I expect their suitors are lining up as we speak." Roger was aware he was being bluntly rude but the ride, coming so soon after his injuries, had been harder than he cared to admit. He was not in the mood for this. He carried on regardless.

"You need not be too concerned. The King will have to give his permission for each match."

Isabella wrinkled her delicate nose.

"And he will. But did you know he has new favourites? Audley and Damory?"

Roger frowned. Perhaps better to have more than one, though.

"'Ee needs your support, Mortimer. To make the right decisions. Along with Pembroke!"

"Our loyalty is not in doubt, Madame. Neither is that of mine uncle – nor the Earl of Hereford, both of whom are held captive. We have proved our mettle on that field and expect their ransoms to be paid promptly."

Isabella touched his hand lightly.

"We know, Mortimer, we know, and are glad of it. But Lancaster and Warwick are secretly rejoicing at our defeat. They are already claiming it as God's will because Edward 'as paid no attention to their Ordinances. So now, you must go to my dear lord and tell 'im of your support in Parliament, as well as on the field."

Roger took this as a dismissal and bowed low again. Making his way to the King's chamber, he reflected that the Queen was, of course, absolutely right. She seemed anxious to make sure he was on their side. Well, indeed he was, but at this precise moment the last person he wanted to see was the King; he had been looking forward to a hot bath and no doubt a great deal of sympathy from myself.

He did not find Edward quite as devastated as the Queen made out, for he was enjoying a sack of wine and dicing with Roger Damory and Hugh Audley, the aforementioned new favourites. His face did fall on seeing my lord, however; especially when the Seal and shield were laid before him. Edward took up the Privy Seal and examined it carefully, as if it might be a fake.

"I was ordered," Roger said hoarsely, "nay, requested, to tell you that they are restored to one true and royal monarch by another."

He thought it politic to reverse the order of the message, but Edward still harrumphed.

"The cheek of the man!"

"Nevertheless," Roger answered, still more quietly, "to the victor go the spoils. He didn't have to return them."

Edward shrugged. To Roger's gratification and surprise, he dismissed Damory and Audley from their presence.

"Sit down, Mortimer. Some wine?"

Roger accepted, gratefully. His shoulder was paining him again after two long days in the saddle, despite his bravado.

"What are we to do? You have heard about Lancaster and Warwick? Still throwing their weight around, despite having got rid of poor Perrot?"

He had not forgotten Piers then, despite his new favourites. Roger relaxed a little.

"There must be another Parliament, of course."

"At York. In September. But I am afraid of what those two will demand."

"Well, they have hardly been loyal, have they, sire? So they will speak from a position of weakness. My uncle of Chirk, Pembroke, and myself will all stand beside you, and make sure the men favourable to ourselves are appointed if there is any demand to reform the offices and household. Hereford will stand by you, too."

"He was not blameless in his attitude to Piers, either," snapped Edward.

"Did he not go down on his knees and beg your humble forgiveness for that? And has he not put his life at risk for you on the battlefield?" Roger thought grimly that if Edward were not a King, he would have been tempted to slap him across the face with his glove.

The King nodded, sheepishly.

"Then maybe it is time to put all this behind us and lay poor Piers to rest."

The King thought about this.

"I miss him so. I need a friend."

"But you have more than one friend now."

It was not the same with Damory and Audley then.

"Time for Piers to rest?" the King repeated.

"I think so, sire. Poor Gloucester too, and Clifford. Hereford also has a young nephew to bury."

"Ah, yes! I should not have taunted young Gilbert so, should I?"

"No use going over that now. He and Henry de Bohun were both impetuous and headstrong. Most likely Gloucester would have done what he did, whether or not."

Edward brightened at this. He had truly regretted his words to Gloucester.

"You, of course, are a sight more clever! But you are right. They should all be laid to rest. Including Piers. Perhaps you would help me arrange it?"

"Of course. I think King's Langley would be an appropriate burial ground for Piers."

"Not Westminster?"

"No, my lord. *Not* Westminster," Roger said firmly. "King's Langley. Where you were both at your happiest."

And also somewhere which could avoid the wrath of Lancaster and Warwick, he thought privately.

"True, true. In the New Year?"

"In the New Year; if the Queen agrees. She has been much comfort to you these last two years, has she not?"

"Oh, yes," Edward agreed. "Indeed she has – and our little boy is growing wondrously well. More are desired, you know."

Roger bowed his head.

"I am glad to hear it, sire. Then all is as it should be."

He forebore to mention that, in that case, Edward would be better off paying more attention to his Queen than to Damory and Audley. But he could not stop a smile crossing his face on leaving the royal presence. Edward might be entirely oblivious of how he had risked his life for him, but at least he could still exert some influence on his monarch, no doubt to the approval of the Queen.

Only everything was not as it should have been, after Bannockburn. The harvest rotted in the fields with so few able men left to gather it in before the rains came. The autumn Parliament did not go entirely to plan either. In general, the men favoured by Pembroke, Hereford and the Mortimers gained ascendancy, but the King decided to marry Margaret de Clare to Hugh Audley and – most worryingly for Roger – another niece, his favourite Eleanor, to Hugh Despenser the Younger. He would have liked to marry Roger Damory off to the eldest de Clare, Elizabeth, in addition, but she was already taken by the widowed Theobald de Verdon, after losing Matilda Mortimer in childbirth. For the time being, Damory must wait. My lord was naturally most worried about the advancement of Hugh Despenser, and his opportunity to claim a part of the Earldom of Gloucester.

Young Gilbert's widow pronounced herself pregnant, however, holding off any challenge for the Earldom. We prayed she would turn out to deliver a boy, for Gloucester was the richest earldom in the country, and controlled the Southern Marches with Glamorgan. We did not want to see it fall into the hands of Roger's sworn enemy.

We attended Piers' burial at King's Langley on the second day of January in the New Year. It was a sumptuous and costly affair but at least it was not Westminster. The Queen also attended, which we felt was gracious of her, especially as she had just received news of the death of her father, King Philip the Fair of France, who was to be succeeded by her brother Louis. Despite her presence, Edward wept openly on Roger Damory's shoulder.

It was a wet and miserable winter. There were still English prisoners in Stirling, though the noblemen had been released, including Chirk and Hereford. Roger had made sure one or two of the lesser prisoners were in his pay before leaving, for he had not forgotten the look on Edward Bruce's face the day of his audience with Robert, and now his fears seemed to be justified. His spies were informing him the Bruces intended to invade Ireland. Or at least, the wily, younger brother did. Although he was heir to the childless Robert's throne, Edward Bruce could not wait that long and fancied himself as King of Ireland.

King Robert, knowing his brother was a hot-head, had held him back till now. But he could not deny that opening up a new front against the English was tempting, given the lack of any acknowledgement to his claim to the Scottish throne, despite his victory. It would squeeze the English further, and there was also the possibility it could encourage the Welsh to rebel against their masters, forming a ring of the oldest Albions against the intruder. For there was always the danger the English would return with another army, cannier than the first, to avenge Bannockburn.

Invading Ireland would mean moving against Robert Bruce's father-in-law, the Earl of Ulster, but so be it. So Robert had agreed, and Edward Bruce was already preparing an army made up of experienced men, many of whom had trounced the English at Bannockburn. Roger's sources also told him Bruce now had the assistance of none other than Sir Philip Mowbray, who was clearly despairing of any further protection from the English King.

Unfortunately, King Edward was disinclined to believe my lord's warnings. He had had his fill of war for the time being. Surely the strong Earl would hold fast in Ulster? And why would the unruly Irish be in any mood to accept a foreign King? No, no, these rumours were most unlikely to be true. No-one else but Roger Mortimer appeared to have heard them, not even the officials engaged in business over the Irish Sea. Mortimer was letting his imagination run away with him after the shock of Bannockburn. He was becoming paranoid about his own Irish lands! So the King said. Of course, he might consider an invasion of South West Scotland by the sea as suggested, if necessary. But then he abruptly changed the subject and turned away to seek the company of his more congenial new friends.

It was then that Roger knew there would be no seaborne invasion of Scotland and no extra troops for Ireland. We would have to look to our own lands there ourselves.

Chapter 23

I WAS BADLY shaken to hear of Roger's experiences at Bannockburn, and for a good while afterwards. I had feared him dead and it seemed he very nearly was. Yes, of course he made his will before departing, but that was considered customary before any campaign. It had not been expected that the flower of English nobility would be put in such danger, certainly not against the Scots, and especially not with their massive army.

It seemed incredible that Gilbert of Gloucester and Robert Clifford were gone. But they were, and Roger was visibly crushed on his return with their bodies. Now it seemed there was no end in sight, and we must look to Ireland for the next onslaught.

Roger appointed attorneys to act on his behalf in England, and persuaded the King to let us go with a royal letter of protection. His brother John would stay behind this time, as he was now a yeoman in the King's household, keen on proving himself at tourney, so Roger granted him appropriate monies.

The weather was dreadful, with the ground too waterlogged to plant seedlings, and the harvest left to rot in the fields last year. Ireland was no better. We had an uncomfortable crossing but installed ourselves in Trim, where I felt secure again, whether this were justified or not.

Roger had secured the constableship of Kildare Castle for Hugh Turpington, so our main retainer was Richard of Monmouth once more, with other equally trusted household servants like Avice, and a new wet nurse for me, as I had recently delivered another daughter we named Catherine. I seemed to be back to my robust state of health despite another pregnancy, and Catherine weighed in lustily, whilst Isabella lived yet. My previous fears over childbirth were now forgotten, as Catherine came into the world so easily and proved to be a contented baby who soon had a winning smile.

There was no more Grandfather for Roger to consult with, sadly, as he had passed away at the Black Friary last year. Perhaps it was a blessing he did not know about Bannockburn nor Edward Bruce's plans for Ireland. He deserved his peace, after all.

Shortly after our arrival, we entertained Sir John Cusack from Killeen. He had proved himself a good friend and neighbour, and I liked him for his easy charm and gentle manners, and looked forward to his visit. Only his news was not good.

It seemed that all the 'Kings' of Ireland – in other words, the most prominent chieftains – had received a letter from Robert Bruce. Cusack had not seen the letter himself, as an Anglo-Irish lord, but he knew many kinsmen who had. Bruce had taken great pains to stress their common Gaelic background with a shared ancestry, language and customs. He expressed a desire to permanently strengthen and maintain such bonds of friendship, and, to that end, he pledged to send an army to Ireland to fight the dominant English, just as Donald O'Neill, the King of Tyrone, had apparently invited him to do.

"No doubt that army will be under the command of Edward Bruce," my lord frowned. "He is likely to land in Ulster with a fleet from the Isles carrying his Bannockburn men."

John nodded.

"They intend to encircle England and Robert Bruce is trying to wrest control in the Isle of Man. They also hope to persuade the Welsh to rebel."

"But Ulster is under the control of the English Earl and surely he will stand firm? He is also Robert Bruce's father-in-law!" I said.

"With little love lost between them," Roger replied grimly. "That won't hold the Bruces back."

"Nevertheless, the Earl of Ulster will fight them?"

"To be sure, he will," John Cusack reassured me, with one of his winning smiles. "He won't want to give up his power base in the north-east, nor his fine castle at Carrickfergus so easily."

"But is he ready, John?" Roger leant forward in his concern. "The Scots lost fewer men than we did at Bannockburn, yet Ulster may still entertain fanciful notions about them not being a threat, as he wasn't there."

"Well, we must disabuse him of that one. Though it's true he isn't prepared. He is away in Connacht this month."

Roger clicked his tongue in annoyance.

"Carrickfergus is left well defended?"

"The castle, certainly – but maybe not the town."

"Do you intend to go up there, my lord?" I asked nervously.

"No. Not yet. We will wait in Meath to see the outcome when Bruce does land, and pray the Earl is back with enough men to stall him. The number of troops we can raise here is meagre in comparison. However, I shall write to the King for more."

"Then let us eat supper and have a little music to take our minds off these worries," I suggested. "We have a new Irish minstrel from the town who is accomplished on the psaltery and sings very sweetly with it."

By the end of the month, we heard Edward Bruce had landed on the beaches near Larne. His army, which was not dissimilar from that fielded at Bannockburn, came in the large war galleys belonging to the MacDonalds of Islay and Ailean Macryan, known as the King of the Isles. There were close on ninety vessels, swelled by a few cogs and plenty of herring boats from Ayr, and so Roger estimated, from his sources, between six and seven thousand men, given the tendency for onlookers to exaggerate. A formidable threat. The experienced Earl of Moray, Sir Thomas Randolph, was amongst them, along with Sir James Stewart, and regrettably, Sir Philip Mowbray. They were joined by the Irish O'Neills, O'Cahans, O'Hanlons and O'Hagans. They certainly meant business.

Edward could have prevented this if he had marched up to the south-west of Scotland. Now Roger could only hope the Earl of Ulster would put up a good showing with his forces, whilst he would stay in Meath with a pitiful rearguard.

But the Earl of Ulster was not there, just as Cusack had predicted. The Scots held the element of surprise, despite Roger's warnings. The Ulstermen men left behind put up a good fight; even so, they were defeated.

Edward Bruce marched on Carrickfergus without any impediment, taking the town itself, and laying siege to the castle. More Irish clans rushed to join him and proclaim him their King. To make doubly sure there was no mistake about this, their leaders even wrote to the Pope to inform him that Edward Bruce was forthwith King of Ireland!

"It appears we are occupied," Roger said drily to me. "At least it's stirred the Earl of Ulster into action. He's marching on Dundalk to defend it. Though our Edward still hasn't sent any men to help de Verdon, who holds that town, even though he also made the case for reinforcements to the King."

"Perhaps it as well your poor Matilda is not here, "I said, sadly. "She is beyond all such cares now, just as my grandfather is."

The Earl of Ulster did not reach the Verdon lands before Edward Bruce and, sure enough, Theobald's fine home at Castle Roche was reduced to ashes and rubble, although he was not present himself. The streets of Dundalk were said to run with bloody havoc. We waited nervously for further news from Ulster, which came in September.

On the advice of the leader of the O'Neills, the Scottish army had retreated north to Coleraine on the River Bann because food supplies were running low. The Earl of Ulster's army arrived on the south bank of the river and there was a stand-off between them. It was Ulster who could gather food stores from the town of Connor; at least, that was until the Scots managed to ford the river and attack the food patrols. Disguising themselves as Englishmen, they launched a bloody attack, slaughtering a thousand Ulstermen. The Earl retreated hastily back to Connor, but was once more defeated in a melee of confusion and bloodshed. Edward Bruce took Connor whilst the Earl of Ulster slipped away back to Connacht. Bruce was now the undisputed master of the northern territories of all Ireland.

As the crow flies – and there were plenty of those in flocks this year, picking over the carcasses of men and animals who had starved to death alike – Trim is barely thirty-five miles south of Dundalk. Whilst Edward Bruce retreated north to Carrickfergus, where he was proceeding to starve the castle into submission, there was nothing to stop him marching south again when his food supplies ran out. The rest of Northern Ireland had been well and truly torched and there was little nourishment there.

The harvest was poor again after all the drenching rains of the summer, with the spectre of worse famine likely to extend into next year. Trim was fortunately well supplied, with its lush pastures supporting cattle, but more pigs were killed to store in the castle, and the order given not to bake white bread every day.

My lord, John Cusack, Hugh Turpington, and the Lacy brothers attended a council of war at Trim to determine their course of action. They would all muster whatever men they could to patrol the border between Meath and Ulster, and they would fight if they must.

Roger entered my solar in the late afternoon to tell me Meath was no longer a place for noblewomen and their children. Catherine and Isabella were sleeping in their nursery. Our eldest daughters, Margaret and Maud, were being taught needlecraft, whilst the middle five children were busy elsewhere with their nursemaids or tutors. Edmund and Roger, the eldest boys, had long gone to be trained as young knights in Hereford's household. For once, it was a day of deceptive warmth and sunshine, but it had come too late to save the harvest, and the nights were drawing in.

I sent the girls away with their maids, and rose to greet my lord with foreboding, well aware of the serious nature of the discussion taking place without me that afternoon. Roger bade me be seated and took each of my hands in his.

"Is there any more news?" I asked.

He shook his head.

"No. But we must ready ourselves for it…I think it would be for the best if you took the children back to Wigmore."

I had to admit my nightmares were full of wild Scottish warriors breaking in, and putting our children barbarously to the sword. For the very first time, I felt unsafe at Trim.

"We can send the children back," I said, "but I am not afraid to stay with you."

"Dear heart, I know. You are never afraid in Trim! But the children will need their mother, especially if it does not go well."

I was alarmed, as I had never heard him say such a thing before. There would be another will made then.

"You think there could be another Bannockburn?"

"Hardly that! We haven't enough men to pick the smallest of fights. We will purely be guarding our lands."

"And if Bruce attacks?"

"Well, then hopefully he'll get a bloody nose at the least. We shall do our best. You know, Joan, the Scottish army will soon be living under famine conditions. That is my hope – that they will just give up and go home. Though I will ask you to carry letters to Pembroke, Hereford and the King requesting urgent assistance."

I sighed.

"He will ignore you again."

"The earls may – nay must – stiffen his resolve if we are not to lose Ireland. I will leave you to make urgent preparations. It would be best to sail before the autumn gales set in."

He took us to Dublin himself, with a goodly detachment of men, taking no chances.

"No heroics," I warned him on parting.

"Of course not. I am no young Gloucester. Don't worry! You shall return to me and all will be well."

I wished I could believe that.

Chapter 24

BACK AT WIGMORE, wintry weather set in early with a dismal gloom heralding November. I missed my lord, but found Margaret a great comfort to me. Roger's mother came to visit from Radnor and pronounced herself very pleased with her eleven-year-old granddaughter and namesake. The visit cheered us both, but I still found the chillier nights cold and lonely, and my thoughts were ever straying back to Trim and what might be happening there. I could not believe the castle would be taken but food supplies might run short and my lord might have to sally forth.

I sent Roger's letters on to court but the only news I had was when Theobald de Verdon, my widowed brother-in-law, paid us a short visit from Alton. I did not relish the visit at first. He had married Elizabeth de Clare very quickly. It was to be expected, but I found myself resentful on Matilda's behalf. He was almost twice Matilda's age when they married at Wigmore, the year after Roger and I wed. Then she had the misfortune to die after giving him four children. Far from uncommon of course, but when I had first met Matilda at Wigmore, she was light and carefree. All of that spirit soon disappeared and was now gone forever.

However, I was interested in Theobald's account of the King sending John de Hothum back to Dublin, 'to co-ordinate the resistance'. We both thought Roger was more than capable of this, providing he were sent adequate men. Verdon had learnt that Sir Thomas Randolph was seeking fresh troops in Scotland and intending to return to Ireland with them for Bruce.

"So why can't King Edward do the same?" I asked, indignantly. "Is he a complete and utter fool now?"

Theobald shrugged but answered my ouburst more diplomatically.

"He seems more engaged in other pursuits."

I began to click my tongue in exasperation and then stopped

myself, suddenly overcome by the knowledge this was Roger's mannerism and not mine. Had we grown so close, then, as man and wife? Was it inevitable? People often implied as much.

"Anyway," Theobald, resumed. "Hothum was beset by problems at sea, and by the time he reached Dublin with the intention of calling a Parliament, Roger and the other lords had taken off to protect their own territory. Connacht is burning now with civil war between the Irish tribes. Not all of them are pleased with the Scottish invaders."

I fell silent, though I supposed this information was mildly encouraging.

"At least Roger can call on me to help in his defence of Meath," Theobald continued, no doubt hoping to cheer me further. Of course, he would say that, but I was far from reassured.

"I fancy Cusack and Turpington will be more reliable," I said, and then, when I looked him fully in the face, I thought he did not seem a well man at all and regretted my harsh words. His complexion was sallow and he appeared to have lost weight, though he had always been a full-figured man in the past. Perhaps losing Matilda had affected him more than I thought. I repaired my manners and urged more hospitality upon him, but he said he would only trouble me overnight, as he needed to get back to Alton.

The worst thing was that all of this was old news. Roger himself was silent, and I suspected this was because he did not want to worry me. I hoped that no news meant good news, but it became increasingly frustrating as the short, bleak days dragged wearily on towards the winter solstice, and the trees around Wigmore lost all their dead, crinkled leaves and scratched the sky with bare branches tossed in the wind.

Something was wrong. It was the middle of a December night at Wigmore when I was awakened by the clatter of hooves and shouting from the inner bailey. The shouting was for the servants to bring lights, and for grooms to come quickly and stable exhausted horses.

I had retired early, weary after dealing with a series of minor complaints in Ludlow that day, followed by major concerns about the scarcity of corn. The King had set an upper limit to charges, which could not be exceeded legally and yet this was being ignored by the more ruthless merchants. My sympathies were entirely with those trying to buy, but the merchants made more noise. It had all been very difficult, though I hoped I had prevailed in the end. I also suspected I was in the early stages of pregnancy again, for my monthly courses had stopped, and I was assailed with the usual symptoms.

I had not slept well and was now wide awake. Dressing hastily, I went down to the Great Hall. My heart lurched to see Richard of Monmouth there on his own, looking dirty and dishevelled, with a bandage round his arm. Even his pleasant face looked haggard and strained. Richard caught me as I staggered with the shock.

"It's all right, my lady! All is well. Lord Roger is here but making sure the men who came with us are properly quartered."

At this moment, Roger himself appeared, looking equally exhausted and dirty. It was clear then all was *not* well. A few of the serving wenches had woken, too, and come peering nervously into the Hall, so I called for wine and bread, and asked for the fire to be revived. At first, both men were quiet, eating and drinking, then the story slowly emerged, with my lord taking the lead.

Naturally, he had organised his men along the northern borders of Meath without the benefit of Hothum's advice. He had also moved to Kells, to the north west of Trim, and fortified the castle there, putting men on the town gates and stocking both castle and town with cattle. He did not want a siege but was planning to fight there to draw the Scots away from Trim; for Randolph had indeed arrived with fresh men and was marching south with Bruce. The Scots left reserves about ten miles away and came on to Kells, as Roger had hoped, seemingly afraid of attacking Trim itself. The armies clashed and there were a few hours of heavy fighting. Then came the decisive blow.

"The Lacys!" said Roger, bitterly. "Those damned, bastard Lacys turned their shields and fled. It left us even more outnumbered, so we had no choice but to withdraw to the town."

"Except they were already torching it," Richard of Monmouth added. "So we had to fight our way out."

"How many of you made it?" I asked.

"A handful."

"About half a dozen."

I swallowed hard.

"Half a dozen! You were lucky to get out alive," I whispered.

My lord inclined his dark head in acquiescence.

"It was within our capabilities, though the situation was, it is true, desperate. I won't dwell on it. We rode straight to Dublin to inform John de Hothum."

"The rest of your army gone?" I was horrified.

"Such as it was, yes. Kells is burnt and Meath, like all Ireland, is open to the Scots. We must take horse again tomorrow and carry the news to the King. He must send more men now so we can fight on!"

"Not until you are rested," I countered. "Even men, like horses, must be fed and watered and sleep well after such events."

Hot water was carried up from the fire, which was now blazing, to fill their baths. When Roger undressed, I noticed his right knee was red and hugely swollen and that he winced when he put his weight on it.

"What happened to your knee?"

"A sideways clout from a mace. Don't worry. Thanks be to God my horse stayed on its feet. The knee will settle in time."

"First Bannockburn, and now Kells. You're getting too old for this, dear heart."

"Nonsense! I'm twenty-eight and barely in my prime. Though it's not been the best of records for military command, these last two years."

"You have come so close to being killed. Twice now."

I was kneeling by the bath, sponging him down, and Roger put a wet hand onto my arm.

"Well, third time lucky! But seriously, you know very well there is always that risk for a soldier, however high up the chain of command. I'd rather die on the field than in bed with the pox!"

"What will you tell the King?"

"The truth! How Scotland and Ireland are lost and Wales could be at risk too, if he doesn't stir himself and give my uncle of Chirk full rein."

"And that the Lacys didn't support you?"

"Of course! But the odds were probably too great against us, even with those cowardly curs. The King has to send reinforcements. Only a very few castles remain in our hands. I am glad to say Hugh Turpington's is one of them, and I don't believe Trim will fall, even with the small garrison I have left. John Cusack's brother, Walter, is in charge and he is a sound man, like John himself."

"Trim could still be subject to siege."

Roger submerged his shoulders and chest in the bathwater into which I had scattered many fresh herbs, and looked thoughtful.

"It is very well stocked. So was Kells, mind, but that idiot Edward Bruce burnt it all. The air stank with the smell of burnt beef and he torched the fields, too. It hasn't stopped raining since you left, so there has been no opportunity to plant fresh seed. The man is intemperate and short-sighted. His men will die from hunger or be forced to retreat. We haven't lost yet, by God!"

"The rain hasn't stopped here either," I said. "The harvest has been rotten again and the people are starving. There was almost a riot at the cornmarket in Ludlow today. Neither English nor Welsh can march without food in their bellies."

"I see I've taught you well," said Roger, his shoulders re-emerging from the bathwater. He managed a wry grin, though his body ached all over and his knee was pounding with pain. He longed for his bed. I had to lend him a hand to get out of the bath and dry himself before fetching one of his best fine linen nightshirts.

"There's nothing to be gained from riding off post-haste to the King, is there? You should rest and let your knee recover. At least, let us spend Christmas here. Nothing will happen now until the New Year."

So it was early in January when Roger finally presented himself at court.

Chapter 25

FEBRUARY 1316 – LLEWELLYN BREN

MY LORD STILL intended to return to Ireland with military assistance as soon as possible, and at last the King agreed. Only first there was an urgent Parliament to be held in Lincoln to discuss the famine. They met on the seventeenth of January in the hope they could convene quickly, but Thomas of Lancaster did not arrive till two weeks later. The burden of feeding a parliament strained the town's resources even more. Lawlessness and robbery continued to be rife throughout the country.

Glamorgan was especially affected. The Earl of Gloucester's widow had failed to produce a male heir, or any child at all, come to that, after insisting she was pregnant for eighteen months. So the lands had been taken into royal custody with royal administrators in charge. At first, Bartholomew of Badlesmere ruled judiciously with some concern for local people. But the King had removed him the previous year and replaced him with a man whose main aim was to beat money out of the local people to enrich the royal coffers. Badlesmere's middlemen, who included some Welshmen, were also dismissed, including one Llewellyn Bren, who was Lord of Senghennyd and a sub lord of the deceased Gloucester.

We Mortimers knew Llewellyn Bren and respected him, as did all the Marcher lords, for he was a fair and just man with a healthy sense of duty and not given to mindless slaughter or constant raiding. But he could not stand by and see his people suffer unnecessarily without making some complaint. The new administrator's response was to accuse him of sedition. So Bren appealed to the King, explaining how his people were troubled and sorely needed some relief. Edward's only response was to order him to Parliament to face the charge of treason.

Up at the Dean's House in Lincoln, the barons and the King were still awaiting the arrival of Lancaster when disturbing news arrived. Llewellyn Bren, at the head of a band of armed Welshmen, had attacked the Sheriff's Court sitting in Caerphilly Castle, burned and looted the town, and captured the Constable and Sheriff of the castle. Edward's face grew dark with anger as he listened to the messenger from Glamorgan.

"Audley!" he declared, impulsively. "Take Montagu with you and recapture the castle."

The Earl of Hereford, sitting opposite, cleared his throat. He had lost respect for the King a long time ago and the loss of his nephew had hardened his attitude. Besides which, his wife Elizabeth, the King's sister, was now expecting a child and he felt a confident part of the Royal Family.

"I don't believe Audley has the resources, sire. His portion of the Gloucester lands is far smaller. Should this not be an independent venture led by the Lords of the March?"

Edward frowned. For a moment, Roger was worried the task would be given to a rising favourite like young Hugh Despenser, for the King's love of Audley and Damory had abated recently. But no:

"Very well then. A concerted attack may be better. You, Hereford, can approach from the north with the Mortimers. John Gifford can come up from the south and Henry of Lancaster – seeing as Thomas is not here – can march with Montagu and Hastings from the east."

Roger was astounded. This was strategic overkill. He had just told the King he needed to be back in Ireland with a significant military force as soon as possible; which Edward had agreed to. What, then, was the point in wasting time pursuing one small rebel on the Welsh borders in such a draconian fashion? But, as usual, there was to be no arguing with the King. Of course, Caerphilly would be re-taken and Llewellyn Bren would have to flee north-west, leading him into the hands of the Mortimers and Hereford. Well, possibly that would be for the best.

It was a chilly dawn in early March when they caught up with Llewellyn Bren and his small band of men at Ystradfellte. This tiny village stood on the River Mellte in a valley which was lush and beautiful in summer but bare and bleak now, although the boulders beside the tumbling stream were rich with green moss and the bare tree branches coated likewise with its silver-grey variant. A slight mist arose from the tumbling water and hung in the air, conveying an air of mystery and suspense.

Hereford and Mortimer had marched south as instructed over the hills of Brecon and were camped near the village, with the Forest Fawr to their backs. It seemed likely that Bren would come this way, hoping to melt unseen into the Great Forest. But he had not reached it in time and certainly would not expect such a large force in the way. Roger had made sure a substantial detachment of men, captained by Richard of Monmouth, was stationed further west to block a sudden dash into the welcoming forest. They themselves were camped only a couple of miles to the north from Bren and his men now.

"I have no stomach for this, cousin," Roger said to Hereford. "Bren has never been aught but loyal and fair to us Marcher lords. The King has wronged him and he has only done what he had to do. I do not want to cut him down as we must."

"I agree," said Hereford, "but look, Roger, look!"

Out of the mist came a figure on horseback in full armour. At first, Roger took it for a herald sent to parley but as the figure drew nearer, he recognised the colours of Llewellyn Bren himself. Undeterred by the formidable array of armed men before him, he was coming forward, entirely alone.

Roger kicked his horse into a walk and went to meet him, also on his own. Their two mounts pulled up just short of each other, close enough to nuzzle together companionably, with their breath steaming in the cold air. It was Bren all right.

"Lord Mortimer," he said. "I have come to give myself up and throw myself on the mercy of the King."

"Know then, we must take you to him and you must be prepared to lay down your life."

Llewellyn looked at the Englishmen behind Roger.

"I understand that perfectly well," he said. "But I cannot also lay down the life of my men. They only obeyed my orders at Caerphilly. I will not have them butchered on my behalf."

Roger nodded.

"I understand that too, Llewellyn Bren. To be honest, I also understand what drove you to do what you did. We will plead for you. The Earl of Hereford is of the same mind. I assume you have given orders for your men to disperse?"

"I have."

"Then I will order my detachment to leave the western fringes of the forest and rejoin us. We will set out to return to Brecon shortly. In the meantime, you may like to break bread with us." For he noticed Bren looked thin, haggard and hungry.

They bowed their heads to each other and picked their way slowly back to the Norman encampment where they were met by a general round of cheering.

In the days that followed, Roger found himself warming further to this stocky Welshman, with his unruly shock of dark hair. He found he was not only literate in Welsh and English, but in French and Latin, too. They discovered they had the same taste in books and much common ground of agreement in chivalry, politics and military matters.

"I wish I could take you straight back to Wigmore, where my wife would gladly welcome you with our hospitality," said Roger. But they were not going as far north as Wigmore or Ludlow. Brecon was in Hereford's ownership, however, so they could rest there awhile. Roger and the Earl both wrote letters to the King on Bren's half, pleading for a lenient sentence and suggesting that the man who had brought all this about, should be replaced by John Gifford.

An imperious answer came by return: it was the King alone who would decide Llewellyn Bren's fate, did they not know, and the man must be delivered to Westminster for trial immediately.

When they arrived on the twenty-first of April, it was clear Edward was determined to find him guilty of treason. Faced with this,

Hereford and Mortimer now argued his life should be spared and the sentence commuted to life imprisonment. The King reluctantly gave his assent and granted Roger leave to visit Bren in the tower, so that his family affairs might be put in order, for Llewellyn had an adopted son and feared he might be attacked by the English and suffer reprisals. Roger gave his word he would protect the boy. Llewellyn clasped his hand warmly and they embraced on parting.

"I am glad to see your quarters are not too dreadful," Roger said, "and I will make sure you receive letters and anything else you need."

"You have been a good friend to me," Llewellyn replied. "But I fear I shall soon weary of this place."

Roger clapped him on the back.

"Who knows? You may escape!"

Bren shook his head and laughed.

"No-one escapes from the Tower, my Lord. No-one ever has!"

"Well then, maybe your sentence will be commuted further and you will be pardoned. I shall endeavour to persuade the King this should be the case."

Back at Ludlow, Roger told me all about Llewellyn Bren but I am afraid I was pensive and a little distracted to begin with.

"My lord, we must speak about Edmund," I said, as soon as he had finished.

"He's back home then?"

For Edmund had been living in Hereford's household, along with his brother Roger, as part of their training to be knights.

"He has been for two days now, and is glad to be so. But he's nervous."

"Of what?"

"Of speaking to you."

"Whatever for?"

Roger accepted the goblet of wine I poured for him and sat gratefully by the fire.

"He's not cut out to be a soldier, Roger."

"Ah," Roger sipped the wine, thoughtfully. "I thought as much."

"He's very clever, though, and studious."

"I know. Well, we did name him Edmund, after all. He clearly takes after my father. But he is the heir and Edmund Senior didn't make too bad a job of it when forced to do so."

"I think he'd like to be a bishop, instead."

Roger groaned.

"No, he wouldn't – bishops are all about politics, certainly not peace-making or even theology until it suits them! Mind you, it wouldn't be a disaster. Far from it. We have Roger and Geoffrey and, if young John carries on the way he is now, he's certainly going to be pugnacious enough."

I sighed.

"Please don't encourage that! We tell him not to torment his sisters all the time, as it is," I said, "and try to teach him some manners. You are correct that our second son Roger is lapping up his training, however, and should prove a most fitting soldier."

Roger was deep in thought.

"Well, then. What Edmund needs is a good marriage. Because I don't see him as a bishop."

"He's still a boy," I protested.

"Joan!" Roger said sternly.

I blushed, knowing quite well what he was about to say.

"He's fourteen. The same age as me when we married."

"Yes, he is. But he's not as…worldly as you were."

"He can learn, can't he? Anyway, I've been thinking about Bartholomew Badlesmere's daughter, Elizabeth."

"How old is she?"

"I am not sure, still an infant. Two or three, I think. Badlesmere is very rich, as you know. He isn't really a military man either, but he's very influential at court. Maybe Edmund could end up as a diplomat, after all!"

So it was settled, and I felt relieved, firstly that our eldest son would not have to cope with the demands of an older woman, and secondly, that not only would Badlesmere guide him at court, but Roger had not taken his different nature too much to heart. I was proud of my son's aptitude for learning, and his gentle disposition, and would have hated to see him forced into a military career like his father.

"You're right," I told Roger, warmly. "As usual."

"Then we will have to think about Margaret."

"Let's get Edmund married first," I said quickly. "I don't want to lose my daughter so soon."

"Very well," Roger conceded, aware that I was with child again and in need of pleasant, almost-adult company.

So Edmund was married to Elizabeth Badlesmere on the 27th of June 1316, in the chapel of our manor house at Kinlet in Shropshire. Roger gave them this manor and also several others at Cleobury Mortimer, Stratfield Mortimer, Arlegh and Bisley. He settled his estates in Somerset and Buckinghamshire on Edmund, in addition, and willed that Wigmore, Cefnllys, Dolforwyn, Radnor and all their surrounding lands should pass to him eventually as his heir, whether a fighting man or no. In return, Bartholomew Badlesmere paid Roger twenty thousand pounds. I was very grateful to him for such magnanimity. Our Irish lands would go to young Roger, and his mother's French lands to Geoffrey in time. So all was settled well.

The wedding was not as carefree as it might have been, however. The famine had worsened, and even Badlesmere could not attend due to riots in Bristol, where he was Constable. Most of the male guests were in conference with Roger much of the time, organising assistance for Badlesmere. The Earl of Hereford was not present either, though for a different reason. He was grieving for his wife, the Countess Elizabeth, suddenly struck down with illness after her childbirth. His entry into the royal family would no longer happen, but it was for the loss of Bess he grieved the most, and I grieved for them both, saying prayers of thanks to God for my continuing and astonishing deliverance from the same fate.

So it was rather a sober wedding party that returned to Wigmore to admire its new building works – intended to make the castle more comfortable and luxurious – before repairing to be entertained at Ludlow. Within the week, Roger had departed to join Pembroke and Badlesmere to lay siege to the rebellious merchants of Bristol. Edmund stayed behind and I was happy to see he seemed contented enough.

Chapter 26

1317 – ROGER'S RETURN AND THE RISE OF DESPENSER

MEANWHILE, ROGER LEARNT from John Cusack that Trim still stood defiant against the Scots, with John's brother, Walter, as its capable steward. However, the Lacys remained on Edward Bruce's side and together they defeated yet another Norman army, commanded by Edmund Butler, near Castledermot. Even so, by the autumn, the Scots needed to retreat north again to seek food. Famine was upon the land.

Nevertheless, Edward Bruce was actually crowned King of Ireland in Dundalk! With Carrickfergus surrendered at last, it seemed an apt enough, though chilling, title. Only Dublin itself, Trim, Kildare, and a few minor castles remained in English hands.

My lord was successful in bringing an end to the Bristol rebellion and plied his advantage with the King, insisting a royal army be sent to Ireland now. At length, the King agreed and appointed my lord the King's Lieutenant, Viceroy of Ireland, putting him in charge of a force of invasion. This was ordered to assemble at Haverford in Wales at the beginning of February but then came the inevitable delays, waiting for promised money, which arrived late.

It was not until early April that Roger was able to land at Youghal, leaving me behind on this occasion. The Scots had reached the Shannon again, near Limerick, way out to the west, but were yet to make a concerted push eastwards, despite reinforcements sent by Robert Bruce.

Back at Wigmore, I was left waiting anxiously for news. Roger's army only numbered about fifteen hundred men although, if he joined up with Edmund Butler, who was now in Cork, it could swell to five thousand. Surely the Irish would rejoice that the looting and destruction inflicted by the Scots were potentially at an end, and prove more malleable as a result? The new King of Ireland had, after all, brought nothing but pestilence and dearth rather than prosperity.

Then Roger wrote to tell me there was no need to fight the Scots straightaway as they had had to retreat north yet again. What was needed was a strong presence to maintain law and order and stop the raiding. The famine would do the rest. He had good reason to believe the Scottish army was suffering from severe malnutrition and disease. Robert Bruce had returned, disspirited, to Scotland, seemingly out of patience with his brother, who had failed to advance to take Dublin.

Roger said Edward Bruce could wait. What he did intend was revenge on the Lacys. It was now May and he was back in Trim, surrounded by the whole army. He sent one of his faithful knights to the disloyal Lacys in a last attempt at reconciliation, bearing letters with the royal seal on them, ordering their submission to the King of England or else face an attack.

No doubt he was in the same room at Trim, where he received news of Gaveston's death, when another messenger arrived with an equally bad story. The knight Roger sent to the Lacys had been butchered by them in a reckless act of defiance. Roger told me he swore and hurled his goblet at the wall. Red wine trickled down the stone and he swore once more that it would be Lacy blood next. Loyalty ran strong in him as always, but any show of treachery aroused a desire for the harshest of revenge.

It did not take him long. In early June, he went after the Lacys with the King's banners unfurled against them, and they were routed. The survivors took to their heels and were driven out of Meath.

Then my lord summoned a Parliament in the King's name at Dublin. The Lacys were banished from Ireland with all their goods, lands and chattels being confiscated for the King. They were still alive, but the revenge was sweet.

Next, it was necessary to sweep through all of Southern Ireland and put the fear of God into any other rebels amongst the Anglo-

Irish and English lords. They all surrendered to my husband's authority.

Back in Dublin, a group of Ulstermen caught stealing cattle were arrested and their heads stuck on pikes around the castle walls. There was to be no tolerance of such behaviour. Four score other heads of defeated O'Tooles and Byrnes were soon to join them. The word went out – Roger Mortimer was back in charge in Trim and Dublin, and was in no mood for mercy.

By October, Edward Bruce was isolated in Ulster, with his claim to kingship looking increasingly tenuous. Roger was confident enough by then to write advising it would be safe for me to join him in Dublin for Christmas and the New Year. He told me he planned to hold a knighting ceremony there, for he had the authority to do so, as the King's representative. All loyal retainers would be rewarded – and I must be sure to bring our child John with me, so he could be included. After this, in the spring, they would prepare a final assault on Ulster. In the meantime, Roger intended to spend Christmas in triumph with his family around him.

Yet shortly after my return to Ireland we received an unwelcome letter from the Earl of Hereford. It began innocuously enough by saying he was happy to continue to accept our son Roger in his household, now that Edmund had gone to Badlesmere. But then he moved swiftly on to court matters. It seemed that Hugh Despenser, father and son, were in the ascendancy, and the younger Hugh had been made the King's Chamberlain. He was now the sole favourite. In fact, Hereford suspected he had become the lover of the king. He said it was like Gaveston all over again, but much worse. No-one was allowed admittance to the king's audience without his say-so and all other close advisers had been sidelined, even Pembroke.

'I also deeply regret to tell you,' Hereford continued, 'that this young braggart, Despenser, has had our friend, Llewellyn Bren, summarily taken from the Tower, without any authority. He took him to Cardiff Castle and put him to death there with the utmost barbarism.'

We were horrified to read the details. Drawn and hung as expected, but then cut down whilst still alive to have his heart and intestines removed and flung into a fire, whilst his limbs were hacked apart and his body quartered. This was the same dreadful treatment meted out to William Wallace and was in no way appropriate for Bren's minor rebellion.

"And the King?" Hereford continued, anticipating Roger's next question. "The King did nothing. Despenser the Younger now lords it over Glamorgan and acts as if he is Earl of Gloucester! The King utters not a word of blame, so besotted has he become. Not one word! I tell you this, Roger: Hugh Despenser is a far greater threat to the Kingdom than ever Piers Gaveston was! He will not rest until he really is the Earl of Gloucester. Damory and Audley are as nothing to the King now."

We were deeply affected by this, and went directly to the chapel in Dublin Castle. To my chagrin, my lord had never been the most pious or regular of men in his church attendance. He always said the company of soldiers suited him better than the company of clerics. But for once he felt the need to pray for Bren's soul, with whom he had felt such a strong bond; except he found he had fallen out of the habit. Nothing but intense anger remained. Whilst I prayed, he made a vow to God instead: to pay back Hugh Despenser in full, like for like, for this treatment of his friend. I did not see how this was possible, but kept my counsel.

Hereford's letter was followed by another from Badlesmere. He told how Thomas of Lancaster was threatening the King again, stung to protest by the King's new favouritism.

Theobald de Verdon had died very soon after his visit to me in the July of that year at Alton. I now believe he knew he was ill then and it had been his way of saying goodbye to the Mortimers. So Edward had lost no time in marrying Roger Damory, who still seemed to support the king, to Elizabeth de Clare. Naturally, Lancaster now saw those three men married to the late Gloucester's sisters as serious threats to his own power. He was demanding all three be banished, and accusing the King of disobeying the

Ordinances again. Of course, Edward refused and even begun to muster an army at York in case of an attack from Lancaster.

Badlesmere joined Pembroke in calling for negotiations to be held. But the King foolishly attacked Lancaster's castle at Pontefract and the Earl responded by angrily refusing to attend Parliament to begin any negotiation. The factions were firmly drawn up against each other now.

Badlesmere and Pembroke had tried to persuade Damory to encourage the King to be more amenable but felt that Roger Mortimer's presence might also be needed. Roger threw down the letter in the most intense frustration.

"Not now!" he railed. "Not now, for the love of God! Not when I am so close to defeating Edward Bruce."

He could not possibly leave Ireland before this end had been achieved. Yes, he answered my remonstrances, it was true he had good men in post now, but he wanted to be the commander that led them into battle. The king's petty squabbles must wait. Although I understood his frustration, I was not so sure he could ignore what was afoot in England.

As the old year began to pass, and there was no further contact from over the Irish Sea, my lord began to relax a little. Late autumn brought the birth of another daughter born to us in Dublin, and we called her Agnes and gave thanks to God. I was concerned there might be some disappointment on my lord's behalf, as the last three children I had borne were all female.

"Not a bit of it!" Roger laughed when I voiced my qualms. "We already have four fine sons, with three of them fit to prop up Edmund. The more girls we have, the more influential marriages we can make! And we really must talk about Margaret soon, and Maud too. But in the meantime, even though our three older sons are away, we can make a knight out of our little John!"

The feast and the knighting in Dublin Castle were as great as any royal occasion. There was much to celebrate in Ireland, and another safe childbirth was grounds for rejoicing too, after the Earl of Hereford's sad loss. I would turn thirty-two in February but my fertility seemed unaffected, my skin remaining clear, my curls thick, and the bloom of motherhood almost always upon me.

John was not the only one to be knighted, of course, though he was certainly the youngest, at seven, and undoubtedly the most thrilled and excited. Roger rewarded all his faithful friends, including Richard of Monmouth, Hugh Turpington, both Cusack brothers, and one John de Bermingham, another Anglo-Irishman who had proved his military worth in their campaigns. To my mind, this was his greatest strength, in recognising such loyalty.

It was, I thought, luxuriating in a beautiful new green velvet gown, flushed and heady with fine food and wine, exactly like the court of a King! Edward Bruce may think he holds the title of King of Ireland but in reality that title is owed more to my husband, Sir Roger Mortimer.

I was happy to pay a brief visit to Trim afterwards to show the younger children my second childhood home, and it had never seemed safer, even when Roger took the bulk of the army up to Drogheda for another campaign. Plans were being made for the final push and we could scent victory at last.

So it was a body blow to my lord when an actual summons arrived from the King in April. Roger must return to England and attend Parliament. He was furious. Some of this was dissipated in making further plans and appointments, and putting the newly knighted Sir John de Bermingham in charge of the army. Even more was vented on the treatment of John Lacy, the son of Hugh, who had been captured and brought to us in Dublin. My lord ordered the young man taken to Trim and told him that, seeing as his family so coveted the castle, he could stay in the dungeon there – and be stoned to death.

I quailed at this sentence.

"Is it not too harsh?" I pleaded.

"No!" my lord corrected me. "Not only did they turn their shields but they killed the knight I sent with a message of reconciliation. We cannot forget that. Those who break the rules of chivalry and show no mercy to others deserve none for themselves."

Chapter 27

THE EVILS OF politics are many, but remain necessary. My lord certainly preferred military campaigns but reluctantly submitted himself to the demands of Parliament. On the 20th of July, he was invited to join Pembroke and Badlesmere in a delegation to Thomas of Lancaster on behalf of the King.

The Earl of Lancaster's obligations were clear enough: Thomas must attend parliaments promptly when summoned, and fight in the north agains the Scots when the King required it. Roger pointed out this was not unreasonable. Had he not spent the last year halting the advance of Edward Bruce in Ireland? He was confident John de Bermingham would defeat Bruce in the battle to come; well then, the same needed to be done against Robert Bruce in the North of the England and the Borders, even if Scotland itself was impenetrable. Lancaster whinged and prevaricated for a while, so that Roger came close to calling him a snivelling coward and a traitor. But eventually there was agreement.

For the King's part, a permanent King's Council should be set up, along with a committee to reform – yet again – the King's household. The barons would be in control of both, and neither grouping would include Damory, Audley or Despenser. Thomas of Lancaster was much more enthusiastic about these proposals.

The delegation returned with the King and several bishops in August, and met with the Earl near the town of Leicester where the two cousins exchanged a kiss of peace. The final treaty between them was drawn up and signed at Leake. Success! My lord found himself sitting on both the Council and the Royal Committee, though secretly he longed to be back across the Irish Sea with Bermingham. At least he had been rewarded for his work in Ireland with the sum of six thousand marks. Back in London, he bought an exquisite ruby necklace for me and a magnificent ruby ring for himself.

He was definitely the man of the moment. So, when he set about marriage negotiations with Lord Berkeley for the union of his son and heir, Thomas, to Margaret, and with John Charlton, Lord of Powys, for his son and heir to be united with Maud, both fathers were exceptionally keen. After all, the Earl of Pembroke was aging, and it would soon be appropriate to replace him with another sound advisor, capable of making the King see common sense. As a strong leader, governor and negotiator, Roger Mortimer of Wigmore might well be that man. His father would have been truly proud of him now!

In October, we received the news my lord awaited so anxiously. Sir John de Bermingham had engaged Edward Bruce at Faughal, north of Dundalk, and utterly defeated him. Sir Philip Mowbray, the King of the Isles, the King of Argyle, and last, but not least, Edward Bruce himself, were all dead. The head of the younger Bruce, smirking no more but set into a terrible, rigid snarl, was sent to King Edward's court by Bermingham. Roger knew that honour should have been his. But the threat to England from the Irish Sea had been removed and that was in no small part down to him. What is more, everyone knew it.

We spent the following Christmas at Wigmore and it should have been the happiest and most triumphant of times. But the hardships of life do not respect great triumphs. My lord's younger brother, John, always so keen to emulate him, was killed in a tournament at Worcester. Given the brutality of the tourney circuit, it is not an uncommon event. Yet, when Roger had survived Bannockburn and Kells and everything Ireland had to throw at him, we felt the irony that John should be killed barely thirty miles away, and not even in battle, deeply. Now we had to arrange for the body to be brought home for burial in the Abbey.

The old Abbot was resigning and being pensioned off, due to his great age, and they were waiting for the appointment of a new man. Brother Benedict may have hoped for promotion but was overlooked in favour of one better connected. No doubt he consoled himself with the self-knowledge that his real skills lay in writing the Wigmore chronicle, and not in leadership.

There was a new Bishop of Hereford in place, too: Adam Orleton, and he came to present and install the new Abbot. We entertained him at Ludlow, where we found him a clever man with more than a touch of cynicism, especially where the King was concerned, though he clearly revered the Pope, having spent a great deal of time at the papal curia. The best I can say about him is that he made me understand my lord's former remarks concerning our latter-day bishops more fully.

"Well," Orleton said, after an ample meal, "I cannot raise my glass to the King but I will raise it to you, Lord Mortimer."

His bishop's ring winked in the firelight and he smiled. I disliked the man instinctively, though he seemed to be getting on well with Roger. There was a certain greasiness, about him. Still, there was no doubt about his oily approval of Wigmore and his family.

"What are your plans next?" he asked my lord.

"The King is sending me back to Ireland as Justiciar," Roger replied.

"So soon?"

"Not immediately. As you know, I have my poor brother John to mourn and to bury first. I also have to attend the weddings of two of my daughters – Margaret and Maud."

For I had been persuaded that Margaret should at last take up married life with Thomas Berkeley, although Maud's union to John Charlton would be in name only, like Edmund's with his bride, because of her tender age.

"A shame that you must go back."

"There is work to be done there after the war – bridges to be built, roads to be repaired, and the houses of many towns to be rebuilt, especially in the outskirts of Dublin. There are also the estates of many dead men to be partitioned."

The bishop inclined his head.

"And law and order to be maintained."

"Exactly so. Thankfully the harvest was successful this year, and the famine is over, which will help. But the eyes of men will always seek the possessions of others."

"Indeed they will. And what of the Irish estates of the late Earl of Gloucester? I believe they are considerable."

"I intend them to remain in my hands for the time being. As Justiciar for the King."

Orleton chuckled, and the folds of his ample chin wobbled with mirth.

"A wise decision. To keep them out of the hands of Hugh Despenser the Younger, I trust?"

"Yes. He is already busy trying to take over the lands of Damory and Audley now they are falling from favour. But I shall reward the Irish Lords who fought with us."

"I hear the Archbishop of Dublin would like a university to be established." Roger nodded.

"Yes, that is certainly something to be encouraged. A seat of learning. Thanks be to God the Book of Kells was removed to Dublin for safekeeping, before the town was burnt. It deserves a proper resting place."

"Magnificent!" Orleton replied. "I applaud your endeavours, past and present, and we must remain in touch."

"Of course," Roger replied. As he knew only too well, bishops could make powerful friends, and Orleton was rising and ambitious.

So we went back to Dublin and my lord set about rebuilding the country and re-establishing law and order, as he had promised. The weather was vastly improved, the famine eased, and I bore yet another daughter we named Beatrice.

Our Geoffrey, a cheeky but popular boy, had left us to be brought up further by his paternal grandmother's relatives in France. I also missed Margaret, who had gone to live with the Berkeleys, and Maud, who was now at the Charltons, but was comforted by the knowledge of the other girls growing up fast. Little Joan was already nine and an engaging, sensible child.

Despite Hereford's fears, the news from England was positive. Queen Isabella bore a daughter after giving the King two male heirs. Edward seemed to be remaining attentive to her and she could exert a good influence on him when this was the case. Arrangements were even being made to begin negotiations with Robert Bruce for a truce, though it was difficult to see them getting far, with Edward still refusing to acknowledge Bruce as King of Scotland. It was necessary to do something, as a siege of Berwick had failed – even with the grudging support of the Earl of Lancaster.

When I looked down from the towers of Trim on our visit from Dublin, it was good to see the bailey returned to normal, with the army gone. The roofs of the town glowed in the sunset after another warm day, with the harvest promising to be good for a second year. The cows grazed on the soft, green meadows next to the clear waters of the Boyne again, and the burbages were busy once more with their fires and fervent industry.

Little John was proving himself quite able as a young squire and was mad on horse-riding, just as young Roger and Geoffrey had been. It even distracted him from teasing his sisters, for he was far too important for them now. I smiled to myself. My lord was right, we did not lack for sons, and certainly not for daughters either. The household remained full of wet nurses and nursemaids. Avice was only nominally in charge now, though I still valued her advice and she showed no wish to retire as my own ladies' maid. Not that I lacked for friends, with Lady Turpington and the two Lady Cusacks in the same country. All three had sent their daughters to me as ladies-in-waiting, and they were pleasant companions.

So, despite the loss of my brother-in-law John, we found ourselves blest with love, friendship and respect. When I heard the bells ring out from the Abbey across the river, I thanked God for this contentment. If only it could always be like this. But it was merely the calm before the storm to come. For we were only to remain in Ireland for one more year.

Chapter 28

1320 – STORM CLOUDS

BY THE TIME we returned to England the following year, the Earl of Hereford's fears were turning out to be well founded. Roger Damory and Hugh Audley were favourites no longer. Neither did the King listen to the Council or Household Committee anymore. He only listened to Hugh Despenser the Younger.

Hugh had prised away huge tracts of land from the former two favourites and also the Cliffords, in flagrant abuse of the law. With the Lordship of Glamorgan his, he might not be entitled to be called the Earl of Gloucester, but he was approaching that eminence where riches were concerned. Damory and Audley were now anxious to ally themselves with Lancaster, John Gifford, Hereford, and the Mortimers to protect their interests.

What happened next is most important for you to understand why I do not consider my lord a traitor, especially after all he had done in Ireland. Everything blew up in the most sudden and unexpected way in the autumn.

William de Braose, Lord of the Gower Peninsula, which is close to Glamorgan, sold his land to his son-in-law, John de Mowbray. He was short of money and his son-in-law would inherit in the end anyway, as Braose had no son. But his action enraged Hugh Despenser, who continued to be greedy, and wanted the land for himself. He complained to the King on the grounds that a royal licence had not been granted to Mowbray. This was a technical requirement in England, though it was often overlooked in similar cases where an inheritance was not in any dispute. It was definitely not a requirement in the Marches under Marcher law.

To the horror of all the Marcher lords, the King confiscated Gower from Mowbray and awarded it to Despenser under royal licence. It was a huge lack of respect to everyone, especially in the Marches, tantamount to saying that Edward would support

Despenser above any others, and any other law of the land, including Marcher Law.

The King knew what he had done. In an attempt to make reparations, he forgave Damory all his debts, and confirmed his and Audley's rights to their lands by marriage. It was not enough. No-one could see him without Despenser's permission or lurking presence, and Hugh had now taken all the 'burdensome' administration out of the King's hands into his own.

The Earl of Pembroke left the country in despair, and most of the Marcher lords likewise left Parliament in disgust. Roger stayed on for a while, hoping to persuade Edward he was wrong. But the King had made his decison. Any dissent whatever made him favour the Despensers all the more. I had never seen my lord so depressed, even in the darkest days in Ireland.

"Is Gower so very important?" I faltered.

"Is Despenser irrelevant then?"

I felt ashamed of my own question.

"No, of course not."

We sat before the fire in our chamber at Westminster, along with Richard of Monmouth, all other servants being at a respectful distance.

"Does he love Hugh Despenser as he loved Gaveston?" I asked.

"That's what they say," Richard answered me.

"Our kinsman Hereford was correct then?"

"Yes."

"And we are most definitely not the friends of Hugh Despenser."

Roger snorted.

"How could we be? Even if it were not for the family feud, the man is no better than a pirate."

"What will you do?"

"Stay on here for the moment, trying to appeal to the King. Then, if that fails, as I suspect it will, we will go home and arm ourselves, as all the Marcher Lords are doing."

"How can this have happened – so suddenly? The King seemed much happier with the Queen recently. She is expecting another child. Why, he even went to France with her, to pay homage to her brother!"

"It hasn't been sudden – as Hereford warned us. It's been growing slowly like a chancre, all the time we've been in Ireland."

"He's nothing like Gaveston," I said. "I always thought the King did truly love Piers, and for all his faults, you could see why. But not Hugh Despenser! He has such a sly smile and is mean-spirited, where the King used to be so generous. He is not even good-looking like Piers or humorous, or generous in any way!"

"There's no accounting for royal tastes."

"I shall speak to the Queen," I said, laying a hand on my lord's shoulder, "maybe she can help us."

So we both stayed at Court until the New Year. But it was a tense and unhappy Christmas, worse even than the last one when we lost John. I took presents of fine lace work and embroidery to the Queen for the New Year, and was solicitous over her pregnancy.

"You are well, Madame?" I asked with concern, noticing that Isabella looked tired and her ankles were slightly swollen.

"Ah, Lady Mortimer! Always so kind to me. But should I not be asking the same of you?" with her eyes straying to my belly.

I laughed.

"But I am very used to it now, my lady, like an old sow with many piglets!"

"Surely not! Come and sit down beside me. I am a mere novice with my fourth! Whilst you – 'ow many is it now?"

"It will be my twelfth," I admitted.

"*Twelve*! So strong," said the Queen in amazement, taking my hand, "and so brave! With all that to and froing on the Irish Sea! Me – I detest sea voyages."

I smiled.

"I confess I am always grateful when we make land. But Madame, although it pains me to do so, I must speak to you about the King. I know it is unpleasant…"

Immediately, tears sprang into the Queen's eyes.

"I know what it is," she said. "It's about that loathsome man who 'as 'is claws into my gracious Lord, is it not?"

I nodded.

"I have no wish to pry, Madame, but is there no way we can convince the King he is wrong to favour him as he does?"

Isabella dabbed at her eyes.

"I 'ave tried. Believe me, I 'ave tried. But Edward no longer visits my bed since I am pregnant again. What is more, I fear 'ee never will again."

"Oh my dear Madame," I said, " I am sure that cannot be true. The King loves you. I have seen how tender he can be towards you."

Isabella sniffed and recovered herself.

"We shall see 'oom 'ee prefers now. My job is done, is it not? I 'ave given two sons and a daughter, and there may yet be another son. And now I see awkwardness when 'ee looks me in the eye. Then when Despenser looks at me, I see pure 'atred. Nothing less."

"I am so sorry, Madame. Be assured the Mortimers will always support you."

"You are a good woman," said the Queen. "I shall not forget it. But I wonder if you, and even your fine lord with his friends, can protect me now? The King 'as stopped listening to me long ago."

Roger was even less successful in his attempts to influence the King. He did actually manage to see him alone, on the pretext of discussing what should happen to the vacant Irish inheritances. But the King was clearly bored. He certainly would not brook any criticism of Hugh Despenser. In vain did my lord mention the Council and the Household Committee, the Marcher Law, the sheer necessity and prudence of avoiding any armed conflict, and even the Magna Carta. He found himself getting more heated as they spoke, and even resorted to comparing rule in England unfavourably with his own in Ireland. That was a mistake: Edward turned cold-blue eyes upon him.

"You go too far, Mortimer," he said. "I relieve you of your position as Justiciar in that backward land. It is my Kingdom, not yours."

"I am aware of that, sire," Roger snapped back. "Do you not remember I saved it for you? I would save England for you too, if I could. Do you not realise how serious this is? The Earl of Hereford, no less, has left Parliament and is raising arms against you. I am sure the Earl of Lancaster, son of your father's brother, will not be slow to join him! Gifford, Badlesmere, many others, even Damory and Audley, will do the same. Whilst the Earl of Pembroke is sympathetic to us and therefore continues to stay abroad in his shame. You have alienated all of your barons!"

"The Earl of Winchester is on my side."

"Hugh Despenser's father!"

"And the Earl of Gloucester!"

"There is no Earl of Gloucester since Bannockburn!"

"Well, there may be soon."

Roger threw up his hands in despair and turned on his heel, ending the audience without permission. He knew when he did so there was no turning back. Not now, or ever again.

It was early January, but we made haste to leave Westminster as soon as we could. The weather was bleak and our hearts full of foreboding.

"This really means civil war, then? There is no other way?" I implored Roger.

My lord shook his head.

"There is no other way. Edward is replacing me with one of Despenser's henchmen in Ireland. I have also been abominably rude to his royal self, as he will see it – even though it was intended to be for his own good. I must gather an army from the Marches, immediately."

I fell silent. This was much more dangerous than anything we had faced before.

"I am far from alone," Roger sought to console me.

"I know," I said quietly. "It is just that it will be the first time you have ever fought against the King."

"For the sake of the Crown," Roger corrected me. "We are still Royalists at heart. But we have been put in an impossible position. Edward has brought this on himself. It's the Despensers we are fighting and we will win. We must save the King from them, whether he wills it or not."

Chapter 29

1321-1322 – THE CONTRARIANT WARS

FINE WORDS AND fine intentions. This was the result: Hugh Despenser persuaded the King to send an army into Glamorgan to defend his lands from attack.

"From the rebels", he told the King. "Rebels against the royal person!"

The rebels are Contrariant barons, as we are now being called.

Roger Mortimer of Chirk was still Justiciar of Wales, though he was an old man now. The King ordered him to make sure all Welsh castles were in a state of readiness to defend and hold for the King. He had certainly never been disloyal to the King before, for all his other faults. But this was an impossible request. How could he desert his own nephew? Of course he had to join the Contrariants.

The King summoned both him and my lord, Hereford, John Gifford, and Berkeley to meet him at Gloucester. They replied they would not go unless the King agreed to put Hugh Despenser in the custody of the Earl of Lancaster and a Parliament be called to discuss all their grievances. It was a while before they received an answer, but when it came, it was resolutely negative.

In May, my lord marched south. He had raised a goodly army, which included some of the Anglo-Irish lords, and all were experienced men. He was joined by Bishop Adam Orleton, Roger Damory, Hugh Audley, John Mowbray and the young Roger Clifford, and they all unfurled royal banners in Gloucester to make the point they were fighting the Despensers and not the King. They numbered eight hundred men at arms and ten thousand infantry. Hugh Despenser proved no match for them and they took Newport, Cardiff, and all the castles and manor houses of Glamorgan with relative ease. Many of the inhabitants of these places joined them in jubilation that the restricted Despenser deer parks were now open to them again.

Our army took all of the horses, cattle and victuals as a matter of course, so that was naturally less popular. With the Northern Lords now openly declaring their support, the Marcher army advanced, even though many men had dispersed in the false confidence they had already achieved what was intended. By the end of July, our army surrounded the walls of London itself and demanded the King negotiate with them.

In a panic, Edward sent for Pembroke who persuaded him he must comply to keep the peace. It was agreed all of the Marchers would receive an unconditional pardon, and that the Despensers would be banished. It seemed a great victory, and was celebrated with a collective sigh of relief by everyone…except the King.

For Edward was incandescent with fury at his humiliation, and now he became more wily, incensed by the banishment of his favourite.

Less than a month later, the King arranged to accompany Queen Isabella on a pilgrimage to Canterbury. The Despensers had left England as promised, and Hugh the Younger was terrorising the Channel between England and France, as a pirate. It seemed confirmation of the wisdom of getting rid of the man. But Edward remained in the grip of his infatuation and arranged to meet up with Hugh secretly on the Isle of Thanet.

The Queen therefore would be returning to London alone. Edward insisted she take a detour and stay overnight at Leeds Castle on the way, where she could ask for accommodation. Isabella was delighted that her rival had gone and had no problem in complying.

It was a damp and chilly October day when the Queen arrived with her entourage at Leeds. The castle was owned by Bartholomew Badlesmere, as Edward well knew, and he was absent with the Marcher army, who were making their way back north and westwards, but were not totally disbanded as yet. Lady Badlesmere was in residence, so Isabella had no doubt she would be received warmly. After all, now that the Despensers were banished, all must surely be well? Isabella was not so naïve as to believe Hugh was gone for good, given her experience with Gaveston, but it was still a welcome respite – for everyone.

She sent a man at arms up to the castle gates to request hospitality, and confidently awaited the answer. To her utter amazement, his face was sheepish on his return, and he told her that Lady Badlesmere refused her entry point blank.

"She says that her husband forbade her to admit anyone, anyone at all, under any circumstances, in these troubled times!"

"But I am the queen!" Isabella cried. Her man shrugged his shoulders uncomfortably.

"You must force the gates," she ordered, angrily. "Then we shall see."

"We are not equipped for an attack, Madame, begging your pardon."

"She would not dare resist!"

Her man still hesitated, uneasy and unhappy.

"That is an order!" Isabella repeated, furiously.

He bent his head and went off to organise the few men they had, choosing ten in number that he chose to advance. As they did, they were met with the hiss and thud of arrows from the battlements and slit windows. Nine of them clutched at their pierced chests with a scream, and fell on the ground, causing the wildfowl to take flight with an answering shriek from the calm waters of the moat. Watching from a safe distance, Isabella's hand flew up to her mouth.

"Mon dieu, mon dieu – God forgive me and God save us!"

She went on her way in a state of the most profound shock.

When Edward returned to London a day or two later, he could barely conceal his delight. The Queen was mortified. Of course, he expressed concern for her safety, but actually doubted her own person had been in danger, though she had been terribly humiliated. It might almost have been planned to end this way, and she began to suspect it was.

The King summoned Pembroke again, along with his half-brothers Norfolk and Kent, who were now of age, and ordered them to lay siege to Leeds Castle with a superior force, which they did. The redoubtable Lady Badlesmere put up a spirited defence in response, and sent a message to her husband, pleading for his help.

Bartholomew was still with Roger's army, which was quartered around Oxford, when he received the messenger. He implored the Mortimers and the Earl of Hereford to help him.

My lord was highly disturbed. This was entirely unexpected. Neither could any action be passed off as defence of the King against the Despensers, now that Hugh the Younger was banished. What course should they take? Badlesmere was our son and heir's father-in-law, and Lady Badlesmere was being attacked in her own castle. If it fell, as it must, she was likely to be imprisoned, possibly along with Edmund's young wife.

Lord Roger of Chirk announced gruffly that it must be his nephew's decision but he would follow where he led. Hereford let his old grudges resurface and was even more strongly in favour. He was also confident that all the men who previously gave their support to them would flock back in return.

Roger was not so sure. He has told me it is always harder to get fighting men back to an army once they have gone home, than to recruit them in the first place. Hereford then argued everyone knew the King would bring Hugh Despenser back as soon as he could, despite what was agreed; it was better to make a firm stand now, whilst they still had an army of sorts. This hit home to Roger, who made his biggest mistake in agreeing. So orders were given for the army to prepare to move south once more.

At Kingston on Thames, Pembroke rode out to meet them with the Archbishop of Canterbury and the Bishop of London. He was his usual elegant and rational self.

"Roger Mortimer of Wigmore, I beg you not to march into Kent. If you retreat, we will ask Leeds Castle to surrender on Badlesmere's behalf and I will mediate for all in Parliament with the King."

Roger had also received an urgent message from the Earl of Lancaster expressing his disapproval that very morning. Thomas of Lancaster had long nurtured a petty quarrel with Badlesmere, and would not support him as a result. They could not expect to succeed without Lancastrian support.

"Very well," said Roger. "I will agree. But the pardon sought must extend to the Badlesmeres as well as the rest of us, including his lady wife and children."

Pembroke inclined his head in relief.

"Of course," he said, warmly, "I shall do my best to make the King see this."

Unfortunately, on this occasion, Pembroke's best was not good enough. There was to be no mercy, given the outrage the Queen had suffered, came back the curt reply. The King was determined to make an example of the Badlesmeres. He even joined the siege at Leeds himself, and, as soon as the castle surrendered, had twelve men hung from the garrison. Following this, he sent Lady Badlesmere and all of her children to be imprisoned in the Tower. This included Elizabeth, Edmund's wife, who was only eight and still living with her mother.

By now our army was retreating, and went up to Pontefract to further explain the circumstances and make a fresh plea for Lancaster's support. If the King could show no mercy to the Badlesmeres, including the lady and her children, then there was unlikely to be any for them, whatever the King said! Lancaster saw the logic in this argument and promised to join them with men, as soon as he could, if the army would march over to their heartlands in the west.

Edward showed an uncharacteristic fervour in raising his own army. He had never done such a thing before, even under threat from the Bruces. But this was personal. He wanted his beloved Hugh Despenser back. The royal army mustered in strength at Cirencester, whilst the depleted Marcher army drew back to the Marches. My lord crossed the Severn at Worcester, burning the bridge, and did the same at Bridgnorth, where the whole town regrettably caught fire and burned, something which would not be soon forgotten, I regret to say.

And so it was he came at last to Shrewsbury, in that January of 1322, where he found himself besieged, and sat down to write to me, before giving himself up into captivity.

Chapter 30

AUGUST 1323 — SOUTHAMPTON

I AM NEITHER a monk nor a scribe of history, and ladies are not expected to keep journals, other than household accounts, even if they are able to read and write...yet what a lot I have written! All thanks to my own imprisonment, and to Richard Judas who has kept me faithfully supplied with pen, paper and ink in secret. You know what followed, and how I ended up in this place. I hope it explains to you more clearly why I do not believe my husband is a traitor. I have transcribed all the events accurately, including those I was not party to, having spoken intimately with my lord and his retainers for many years.

But I have no idea how it will end, so can write no more for the moment. In my darker moments, I fear I will have to tell the news of my lord's execution, and that very soon. Will the King release us then, or will his enmity know no bounds?

We have been in our new quarters for six months now, and it is well into the second year of our imprisonment. In April, I was informed my mother had died at the age of sixty-three, but given little detail. It was dreadful to know I had not been there. Neither was I allowed to attend the funeral. They informed me that my sisters, still in residence at Aconbury Priory, had arranged for her burial in France, at the Abbaye de Valence, close to Lusignan itself, so it would have been impossible. No doubt they held a memorial service at Aconbury for her first, but I was not granted leave to go. Although it was only right my mother should return to her family home in France, I felt cheated of my own expectation of mourning in public. I received a rather cool letter from Maud and Beatrice, explaining the arrangements. It was as if they blamed me for lack of contact, though I had always been attentive to their needs before my captivity. They had clearly not received any of my letters from Southampton.

Now I was truly alone in the world, with my father, grandparents and mother all gone, my sisters estranged, and my husband and children in the Tower or elsewhere. Only Joan and Isabella remained with me…and Avice. I wept for my mother, but in all honesty I also wept for myself.

In the meantime, I learn that Hugh Despenser has completely taken over the running of the country. He is Edward's first and only minister of state, which is a huge insult to the Earl of Pembroke, and indeed, the King's own half-brothers. He has imposed the most crippling of fines and seized many lands he is not entitled to, persuading the King to maintain an immense treasury, out of greed.

The widow of Roger Damory has Usk taken away from her, and has hardly any money left, with all of her rightful inheritance removed. As if Elizabeth ever asked to be married to Damory after Theobald died! Margaret de Clare is likely to fare no better. Only Eleanor is rewarded, having married Despenser.

There are even worse rumours that the Queen herself is being deprived of manors, monies and gifts at Despenser's instigation. Naturally, they are said to loathe each other. No wonder, as he maintains his sway over the King and has trespassed on her marriage. The Queen seems to have lost all power over her consort, in which case any further petition of mine will be useless. And there is persistent expectation that the King will not let the Mortimers in the Tower live much longer.

I am in a fever of anxiety over all this. For the first time ever, I received a letter from Roger himself only a few weeks ago. Father Judas brought it to me from the friars and says they had it from Bishop Orleton, who remains in the protection of the church and in support of Roger. Somehow, it has been smuggled out from the Tower.

It was good to see his hand again. Of course he sought to reassure me, said that he is not that badly treated, that he still has friends on the outside amongst all of those who are angry at Edward's vicious behaviour toward their families. He even seemed to think the Queen might speak on his behalf. But I am not fooled by any of this. Dear heart, you must know the King no longer listens to the Queen, nor to anyone else, not even to Pembroke, but only to Hugh Despenser, who always gets anything and everything he wants. He has colluded with the King to rob and imprison so many noblewomen and to raise taxes so highly. And now he wants Roger Mortimer dead, along with his uncle.

So I fear the worst, but must compose myself to pen a cheerful reply. No sooner have I begun when there is a frightful commotion outside. Avice runs to tell me that Sir John Arundel is here with far more armed guards than is usual on his visits. I make haste to hide my writing materials in a chest, and prepare to meet Sir John. He is even more redly flustered and choleric than normal.

It appears I am to be uprooted and moved away from here! Way up into the north of England! Why should that be?

"King's orders, King's orders," is all Arundel will say. "That is enough."

But that is far from all. That evening, Richard Judas pays a visit to our friars and comes back, agog with the news. The word is that Roger Mortimer has escaped from the Tower. Over a week ago! On the feast day of St Peter ad Vincula. We do not know exactly how, but there are stories of guards being drugged and the Deputy Constable, who went with him, being involved. The King's men expected he would ride to Dover, or back to the Marches.

But my lord is cleverer than that. And now they know he came to Portchester, scarely twenty miles from here, and is believed to have taken ship for France from there. No wonder Sir John is in such a state! As close as Portchester! Was he coming for me? My heart jumps at the thought, though I realise it would have been impossible. Still, he has got away. And he will come for me one day. I know he will.

Now I realise why I am to be sent north. Edward thinks Roger will come back for me. So I must be moved. No matter. It is excellent news that my dear lord has saved his life. He will manage my release somehow – that will be nothing compared with escaping from the Tower. No-one else has ever managed that, as far as I know. I feel elated and thank God, for I am sure this heralds the end of all our troubles. How could I know it was merely the beginning?

PART THREE
THE GATHERING OF THE KITES

Chapter 31

1325 – Skipton Castle

IT IS TWO long years since I arrived here. Whilst awaiting my removal, Sir John Arundel was ordered to increase the guard and I was not allowed out again. The children were taken first, and that tore my heart out. Joan has gone to Sempringham, and Isabella to Chicksands Priory. Isabella was still coughing as usual, and far from sturdy. If only they had gone together! I know Joan would have comforted and taken care of her.

I learn that even my Margaret has now been taken to Shouldham Priory in Norfolk, because her husband Thomas has been imprisoned along with his father, Lord Maurice Berkeley. They say the Berkeleys assisted Roger's escape.

Only Maud and Geoffrey remain at liberty. Edmund, Roger, and John are still in captivity at Windsor. Roger married Joan Butler of Ireland four years ago but he has had little knowledge of her, having fought with his father and being incarcerated immediately afterwards. Whilst three of my daughters are now detained in separate convents. How cruel that is! Only Catherine, Agnes, Beatrice and tiny Blanche, my very last daughter, remain with their grandmother. For the moment, I am told, contemptuously. For the moment, my lady! Catherine is almost nine and may soon have to follow into a convent. I am not allowed to write to any of them.

Perhaps Margaret de Fiennes has been able to take my youngest to France if she is permitted to leave the country? I know she will be caring for the little ones as best she can. Nevertheless, they may have forgotten me. Margaret will try to keep my memory alive, but what are they to think of their mother being imprisoned? It is very likely Blanche and Beatrice are too young to remember me at all, and this is a wound which cuts deeply.

These are my children, I wanted to scream at the guards, heaving my heart out before them. And we have done nothing wrong! We do not deserve to be locked up. But it was of no use, and would only have upset Joan and Isabella further. The King has sent me almost as far away as he can – to Skipton in the North of Yorkshire.

My lord is thought to be at the house of his French cousin, John de Fiennes, along with Geoffrey, who was already there. Geoffrey will be sixteen now. Almost a man! He must have changed a great deal. My lord's cousin will be bound to support them financially. I am glad they are together again. Uncle Roger of Chirk did not escape. He is said to be very frail, and is likely to die soon anyway. It is hard to imagine that bull of a man dwindling into something frail, but that is what they say.

My household is reduced again. My groom has been relieved of his duties as I am told I am no longer permitted to ride out. So now I am only allowed Judas, my confessor (being such an evil woman), Avice, and a laundress. Recently, I demanded a cook from the town. I am told this will be granted…eventually.

As I say, my confessor is still considered of the prime importance. I have no actual deeds to confess, as I have very little to do here. But I have thoughts aplenty, and I must admit they now include a fierce hatred of the King. Judas tells me he remains susceptible to the evil influence of the Despensers and offers this in his mitigation. He says we must pray for the King's deliverance and a return to his senses. I am afraid I find this too hard a counsel, may God forgive me.

King Edward has granted Hugh Despenser the Elder the Earldom of Winchester, and yet has seen fit to hole my daughters up in convents. Ah, says Judas, but he has not made the Younger Earl of Gloucester yet: that is a good sign! I do not agree because we all know he may as well *be* Gloucester, given the vast amount of wealth and land he holds there. I also expect he has his eyes on bigger prizes, like the Earl of the whole of the Marches, no doubt, even though that would be a new creation.

I know I have become more bitter and angry here. It is since Joan and Isabella were taken away; I did not expect that. They became so close to me and were such a comfort when we were imprisoned in our little house in Southampton. Looking back, life there was almost normal, if very poor, and lacking privilege. This is far worse.

The raised allowance of thirteen shillings and fourpence a week is supposed to continue, thanks to the Queen, but is often not paid. I am also supposed to have an allowance for new garments every year, but it does not come and I let my dresses go threadbare. It is not as if I am receiving guests, so what does it matter any more? There seems no point in maintaining appearances, and it means we can eat a little better, though I make sure Avice is warmly dressed. She wants me to take better care of myself, but I do not take heed.

When I first arrived at Skipton Castle, its drum towers reminded me of Windwhistle Tower in Southampton. Unlike Southampton Castle, it remains empty however, apart from its keeper, John de Ryther, his servants and garrison, and two other male prisoners. Rightfully, it belongs to the Cliffords, who were so well known to us. Lady Maud's eldest son, Roger, was hung, drawn and quartered at York when he was barely twenty-two, for the crime of assisting my lord in his rebellion against the Despensers, and so it passed into royal hands. My dear friend had much sorrow to bear so soon after her widowhood. She has a younger son, another Robert, but the King continues to deny him his inheritance, to punish the family further.

So the Cliffords are absent. I heard that Lady Maud absconded with one of her rescuers from an outrageous kidnapping, and married him against the King's will. I hope she is happy now and out of Edward's clutches, and I often think of her, as I am housed in her solar with a withdrawing room off it for our personal use. These rooms are at least comfortable, though very lonely without the children.

Sir John used to be a gamekeeper on the confiscated lands of the Earl of Lancaster, and is a King's man through and through – even though he looks mighty like an old Dane. He conducts his business in the Great Hall below, and the garrison is quartered in the gatehouse. I gather the male prisoners languish in the dungeon there, so I suppose I should be grateful I am not held with them.

My quarters do not allow a view down the High Street, with its busy market and comings and goings. The solar looks out upon nothing at all, and the withdrawing room looks to the rear, with a precipitous drop to the Eller Beck below. A little countryside is visible beyond, but it doesn't include the deer parks – only sheep, and moorland. All too often, they lie under a bleak, grey sky sheeting down rain. The days in winter are almost as dark as the nights.

I am never allowed out now, except to the Chapel of St John the Evangelist, which is within the bailey, to hear Mass. When I leave the chapel, I turn my face up to the sky to feel the soft air and wind on my cheeks. I miss looking up at trees in leaf, riding through a forest, seeing and hearing birds of all kinds (and I wonder what ever became of my beautiful gyrhawk with its gorgeous white feathers?). I miss sunlight, which does not come filtered through a window or slit. I miss the smell of herbs growing in the ground and the company of dogs lying by the hearth. I endlessly miss having my family around me.

There came a low point last winter when I thought about throwing myself down to the beck. It came after I heard the Earl of Pembroke was dead. I suppose I had always entertained the notion that he would somehow obtain a pardon for my lord. Typically, Aymer de Valence, the Earl of Pembroke, was in France at the time, trying to make peace between Edward and the French King, for there is trouble in Gascony again; they say he died from an apoplectic fit. With his passing, everything seemed completely hopeless.

As I finished my third full year of captivity, I saw the events of my life circling round cruelly, in the same jaded manner, without end. My days are all alike now. How long must I endure this, I pray to God? Yet the outside world seems cruelly repetitive too. The King has been defeated in another Scottish campaign. There is further unrest in Gascony. No doubt Ireland is less well ruled now. Nothing changes. Except that, as soon as my youngest daughters grow old enough, they will take them away into convents and I may never see any of them again. This way, the black hole beckoned.

It was Avice who pulled me away from the window. I threw my arms around her and sobbed my heart out in despair. She hushed me, gently stroking my face.

"Remember, Madame," she said, "how our Lord Mortimer wrote you must hold fast whatever they throw at you, even though none of it has been deserved. Hold fast for the children! They will need you in the future, and we will see them again, I am sure of it."

I felt ashamed then.

"Poor Avice," I said. "What about you? You don't deserve to be locked up. Why, you could have your freedom tomorrow if you asked to be let go!"

"No, Madame!" Avice protested. "What a foolish thought! Wherever could I go and whatever would I do, without my lady to look after?"

That made me cry all the more for comfort, though perhaps it was a good thing, a catharsis of sorts, as I had never allowed myself to break down so completely before.

When I had calmed myself, I went to the chapel to pray for forgiveness. It does comfort me, with its still calm, although it is bare and spartan compared with most, as if it is only half finished, and the painters had to leave suddenly. It is my only sanctuary and the only place open to me outside my rooms.

What an active life I used to have, managing both Wigmore and Ludlow when Roger was away, not to mention all the manors, crossing and re-crossing to Ireland, visiting and being visited by so many ladies, riding and hawking when I could. Reading even. I am still allowed no books. It seems so far away now, and I feel like another person, broken, humiliated and cowed.

Father Judas recognised my despair at confession, for, of course, I had to make my great sin and contrition known to him. I even told him I could no longer love God – surely the most blasphemous of thoughts? He told me that God still loved me, even though I could not see that in this present time of hardship, but would know it again in the future. He said he would ask the monks to pray for me, for he is allowed to visit the Augustinian priory at Bolton. Once again, he can provide me with some insight into the world. The Augustinians are always in the know.

Chapter 32

WE LIVE ON rumour in our northern fortress, and now Judas says rumour has it that Roger Mortimer will return to England at the head of an army, and be welcomed as a liberator. He has promised to build a chapel to St Peter ad Vincula, who looked so favourably upon him, and believes that St Peter saved him for the blessed purpose of saving England. This does not sound like my Lord Roger to me. Revenge, yes, but becoming a saviour? Maybe the time spent in the Tower has changed him. Captivity does change people. I know it has changed me now I am in the fourth year of my captivity.

The rumour seems to have panicked the King, anyway. He has taken to referring to my lord as 'The Mortimer' and demands that the new King of France, Charles, should banish him. Yes, that is another part of the recurring cycle of events: Isabella's brother Louis did not live very long, and so her younger brother has taken the throne, requiring further homage to be paid to yet another French King. Charles is not in the mood to listen to Edward when this homage has been withheld, especially in view of another quarrel over Gascony.

Things have gone from bad to worse there, with a French sergeant at arms driving a stake into the ground at St Sardos to claim it as his land, so he can build a French fortress on the site. The neighbouring English lord promptly responded by hanging him from the very same stake, and burning the village down. So the threat of war has raised its head again between the two powers, with King Charles sending an army, under his uncle Valois' control, into Gascony. The Earl of Pembroke, who might have sorted this out, is dead, and Roger Mortimer continues to receive hospitality from the Count of Boulogne. Edward has flown into a rage and ordered all French subjects presently in England to be arrested and their goods seized.

"What?" I exclaim when Judas tells me this. "What about all the Queen's ladies and servants?"

Judas shakes his head in sorrow.

"Some have already left in fear of the consequences. Hugh Despenser is urging the King to ensure the threat is carried out. Of course, he may be sniffing more profit. He is already harrying the Earl of Pembroke's widow, and his nephew, to pay off their debts and surrender their lands to the Crown."

It is so unlike Judas to make any judgemental comment that I know this must be true.

"The Earl of Kent is presently the King's Lieutenant in Gascony, but he is under siege in his castle at La Reole, whilst the Count of de Valois is demanding that the city of Agen be surrendered to him."

"Gascony would be virtually lost then."

"That is what people are saying, Madame. It will go very badly for the King if he is seen to lose Gascony, so he has decided to send the Queen to plead his case with her brother and negotiate a settlement. The Pope has recommended it."

"Poor Isabella! It sounds like an impossible task...although she is diplomatic."

"Indeed she is, my lady."

"If she succeeds, might she not also secure a pardon for Roger?"

"I shall pray for it."

But I know this is my dark little confessor's way of saying he does not think it is a likely outcome. I sigh.

"So where does that leave us?"

"Madame, we must continue to pray to God for the deliverance of your innocent self."

I am afraid I turn on him sharply.

"Are you saying my husband is not innocent?"

Judas does not blush but coughs hastily.

"It may become…complicated, Madame. We must pray for a good outcome. Let me read from the Bible to distract you from all of this anxiety."

"Not now. I feel tired. You have told me so much. I am a little overwhelmed with it all."

"Pardon me, my lady."

No, it is not your fault. Of course I welcome any news. But let us…hope the situation improves."

I realise the word 'pray' sticks in my throat.

In a way, the news does improve. In July, we learn that Queen Isabella has managed to negotiate a truce, though the terms are not good. Gascony must be surrendered to France and then partially re-granted, providing Edward pays his homage to Charles. Now everything seems to have grown quiet again, though there must surely be arguments going on at court.

Edward has made no preparations for a voyage to France. Judas says he is very loathe to leave England for France. He has been told 'The Mortimer' and other English exiles are no longer there but are in the neighbouring state of Hainault; this is meant to reassure him. He must be truly frightened of them.

Of course, he is even more frightened about what may befall Hugh Despenser if he leaves. Henry of Lancaster has taken over his deceased brother's earldom and is known to openly oppose Despenser, along with many others. I can see the ghost of Gaveston must be tormenting the King once more.

The summer wears on, with each day like the last, and I see the rowans by the beck heavy with red berries again. Another winter will be on its way soon.

Then, to my great surprise, in late November, I receive a most welcome visitor. It is the Dowager Lady Clifford herself, though her married name is now Wells. We embrace fondly and laugh and cry together at the same time.

"My dear lady Maud, how can you ever forgive the Mortimers for the cruel loss of your son?"

"That was not your fault, dear Joan! My husband would have taken the same action against the King under the same circumstances, had he been spared by the Scots. Fortune has treated us both cruelly as wives and mothers. But I am glad to see you here in my old rooms, at least, though certainly not as a prisoner and held in such poverty, with no gentlewomen around you."

"My load would be so lightened if you were here too. Are you allowed back?"

"No, I am sorry. I am no longer Lady Clifford. My husband is a much lowlier knight now."

"You married without the Royal consent. How brave you were! Are you happy, Maud?"

"Indeed I am, and lovingly cared for."

"And you are still a great lady, having been born a de Clare!"

"Though sadly not as well favoured as cousin Eleanor, who had the King's ear even before she married Despenser," Maud says sourly. "Every one of those girls married off to a royal favourite in their time, and now Eleanor queen of the lot! Not that I envy her that noxious husband, believe me. But I believe she revels in her new position."

"Did she go with the Queen to France?"

"Not this time. She is charged with looking after the royal children instead. I imagine that grates somewhat with the Queen."

"Is the Queen not yet returned?"

"Far from it! But let's sit down and I shall tell you all about it."

"You must have some food and drink after your journey."

Lady Maud raises her hand.

"No, my dear, I will not hear of it. I have brought you fish and a haunch of venison, and ordered my servants to take them to the kitchen, with express instructions they are to be prepared for your little household alone," and then she clears her throat. "Also, my dear, I have brought you some money. Please do not demur! You may look upon it as a loan, if you wish."

Tears spring to my eyes as my hands stray involuntarily to the bosom of my old, frayed gown with its faded and worn blue cloth.

"What a pretty pass I have come to!" I say regretfully. "But at least my husband and sons are alive, unlike yours."

Maud raises a finger in admonishment.

"As your elder by a good few years, I must forbid you to dwell on such matters. Not that there is anything else to do but dwell in this place, if you are not allowed out. Do you want to hear the news or not?"

I wipe my eyes and nod eagerly.

"Please! My only news is filtered through monks and clerics."

"The worst gossips in the world!" Maud says tartly. "Well, as you may have heard, our gracious King Edward has not been enamoured by the thought of going to France to pay homage as he ought. All because of his beloved little bedfellow!"

"We don't actually know that," I say, feeling I ought to be magnanimous. After all, it is treason to say such a thing out loud. But Maud is incorrigible. It makes me wonder if this new spleen is the conduit for her grief on losing her former husband and son.

"Come dear," she says contemptuously. "We were not born yesterday, were we?"

This makes me laugh. It is hard not to feel cheered by Maud's attitude.

"So the King decides to make his son and heir Duke of Aquitaine and Count of Pontieu, and send him off to pay homage instead."

"Was that acceptable to Charles of France?"

"It was. But now the King writes to Isabella and young Edward demanding their return."

"They haven't come back?"

"Not a bit of it," and now Lady Maud launches her gleeful denouement. "Queen Isabella appears in widow's weeds to make a public statement instead. Now, let me see, I must get this right: she says that 'someone' has come between her and her husband, trying to break the sacred bond of marriage. There is a third person in the picture, in another words! She declares she will never return, unless this intruder is removed and she is avenged against him."

I gasp in utter astonishment and Maud is gratified at my reaction.

"Furthermore, her royal brother Charles refuses to expel her on Edward's behalf, saying she came to him of her own free will, and is free to return as and when she wishes."

"And the young prince stays with her?"

"Their son and heir. Yes, of course. You probably don't know but Edward has been negotiating a Spanish marriage for him. This has not pleased the French. So there is talk that Isabella is now looking elsewhere on his behalf."

"In France?"

"No, but close by. In Hainault. The Count there has three eligible daughters."

"Edward will never allow it."

"Perhaps he will have no choice in the matter? Now, who do we know in Hainault who is an expert in arranging advantageous marriages?"

"My Lord Roger?" I say his name almost hesitantly.

"Yes indeed! There is also talk that he leads all the English exiles who have given up hope of being pardoned by Edward. They have followed him to Hainault and, if he does succeed in betrothing the prince to a Hainault girl, her father will raise an army for them."

"But where will it all end?" I ask in sudden alarm.

It was like asking my mother or Avice if all would be well many years ago. Maud can give me no better answer.

"That remains to be seen," she says. "Hopefully in Edward being forced to give up Despenser and banish him completely, restoring the Queen to her rightful place."

"That does not mean Roger would be pardoned."

"Oh, I imagine that if he appears at the head of an army of invasion, with the Queen and the heir at his side, Edward would soon capitualate and change his mind. You probably don't realise, dear Joan, but there is precious little support in this country for the Despensers now. They are loathed and reviled. Henry of Lancaster opposes them, and I believe the King's own half-brothers, Norfolk and Kent do, too."

"Let us hope we live to see it," I say faintly.

Maud leans over and takes both of my hands in hers.

"Oh my dear, take heart! This has ground you down, of course it has. But I do not think better days will be long in coming now. That is what I came to tell you. You must take heart!"

After she has gone, and I have time to digest everything she has told me, I do. I do take heart, at last. But that is only during the day. At night I begin to have terrible nightmares.

It is always the same dream. Roger is in full armour riding beside the Queen's standard bearer at the head of an army, tall and proud on a magnificent destrier. I know it is poor Marcher, who died long since at Bannockburn. They ride on for hour after long hour and, gradually, the other soldiers begin to melt away into the woods. There is a terrible battle – the most bloody I can imagine. Suddenly, I see my lord on the ground with his helmet knocked off and the King's men moving in to hack him to death. His head rolls off and I wake sweating and crying out.

Chapter 33

THE SAINTE-CHAPELLE IS the chapel of the Royal Palace on the Ile de le Cite. It is one of Queen Isabella's favourite places from her childhood. The high Gothic roof is painted with white fleur de lys against a bright blue background. As a little girl, she thought it was a sky full of French stars. Even then she knew she was destined to marry the future King of England.

During the day, the tall, stained glass windows cast pools of colour and blue light into the aisles, as brilliant as the jewels she loves to wear. But tonight it is dark apart from the flickering of candles. Isabella has come to pray with her ladies in waiting. These are sadly depleted. Most of them are chosen now for their loyalty to the King, so she feels abandoned. She leaves them kneeling in the aisle and approaches the altar alone in her black robes, like a grieving widow. She is upset.

It is two months since she made the public declaration concerning her marriage, in front of her brother and Bishop Stapledon, sent by Edward to demand her return to England. Edward has sent her no further monies – only letters to their son, begging him to obey his father and return. The boy is confused and unhappy. But she has no fear he will leave her. He does not admire his father and, even at the age of thirteen, wants to model himself on his warlike grandfather instead. He is also angry about Hugh Despenser's treatment of his mother.

Edward has made no acknowledgement of Despenser's role in all of this. Nor has he agreed the man should go. On the contrary, he had the audacity to write to her claiming that Hugh has always held her in the highest esteem, and she should be grateful for this. Grateful? The daughter of a long line of Capetian Kings? Grateful to this ugly monkey, the spawn of a mere baron? She is infuriated. Let her waiting women take themselves off; they are no better than spies and she cannot afford to pay them anyway! But how can she make Edward listen to her again? This is the subject of her prayers.

A tall, thin figure detaches itself from the shadows of a side chapel and comes up beside her. Even before she turns to see the man, who is now on bended knee, she has guessed who it is.

"Mortimer! You are not supposed to be 'ere."

"With respect, Madame, neither are you!"

Despite herself, that makes her laugh briefly, and she bids him rise.

"I must thank you for what you did for Joan – in improving her conditions," he says.

"But she is shut up in Skipton castle now and is not always paid. The King no longer listens to me."

"I know. But Madame, I am on your side and so are many others, including Kent and Norfolk."

She is appalled to find herself breaking down into sobs, which are not at all queenly. She has hardened herself against harsh words, but kindly ones are unexpected, even if only from another mere baron.

"But what can I do? What can anyone do?"

Roger takes her small hand in his large one and leads her to a seat reserved for the celebrant. A faint murmur of outrage arises from the distant ladies in waiting but he ignores it.

"There is a great deal we can do, Madame. You have control of the heir and I do not imagine he will desert you."

Isabella is still sobbing, though more quietly now.

"We wanted the Prince to marry into the Valois family. But now Edward has turned himself against everything French and wants to marry my son to a Castilian!"

"Does he now? Well, I fancy the Prince would like some say in the matter. The Count of Hainault is very anxious for him to meet his three daughters and choose one of them. And if he does, for that very great honour, the Count is prepared to raise an army for us."

Isabella stops crying.

"Are you certain?"

I am. I have spent months in Hainault working towards this very end."

The Queen sniffs and tries to regain some of her pride.

"I do not think I can command an army," she says despairingly.

"No, but I can. I am not the half-starved wreck of a man you last saw from a distance in the Tower."

"I did not notice you then."

"No, but I saw you from afar in the gardens whilst you were still carrying this accursed King's fourth child."

"Your talk is treasonable."

"Madame, I am already known as the greatest traitor by the King. He calls me 'The Mortimer'. Yet," and he slams his hand down hard against the arm of her seat, startling her, "I was always his greatest servant and most loyal lieutenenant. Until he finally took leave of his feeble senses!"

"I know," Isabella whispers. "Only do not talk so loud! The walls 'ave ears."

"The walls wear gowns and jewels," Roger agrees. "You are correct. But I have no choice other than to be treacherous. Edward will keep me in permanent exile now, until he dies. By then I shall be an old man or dead myself. I will never see my homelands again, nor my wife and children excepting Geoffrey. What kind of a choice is that?"

"You are determined on this course then?"

I am, Madame. You need not come with the army but I will invade England on your behalf. Should I fail, I would rather be executed than not make this attempt. But I do not believe we will fail."

Isabella is silent for a while, whilst he waits. At last, she speaks.

"No. I also 'ave no choice and I will come with your army, Roger Mortimer. You will need my backing to succeed. The people still love me. If we fail, then we will see if the King dares to execute a Queen!"

Her blue eyes are completely dry now, and flash with anger as she turns them up to his.

"It will not come to that. I promise you. So let us swear a pact to do it."

He bends his knee to her again and takes both her hands now, with his clasped over them.

"I swear," she says.

"And I swear too."

The queen rises to her feet and Roger follows her. She offers him her free hand and he kisses it.

"You must stay at court," she orders him. "We have plans to make."

He inclines his elegant, dark head and smiles.

"But of course."

"You may come to my solar to discuss them. But we must be discreet."

He nods and melts away into the shadows again. The Queen steps lightly down the nave of the dark chapel, back toward her ladies. Her tread is more buoyant now as she thinks fondly of the starry sky above her head.

It does not take long for the remaining ladies in waiting to be all of a flutter. Roger Mortimer of Wigmore visits the Queen's bedchamber and does not leave until late. What is more, they are dismissed from the solar during this assignation. In their minds, this can only mean one thing. The Queen has taken a lover.

The truth is in fact more prosaic. As well as planning their strategy, Roger spends many hours listening to the Queen berating Despenser and yearning for Edward to return to her affections.

"When we capture Despenser, I want him executed," she repeats for what seems like the hundredth time.

Roger agrees.

"It is the only way to get rid of him," he says. "What is more, it will be in the manner of Llewellyn Bren. I have not forgotten what he did to my friend. There will be an eye for an eye and a tooth for a tooth."

"And then Edward will come back to me!"

Roger hesitates.

"He will not forgive those who bring Hugh to his death, my lady. Just as he never forgave Thomas of Lancaster for Gaveston. I think you must prepare yourself for that."

Isabella knows he speaks the truth, though it is unpalatable to her. She bursts out into loud, wailing tears.

"Come now, Madame," Roger says, wishing she could be a little more temperate with her emotions, as Joan used to be. "Let us seize power first, and then see what comes of it. Remember, you still have the heir to the throne."

In February, the Pope writes to Edward and Isabella, expressing grave concern at their separation. He even makes a formal request to Edward that Hugh Despenser the Younger remove himself from the court. It falls on deaf ears, as Roger knew very well it would. Instead, Edward writes many letters to his son but none to Isabella. He tells the boy he is shocked that 'the Queen of England, our wife', should have taken 'The Mortimer' as her chief counsellor and adviser, thereby exposing his son to a traitor's presence. Isabella is hurt at his mode of address. Formerly, he has always spoken of her as his most dear, or very dear consort.

In May, Charles, King of France, crowns his wife, Joan of Evreux, Queen, in the glorious Sainte Chapelle. Naturally, his sister Isabella attends, putting aside her widow's weeds for the occasion in favour of a rich, vermilion velvet. Prince Edward had not been invited, out of diplomatic respect for the King of England's feelings. But Isabella insisted he attend, and this time Mortimer is not lurking in the shadows but carrying the boy's train, in an inflammatory echo of Edward's own coronation, long, long ago at Westminster.

When King Edward hears, he is incensed. Papal envoys had sought guarantees for the safe return of his Queen, the Prince, and the Earl of Kent, by then. King Charles retorts sharply that this is entirely unnecessary, as any of them can return safely, at any time, if they so wish, including the absent Queen. She wavers and wonders publicly if she ought to return.

Roger loses his temper as he sees all his grand plans slipping away. In a room full of courtiers, he forgets himself and yells at the Queen.

"Don't be ridiculous! Have you gone mad? If you go back, you will be killed."

She stares at him in shock, then turns on her heel and leaves with her ladies in waiting following. That night, he does not receive an invitation to her solar. In fact, it is a few days before she asks to see him again, though it is very late and all her ladies have been dismissed. This time he approaches more humbly, with an apology ready on his lips. But she forestalls him by raising her hand.

"I am sorry, too."

He realises her eyes are red rimmed and puffy from copious amounts of weeping.

"I 'ave 'ad time to think and I can see I was weak. I wanted so much to believe it could all end well between me and the King."

"Even so, Madame, I overstepped my role and I do truly apologise…"

She stands then and approaches him closely, a little too closely.

"No, you were right. And you 'ave been very patient with me. But now I must grow up and face facts, no? We are lost souls, you and I. If we are to see England and the rest of our children again, we must keep our courage and stay with our intentions."

Roger knees and kisses her hand, genuinely touched.

"I said what I did because I care about your wellbeing," he says simply.

She bids him rise and stretches up to put her ams around the neck still bowed towards her.

"I am lonely, Roger Mortimer," she says, disconsolately.

It is an invitation and he knows it. He kisses her again but this time more forceably on the lips and feels aroused.

"We are both lonely," he says. "Paris is a long way from home – my home at least."

He becomes uncharacteristically nervous, because of her undoubted royalty and pre-eminence over him. Nevertheless, she allows him to scoop her into his arms and carry her to bed. That night he stays until the morning. Soon afterwards, he leaves for Hainault to prepare the ground for Isabella and her son's visit to Count William of Hainault.

In the days which follow, he can scarcely believe what has happened: that this highly bred Queen could even consider taking a mere Baron to bed! Yet he knows it will happen again, remembering how she clung to him. Now he can feel the wheel of fortune turning once more. Not only are their plans in the Low Countries likely to succeed, but he has cemented a most intimate alliance with the Queen. They are not to act in any different way in public, of course. Discretion must rule. But she needs him on so many different levels now. He cannot deny it adds an extra spice to the mix to know he has cuckolded the King.

He feels guilty about Joan when he thinks about her, which is not as often as he used to. It has been so long since they were together. She will be entering her fifth year of captivity soon. Well, he would secure her release very soon. He could hardly tell her what had happened in the royal bedchamber. But how could she complain if he restored their family fortunes and reached the heights of favour? God knows, the King had been permitted to have his favourites – so why shouldn't the Queen have hers? Especially one of such undoubted administrative and military skills.

In this manner, Roger is able to tackle his conscience and tuck it away to one side. He has never subscribed to the idea that a married man should be completely chaste. Of course, bedding the Queen of England is not akin to sating your lust with a prostitute. It was going to be a hundred times more complicated.

Despite this, Roger can smell money and power. With Pembroke gone, who else was there to exert a steadying and wise hand on the realm? He had no doubt they could rid it of the Despensers. Edward himself would be more of a problem and Isabella would need careful handling over her liege. Yet with Lancaster, Norfolk and Kent all on board, surely some suitable arrangement would be possible? The thought came unbidden. Why should the boy not rule in his place? With a Regent, of course, to guide his hand.

It was all about the boy. In truth, Roger had taken little notice of him up until now. That would have to change.

By the end of the following summer, Queen Isabella and Prince Edward arrived in some style at Hainault, to be entertained by the Count in his chateau. The betrothal negotiations had gone well, even though Isabella technically had nothing to promise. Nevertheless, she agreed to pledge all the revenues of Ponthieu to the Count on her son's behalf, with her brother, Charles IV of France acting as her guarantor.

The eldest of the Count's unmarried daughters was called Philippa. It only remained now to see if the young pair took to each other. Roger told Isabella it really did not matter either way, as there were two others behind Philippa who were equally eager and compliant.

Mortimer greeted the boy with a deeply respectful bow but sat well away from the royal family at the welcoming banquet, at the end of the long table with servants scurrying between them all. He took good care to watch the Prince and Philippa closely, however. She was only twelve, but then so was the Queen when she married Edward. He thought her rather plain in contrast to the Queen, but she had a merry smile and an open face, which promised a good disposition. Inevitably, he was reminded of Joan.

At that moment, Isabella looked up and glanced directly at him down the table, nodding her approval. He smiled briefly in return, but returned hastily to converse with his dining companions, the Earl of Kent, and one John Maltravers, who had a question about the troops.

For there were indeed already troops assembling at Dordrecht. Count William of Hainault's brother had raised an army of seven hundred mercenaries and was busy acquiring more, with ships to carry them. It would be a small army but Roger was sure it would swell in England, when others joined them at landfall.

That night he was summoned once again to the Queen's bedchamber. She had forsaken her widow's weeds for the vermilion gown and robe to impress Count William. Her long, golden-blonde hair, which he had grasped and run through his hands so recently, was bound in a gold, embroidered net. Her cheeks were flushed with wine and there was a sparkle in her sharp, blue eyes.

"They like each other," she told him in delight. "They are getting on very well. Me, I found 'er a bit plain and boring, but Edward likes her."

"That's all that matters then, my Lady. You wouldn't want her to eclipse your charms. Not that that is any way possible, of course. I am very happy to hear they like each other."

"And the troops?"

"All going well there. Now the Prince is betrothed to his daughter, the Count will be happy to commit more men for say, ninety ships. We can be ready to sail within a matter of a week or two."

"Am I to wear armour?"

Roger smiled at her indulgently.

"I shall see to it you are protected in the finest chain mail and helmet. Never will the world have seen such a beautiful commander. But I will also make sure to keep your gracious person away from any danger."

That greatly pleased her so she invited him to stay the night again, and this time he needed no encouragement. Except that afterwards, the numbers of men, horses, weapons and tents to be taken to England came back a little too readily to reel through the back of his brain, despite their lusty coupling.

Chapter 34

NATURALLY, I KNEW nothing of this then, and even now do not like to think of it. So you may think me a fool for much of what I write next.

By the end of September, I notice a subtle change in the attitude of my guards. They seem more conciliatory, even a touch nervous in my presence, whilst Sir John, the Keeper, has taken to enquiring about my welfare in as solicitous a tone as he can manage with his gruff Northern accent.

By the middle of October, this becomes even more pronounced. I have sent Richard Judas off on a visit to the Augustinians at Bolton, so cannot sound out his opinion. However, I receive a short letter from Lady Maud, which is brought directly to my room and has, surprisingly, not been opened or tampered with in any way.

'My dear Lady Joan,' I read. 'He is here! He has landed! We know of whom we speak! The Queen of England is with him. Your son Geoffrey too. They are encamped at Bury St Edmund's after landing in Suffolk on the 24th last. They say there are almost a hundred ships. Take heart, dear girl, take heart!'

This must be the reason for the Keeper's sudden concern. I show the letter to Avice, who gives thanks to God and is instantly full of joyful spirits.

"We must not speak of it," I warn her. "The guards hadn't broken the seal. But it may not be common knowledge, and we do not yet know the outcome. A hundred ships is not that many. All may still be lost."

Despite my caution, I give thanks in St. John's Chapel, spending a long time on my knees, telling my rosary beads. I hope Judas will return from Bolton Priory soon with more news. Every morning I wake, not with excitement or keen anticipation, but a strange and pervasive sense of dread, and the memory of that nightmare.

My mind keeps on straying throughout my prayers. For some reason, I think about the comet we saw blazing above Wigmore, shortly after our wedding. What a confident, eager youth Roger was then! Surely his imprisonment and all the wars he has fought (and lost) must have dented this confidence a little? Yet now, here he is at the head of another army, challenging the King directly.

A noisy clattering brings me up short. I realise I have been gripping my rosary so tightly it has broken, with all the golden-brown beads spilling and rolling over the stone floor of the chapel. It was made in Paris by the Paternosterers' guild and I feel a pang of regret. I hope it is not a bad omen.

So much for my devotions. Would my daughters be chastised, I wonder, for such laxity, in their isolated convents? I expected so, and doubted if any liveliness of spirit would be tolerated. Had not my sisters at Aconbury turned out meek and mild, despite all my visits and gifts, and my attempts to make sure they were well cared for? I do not think God is very fair on women, though it is obviously disrespectful to say so.

As if on cue, Richard Judas enters the chapel in his black skirts and looks alarmed to see the scattered beads, which he begins to pick up.

"It was not," I announce stiffly, "intentional."

But it turns out Father Judas is in too much of a lather about his news to care one way or the other. He speaks in a hoarse whisper, in deference to his surroundings, but very rapidly.

"My lady, there is great news!"

"I know," I say calmly. "Roger has invaded. Along with the Queen and a small army. Lady Maud Clifford, that was, wrote to tell me."

"More than that, my lady. Much more than that!"

He abandons his thankless task to kneel beside me, smiling.

"The Earls of Kent and Norfolk are with them, and all the people of Anglia have joined in. Henry of Lancaster is also on his way to lend support. Bishop Orleton has denounced the King as a sodomite from the pulpit! There is no resistance!

"Only the Despensers, Chancellor Baldock, and the Earls of Arundel and Surrey hold fast for the King, and they have all fled London for the west. The capital is in chaos and, oh my dear God, Bishop Stapledon has been hounded from his London house by the people, and killed in the street. God rest his soul and have mercy on him!" and he crosses himself urgently, before continuing.

"All the prisoners in the Tower have been released, including your sons and Thomas Berkeley, but lately moved there. Except for Roger Mortimer of Chirk, your husband's uncle, who died there six weeks ago. God rest his soul and grant him mercy for his deeds! They have locked up Eleanor de Clare, Despenser's wife, and taken the royal children off her to be reunited with their mother!"

He draws a quick breath.

"There is more, too, Madame. The Queen, who is now at Wallingford, has ordered a proclamation that Hugh Despenser the Younger is guilty of damaging the realm and the Holy Church by sending good men to their deaths, acting as a tyrant, and usurping the royal power. A ransom has been issued for his arrest."

"He will be with the King," I exclaim. "But where is the King?"

"They say he has left his realm by boat from Chepstow, in which case the young Prince Edward must now be the Keeper and Sovereign of the Realm. The Queen's army is heading for Bristol, as there is a rumour the wind may have blown the King and his party back to shore."

At last, the exhausted Judas falls silent and we both look up at the gilt crucifix in the chapel in utter astonishment.

"Where will it all end, Father?" I ask, wonderingly. "Where will it all end?"

By the end of the month, Sir John Ryther is falling over himself to placate me by advancing extra monies. Soon afterwards, he receives a visitor of some importance.

I am shut up in the back of the castle as usual with Avice, weaving woollen cloth on a new loom I asked for, so we may all have warmer clothing for the winter. I do not hear the clatter of hooves nor the roll of waggons entering the bailey. The first I know of the arrival is the sound of the key turning in the lock and the appearance of a once-familiar face standing next to Ryther.

"Richard! Richard de Burgh? Is it really you?" I ask in bewilderment.

My former knight, Sir Richard de Burgh, drops to one knee as I take his hand.

"My dear Lady Joan," he says with moist eyes. "I am come rejoicing to secure your release."

Immense relief surges through me, and then I wonder if this is a dream, or even worse, a vision arising from madness. I close my eyes but when I open them again, my old knight is still kneeling at my feet.

"My release?" I echo him. "Is the Lord Roger here?"

"No, Madame. He has been much occupied in Bristol and now in Hereford. There is much to tell. But he has ordered me to make haste and take you to Pontefract, in the first instance."

"Not Wigmore?"

"Alas, no. Wigmore is scarcely habitable at present. But Ludlow has been well maintained, and you can proceed there as soon as it can be made ready for you and you feel fit enough. It was thought best to break your journey at a closer point to Skipton to begin with. Your Lord did not know the condition of your health, after such a long captivity."

"That is indeed thoughtful of him," I say, overcome by emotion. "I am quite well, but certainly not used to travel!"

Sir Richard looks concerned. He must notice how pale and thin I look, despite my fine words. I have cast off my wimple because it is too worn, and I am aware there are many grey hairs straggling amongst my brown curls. My gown is grubby and old, and the hollowness of my cheekbones has come to emphasise the sharpness of my nose and chin. I have been imprisoned for almost five years, virtually alone apart from my confessor and serving women, and I know it must show. I feel deeply embarrassed before him.

"Lady Elizabeth is here with me. My wife, you remember?"

"But of course!"

"She has brought fresh clothing with her. May I call her up to wait upon you?"

I nod.

When Lady Elizabeth appears, she is no longer weeping but beaming.

Chapter 35

ALL OF THIS has been a huge shock, no matter how dreamt of or desired. Over the next few days, I am dutifully bathed, perfumed and dressed in rich velvet and warm furs. Lady Elizabeth washes and combs my tangled hair before sorting out a freshly laundered, crisp wimple. She does the same for Avice, selecting less rich, but warm and clean clothes. She asks the village girl to take away the loom, seemingly shocked at its presence. All the while, she chatters away brightly and is full of news. Roger has marched on Bristol and taken it from the Earl of Winchester – "Hugh Despenser the Elder to you, Madame".

Winchester was given a trial but not allowed to speak on the grounds that he and his son had not allowed Thomas of Lancaster to speak at his trial, after the Contrariant rebellion. The outcome was never in doubt. He was hung and his body fed to the dogs. Fitzalan, the Earl of Arundel, had also been apprehended and executed.

"Roger's cousin?" I ask, sadly.

"Yes, and they say it was done very clumsily, too – by an inexperienced executioner, with a blunt axe."

I sigh.

"He has been against Roger for many years, but I can hardly believe that – they were in the royal household together as young men once."

"Well, they do say Lord Mortimer did it out of spite."

"He's a hard man, but he would only do that if Arundel had done the same to somebody else."

"Oh well, you know how people talk, Madame. Who knows what to believe these days? I am sorry if it upset you."

"Where is Roger now?"

"With the Queen, staying at Bishop Orleton's palace in Hereford."

Lady Elizabeth is well aware of the gossip being passed round by the 'people' she likes to mention so often, but is discreet enough not to repeat it.

"Ah yes, I never really took to Orleton, but I must admit he has been a good friend to my lord. And where is the King?"

"Well, his boat was blown back to shore and he took refuge, with his young Hugh Despenser, in Caerphilly. But, as the Queen's army grew closer, they panicked and fled, leaving Hugh's son, Huchon, to defend the castle as best he could. The Earl of Surrey decided to desert and switched sides to join the Queen. So the King and Despenser's company became very small. Only six men, and those of the most ordinary kind, apart from themselves and Chancellor Baldock were left.

Henry of Lancaster's men picked them up at Llantrisant Abbey. He let the six men go. But Hugh Despenser is the next one for execution. In Hereford. Quite soon now. That is why Lord Mortimer and the Queen are there. The Queen wants to see it done."

I shudder.

"I have never understood why people love these spectacles. Of course, that is the way of the rabble, perhaps it comforts them to see how the high and mighty can suffer, too. But the Queen?"

"Well, they do say she is very bitter against the man."

"That does not surprise me. I don't suppose they will allow him to speak either. Well, I am not sorry for him. Although I am afraid Roger will treat him as Despenser treated Llewellyn Bren, and Edward I treated William Wallace."

"They say some of Bren's men were with Lancaster when Despenser was captured."

"Really? How strange life is, Elizabeth! What do we say? The Wheel turns round but will always turn again?"

"Something like that. It certainly has for the Despensers and the King."

"I am glad Warenne of Surrey is back on Roger's side, at any rate. Of course, if the King has been captured in Wales, he cannot be said to have deserted the realm now, can he?"

"I don't know about that, Madame," Elizabeth said, fastening a gold necklace studded with sapphires around my neck. "He is in the custody of the Earl of Lancaster, and will be taken to Kenilworth Castle, where he is to be treated with all courtesy and care. But he was required to give up his seal to Bishop Orleton, and the Queen has taken all of his money and jewels from Caerphilly."

"The King will not be able to forgive Isabella for executing Hugh Despenser."

"I really don't know," says Lady de Burgh.

"There!" she says, giving my cheeks a little pinch to bring some colour into them, and standing back to admire her handiwork. "Now you look more like your old self."

"Do I?" say I. "Somehow I don't feel it…yet. But thank you, Elizabeth. I need to enquire about my convent daughters. Have they…?"

"Been forcibly veiled, Madame? No, I believe they have not."

"That is good news. It warms my heart!"

The following day, we set out for Pontefract with Lady de Burgh at least happy I am looking like a lady again. She says I need to eat more to fill out – why, I had only picked at the food I had been served, like a bird! Lady Elizabeth, who has an ample figure, is not aware that once you have trained your stomach to expect less, it is not easy to reverse the habit straightaway.

Ockley and Bullesdon also returned as my men at arms with Sir Richard, so we have a small retinue to guard us on our journey.

"Not that anyone would dare attack Mortimer's wife under these circumstances," Sir Richard says, smiling.

I fall quiet as the waggons rumble down the setts of Skipton High Street. I have just said goodbye to Richard Judas, who has asked to be released to stay at Bolton Priory, which request I naturally granted after all his faithful service. How odd it seemed to be able to grant anything again! Yet I found his departure surprisingly emotional.

"You do not need me anymore, my lady," he said.

"Oh yes, I do," I retorted.

"No, you don't, Lady Joan. You will be well. I shall, of course, still pray for you every day."

A lady could not kiss a priest but I felt he knew of my affection, none the less.

"We would not have survived without you," was all I said in the end, with a catch in my voice.

He smiled his dark little smile.

"Maybe, me neither," he said. "God bless and keep you always, Madame."

The High Street in Skipton is busy as usual and I am surprised to see so many of the townsfolk standing to attention, cheering and doffing their caps to me. I had not known any of them, apart from the damsels, who brought in the laundry and cooked and served the meals, and have now returned to their own homes. Yet they have clearly known about me and possibly felt for me. I feel touched because I did not expect such warmth.

My nostrils fill with the warm, horsey smell around the waggon.

"I wonder," I say to Lady de Burgh, "if I shall remember how to ride again?"

"Of course you will! But it is much better to be in the waggon for this journey."

The weather is indeed miserable, grey and wet. However, Sir Richard has arranged frequent stops at priories and manor houses, instead of pressing on through the cold of the night, as I was forced to endure on my journeys to and from Hampshire.

It is strange to think the King is being taken north whilst we travel south. I cannot forget his ill treatment of me, but confess I do feel the return of some sympathy. I remember how devastated he was when Gaveston died. But Piers never really did anyone any harm, other than puncturing their pride. Hugh Despenser is not like that. He deserves his fate.

I was not to know that, on the very morrow, Hugh Despenser would be dragged into Hereford, following a mangy horse and wearing a crown of nettles, with biblical verses carved into the flesh of his arms. He would be drawn up onto a fifty foot-high scaffold, partially hung, have his entrails cut out and burnt before the crowd, his penis and testicles cut off, and, finally, his heart torn out. It was said to be still beating. The penis and testicles had not been part of Llewellyn Bren's execution. That seemed to be Isabella's especial punishment.

All the while, the spectacle would be watched by my lord and the Queen, drinking and dining on rich food, laughing and flirting on a raised dais above the howling crowd. It was Roger who made this triumph possible for the Queen, and he would watch the quartering of the body take place without flinching. The red kites would swoop swiftly to earth then, to pick up and carry off pieces of any body meat not consumed in the fire, before the guards scared them off.

Chapter 36

1326-1327 – LUDLOW

PONTEFRACT PROVED A comfortable stay, though it seemed my resting there went completely unnoticed by the nobility. Neither the Queen, Roger, nor Henry of Lancaster, who owns the castle, were there to welcome me. Well, I supposed Lancaster must be with the King in Kenilworth. But I had hoped my lord would join me here from Hereford.

Sir Richard said he would no doubt be heavily occupied with matters of state. If that were the case, there did not seem to be much point in remaining in Pontefract, and so I asked to resume my journey as soon as I was rested, pointing out I was no longer a captive so could presumably do as I liked? For a moment, I detected an undercurrent of alarm in both de Burghs but when they hastily concurred, I decided I must have been overly sensitive.

By the end of November, I was back in Ludlow to be met by more cheering townsfolk as the waggon rolled up Broad Street and through the market place. At least, the common people seemed glad to see me return. Now it is all a question of settling in and preparing for the Christmas season, which I want to be especially wonderful for the children. By then, surely the King will be back on the throne and some semblance of normality returned. My lord will certainly come then.

But my lord does not come at Christmas. Instead he writes to me, addressing me as 'his dear wife'. He wishes me well and expresses his delight I am back in Ludlow, which he is sure I will manage and maintain well in his absence, as I always have. He explains he is sorely taxed with the affairs of Parliament but sends his warmest regards. 'His regards!' After all those enforced years apart? If he is so engaged in Parliament, why does he not send for me, as he used to so many times before?

Then I read that he is required to spend Christmas with the Queen and her court at Wallingford, and Edmund and Geoffrey will attend him. A very special and private Council Meeting will be held there, to decide matters concerning the King. The Pope had written expressing an earnest wish that the King and Queen be reconciled. Sadly, this did not seem possible. Edward was not in a mode of forgiveness.

Lady Margaret de Fiennes brings my little ones back to Ludlow, and that is the occasion of much crying and kissing. Yet they are not tiny anymore. Catherine is twelve and has been lucky to escape being sent to a convent. She seems very self possessed and independent. Agnes and Beatrice are ten and eight years respectively, and also well on the way to growing up. Even Blanche, who was in swaddling clothes when I left her, is now six. It hurts me to think of all the years I have missed. They are distant from me, at first: this mother they have hardly known, and are suddenly expected to take back as a stranger. This is hard, but must be borne. Gradually, they begin to thaw. Blanche is the easiest and the most willing to accept my cuddles. I make Christmas for them, but there is no father, and no older sisters or brothers who would have helped me bear it.

After my initial joy at returning to Ludlow, I find it over-large and feel somewhat lonely. I am still waiting for my 'convent girls' to come home, though I have been assured that the necessary arrangements are in hand. There is a renewed coterie of gentlewomen around me, but I find their constant prattle and laughter often grates on my ears. Very often, I retire to my solar alone with Avice, and spend my time quietly sewing. I know that my women find this unhealthy and perverse, but explain I have been alone so long that I need time to accustom myself to the change.

Lady Elizabeth de Burgh is chief amongst the prattlers, of course, but I notice they all fall silent when I join them, when they have been laughing merrily before. Initially, I thought this was out of concern for my sensibilities and intercepted several sideways glances of sympathy. Yet these glances have become more apparent, rather than less, as time has gone on. One day, I call Lady Elizabeth to me and ask for her company on a stroll outside, despite the chilly weather.

"Elizabeth," I say, when we are out of earshot of the others, "what is wrong with you all?"

"I really don't know what you mean, Madame. We are all perfectly happy."

But Elizabeth is not stupid and there is the tinge of a blush on her cheeks.

"You are happy till I walk in the room, and then you fall silent. I feel there is something you are not telling me. Maybe about something happening at court?"

Well, Madame, they do say that the King and Queen cannot be reconciled and that is very sad."

"Yes, I know that, Lady Elizabeth. But what about my lord? Is he to be pardoned? The Queen must surely have spoken for him."

"Oh yes, Madame. Very much so!" and Lady de Burgh allows herself a small but fatal smile.

"What do you mean? *Very* much so?"

"Well, of course she is grateful to him. He has become her favourite. But I don't mean anything else by it. Of course not. Nothing at all."

That word 'favourite', with all of its past connotations, blazes out at me like a banner.

"I don't entirely believe you, Elizabeth. You must tell me the truth."

Lady de Burgh is positively squirming now.

"There's just a lot of silly rumours, that's all. No-one really knows what's going on."

"What do they say is going on?"

"Well..."

"Elizabeth!"

"Well, they say Lord Mortimer and the Queen have become very close. But it's only gossip, Madame. They don't really know if they are lovers or not!"

I feel as if I have been struck by a thunderbolt from heaven.

"Thank you, Elizabeth. I value your honesty."

"But it's only rumours, Madame," she says desperately, no doubt seeing how the colour has drained from my face.

"So you keep saying. I would like to be alone now, Elizabeth. You may go back inside."

"Aren't you coming too, Madame? The wind is awful chill."

For answer, I wrap my fur-lined cloak of blue velvet closer around my shoulders, turn up the collar and walk on, making for the circular chapel of St Mary Magdalene in the inner bailey. I make sure I hold my head high.

"Wait Madame! Don't go!" Elizabeth cries out in a panic.

I do not reply.

At New Year, I receive a present via a messenger from London. I am astonished to find it is a chain bearing four massive rubies, set in gold in the shape of a cross. A letter from Roger accompanies it. I am relieved to find he still addresses me as 'his own very dear wife'. He is sorry he was unable to come to Ludlow at Christmas. The Council Meeting at Wallingford concluded satisfactorily and now he has returned to London for an even more crucial Parliament. He cannot say for certain how that will go, but he has reason to believe it will culminate in the abdication of the present King in favour of his son, and the setting up of a Regency Council. As soon as these pressing matters are settled, he promises to visit. He is anxious to begin further building at Ludlow and plans a brand new chamber block and garderobe tower, for he envisages much entertaining in the future.

I feel confused and uneasy as I turn the valuable ruby cross over in my hands. Once, I had a ruby necklace which Roger bought for me to celebrate our success in Ireland. But that was a pretty and delicate thing, which I loved. Of course, it had been confiscated at Wigmore along with everything else. This piece of jewellery is huge and vulgar in contrast – more like something a bishop would wear. It would weigh my small frame down and look ugly. If Roger was seeking to compensate me for the loss of my former trinket, the choice of this bauble was inappropriate.

I remember Richard Judas telling how Bishop Stapledon was dragged out of his house in London and murdered in the street. Had his goods been claimed by the Queen? Had she then given this to Roger as a reward? I shudder. I would never know the truth, but it could be so. The very idea increased my distaste for the object. I would not wear it, but keep it wrapped up in a drawer in case I ever needed to sell it.

Yet despite my embarrassment, I take it first to show my ladies before I put it away, so I can publicly demonstrate this mark of my husband's great esteem and regard for me.

Discomfort grows in my mind about Roger's proposed building works. After Skipton, Ludlow feels vast enough as it is. Nevertheless, it does seem my lord intends to come back here then, and this gives me hope for the future.

Another sadness comes at my rather melancholy Christmas. I wrote to Lady Maud Clifford (that was) to ask her to come and stay, along her new husband, but was shocked to receive a letter back telling me that Maud had died suddenly, before the end of the year. This was an unexpected blow. She had been so kind and I had so looked forward to paying her back what I owed and seeing her cheerful face again, as my guest. Oh Maud, I am so sorry your new found happiness did not last long, and I thank you for all the hope and kindness you gave me. How much easier it is to pray to God for the soul of a greatly loved friend than a cruel king!

January brings happiness, with the return of Joan from Sempringham and Isabella from Chicksands. I hear Margaret is back with Berkeley, too. Joan has shot up in height and is looking very comely and robust, but, oh dear, Isabella looks so pale, thin and ill. We must take extra good care of her now. Both girls are overwhelmed with delight to see how Catherine, Agnes, Beatrice, and even little Blanche, have grown up, and to be in their company again, as well as each other's.

Chapter 37

WHAT FOLLOWED, I learn later from Edmund and Geoffrey. Roger was commanded to stay at the Queen's court in Wallingford for Christmas, and his friend, Adam Orleton, was also invited. The bishop enjoyed it all immensely. With the exception of William Melton, Archbishop of York, all the senior clerics of any stature, including the Archbishop of Canterbury, were now reconciled with the Queen and giving her their support. Orleton congratulated himself over this. The Council convened with one notable absence from the Church — that of Stapledon of Exeter, whose limbs were indeed torn apart by the mob in London, just as Judas told me.

The tide had turned so far that a few rash individuals were actually calling for the execution of the King. Queen Isabella was horrified, and Roger Mortimer spoke up for her. There was no precedent for such a dreadful act, he said. Neither was it in any way practical. There was no precedent for deposing a King either, but Adam Orleton had other ideas.

"How can we tolerate a sodomite for a King?" he asked. "It is a mortal sin! How can we tolerate a King who has not acted with one scrap of wisdom? How can we tolerate, in fact, a most un-kingly King? How much better it would be to put his son on the throne, and keep the old King in comfortable captivity for the rest of his life, as befits his royal person and status of paternity!"

"The boy is not of age," objected Henry of Lancaster.

Orleton smiled thinly, but it was Roger who answered back.

"There is a precedent for a boy King," he said. "Henry III was only nine, five years younger than our Prince, but was ably guided by William Marshal as Regent."

"And I suppose you offer up yourself as Regent?" asked Norfolk, sarcastically.

"Certainly not," countered Roger smoothly. "But the boy has a wise mother and two able half-uncles. Not to mention his noble cousin, Henry of Lancaster."

"And a council of bishops," interrupted the Bishop of Winchester.

"Perhaps the solution rests in a Regency Council," Roger agreed.

"But we must put it to Parliament first," Kent said nervously.

"Of course we must. To that end, I suggest a Parliament be called in Westminster in January."

And suddenly, everyone seemed to be in total agreement.

There is a new Mayor in London, who is one of Roger's men, and he has managed to restore the city to some semblance of law and order. Parliament was called to assemble on the 7th of January and all the lords, knights of the shire, and representatives of the boroughs and Cinque ports, duly assembled in the Great Hall at Westminster. Only representatives from Wales were absent. They had not been summoned, for it was well known they remained partial to the King. The bishops sent to Kenilworth for the King himself to be brought, but returned empty-handed. It was Orleton who made this shock announcement: the King refused to come to Parliament! So what was Parliament to do? Did they wish to continue to be ruled by a feeble King who would not even attend their meetings? Or would they prefer to be ruled by his son who would attend? There was a stunned silence.

The Archbishop of York quietly suggested that if the King were to abdicate, he should do so voluntarily, and should be seen to do so in Parliament. There was a low rumble of assent like distant thunder.

"But how can we proceed if the King will not come?" cried Orleton, with his arms raised in exasperation to the heavens. "Perhaps it is as well he will not! For if he did, he would be bound to intend the Queen some harm."

This unwarranted comment was received by another silence, but it was tense and nervous this time. So Parliament was dismissed until the following morning to consider its decision.

My lord was first up to speak the next morning. He had been up most of the night but still looked fresh. Inside, my sons knew he was on fire, but outwardly he remained cool and calm. He showed a letter from the Mayor of London and 'its citizens', asking Parliament to depose the King and swear an oath of allegiance to the Queen and her son.

"Last night," he said, "I had the honour to be present at a meeting of the greatest Lords in this land. We discussed this matter long into the late hours, looking at it from every possible angle. Regrettably, we came to the conclusion that the King must abdicate. The decision was unanimous. We have suffered his rule in silence and with the utmost patience for far too long."

Thomas Wake, another of Roger's cousins, immediately leapt to his feet to declare that he, for one, did not think the King should be allowed to rule for one day longer. The rumblings rising to the rafters of Westminster Hall were now of general assent.

Orleton stood up again.

"An unwise King destroyeth his People!" he proclaimed, and proceeded to deliver an impassioned sermon to prove the point.

By the time he came to the end, he was greeted with shouts of "Away with the King! Away with him!"

The Bishop of Winchester then took up the reins, stating that the King had become feeble in mind. He was followed by Walter Reynolds, Archbishop of Canterbury, once a friend to the King. But now he spoke about the long oppression of the people under this monarch and declared that if it was the will of the people to cast off this yoke, then it would also be God's will the reign should end.

Thomas Wake sprang up once more.

"Is this the will of the People?" he hollered. "Is it the will of the People that the King should be deposed and his son put in his place?"

The answer was tumultous.

"Let it be done! Let it be done!"

Reynolds raised his hand for silence.

"Your voice has been clearly heard," he said. "Edward of Caernarvon is deprived of the government of this realm, and his son, Edward of Windsor, is made King of England by unanimous consent."

At this point, Prince Edward was ushered into the Great Hall, looking somewhat dazed and bewildered.

"Behold your King – King Edward III!" said the Archbishop.

Most of the assembly began to sing 'All glory, laud and honour' in response.

The Mayor of London called for a ceremony of oath-taking for fealty to be held at the Guildhall that very same day. Roger was one of the first to swear the oath, but was followed by a crowd of noblemen and peers of the realm, all anxious to prove themselves willing.

And so it was done. Now, all that remained was to inform Edward at Kenilworth that he was no longer King, but Lord Edward of Caernarvon, and only 'the Father of the King'.

When Edward was led into the Hall at Kenilworth a week later, he hardly needed telling, for he could read it in the faces of his visitors. He fainted and had to be helped to his feet by the Bishop of Winchester and Henry of Lancaster. It seemed apt he was wearing a black robe as he stood trembling before Bishop Orleton, who read out a long list of his crimes.

Chiefly, he was not fit to govern, through his incompetence and letting others govern for him to the detriment of his people, his realm and the Church. He had refused to listen to good advice. He had lost Scotland, most of Gascony and almost lost Ireland. He had unjustly executed or imprisoned, exiled and disinherited many of his nobles, and governed for his own profit. He had fled the country with a traitor when challenged. He had lost the faith and trust of his people, and they all agreed there was no alternative but to cast off his reign.

He now had a clear choice: either he could abdicate the throne in favour of his son or, if he resisted, he would have to relinquish the throne to one who was not of the royal blood, but was experienced in government and would guide the Queen.

Our sons, watching all of this in the background, winced at that. The man who was not of royal birth could only be their father. They could see the King was shaken to the core and weeping with genuine remorse that the people should hate him so. They were heartily relieved when he muttered his agreement to abdicate.

Sir William Trussel stepped forward then to renounce homage, on behalf of all the Lords of the land, and Thomas le Blount broke the staff of office before him, with a loud crack, to announce this royal household was no more. Now they could say in London that the King had not been deposed, but had chosen to abdicate. A new reign was begun.

In the middle of February, we are joined by Edmund with his little wife, Elizabeth Badlesmere. She is still only thirteen but has been sent into his care after her release from the Tower. It amuses me to see her follow Edmund round like a puppy dog. She is a sweet girl and clearly looks up to him adoringly since her father was executed.

Edmund is fresh from the coronation of the young Prince Edward at Westminster. I feel hurt I was not invited to attend, especially as all three of my elder sons were, but I say nothing to Edmund about that. He has to tell the story to the girls many times over – how the Archbishop had to hold the crown above the boy's head because it was too heavy for him to wear! Their father, Lord Roger, bought his sons robes fit for an earl for the occasion. I wonder where he found the money to do that, but again say nothing. Young Roger has gone straight back to Ireland to see his wife and offer John Butler, who is now Justiciar, his military services, so I do not see him. Geoffrey remains in his father's employ at court. John is there too, desperate for his father to advance his further training as a true knight.

Chapter 38

GROWN CHILDREN

ONE EVENING, I ask to see Edmund alone. I want to hear a truthful account of his captivity, out of the girls' hearing, and also to ask what is happening to his father. The former he dismisses with a shrug. Windsor was not so bad, though they did not appreciate being moved to the Tower, after their father's escape.

"But it was easier for me than the others," says Edmund. "I had some books and you know I have always enjoyed study. It was Roger and John who were climbing the walls and always at each other." He pauses. "I was allowed to see Roger of Chirk, too, shortly before he died. He was very glad to see me, though I think, no, I am sure, that he mistook me for his brother Edmund. It was strange, mother. I used to be so frightened of him as a child, you know? But he had become so bony, shrunken and frail."

"I used to be frightened of him, too, once. He was not a good man," I say. "It must have been strange for you."

We are silent for a moment before the firelight in my solar, drinking our wine together companionably.

"I am sure you suffered just as much as we did, mother. If not a great deal more, without as much company. We had the Hereford boys at Windsor in addition. Thanks be to God it is all over now though!"

"And how is young Elizabeth? She seems to be happy to be with you in your home?"

"Yes, she is," Edmund says. "We are not quite sure what to do with each other yet, apart from playing at being lord and lady in our manor house, but I think we are getting on well enough and we do hope to give you grandchildren in time."

"She is still young and has been through a great deal, losing her father in such a cruel manner, and being cooped up with her mother in the Tower. No wonder she follows you around everywhere."

"I am content with that, mother, and I intend to spend more time at the manor house in Stratfield. I can help you with the estates from there. You know I have never been one for warring or tournaments."

"Like your grandfather and namesake. I think your father hoped you would make a courtier and a diplomat, though."

Edmund looks slightly awkward.

"Oh well, he has Geoffrey for that."

I choose to ask the inevitable question now.

"And how is your father?"

"Very busy. Very sure of himself. I didn't say earlier, but our fine robes were ordered even before the abdication took place."

"My goodness – that was bold! What do you make of it, Edmund? I never thought King Edward would agree to such a thing."

"Geoffrey says he is a broken man and had little choice. So, now his son is King."

"But the Queen will want to control her son."

"Yes. She is much concerned to restore her lands, and more. She has just been awarded a massive income…I mean really massive, mother. More than old Thomas of Lancaster had."

"I expect she feels it is her due. But what about your father? Does he look for grandeur and riches too?"

"Geoffrey thinks so, and is closer to him than I am. Possibly even an Earldom, if all goes well."

"I have heard it said that your father is the Queen's favourite," I stop short of declaring the full extent of the allegations.

Edmund fiddles with the stem of his goblet, and looks embarrassed.

"I have heard that, too," he confesses, "but royalty can be fickle."

"Lovers may not be…I have also heard that. Is it true?"

"I don't know, mother. I really don't know."

Edmund is blushing now, and I realise it is unfair to question him further.

"I think I will write to Geoffrey," I declare. "He was in France with your father all that time, and during the invasion. He must know the truth of the matter."

I soon gather that my daughter, Lady Margaret Berkeley, is hoping her mother will go and see her, now that Edmund is back to see to estate matters, but I tarry at Ludlow, hoping for a visit from Geoffrey.

I have always been the closest to Edmund and Margaret as my first born, even after they married, despite Edmund spending so much time in another household, as is the custom for sons of noblemen. My daughters behave more predictably, but I never cease to marvel at the difference between my sons.

Edmund is studious and kind. As the second son, young Roger has always shown a fiercely independent streak, which seems to have intensified since living with an Anglo-Irish lord, and at times I am uncomfortably aware I hardly know him anymore. His wife, Joan Butler, died very soon after their reunion, and I feel extremely sorry for him, especially as he remains childless. He does not seem to feel the need to come home to seek comfort and will probably marry another daughter of the Anglo-Irish aristocracy in time. I hope so. He has a fair slice of our lands over there now. I think I ought to go to Ireland and see him soon.

John has always been impatient and full of himself, a bit of a nightmare as a child, but is now happy, actively pursuing life on the tourney circuit.

Geoffrey, on the other hand, is different again. He is the expansive extravert, the frank, charming, popular man. So I expect him to be more informative about his father's doings than Edmund, whom I guess is anxious to spare my feelings. If only Geoffrey can spare the time to come! Which he does, shortly after Edmund and Elizabeth return to their own manor house in Stratfield Mortimer.

He embraces me warmly on his arrival, as is his wont, and, over dinner, does not hold back on his description of the previous King's abdication.

"But what did Bishop Orleton mean?" I ask, "when he said the throne might pass to one not of the royal blood? Surely, it could only go to Kent or Norfolk, and they are of royal blood."

Geoffrey turns to me and wraps my hands in his large, warm ones.

"Mother, you may have to get used to wearing widow's weeds, just as the Queen did in France."

I withdraw my hands in horror.

"It's true then? He is her lover as well as her favourite?"

Geoffrey nods sympathetically.

"But he won't desert you entirely, mother."

"She'll get tired of him!" I declare – for of course it is impossible for anyone to tire of a queen, even if they feel that way.

"She may not, now the King has been deposed. And he will not, because he will think of himself as King. A King of pure folly!"

"You must not speak of your father like that!"

Geoffrey looks at me pityingly.

"Mother, I have seen the way he is acting now, with my own eyes, and it can only get worse."

"That may be so, but everything he does will be for the family. Only for us. You will see."

Geoffrey sighs.

"Do you know he wants this solar block built at Ludlow so he can entertain the Queen and the new King here?"

I falter at that.

"I guessed as much. But there is nothing wrong with that in itself."

"No, not in itself, but I know this power will go to his head and he will become greedy and arrogant. I am sorry, my dear mother. But why hasn't he come to see you yet?"

"He will come," I say firmly. "He will come very soon. On his own. You know nothing of marriage. Nothing at all. You are still too young and confident. It breeds carelessness; you must take more care of yourself!"

Geoffrey's eyes glaze over as if I am talking nonsense. After he has gone, I feel ashamed and wonder if in fact I have been doing just that.

Chapter 39

AT LAST HE comes. Not to Ludlow, but to Pembridge. I was asked to attend the manor house in April, and to take 'only the most necessary of retinues'. He would attend with Richard of Monmouth and a very small number of men; it was clearly meant to be a private reunion. I cannot help but wonder if it is also a sentimental choice, for Pembridge is where we married.

Since Geoffrey's visit, I have found myself the victim of a maelstrom of emotions. I was angry at his denunciation of Roger, and stung into quick defence. It is true my lord has always been ambitious and sought power. But he has not been foolish. How many times did we deprecate Gaveston's behaviour between ourselves, and fear the outcome? Could he really become the Queen's 'Perrot'? Surely not! Perhaps the rumours are untrue and spring entirely from jealousy?

He has sent me generous amounts of money and a stupendous New Year gift, even though I did not take to that. It appears that Henry of Lancaster has the chairmanship of the Regency Council and Roger is not even amongst its number. So, he cannot be another Despenser.

Then, the next moment, my certainty wavers. He has left it the best part of a year before coming to see me, and not once have I been summoned to court. The tone of his letters has changed, even though it is subtle. He has enquired after the health of his daughters but not visited them, despite their long separation. Most damning of all is the knowledge that Geoffrey is certain he shares the Queen's bed. Had I not myself sought out Geoffrey, as the one who would know, if anyone did?

I go to Pembridge in good time, having made sure to take the finest of my new clothes. I have regained some weight since returning to Ludlow, but I am aware the last few years have not been kind to me. Only my fine eyes remain a feature to be proud of. My face is still pale and drawn with anxiety. My hair beneath its wimple is now completely gray. After twelve full-term pregnancies, all the tone in my abdominal muscles has vanished and my skin sags in that area and looks like the peel of an orange. I am also thickened around the waist, even though my body overall remains small. They say the Queen, in her thirties, is more beautiful than ever.

I am forty-two and have lost the last five years. Whilst I did involve myself in estate management at Ludlow again to begin with, I am happy to relinquish the task to Edmund now. I have ridden a horse and enjoyed it, but lost interest in hawking. I have more books but have yet to read them. I find my ladies' chatter tiresome and I have delayed visiting Margaret at Berkeley.

Some of my confidence in travelling seems to have disappeared. I persuade myself this is due to worry over Isabella's health. But I found myself reluctant to leave the castle grounds at all this winter, even though I could. Everything seems too much effort. All is not well with me, but I cannot put my finger on any cause other than my lord's absence.

On my arrival in Pembridge, I am dismayed to find the house looking tired and shabby, and decide it needs some time and money to restore it to its former comfort. It should be more like Stokesay, whose space and comforts have previously impressed me. The church also needs attention if it is not to decay through neglect. That cannot be allowed. But there are only a few days before Roger's arrival.

At least I can give firm instructions to the servants regarding cleaning and mending. I order the best food and wine available and ask for fresh rushes to be brought, fires to be built up, and the beds made with good linen. Lord Mortimer should lack for nothing.

Richard of Monmouth comes first, having ridden on ahead to warn me of Roger's imminent arrival. I greet him warmly as the long-lost friend he is. Richard's face has always been open and accessible. Is it only my imagination, then, that his eyes cannot quite meet mine?

I have been consumed with apprehension all day, so order my horse to be rapidly saddled and brought round to accompany Richard back down the lane to the outskirts of the village, where we see riders approaching in the distance. I ask Richard to wait and nudge my palfrey to walk on alone. The party have stopped on sight of me, and Roger must have given the same instructions, for he too comes on alone. We halt a few feet from each other but remain on horseback.

It is a surprise to see him thinner than ever, though his hair and beard are still black as a raven. I am relieved to find his deep-brown eyes look at me directly, but struggle to see any real warmth in them. He is dressed very finely, so finely there seems little of the tough soldier left.

"Welcome, my Lord," I say, in a thickly choked voice. "Welcome to Pembridge."

"Dear Joan," he says.

That is all, though I fancy there is some sadness in the words. Maybe he is thinking how much easier it would have been if I had died in captivity. He will know that is a shocking thought, but I am sure it is what he will think. I am not so bonny anymore. His horse is restless and fidgety, and tosses its head under his hand.

"Shall we ride on together?" he suggests, and we do so with slack reins, letting the horses amble back towards the village through the woods, which are just beginning to leaf out.

"I am afraid Pembridge is not what it was," I tell him.

"No matter," he says.

I suddenly realise he is nervous, and it gives me the confidence to speak more brightly to hide my distress.

"But we shall dine well nevertheless, and be comfortable."

"The peasants are coming out of their cottages to gawp. Shall we ride on more quickly?"

There was nothing else said until we crossed the drawbridge to the manor.

But I knew. I already knew the truth.

He regained his composure over our supper, and even entertained me with his accounts of all the portentous happenings at court since his entry into London.

Afterwards, we take a turn in the air, which is mild and spring-like. I say I want him to see the state of the church and belltower. He agrees it needs money to be spent, and says he has no problem with that. It is when we leave by the porch, pregnant with memories, that I speak sharply for the first time, feeling anger burst out of its cage.

"Is it true what they say, then? That you bed with the Queen?"

This startles him. He clearly did not expect a confrontation.

"You think that of me?" he tries, cautiously.

"I think I am like a penitent in a turf maze. The closer I get to the centre, to be with you again, the further I seem away!"

"The Queen is not to be disobeyed, Joan. But she will be good to us, I promise you."

I laugh with undisguised contempt.

"So you are her Perrot then?"

"A better advisor than Piers, I hope."

My voice breaks down.

"My God, what have you done? How could you?"

He reaches for my hand but I snatch it away and lean on the stone parapet of the bridge to the manor, staring wildly into the growing shadow of the moat.

"Joan, she has promised me an Earldom in time. A newly created one. I shall be the first Earl of March and all of our unmarried daughters may then marry Earls in their turn!"

"Oh, not just Perrot, then, but a Despenser, in addition?" I know this will cut him to the quick, and it does. "No marriage to an Earl for poor Isabella. She is not strong enough for any marriage! You should see how ill she looks now, after being cooped up in that cold, damp convent!"

"I am sorry to hear it. But she has always been a sickly child with a weak chest. Her condition may have worsened, whether in or out of a convent. I shall see she has the grant she deserves to be well cared for, all of her life."

I begin to scream at him.

"Do you love her?" I speak completely out of sequence, but he knows very well whom I mean.

"There are different kinds of love."

"Oh, so you lust after her, then?"

"Perhaps. Some of the time. Certainly in France, on my own…"

"What a shame! Oddly enough, I wasn't provided with a male stud in prison either!"

Despite himself, he smiles at that.

"Would you have wanted that, my love? I thought you may have had enough of all that childbirth."

I melt at the endearment, but then hot tears trickle down my cheek unbidden.

"Too late for that now, anyway," I say.

He seeks my hand again and this time I do not take it away.

"Oh, Joan. I am sorry. Truly I am. Especially about your harsh imprisonment. And the girls. But there's no going back. Not now. I shall use my – position – entirely for the family."

I dash away my tears, angry and ashamed I have ever allowed them to fall.

"Why can't you be like Pembroke – the elder statesman everyone respected?"

"Because I am not Pembroke! I invaded the country and persuaded it to depose the King. Anyway, look at what happened to Pembroke's widow and nephew – dispossessed by the younger Despenser. That was no reward for loyal service! I shall see the nephew re-instated and fancy him for Agnes' husband."

"Geoffrey says you will become a King of Folly."

"Does he now? Well, he has always been an impudent fellow."

"It will not end well, my Lord," I feel calmer now and genuinely concerned, but speak firmly.

The light is fading fast and a bat darts out of the church tower, flitting over our heads.

"Life rarely does," Roger says quietly. "We must take what we can whilst we can."

"Does that include what is not ours?"

"I have only taken back that which is rightfully mine so far, though I shall take Chirk, and Denbigh in addition, as the new Justiciar of Wales."

"What about the Lord of Chirk's own son?" I say in dismay. "His Roger?"

"He would not want him to have it. His son will be happier with Tedstone Wafre. Uncle Roger always thought I was more like his son, and treated me as such."

I shiver at the allusion. Were they becoming more alike?

"You are getting cold now. Shall we go in?"

"Yes, but not to bed!"

"We can still be companionable, without rancour. Can't we? Now we have come to a better understanding?"

I was not sure we had, nor that I could let go of my rancour, but I allowed him to take my arm and guide me toward the torchlights at the manor's door. I felt utterly powerless and crushed.

He halted just before the entrance.

"Oh, and one more thing. Do accept Margaret's invitation to go to Berkeley. Young Thomas is very occupied now his father has died and he has inherited. Margaret misses her mother, and has some very good news as she is with child again. It will do you good."

"I shall go. I have just been much…preoccupied, and sick with sadness in my heart."

"It will be good for you to go," said Roger. " I may have need of you there soon, and I promise to visit."

Chapter 40

SUMMER 1327 — BERKELEY

BY THE TIME I organise restoration work for Pembridge, it is almost the end of July before I reach Berkeley. Once more, I take the smallest of retinues, under the protection of the men at arms, Ockley and Bullesdon, whom Roger has put at my disposal. I include Avice, as my oldest and most trusted, if not noblest, companion, and leave Lady Elizabeth de Burgh in charge of my daughters.

Margaret is so overcome to see me again that I do indeed feel remiss at neglecting her. I realise I have been in such low spirits, and for so long, that it has sapped my strength and willpower. Now I really must strive to put all sorrow behind me and concentrate on my duties as a mother and grandmother.

So here is Margaret, hugging me, laughing and crying, at our reunion. She is heavy with child — her third now — conceived since her return from Shouldham Priory. She assures me the nuns were kind to her there, and not at all restrictive. For she had been carrying her second child, Thomas, when she was taken there, and that was where he was forced to enter the world. So the nuns made a great fuss of mother and child, as I could well believe.

Her father-in-law died in captivity at Wallingford a few months before Roger's invasion — shortly before Roger of Chirk passed — neither of them able to see the outcome of the invasion. So Margaret's husband Thomas inherited the title, along with Berkeley Castle, and Margaret was Lady Berkeley now, with a whole raft of new responsibilities.

I had not seen her eldest son, Maurice, since he was two, and my eyes mist over at having missed all the years inbetween. He is the most delightful child who is only too ready to get to know his grandmother, despite the intervening years. Little Thomas I have never seen, so this is another delight and surprise. Certainly,

Margaret needs me now and I promise to stay until the end of her confinement, at the very least.

"You look careworn, mama," Margaret says to me with concern. "You can have had no rest since your release, with all your responsibilities at Ludlow! You must rest and restore yourself with us now."

"Well, I don't think it has been that irksome," I say. "There were others to count on for advice, and Edmund is back now. But it is true there has been a great re-adjustment to make…in many ways. Have you seen your father, lately?"

"Yes, he was here in March before he left for Pembridge. When Lord Edward came."

"Lord Edward who?"

"Lord Edward of Caernarvon, the Father of the King."

I draw in my breath sharply.

"The former King?"

"Why, yes! Did father not tell you he had arranged for him to be brought here?"

I shake my head.

"I thought he was at Kenilworth."

"He was, but Father said that was no longer safe when he discovered there was a plot to rescue him."

"Was Henry of Lancaster involved in that?"

No, I don't think so. There are some brothers, both named Dunheved, who are Dominican friars, and they are suspected. Although Father did tell Thomas he does not trust Lancaster as Keeper. There has been a falling out between Lancaster and the Queen, so Father has made my Lord Thomas the keeper now."

"So Edward is already here?"

"Yes, in a sort of cell, but it is not a bad room and he does not lack comforts. The Exchequer has granted Thomas five pounds a day for his upkeep."

"Huh!" I cannot stop myself retorting in disgust. "Exceedingly generous!"

"Yes, I know! But he is locked up and we no longer let him into the castle grounds without a strong guard. He actually did manage to escape from us at the beginning of this month! The friars were to blame again. Fortunately, Thomas' men managed to apprehend him. They took him to Corfe for a while, where John Maltravers is the custodian, but he's back here now and says he is glad to be so, for Thomas is much kinder to him than Maltravers was."

"Your father has told me nothing of all this!"

"Well, he's in Scotland, on a campaign with the young King and a royal army. Thomas says Father wants to show the boy it's not possible to conquer the Scots so easily, so he has been preoccupied. He said he would come back to see us in September, so he can't be planning to stay that long in Scotland, whatever the outcome." Margaret pauses and looks at her mother's face. "Are you alright, mama? You seem upset. Would you like to see the Lord Edward?"

"Whatever for?" I ask, bitterly.

"Naturally, he hates Father for what he has done. But he may be more sympathetic towards you."

"I really don't think so, and I don't know what would be the point of me seeing him."

"You don't have to, mama. Not if it distresses you. But Father is worried he may try to escape again. He would like to send him to Ireland to be more secure. He did say you were more likely to make Lord Edward comply with that than he was."

"By selling him the delights of Trim? I doubt it," I say, tartly. "Anyway, surely your father could just have him moved there, if he wanted to? Lord Edward is *his* prisoner, by the sound of it."

"I think he has to be careful how he manages things at court. If Lord Edward said he wanted to go, it would make his life easier."

I swallow hard.

"I am astonished you have talked about this together, Margaret – and mentioned me. What is your father trying to do?"

"To secure the old King and protect the new one."

"And the Queen?"

Margaret blushes.

"There is that, too," she admits. I remain silent and quietly furious.

"Father said he would explain it all to you."

"Well, he didn't. Though looking back, I can see he made a cryptic remark to the effect, when he hoped I would visit Berkeley soon. But he was too occupied in trying to explain away his appealing new way of life."

I try to sound cold but have to brush away a tear hastily.

Margaret leans over to squeeze my hand.

"Do you mind very much, mama?" she asks gently.

"Mind? Of course I mind! He's my husband and my lord!"

"But it is the Queen, after all. And now you can rest, you know…without being bothered all the time."

I am silent for a long time. It is hard to believe my eldest daughter seems so casual and forgiving of her father.

"Do you love Thomas, Margaret?"

She is taken aback. After all, she has been brought up not to consider love an option where marriage is concerned.

"He is quite handsome," she says, "and he is kind to me – and happy to have heirs. Yes, I am happy, mother. All is well."

I can see Margaret is dismayed to see my eyes fill with tears. She has never seen me like this before. I have always been a strong and jovial mother, as far as she is concerned. She must feel embarrassed and awkward. This is not how a real lady or mother behaves.

"Anyway," she says briskly. "You are going to have a lovely time here, mama. I will make sure of that. Plenty of rest! And we won't talk about that awful Lord Edward ever again."

But rest is the last thing I need.

Nevertheless, after a few weeks at Berkeley, I do begin to feel more relaxed and even to enjoy myself. The castle is well built and comfortable with a turreted solar block attached to the keep. Set amongst green pastureland, it overlooks the banks of the Severn in the far distance. There are many common cranes, which fly over at dusk on their way back from the estuary, and I marvel how such a large bird can fly so effortlessly, with its legs and wings extended in the shape of a cross.

Berkeley lies midway between Gloucester to the north and Bristol to the south, and the land is very flat. More boring than the rolling hills of the Marches, yet somehow its very dullness manages to soothe. The days are long, warm and still, and the Berkeleys have a lovely garden. Young Maurice also makes a good companion, as he is thoughtful but talkative, with all the wisdom of a seven-year-old. Slowly my heart begins to approach some healing.

And as it does, I begin to feel more curious about the King. Try as I might, I cannot get used to calling him 'Lord Edward, the Father of the King'; I do not feel ready to bestow the crown on that fourteen-year-old youth whom Roger has taken to Scotland to baptise with warfare, even if everyone else has.

I have glimpsed the King once or twice under guard in the gardens, whilst entering or leaving, but only from a distance, and have not approached him. Thomas Gurney, who is the chief of his daily custodians, has told the Berkeleys that Edward is very moody, veering between bitter and angry recriminations and tearful self-pity laced with self-blame. I ask Gurney to let me know when it is one of his quieter days, as I do now intend to pay him a visit. Within a week, Gurney notifies me this time is as good as any, and escorts me up the uneven stairs to his holding cell in the keep.

Once admitted, I drop a deep curtsey, partly out of habit, and partly in prudence. Edward is sitting at a table next to his truckle bed, and is engaged in writing a letter. His straggling locks and beard are still mostly golden and untouched by grey, his good-looking face only a little more lined. He looks up, laying down his pen, and seems astonished. Of course he recognises me at once.

"There is no need to curtsey," he says gruffly. "Have they not told you I am only Lord Edward now?"

"You will always be a King to me," I say, rising. It is a statement of fact, and not borne out of any reverence.

"Have you come to gloat, Madame?" he demands.

I hope Gurney, who has left me alone as requested, was accurate in the assessment of the King's mood.

"I would not do that," I say, "for I, too, know what it is like to be locked up, apart from your loved ones, and how long each day can be."

My eye alights on the fine, fresh linen on his bed, the expensive carpet covering his table and the flagon of wine in front of him. He has pushed aside a plate of half-eaten meat, but I recognise it as the same fine fare our household was given that day.

"Although," I cannot resist saying, "my allowance was not as generous as yours."

He has the grace to look uncomfortable.

"Harrumph! Well, that wasn't my doing, you know."

"No? Well, I daresay you were led astray, as you were so often. Your Queen was kind to me in persuading you to relent ever so slightly."

"My Queen! Isabella! So beautiful, so pious and so charitable. And now she loves me not."

He buries his face in his hands and gives himself up to violent sobs. I allow some time for the heaving of his shoulders to abate and his convulsions to lessen.

"I am sure that is not true, sire," I say. "I have served your lady queen long enough in the past to know the affection she holds for you. Why, even today, my daughter informs me a parcel of sweetmeats has arrived for you from the Queen."

"Really?" he asks, uncovering his face. "Is that true?"

I nod but another spasm crosses his face.

"Cuckolded!" he shouts, banging his fist on the table. "Both of us cuckolded, Madame, by your damned husband."

I bow my head meekly and utter a quiet "yes". To my great surprise, Edward springs up from his chair and comes to stand next to me, taking my hand and chafing it in his own.

"What are we to do, my lady? My poor, poor lady! What are we to do?"

"I think there is very little we can do, sire. Except to remain calm, perhaps."

"You are right," he says glumly. "But you have your freedom now, Madame, and the comforts of your daily life with family around you, and I do not…"

His voice tails off in despair. He has said it as if he alone is responsible for my release, but I try not to mind, though I withdraw my hand.

"My confessor was a comfort to me in my imprisonment. I believe you have a great love for the Dominicans?"

"I am banned all contact with them now."

"Only the ones who assisted your escape, surely? They were not acting in your best interests. But you might benefit from the solace of a simple life in a more well-intentioned community. My grandfather, Sir Geoffrey de Joinville, spent his last years in great contentment with them."

He turns his back on me and throws himself down in his seat again with disgust.

"Ah, I see now where this is going! You are here on behalf of 'The Mortimer', after all: to persuade me to suffer myself to be locked up in a dungeon in Trim!"

"I was not speaking of the castle. Neither am I here on Lord Roger's behalf."

But I knew I could not be sure of either. Roger did want to lock him up in Trim, or elsewhere in Ireland, rather than permit him to go to any religious community. Was it fair, then, to mislead the Lord Edward into a fantasy?

"I only meant," I falter, "that maybe one day...it might be possible, in time, to lead a different life."

"You are right that I would welcome it. So right. I never asked to be King. I never wanted to be a King."

He puts his head in his hands again and I see this is true. He would have been happier as a common boatman or thatcher. If only he had not been heir to the throne. Despite everything, I feel genuinely sorry for him for the first time. I go up to him and lay a hand on his shoulder. You cannot do that to a king. But he is no longer the King.

"Lord Edward," I say, and now it is as if I am speaking to a child, "God knows I have very little influence over my husband these days. But I promise I will try my best for you."

I am not sure he has heard me.

"Oh, Hugh," he is muttering. "My poor, dear Hugh!"

"Forget Hugh!" I snap. "He was a cruel bastard. He got you into this trouble in the first place. If you must grieve for a man, then grieve for Piers."

I remember I do not have to wait for his dismissal anymore, and make for the door to call Gurney who is waiting outside.

"But I do," he moans piteously. "I do. Lady Joan, I do!"

Chapter 41

ROGER ARRIVES ON the 17th of September in the company of Richard of Monmouth. He is tired and irritable, and tells us he cannot stay long.

"I am needed at court," he says imperiously. The court is presently sitting at Nottingham. So it has been a long and arduous journey across country. In addition, he has only recently returned from the Scottish campaign, which has been an unmitigated disaster. The boy King is apparently furious with him, even though my lord was not in command all of the time. Roger is unrepentant.

"I told him so," he says contemptuously. But, apparently, there are other courtiers also pointing their finger at the unexpected failure of a seasoned campaigner.

"What they do not understand," he tells Thomas at the high table in the Great Hall, "is that Robert Bruce is an old man now and anxious for peace. He only gave orders to raid the North again when the new King was crowned, and we hadn't made any overtures to him as we did indeed promise him we would – from Hainault! He is a man you can negotiate with. He held back on our account during the invasion, but now he wants peace."

Lord Thomas seems surprised, but I, sitting near enough to hear, though not alongside Roger, am pleased. Our whole life has been blighted by war with the Scots. Why not make peace at last? How many future lives might be saved? No more Bannockburns or Kells. I speak up with conviction.

"My lords, I think peace is an excellent idea."

Roger nods and smiles at me warmly for the first time since his arrival. His clothes are still dirty from the road as he had no time to change before eating. But he is beginning to relax, as his face is flushed in the firelight and torchlight, for we are dining late on his account.

"You see, Lady Joan understands the sense of it, as always!" I am glad to hear him say this, but cannot help noticing how often he goes on to use the pronouns 'we' and even 'I' when he speaks of what should happen. He must be firmly in control then. I might be proud of him under other circumstances.

That night he comes to me. I thought I did not want him to, if he had the smell of the Queen on him, but find I do. He undresses, but only seems interested in private conversation.

"Gurney says you saw the King – I mean the Lord Edward, of course."

So he trips himself up occasionally on that one, as well!

"I did," I admit.

"I am very pleased. How was it?"

"I felt more than a little sorry for him."

Roger waves that away with an angry gesture of his hand.

"He locked you up for almost five years, Joan!"

"I know. I used to feel terrible anger towards him. But it has gone now and I feel better for it. He was, after all, under the influence of Despenser."

"He would never have changed, Joan. You know that – even with Despenser gone. He would have found another ill-chosen favourite."

"I suppose so. But he does make a pitiable sight. To have been brought so low! He does love the Queen in his own way. Did you know she still sends him presents?"

Roger scowls with bad temper.

"Oh yes," he says, "and now she thinks she might like to see him as well!"

"That would be good."

"No, Joan, it would not. It would be disastrous. Fortunately, Isabella also realises that any such action on her behalf would prejudice her son's position, and she dotes on her son."

"But her son is angry with you over Scotland, isn't he?"

"Oh yes. Because I made sure there was no major battle, and he was itching to cover himself with glory. I also made sure the life of the young brat was in no danger, and saved the lives of our English archers into the bargain. Unfortunately, there was an embarrassing night raid on our camp by the Scots, which made it all seem much worse than it really was."

"But you do want the boy to remain King? You have taken your oath of allegiance to him."

"Yes," Roger admits, drawing himself back from the brink of treachery. "What is more, he will make a better King than his father one day. He does not lack courage nor intelligence, even if he is wet behind the ears right now."

"And in the meantime you are ruling for him. Through the Queen. Not the Council! Does she do everything you tell her?"

"Pretty much. She has agreed to marry one of her daughters to Bruce's son. That's good."

He sits in his nightshirt before the fire, morosely nursing a goblet of wine. I realise he is not happy. In no way is he happy. I wait for him to speak. Finally, he does.

"I shall see him tomorrow."

"The Lord Edward?"

"Yes. We need a solution. There are still too many damned plots concerning him. William Shalford has written to me from Anglesey to warn me of yet another."

"Does the boy realise that, too?"

"Oh yes. As I say, he is not stupid."

"Edward is not willing to go to Ireland to be locked up in a castle. I thought maybe the Black Friary..."

Roger shakes his head, vehemently.

"We cannot trust them to keep him. No-one must know where he is, especially the friars."

I sigh, realising Roger had never intended to offer that as an option.

"Would it matter so much if he escaped? He is such a weak man, really."

"Don't be ridiculous! Of course it would. He may be weak, but he would be used as a pawn by those wanting to challenge the new King."

I have to concur this is true.

"Well, I think you will find him reasonably compliant tomorrow."

"Compliant? Therein lies the problem. He has never known his own mind. He can be so easily used by others. It would be better if he were dead."

I am shocked to the core.

"You cannot mean that," I say. "You cannot possibly mean it. Not the King. What about your oath of fealty to him? What about your mortal soul? Roger!"

But, when I look at him, his head has sunk onto his chest in sleep, and his goblet has fallen and rolls over with a tinny sound. He does not waken, but the last of the wine spreads across the tiles like a bloodstain. I cover him with a blanket and get into bed alone, full of foreboding.

The next morning he is up bright and early, calls for hot water to wash off his travel grime, and dresses in sumptuous black velvet. He wears his great ruby ring and also puts a thick, gold chain round his neck. This must be a gift from the Queen. It is a statement of office. He is full of urgency and says he will go and see Edward immediately. I offer to go with him but he says no. So I watch him cross the courtyard, with his black cloak billowing out in the autumn wind. The bright sun casts a shadow behind him like a giant black bat. Then he disappears up the stairs to the Lord Edward's cell. He is there a long time.

In the Great Hall later, I ask him how the audience went. Of course it was not his audience with the King, but the other way round. He laughs and says the King used a lot of words he could not possibly repeat, but in the end had been compliant.

"Compliant all round," he says with some satisfaction. "Given a hard choice."

I feel some relief but cannot question him further with the family all around. He is to leave on the morrow, and Thomas and Margaret have laid on a grand feast in his honour with dancers, minstrels and jesters – though to tell the truth, he has never cared much for the latter. Uncle Roger used to accuse him of being humourless. He does not come to my room that night.

But, in the morning, he seems sorrowful, and asks to see me before leaving. He has a present for me, which he forgot to bring me before. It is not a ruby I have no use for this time, but a pile of books, including the Roman Brut containing the history of King Arthur.

"They told me they took all your books," he said simply. "So I am returning them."

We embrace briefly but, when we part, he keeps hold of my hand.

"Tell me, Joan," he says. "I saw the other night you still have Avice with you. How old is she now?"

"I am not quite sure. In her seventies, at least."

"I cannot believe she is much use to you, my dear. Why, she is toothless and almost hairless, I imagine. Can you not get yourself a better serving woman?"

"No, you are wrong, Roger. You forget she was with me in prison all those years," I say firmly. "She is still my closest friend as a result, and completely trustworthy. Besides, she is so wise and knows so much, all about the best medicines and all the old skills and remedies."

"Well, I suppose that is true – she is certainly a useful woman. I had forgotten her many advantages," Roger conceded. "Though I am told Lady de Burgh finds it hard to understand."

I grimace. So there has been a complaint. I am not going to be disturbed by that. I am still mistress in my own house.

As I take my leave of him, I see him call Ockley and Gurney, and they converse earnestly together in the courtyard for a while. Then he is gone, as swiftly, hurriedly and irritably as he came, bound for Lincoln into which city the court has recently progressed.

After his departure, everyone seems a little fretful. Lord Thomas is not well and has to postpone a visit to the nearby manor of Bradley. Margaret is finding her pregnancy more burdensome, the children are querulous, and even the weather has turned wild, with the first of the autumn gales blowing up the river, and the noise of geese crying out in complaint. Avice says it is always so at the end of summer, but everyone will be right again soon.

On the next day, Sir William Beaukaire, a royal sergeant of arms, pays an unexpected visit, bearing a letter from the court for Lord Berkeley. Thomas is still not well, but spends a long time closeted with his guest, along with Ockley and Gurney.

That night, I am awakened by an odd, startled cry in the courtyard. It sounds muffled but unmistakably human. Avice is sleeping at the bottom of my bed but is not disturbed. She has become rather deaf of late. At any rate, if it made any impression on her at all, she soon settles back into her snoring. I slip out of bed and cross the floor to the window of the solar. The wind has dropped and there is an orange harvest moon, which is almost full, though part of it is obscured by clouds. An owl hoots in the distance. There is no-one in the quadrangle of the courtyard.

I am about to return to bed when two men appear below, from the direction of the outer bailey, coming towards the keep. They are carrying a long bundle of cloth between them. It must be heavy because they are struggling with it. They disappear into the tower where the King is kept. I wait a while, feeling uneasy without knowing why. Then one of the men returns. His hood has fallen from his head and I guess it is Ockley from the pallor of his bald head in the moonlight. He retraces his steps from the keep, around the corner and out of sight into the outer bailey. I wait some more but nothing else happens, though I can hear the low rumble of a horse and cart leaving. It takes me a goodly while to get back to sleep, wondering what could have been delivered to the keep at this time of night, but eventually I doze off.

In the morning there appears to be nothing amiss, until I am asked to attend Lord Thomas in the Hall and bring Avice with me. This is not surprising – perhaps his gastric complaint is worse and Avice can provide him with a remedy, though he has not used her before. Maybe Margaret has suggested he should.

I ask after his health with some concern, but he puts my fears at rest by saying he feels much recovered today, thanking me kindly.

He says he has something of importance to tell us, but clears his throat several times first, which I find intensely irritating.

"It's not my Margaret, is it?" I cry. "Or the baby?"

He shakes his head vigorously.

"No, no. Calm yourself, mother. They are both well." He clasps his hands together in front of him, clears his throat again, and leans forward across the table where we are seated.

"We have, however, had a most untoward event in the night. The Lord Edward has been commanded to God."

"Dead?" My heart lurches.

"I am afraid so, yes. Gurney has been telling me the Lord also suffered some gastric symptoms over the last few days. Yesterday, he complained bitterly of stomach ache and took to his bed. To my shame, I did not take much notice, having experienced the same thing myself. As have the boys, as you know."

"But you are fully recovered, and so are they!" I point out.

"Thankfully yes. But, this morning, the Lord Edward was found dead in his bed. He is still a royal personage, of course, and will need to be embalmed as quickly as possible. I wondered if there was any chance your woman Avice could be up to the task?"

I am astounded, but look at Avice who nods confidently. She has not done it herself, she says, but has seen it done many times before. In fact she assisted the surgeon with Lord Edmund, God rest his soul, if her mistress remembers? Only she does not have the same implements as a surgeon would – she must have knives, a saw and pliers too, if the heart is to be removed, as she expects it should.

Lord Thomas agrees the heart must be treated with especial care, as it is likely to be sent to the Queen. He assures her all will be supplied. The herb garden can supply lavender and rosemary in abundance to make the necessary oils, and the Berkeley kitchen is well stocked with spices. So Avice bustles off to the household servants to give instructions regarding everything needed. She is bristling with importance.

I stay on, however, to question my son-in-law further.

"Thomas," I say firmly. "Avice is a wonderful woman, and I love and trust her dearly, but she is very lowly in her station. We are talking about a former King's body here. Why cannot you wait until someone more qualified and eminent can be sent for?"

"I have my orders it should be done as quickly and discreetly as possible," says Thomas, quickly.

I stare at him incredulously.

"You have your orders? But how can you have any orders? The King has only just been found dead. This very morning!"

Thomas colours.

"Lady Joan, I must ask you not to question my judgement here."

I put a hand to my mouth to avoid retching.

"Dear God," I say, appalled. "Your orders came before he died. They did, didn't they? And his death is too sudden, too unexpected, for such a strong and healthy man."

"Lady Joan Mortimer. I must ask you not to speak in this manner! It is possible... I have known men die after a bad stomach ache for a few days! I must go to Bradley now. Then I have to write a letter to the King. Send word when all is done. I will provide a silver cup for the heart."

But he cannot repair his blunder over the orders. I leave him with turmoil in my heart.

It takes Avice all day. I do not dwell on the details of what she will have to do. All the soft organs must be carefully removed. Then the inner cavity of the corpse must be washed with alcohol and rosewater before being filled with spices, herbs, and cotton. Finally, there will be many layers of cloth to wrap around the reconstituted and newly sewn up body, to prevent the worst of the decay, finishing with waxed cloths. Avice is strong in body despite her years, and will not baulk at the task. I have no doubt she is able to do it competently enough. I am far more distressed at my suspicion the King has been murdered.

Inevitably, I remember my night-time vision, and ponder again over the heavy cloth taken into the keep by Ockley, and probably

Gurney. Then there was that cry. Could it have come from the Lord Edward? It must have been very loud to have been heard outside the keep, but then Edward had been a strong and healthy man.

In the evening, I climb the stairs with a heavy heart to the cell in the keep. William Beaukaire is on guard now. He must have brought the orders, I realise. And who would have sent him but Roger? For a moment, I think he will not let me in but, seeing who it is, he gives me a cursory nod.

The room is heavy with the smell of cloves and lavender. Avice is almost done. Thankfully, all the entrails have been taken away, along with the heart in the silver cup. Avice looks up as I enter. She looks tired but satisfied.

"There's only the cerecloth for his face now, Madame," she says. "Seems a shame to cover such a handsome one. I would have thought the King's face should be left exposed – at least for a little while. But these are my orders, Madame."

I nod and move over to the wrapped corpse, looking at the sad face of my erstwhile king one more time. Then I gasp.

"What is it, Madame?" asks Avice nervously. "Have I not done well?"

I collect myself and beam at her, hugging her tightly to my bosom.

"Avice, you have done wondrously well. I am very proud of you!"

Then I drop my voice to a low whisper, aware that Beaukaire is listening outside the room.

"There is only one thing, Avice, but say nothing now."

"What is that, Madame," asks Avice, still worried.

"This is not the King!"

We confer together back in the safety of my solar, with everyone else dismissed. At first, Avice does not believe me. She has been told he was the King by someone in authority and that is enough for her. She knows he is tall with long fair hair and is said to be handsome, and so was the corpse she has pored over so carefully today.

"But Avice, my dearest one, you have never seen the King!"

" I think I did once – before he was the Prince of Wales. I was quite young, but my father took me to London, and we saw him in a procession, far off like, but my father said it was him."

"Exactly! Far off – and it was years ago! But I have been at court, Avice, with Roger. Edward was the Prince then, at Langley. He took me to see his camel and I was as close to him then as I am to you now."

"What's a camel, Madame?"

"A fabulous beast. You would have loved it, Avice. But what I am saying is that I knew the King very well. That poor man in the cell was a reasonable likeness in age and build, and had fair hair, but it was not the King."

"You know best, Madame," Avice said in the end, only half believing me.

"You must not speak of it though, Avice. Not to anyone! I think we must pretend it was the King."

Thomas Berkeley spent the whole morning writing to the boy-King with his sad news. Would the son come to view his father? He does not. Neither does the Queen. A handful of local nobles visit during the next few days, to pay their respects, but none of them are particularly cognisant with the King. James Berkeley is Bishop of Exeter and he comes, but of course he is kinsman to Thomas. Then the cerecloth goes over the face for ever, and the body is placed in a shroud prior to its removal to Gloucester Abbey. Edward has always been fond of this abbey, so it comes as no surprise he is to be buried there, and not Westminster. After all, he is no longer the King, but a mere lord of the realm.

I say nothing, but have second thoughts about Avice's involvement and confess to her I may have been mistaken. After all, death can alter the features. I could have been wrong. Avice is more than happy with this.

But I know I am not wrong. I think once more about the heavy burden wrapped in cloth that Ockley and Gurney carried *into* the keep that night. I remark the news that a porter has gone missing, run away, says Lord Berkeley, though there seems no reason why he should. More than anything, I remember that low rumble of a cart leaving the castle in the night.

Chapter 42

DECEMBER 1327 – GLOUCESTER AND WORCESTER

THE FUNERAL CORTEGE left Berkeley for the Abbey of St Peter in Gloucester, sixteen miles to the north, on the 19th of October. The abbot supplied his own carriage, which was draped in black canvas. Inside, the embalmed body was dressed in royal robes and laid in a lead coffin placed inside a wooden one. Layer upon layer of deceit, I thought, watching it rumble off into a low-lying autumn mist. It seemed poignant when a group of cranes flew overhead in the shape of crosses, as if they were paying their last respects, though I knew that was fanciful.

But I had other pressing matters to occupy my thoughts when the hearse disappeared, for Margaret was in labour and in sore need of my comfort and assistance.

Thankfully, all went well for Margaret and her new son, whom she named Roger; so two months later, I am present in Gloucester for the Lord Edward's funeral, having made it known to my lord I strongly wished to be there.

It might not be Westminster but it is certainly a grand affair. The hearse now bears the gilt images of the lions of England on its side, with the four evangelists at each corner. Around it stand eight sculptured angels, covered in gold leaf, appearing to waft incense. On the bier itself there is a finely carved wooden figure of the former King wearing cloth of gold and a gilt crown. There are hundreds of candles burning all around and it is a sumptuous sight.

Oak barriers have been erected to keep the crowds away, for there is already much weeping, and imaginings of martyrdom from a fickle public. The requiem mass is sung by the monks of the abbey, and I think how amazed the man really lying here would be to see all this pomp for his demise!

My lord himself has made the arrangements, and made a pledge that the eventual tomb will be even more beautiful. He is wearing a black tunic to express his deep mourning when he comes to the west door of the abbey to greet me and escort me to my rightful place as his wife, sitting next to him. The Queen enters last, with her son, and is seated several rows in front. No doubt the appearance of the Mortimers together will lead to whispered tongue wagging in the rest of the congregation. Well, I will play my part – up to a point. When the ceremony is finally over, I lean towards my husband and hiss in his ear.

"How can you get away with this? What on earth are you thinking of?"

I know I have succeeded in startling him, but he manages to smile and bow and play his allotted role. I leave the abbey alone, with my head held high, without looking back.

My questions bring him to my lodgings for a private meeting the very same evening.

"How did you know?" he asks me, curtly.

"I went to inspect Avice's work."

"I should have guessed you might," he says, remembering, no doubt, I have always been robust in such matters. "Does Avice know?"

"I told her. But she does not know what to think."

"You must tell her you were mistaken!"

"For her own good!" Roger adds.

"I already have."

Roger relaxes slightly.

"Then it will only be us who know."

"And Sir William Beaukaire, and Ockley and Gurney presumably?"

"Yes."

"And Thomas, our son-in-law?"

"Of course."

"He will perjure himself on your behalf then."

"If asked."

"What about Isabella? She did not seem overly sorrowful at the funeral."

"Yes, the Queen knows. She was most insistent he be spared."

"And the young King?"

"Not yet."

"Do you intend to tell him?"

"Yes, I do. It will be essential, to keep him on our side. He grows more kingly every day. Or would like to."

"That is only to be expected. He has turned fifteen. Ready to be married. Hardly a boy anymore!"

"But still six years off his maturity. Much may be done in that time."

I consider this, quietly.

"And where is the Lord Edward?"

"Where do you think?"

I remember the low rumble of the cart leaving Berkeley in the night.

"In Ireland. I think he was taken to Berkeley Quay, and sailed down the Bristol Channel from there."

Roger chuckles.

"He was, but has not gone as far as Ireland. He is back in Corfe, for the time being."

"Maltravers is not as gentle with him as Thomas. He would be better with the Black Friars in Trim."

"No. I will move him to Trim Castle if there is any more trouble. But there shouldn't be, providing this doesn't get out."

I exhale long and hard at the knowledge of his audacity.

"Your concern for him continues to amaze me!" Roger says. "But then you are a better and more godly person than I."

"I am concerned for you, too. For your mortal soul. I cannot tell you how relieved I was to see Avice had not worked on the King! Can you really tell me you only stayed your hand because of the Dowager Queen? Or did you baulk at regicide, in the end?" I do not intend to address Isabella as the Queen anymore, though I note Roger always does so.

"Perhaps. Of course, they will all think I did it, anyway."

"You ordered someone else's murder without cause. I think it was the porter. He was a tall, fair, strapping fellow and disappeared the next morning. Thomas said he must have run off, but I saw a body being carried into the keep that night."

"He had no family." Roger says.

"That doesn't make it right."

"Perhaps not. But it had to be done." Roger hesitates. "No-one must ever know, unless I command it. Mind that Joan! I order you to obey," and he grabs my arm fiercely, "I have to be able to trust you too."

I am shocked and pull my arm away. My lord has never done anything like this before. He is much changed.

"It seems it will not benefit anyone to be told the truth," I say, sadly. "Unless you do, one day."

"No, never. It would implicate Isabella."

"Will you stay with me tonight?" I ask suddenly. "That would be seen as seemly after escorting me to the requiem."

"No, I cannot. I am expected back. We leave for Worcester tomorrow, where the court will spend Christmas."

"You too?"

"Yes. There is much to do in arranging the boy's wedding and arguing for terms with Scotland to be agreed."

The following day, I am making my own dispirited preparations to return to Ludlow, after the long sojourn at Berkeley, when a royal messenger arrives. I am commanded to take Avice with me to Worcester, where the King will reside that night. I am further instructed, by Lord Mortimer himself, to prepare the servant woman to speak the truth – the whole truth – before the King and to corroborate her account if necessary. So help me, God, I thought! He has decided it is time to tell the young King.

I call Avice to me at once and give orders for my small retinue to change its plans.

"Avice," I say, "you remember what I said when I found you about to lay the cerecloth on the Lord Edward's face at Berkeley?"

"Yes, my lady. You said it was not the Lord Edward at all. But then you told me you must have been mistaken."

"Yes, Avice, I did. But I told you that to reassure you and calm your anxiety. What I told you first was the truth. It was not the former King. Now my Lord Roger has summoned us both to Worcester, where you are to tell the present King the truth in private. That his father is not in fact dead."

Avice clutches at her cheeks.

"It's not my fault, Madame!" she cries.

"No, of course it is not. You were asked to do a job in good faith and you did it well. Don't be frightened, my dear. Nothing will happen to you. I will be with you. We are required to tell the King the truth now. But no-one else. Never, ever anyone else. Do you understand?"

Avice nods but is not reassured.

"Will they put me to death, Madame?"

"No, no, they will certainly not do that. I would not allow it! The Dowager Queen knows already. That's why she did not appear as grief-stricken as she might in the Abbey, when she was presented with the silver cup in which you had placed the heart. She must have told her son, but he wants confirmation from, well…you, as an independent observer."

Avice continues to clutch herself, around her scraggy breasts this time.

"It's wicked to tell lies, Madame!"

I sigh.

"I know, Avice. But it was the Queen and my lord who did that! We will only be telling the truth. And at least they have not foreshortened the Lord Edward's life, as some people are already saying behind their backs. He is quite safe. It is better for all that he is thought dead, to keep him safe. Only the present King needs to know. I imagine he will be very grateful to you."

Avice hesitates.

"And I shan't get into trouble for it?"

"No Avice, you really will not."

So we went to Worcester. I was not asked to be present with Avice at her private audience with the King, to my surprise and anxiety. Perhaps they thought me too close to Lord Mortimer to believe me. Or else, the boy King was not aware Avice was my serving woman, and my lord wanted to keep it that way. That was more likely.

I was glad when she returned with a smile on her face. I did not question her unduly about what was said, and we promised we would never speak of it again. Avice was more than happy with the two silver groats the King gave her for her trouble – almost double what a mason might earn in a day, she said proudly. All for her, and my, how kindly and graciously he had thanked her! I was heartily relieved. For all their reassurances, it was not inconceivable that Avice could have been arrested and tortured, though I had trusted Roger would not allow that. There seemed to have been no doubt cast on her story from the King.

How shocked that young man must be. He must be so angry in his heart at having his fate even more closely bound with Roger Mortimer and his mother now; even angrier than over Scotland! I doubt he will ever truly forgive them.

Worcester is getting ready for Christmas but I make my own way back to Ludlow, keenly aware I am no longer welcome at court. At least some of the family will be with me. Not Margaret, for it is too soon after her confinement to travel. Maud is not in Powys either, because her husband John is now Lord Chamberlain of the Royal Household, a good advancement for him, and so they will stay at court with Geoffrey. Young Roger remains in Ireland but John will be paying a short visit, and of course the younger girls will be there, along with Edmund and Elizabeth.

All are well, with the exception of Isabella. The four-month absence emphasises how weak she has grown, worse than when she returned from the priory, so I can no longer blame her confinement there. Her cheeks are flushed with an unnatural redness, and she is breathless at the least effort. I grow increasingly concerned, for I know that, whatever else I think of Lady Elizabeth de Burgh, I know she would have given my sickly daughter the best of care in my absence.

Chapter 43

WINTER 1328 – MY ISABELLA

ON JANUARY THE 26th, King Edward III was married to Philippa of Hainault in the Minster at York by Archbishop Melton. There was an audience of thousands but I was not invited. Nor would I have gone so far, with my Isabella so ill. Nevertheless, I was glad the young King now had his own confidant.

Shortly afterwards, Queen Isabella's final surviving brother, Charles, took ill and died. He was the last of the Capet monarchs, for Isabella herself obviously could not claim the throne, as a woman. She claimed it for her son instead. The French preferred to hand it on to Philip of Valois, Charles' cousin. I foresaw endless troubles over this and the potential for yet more warfare.

However, an official delegation was sent to Robert Bruce, offering to recognise his Scottish independence, and to cement it by marrying Queen Isabella's daughter, Joan of the Tower, to Robert's infant son, David. The borders would be restored and monies paid in reparation for damage, by the Scots. It appeared the young King had submitted to Roger's plan, however unwillingly, trapped by the secret knowledge they now shared. Henry of Lancaster was displeased but could do nothing.

I thought it a fine decision. My son John, staying in Ludlow into the New Year, most emphatically did not. Fiery and combative as ever, he professed himself disgusted at his father's influence in this treaty. He accused him of losing his backbone and was sure the new King could not really approve of Scotland being allowed to 'win the war', as he put it.

"When Father is dead," he declared with youthful belligerence, "King Edward can fight back and I shall support him. So will Henry of Lancaster! We will get Scotland back."

I was mortified.

"How can you speak of your father like that? May I remind you he fought most bravely at Bannockburn? And that Scotland has never truly been ours? The Lancastrians have always complained about the Scots, but they rarely lifted a finger to assist our royal armies against them!"

John was unrepentant and merely informed me, arrogantly, that this was all ancient history now, and that he would do better than his father at tourney and eventually in battle! Was this the child I had raised? I felt cut to the quick and we parted coolly.

It did not help when Geoffrey sent me a sardonic letter along with his New Year gift and all his good wishes.

'He is using the Royal seal now, and against Henry of Lancaster, no less,' he wrote. 'Appointments here and appointments there. Expect great building works to disturb your peace, mother. Let the folly commence!'

I am frustrated that I am continually having to defend their father to his sons. To be fair, I really cannot see anything wrong in the appointments and grants which Geoffrey mentions. I am especially delighted that the young Robert Clifford has all of his lands and estates restored, including Skipton Castle. I am relieved that Lady Eleanor de Clare, the widow of Hugh Despenser, has been released from the Tower with her children.

Furthermore, I am pleased to hear Sir Hugh Turpington has been made keeper of Newcastle Emlyn in Wales, after his long and dedicated service, and that John Hothum, whom we long relied on in Ireland, has all his debts excused and is appointed Bishop of Ely. No doubt Adam Orleton will be advanced in his ecclesiastical ambitions as well, in time, with the agreement of the Pope.

Another long-time ally is made Treasurer, and another has become the King's Chamberlain. Both good men in Roger's eyes. It also seems fitting he should reward the Deputy Constable, who secured his escape from the Tower, an annual income of forty pounds for life, and grant his own cousin, John Fiennes, the right to sell his English lands to make up for the debt incurred whilst Roger was with him in France.

Thomas Gurney is given the right of free warren on his estates, and John Maltravers made Steward of the Royal Household. Perhaps those favours could be seen as more suspicious, but it was not as if they had done anything wrong, whatever anyone thinks. The Earl of Kent, who is now married of his own free will, to Roger's cousin, Margaret Wake, is given most of the Despenser manors, but is surely entitled to them, having supported Roger and the Queen in their invasion.

As I say in my reply to Geoffrey, it was not as if his father was rewarding himself unduly, though I did wonder where all the money for the new building was coming from. Neither is he Earl of March as yet. He has only made himself Keeper of the Peace in the local counties and been awarded a small manor in Church Stretton.

I knew he had great plans for the marriages of Catherine, Agnes and Beatrice, but he had kept his promise to endow Isabella with a small grant in view of her chronic ill health and the unlikelihood of her ever attracting a husband. Geoffrey said a request had been made for his brother Roger to marry Pembroke's widow, the much older Marie St Pol, but I thought that unlikely to be granted, given my second son's preference for the mercenary life in Ireland.

Geoffrey went on to assure me there was plenty of money to be had. Perhaps it was this, more than anything else he said, that gave me some disquiet.

Geoffrey was correct about the building works. They begin immediately after my birthday, on the Feast of the Purification, at the beginning of February. A new solar and garderobe tower are to be added to the north range at Ludlow. So then there will be a solar block on either side of the Great Hall. In addition, a new chapel, dedicated to St Peter ad Vincula, is to be built in the outer bailey, keeping Roger's promise after escaping from the Tower on St Peter's feast day.

The erection of this chapel does not interfere with the daily life of my household, but the building of the new solar block certainly does. To begin with, the kitchens had to be moved to the other side of the courtyard. Then, from dawn to dusk, the inner bailey is filled with dust and the incessant hammering of masons, as carts bearing limestone roll in and blocks are unloaded for shaping. The earth dug from the foundations is reloaded onto the waggons for removal in return. A temporary wooden lodge is erected in the bailey for the use of the masons, whose job it is to cut and shape the stones whilst their labourers mix the lime mortar.

The white dust seems to get everywhere, penetrating into the Great Hall and even the upper floor of our original solar. By March, Isabella has developed terrible fits of coughing in which she brings up fresh blood. They leave her exhausted. Her cheeks remain flushed but her slight body is wasting away so that her eyes seem enormous in a girlish but gaunt face. She is fifteen but still has the appearance and body of a child.

I demand repeated visits from our physician but there seems little he can do. He tells me he believes my daughter's heart is failing now, and this is making her breathing worse.

Isabella is a pious girl who never complains, but I can see her developing an almost translucent quality to her face, which seems to increase daily. In a panic, I surmise this indicates the final stage of life. I must take her away out of this noisy, dust-laden atmosphere. But where? Wigmore would be little better, as it is suffering its own building works and repairs to restore its former comfort. It is most unlikely Isabella would survive any major travel, especially to Ireland, or to London where the miasmas are bad. Even the mild and gentle Berkeley airs might prove a journey too far.

I am pondering the relative benefits of the manors of Pembridge or Stanton Lacy when Avice tells me there is a healing well just off the road to Church Stretton, near Minton. Roger has recently received the manor of Church Stretton, so we could go there. It is a bare fifteen miles on a good road. I will send a party of servants there in advance, to make sure it is comfortable. Most importantly, Avice can take us to the well that she says has been known to perform miracles through the excellence of its assuredly holy water.

We set off within days, having received good reports from the servants. The manor lies to the south of the small town, but off the Bristol Road, so all is quiet and peaceful. It is sheltered by the hill of the Long Mynd and only a few miles from the healing well itself. Isabella is cheerful, excited even, in the waggon. She is not for eating much, though I try her with the daintiest titbits and delicacies. Nevertheless, she declares herself feeling better already, having left the dust-ridden castle behind. We are only a small number, escorted by a few men at arms. Isabella has my full attention and that of old Avice, whom she has known so well. Her own maidservants have been sent on ahead to the manor to make all ready and comfortable for our arrival.

We reach the manor without event and settle in, but on that night Isabella takes a turn for the worse. I sit up with her, gently sponging her dark curls, which are plastered down with sweat. In the morning, I realise she is too ill to be taken to the well and bid riders go there to fetch the water back, under Avice's direction.

Whilst we wait, I talk to her of everything that has happened in her short life. How hot and beautiful it had been in Gascony when I was carrying her, about the nursery days in Wigmore, the peacocks which intrigued her so as an infant, the Christmases, the dogs and horses, the visits to Trim. I cannot hold back a sob when I recall Southampton and the Windwhistle Tower.

"But I only really remember the dwelling house there," Isabella says with an effort. "I liked it there. Especially after John left. You were always with us and I didn't mind being poor. It was a good time for me, mother, and so exciting when Father Judas was allowed to take us out into the town."

Avice returns with the healing water in the afternoon and Isabella drinks deeply of it, saying she does indeed feel very thirsty. Afterwards, she smiles at me as I prepare to sit up with her another night.

"You must let me go, mama," she says. "The nuns at Chicksands taught me not to be afraid of death. I know you think they did not take enough care of me but they did, you know. There is worse than death – much worse – in the world around us. If the water does not work, you must let me go." She closes her eyes and sleeps then, better than before, although her breathing is still laboured.

After a few hours, I am initially relieved to see the flush leave her cheeks. But it is replaced by an icy pallor. By dawn, she is scarcely breathing at all, and there are no more words. A priest is sent for, to administer Holy Unction. By terce, she has slipped away and lies cold but peaceful, no longer racked by coughing. It is as if the healing water has at least eased her passage out of this world and into the next.

Avice holds me, weeping and wailing with me. After a little while, she asks if she should carry out the embalming. I shake my head.

"No, Avice. Please no! I could not bear it. She must remain undisturbed. We will go to Wigmore straightaway and I will send a messenger on to the abbey so they are ready to receive her body for prompt burial."

Wigmore Castle was still under maintenance and repair, so I stayed in the abbey, in rooms I had occupied once before, during domestic improvements. It seemed more fitting. Despite all the new activity, I was saddened to see the little town somewhat shrunken. Folk had moved out during our six-year absence with their source of revenue dried up. I wondered if it would ever recover. The work being carried out must be encouraging, at least. Once again, I wonder how it can be afforded, in addition to the new building at Ludlow.

Edmund, who joins me at the Abbey, says there are no worries on that score; his father has been awarded all the land in Shropshire formerly held by the Arundels, as well as Chirk, and the great Lordship of Denbigh, which the Despensers once held. He also has temporary custody of Glamorgan. Naturally, the rewards are said to come out of the King's gratitude, but the Dowager Queen is generally held to be responsible. I suppose I should be glad of this sudden access to good fortune, but only feel more saddened. Perhaps Geoffrey was correct in his assessment after all.

The Prior receives us with the greatest deference and dignity. It is a very simple, quiet and private committal. Besides myself, Edmund and his wife, only the younger daughters: Joan, Catherine, Agnes, Beatrice and even little Blanche attend – it seems appropriate. Joan has the most intimate memories of their sister. I would have wished Edmund's brothers and father to be there, of course, but it was impossible, given the distances involved and my desire for a speedy burial. It was a solemn Requiem Mass and Brother Benedict will record it in the Chronicle. Afterwards I sit down to write to Roger with the bad news, knowing it will not be unexpected or come as a great shock to him.

Before their departure a few days later, Edmund ushers a bashful and blushing Elizabeth Badlesmere into my presence to give me some good news. It is rather early to say, but she is sure she is with child and hopes it could prove to be a Mortimer heir.

"God bless you both!" I say. "This is happy news indeed." It is true. I already have several grandchildren, but they are all Berkeleys or Charltons, whereas this one will be a Mortimer.

"Thank you for telling me at this time. It will make my grief a little easier to bear."

"Only we thought we would not tell Father immediately," Edmund says gruffly. "Just in case. In his present mood, he would likely be after lands and titles for the poor child already!"

I smile.

"You too, Edmund? Do you also condemn your father like Geoffrey and John?"

"We only wish he would pay you more attention, mother. Me and Geoffrey both."

"I did not say you were not justified," I reply. "No, far from it. But this period cannot last forever. Just as the King – I mean the former King – became tired of Damory and Audley in time, perhaps the Queen will find a new favourite."

The only flaw in this argument was that I felt our best years slipping away. They already seemed to have slipped away from me, after everything that had happened.

"In the meantime, I am afraid we must be content with what we are given."

Chapter 44

BY THE TIME MAY arrives, I do not feel as sanguine – my Lord Roger has not come to visit me in our grief. The building goes on apace, with the masons paid extra to work every daylight hour and finish the garderobe tower. The carpenters, tilers and glaziers have already moved into the solar, closely followed by the painters and sculptors.

Roger has confirmed that Joan, who is now sixteen, will marry his fifteen-year-old ward, James Audley, in Hereford Cathedral on the 31st of May. This has been arranged for some time. But now it appears there will be a double wedding, for a match has been arranged between twelve-year-old Catherine and the fourteen-year-old Thomas Beauchamp, also lately one of Roger's wards. It does not come as a total surprise, as Catherine's presence was requested at court last month so she could visit her father and meet the young Warwick.

Thomas was granted the title of Earl two years ago, after the invasion, but of course remained in wardship. He had a long wait for the title, as his father, Gaveston's 'Black Hound of Arden', died when Thomas was but an infant. At the time, there were rumours Edward II had arranged for the old Earl to be poisoned in revenge for Piers, and for not supporting him at Bannockburn, but this was long forgotten. His boy now appeared sturdy and healthy enough to merit the title, and was likely to be among the first cohort of the new King's knights in due course.

So here it begins, I think: the first of the earls, as Roger told me. If young Joan was a little put out that her big day was to be shared, and the choice of bridegroom likely to eclipse her own, she tried not to show it, having, I don't mind saying, inherited much of my good sense. Catherine, on the other hand, was thrilled and positively aglow on her return from court.

I fear she is too young to know her own mind and is swept away by the excitement of it all. But Catherine insists she really did like Thomas Beauchamp and knew they would be happy together. Knew! I had not been as confident at her age, though I had been happy...once. Still, there was no point in deflating the child.

Of course, the whole family will attend and Ludlow must be ready for the feasting and entertainment of illustrious guests afterwards, even if the paint on the walls is scarcely dry. I understand this and am already being driven frantic by the dual arrangements.

Then I learn from my lord that Queen Isabella will be attending, along with Edward and Philippa, the new royal couple. This means I will be required to give precedence to the Queen at the event, even though I am the mother of the brides and the lady of the castle. Now I realise the real reason for all that urgency in preparing the new buildings. It is for the Queen, though that title belongs by right to young Philippa, married yet still waiting to be crowned. I know I will not be admitted to the new block, with its exceptionally commodious sanitary arrangements of no less than four chutes.

I watch without comment whilst silken bed linen, embroidered with castles of love, and matching hangings, arrive and are borne inside, along with splendid tapestries and expensive rugs. They are not for my use. I will remain in the opposite solar block, separated by the expanse of the Great Hall. But my husband's mistress will be under the same roof. The shame of this stings like a wasp, and sickens me. Ludlow is my inheritance as a de Joinville, even though I gave it away at that church door. I could have refused hospitality to any other woman but not the Queen.

In a fit of uncharacteristic anger, I tear the cloth containing my supper, and that of my ladies, off the table in the solar, sending food and plates crashing to the floor. Avice comes in, startled, and makes to pick up the pieces.

"Leave them!" I scream at her. "You shall not do it. Send for one of *his* lackeys instead to wait on us!"

Avice scuttles away in shock. She has never seen me like this. In her haste to fetch help, she misses her footing and falls down the last few stairs from the solar. I hear her cries for help bleating out like a modest sheep who does not really want to bother you, but who is nevertheless in pain and cannot help it. I am mortified and blame myself bitterly when I am told Avice has taken to her bed, unable to walk. I send for Gilbert of Ludlow, who is cautious in his appraisal, saying her leg will heal in time, though she will be afflicted with a pronounced limp. He reminds me needlessly of the woman's great age.

And still the finery and sumptuous goods pour in. There is silverware for the hall, with gilt cups. At least they bear my arms, as well as my lord's. A great curtain, depicting scenes from Welsh history, also arrives for the hall, with another arras tapestry embroidered with butterflies. Tunics and armour come, intended for a celebratory joust. Then, on the very day I am due to embark for Hereford with my excited daughters, finally the peacocks appear! They make me feel like crying. Of course, the girls are hugely impressed with all this finery, thinking themselves the cause, and I do not disillusion them.

There is a new Bishop of Hereford, as Adam Orleton has moved on to the see of Worcester, launched on an upper trajectory both within the Church and its temporal realms, having also become Lord Treasurer. I am glad he has gone. For the wedding party is housed within the Bishop's Palace at Hereford, whilst the royal party lodges in the castle, to the south east of the Cathedral, close to the river.

I am relieved when Roger joins the family the evening before the wedding. Although he does not stay the night, he sits with me in the Cathedral to watch Joan and Catherine wed. Everything is managed discreetly so no-one would have known of any difficulty for the family or royal party.

It is very different on our return to Ludlow, even though I have most of my children around me, except for young Roger who stayed in Ireland, and John, still sore over Scotland, who refused to attend his father's triumph.

Ludlow shines like the legendary Camelot in sunlight. Its brand new solar block impresses all the guests. They exclaim at the lavish decoration of the Great Hall, with its tables so splendidly dressed with silverware and gilt. The new arras is much admired, and the food and wine pronounced second to none. The most accomplished minstrels play from the gallery.

Only the young King does not seem to enjoy himself. Naturally, he sits at the head of the table, but his mother occupies the seat on his left with Roger Mortimer on his right. She therefore displaces not only myself but also Philippa, who is relegated to sit beside the newly married Audleys, next to her mother-in-law. At least I can sit between Roger and the Beauchamps. Only Roger is continually leaning rudely over the King, to speak to Isabella. No wonder the young King scowls. I spend most of my time chatting with my new son-in-law, the young Earl of Warwick, and am pleased to find him intelligent, courteous and charming, for all his youth. Maybe Catherine was right after all. They certainly pay each other loving attentions.

When the dancing begins, I excuse myself on grounds of the heat, but in truth because I have no desire to stay and watch Roger lead a laughing Isabella onto the floor. I take some tasty morsels of food with me, wrapped up in a bundle, intending to take them to Avice in her sick bed, but stop by the Chapel of St Mary of Magdalene first, to say a prayer for her. I thought it would be deserted at this hour, for the chaplains are paid to pray in the newly consecrated Chapel of St Peter ad Vincula.

So I am surprised to see a tall, fair figure rise from his knees in the gathering gloom as I enter. When he turns, I see it is Edmund, the Earl of Kent, half-brother to the old King. How alike they are, at least physically! He is a wedding guest in his own right, as the husband of Roger's maternal cousin, Margaret Wake, as well as being part of the royal cohort.

He looks slightly abashed at being found absent from the feasting by Lady Mortimer herself, and bows to me humbly when I bob him a curtsey.

"Forgive me, Madame, for trespassing in your lovely chapel."

"Not at all," I say. "It is for anyone who feels the need for prayer."

He smiles ruefully.

"Well, as you can probably guess, my prayer was for the soul of my poor brother, the Lord Edward. I could not help but wonder what he would have made of this night."

Afterwards, I could not say whether it was compassion for the Earl that drove me, or revenge on the dancing couple next door, but the devil suddenly took my tongue.

"Don't grieve so, my lord. The Lord Edward is safe and well."

The Earl starts, and his eyes narrow. There are those who say he lacks brainpower, but I believe this is because he has such a pleasant and open face. He is certainly no fool.

"What do you mean?" he asks me, sharply.

My heart beats palpably against my ribs. I feel suddenly afraid at the enormity of what I have said.

"I meant only," I explain, with some difficulty, "that he will be safe and well in the arms of God. That is all."

But I can tell he does not believe me. He offers me his arm.

"May I escort you back to the revels, my lady?"

I shake my head.

"I think not. I am not enjoying the dancing. There is also a very old and dear servant of mine who is sick and I promised to look in on her."

"I do not blame you." Kent says simply. "You are a most loyal lady, are you not?"

I knew he was not referring to my devotion to Avice. He is an understanding and compassionate man.

"I try to be, my lord."

"I imagine it must be extremely difficult," he replies, softly.

We part outside the round chapel, but I am aware of his eyes boring into my back as I make my way back to my own quarters.

Avice was the one person I might have told about this unguarded conversation, but I find her flushed and a little distracted, plucking at the bedclothes. She is not in pain, she says, no not at all, but would welcome a glass of watered wine. I saw the woman I have engaged to look after Avice has already given her one. So I feed her the tasty morsels saved from the feast instead.

"That's very good," Avice says, nodding her head merrily, like a mildly demented doll. "Very, very good. Fancy my little Joan and Catherine marrying earls!"

I do not correct her by saying that only Catherine has become a Countess.

"I want to hear all about it, mind. But what are you, their mother and the Lady of Ludlow, doing away from the ceremonies, coming to see plain old me? You must go back straightaway."

Only I did not have the heart. I feel tired and unsettled by my encounter with Kent, and seek the privacy of my own room, as all the ladies are at the feast. Would Roger notice my absence? If he did, he would probably be relieved.

Could I possibly expect him to join me tonight? Surely not.

He does not, but I maintain a dignified air on the morrow.

Chapter 45

LATER IN 1328 – SONS COME HOME

IN THE MORNING, Edmund and Geoffrey both assure me their father stayed up all night, drinking with the guards. I do not think Edmund a good judge of this, as I know he would have retired early with his pregnant wife. Geoffrey is more credible but clearly trying to spare my feelings, as he had not stayed up the whole time himself.

There is riding out and hawking the next day for entertainment, before a joust in the afternoon. I do not go to either, as I see Avice take a turn for the worse, and am beyond caring what people think of me. The next day, the royal party are away to Worcester via Bromyard, gone as suddenly as they came – and Roger was gone with them, leaving me behind.

Their next journey would be to Scotland for another wedding: that of Princess Joan to Robert Bruce's infant son. Little Joan Makepeace, as the Scots have begun to call her, is only seven. Yet Isabella seems resigned to let her go. Her sulky royal son will stay with Henry of Lancaster, though she will take good care to take the Privy Seal with her. Lancaster shares the boy's opinion of the Scottish treaty. He demanded a parliament be held in the north to discuss it. Except he did not attend, having learnt such tactics from his late brother. But he was not the only earl to disobey the summons. Neither Kent nor Norfolk were there either.

Back at Ludlow, I am hardly aware of these matters, as I have assumed the nursing of Avice myself. It has been too long for such an old woman to take to her bed, though there was little choice as her broken hip bone remained too painful to allow walking. She sinks quickly with an infection in the end, though passes away peacefully.

I am inconsolable and blame myself repeatedly for her fatal fall. Of course, Avice was very old and, apart from our time together in captivity, I had given her a good life. But that fails to comfort me. I have lost my most loyal, faithful servant and my truest friend. Avice has gone forever, and I feel truly and terribly alone.

Worse was to follow: Geoffrey went to Scotland with his father but returned to Ludlow in August with more bad news. He collected Edmund on his way so they could tell me together. Young Roger was going to join his father and brother in Scotland but now he was dead. There would be no marriage to Marie St Pol, even though he had agreed to it in the end, and the King had granted his permission. Geoffrey had few details but said the death was sudden and unexpected – as if he had been taken by the swiftest hand of God.

"Father is arranging for his body to be brought back to Wigmore," he told me. " He will join us as soon as he can. And he will settle Roger's Irish lands on John."

This seemed fitting, as Edmund would inherit the lordship of all the English lands, and Geoffrey his grandmother's French estates. Geoffrey pronounced himself perfectly content, even though he was older than John, for he had no love for Ireland, and Edmund agreed.

"Why has my lord not come at once?" I asked in my misery. Even though my son Roger had grown apart from us all, I still remembered the child he had once been, and grieved for that. How I wished I had visited him sooner!

"Father needs to take precautions against Lancaster," Geoffrey explained. "He has advised the King to ban all armed meetings and followings, and is busy making sure all those in a position of authority can be trusted."

"Is it as bad as that?" I said in alarm. "Does Lancaster have so many followers?"

"We are not entirely sure. But his behaviour when the court was at Lincoln was threatening. He had a small army with him then, and was shouting abuse at Queen Isabella."

"In the presence of the King?" asked Edmund in surprise.

"Yes. Though that was no bad thing. It shook the lad and he knows he must rely on Father now, should there be any rebellion."

"But what are the grounds for it?"

"Oh, Lancaster has a long list of grievances. He says that Princess Joan has been married to a traitor. He also complains about the Queen's expenditure and Father's taking too much land – with some justification. Finally, he accuses them of doing away with the old King, as many now say they did."

"Doing away with the King," I broke in on my sons' conversation. "That is not true!"

They both look at me with shameful faces.

"You have to admit his death was very convenient," Edmund says, as gently as he can.

So they do not know, I realise. They do not know, and I am not to tell them if Roger has not. Perhaps they need protection by not knowing. I change my mode of attack abruptly.

"And how can David Bruce possibly be a traitor at the age of three?"

"Well, his father certainly was," counters Geoffrey.

"Was he? Was he really? For fighting over his own lands? The Lancasters never fought at Bannockburn you know. Wasn't that treacherous? I am pleased your father has made peace and that you, and Edmund, and John, will not have to spill your blood on any Scottish or Irish soil. At least your brother Roger did not die in battle!" I had held back my tears until now, but suddenly they burst forth.

Edmund took me in his arms.

"Come, mother! Sit yourself down. Shall I ask Elizabeth to come to you?"

"No," I say. "She must not be upset in her condition. I shall be calm again."

"He will come soon, mother," Geoffrey reassures me. "It has hit him hard, too. But he needs to come armed and to raise an even bigger army at Gloucester, before the next Parliament. Lancaster is raising men in London, so Father will take them from Wales and the Marches. I believe the King and his mother will prevail with his help. After all, why would anyone seriously want to put Henry of Lancaster on the throne? Edward III is the true King."

He did not add that his father and Queen Isabella were unlikely to have their way forever – though he thought it, having seen the boy King's mettle at close quarters.

Roger is to arrive a month later. Geoffrey goes to rejoin him but Edmund stays at Ludlow. He receives advance notice of their arrival by messenger. He requests to see me immediately and I see at once he looks terribly grave and shocked.

"Mother, we are to ready ourselves for Wigmore."

I nod, looking up from my needlepoint, which continues to calm me, even after all those long hours in the past with nothing else to do.

"My boy's body is here now?"

"Yes." Edmund hesitates. "Father and Geoffrey are coming down from Shrewsbury."

"Then John will be with them," I say, for we knew he was taking part in a tournament there. "I am glad of it. He has been away too long. It is time he was reconciled with his father, especially now he will be receiving the Irish lands."

"No, mother…," Edmund puts his face in his hands, not knowing how to tell me.

"What is it?" I ask. Then an awful premonition hits me. "Not John as well? Surely not John?"

"He was killed at the tournament," Edmund admits. "He fell from his horse, catching his foot in the stirrup, and was dragged and trampled underfoot."

I drop my embroidery. The exact horror of this did not bear thinking about.

"We are being punished," I say in a still, small voice. "God is punishing us. Your father and me both."

Edmund spreads his hands in despair.

"You, at least, have done nothing wrong, mother," he exclaims.

"You don't know that," I say, half thinking of my conversation with Kent. "I was cool the last time I saw John, and I should have gone to see young Roger long ago. Then Avice's death was all my fault. I startled her and put her into a hasty descent of the stairs. I might as well have pushed her!"

Edmund sits down next to me and takes my hand tenderly.

"None of those things were planned, mother! Avice could have fallen down the stairs at any time, she had become so doddery. You had more than enough to do here, without going back to Ireland. Roger could have visited you here, after all, and even though he was my brother and I do not relish speaking ill of the dead, John was always troublesome and became arrogant, and he did speak ill of Father. I heard him, too."

I remain silent as he chafes my hands.

"Isabella, Roger and John. Avice, too. All in the same year. It must be God's will."

"Maybe. But he is not punishing you, mother. We do not know how He works. Remember He is also giving me a child and maybe even an heir."

I put out my hand and ruffle his hair.

"Elizabeth is well?" I ask.

"Yes, very well. And she is much stronger than she looks, mother – you shall see. We will take care of you."

The cortege proceeded to the abbey, but my lord rode on to the castle at Wigmore, where I go down to meet him in the inner bailey. I notice his shoulders are stooping as if under a heavy burden, and there is grey in his beard for the first time. He looks like a broken man as he dismounts wearily.

Roger and John were the sons most like him, and this last death must have brought his brother John back to mind, too, as it had occurred under the same circumstances. When he turns to greet me, he tries to put on a brave face. Richard of Monmouth takes his horse away and he embraces me with real feeling.

We climb back up to the newly refurbished castle apartments, but he stops me before we go in and bids me sit down awhile, taking my hand and looking down the hill towards the curtain walls, the gatehouse and the rolling green hills beyond. The trees are beginning to turn but it is a still and sunny day.

"I have not been here for so long," he says. "How calm it all seems!"

"It is certainly quieter since the workmen left," I agree.

"Quieter by far than it used to be. In the old days."

"Your men at arms will soon put paid to that. Geoffrey says they will rally for you at Gloucester."

"I believe they will."

"It's a long time since you were in a battle. The invasion hardly counts when it was so easy."

"I hope this will prove the same," Roger says. "I pray to God he will not also thwart me in this." There is a short silence, then he continues. "I am going to make an endowment to the chapel at Leintwardine. The lands and rents of a hundred marks annually will pay for a college of nine chaplains, to sing daily masses for the souls of all our family, and those of the royal family. For our ancestors, too, in perpetuity. I may not live to see this child of Edmund's grow to be an adult."

I am amazed.

"Are you so worried about Lancaster?"

"Not Lancaster, no, though he is demanding my banishment. I think he will cave in. But everything is becoming more complicated. Kent knows that Edward is still alive."

"How can he?" I ask in alarm. "He may suspect, but cannot prove anything, surely?" My heart drops a beat.

"I think the boy confided in him whilst we were in Scotland."

It seems unlikely but I am grateful Roger believes this.

"That was not in his best interests."

"No, it is not, but who knows? He may have been tempted to share his secret, thinking his uncle would keep it quiet. Kent has no obligation to do so, of course. I notice his manner toward me is changed of late, and I believe he is bound to tell Norfolk, and maybe even Lancaster."

I sigh.

"Perhaps it would be better if the court knew the truth rather than thinking you had the king murdered?"

"Having persuaded everyone he was dead and given him a funeral? I doubt it, Joan. Young Edward could easily claim it was all my doing, and he had no knowledge of it at all."

"He would be loathe to give up his crown though."

"Yes, there is that. But you see, I must keep a tight rein on him."

We fall silent again. I think that our conversation is like it used to be. In the distance, a pair of red kites glide on the thermals above the hills, the sun lighting up their forked, red undertails as they circle each other and search for prey. What a tangled web my lord has woven! I am not sure the endowment for Leintwardine will be enough to placate God.

That night, I am surprised to find my lord comes to my solar and wants to stay. He is in his cups of course, but so had he been at Ludlow, and that made no difference then.

"I am not going to spread my legs like the Queen," I tell him, bluntly.

I am even more surprised when that makes him smile wryly, instead of angering him.

"I know that," he says. "Neither do I expect you to, if you do not wish it. But, oh Joan, I do not want to be alone tonight. On the eve of two of our son's burials. Neither, should I imagine, do you."

I relent then because it is true, and my heart is equally heavy.

"I thought you would try and divorce me," I say sadly.

"After bearing me twelve children? Never. The Queen is important to me, of course she is, but the family is more so."

I am gratified at this.

"Can you not persuade her to give you up? Let you return to your estates?"

"You do not know how changed she is now. She wants everything and everyone to be hers. Especially me. I need to stay for our advancement."

"She does seem much changed. But she is no longer the Queen. She is the Queen Mother. Will her son not grow to resent you?"

"Oh, he does already! You saw his face at Ludlow."

"And he will not remain a boy forever! Can you not draw back?"

Roger shakes his head.

"There is no way of going back. Only forwards and keeping tight control. He will be grateful when I subdue Lancaster."

I sigh, ever more deeply.

"Then I must pray for you, too, as well as the chaplains at Leintwardine," I say.

"And for the Queen? You used to be great friends."

I will not let him off that lightly.

"That was before she stole you from me and her heart grew cruel."

So that night we shared a companionable, if not a passionate bed. He stayed on for another two days after the funerals, before leaving for Gloucester, and this small solace continued.

"You must let me know what is happening," I beg him on his departure. "You don't know how terrible it is not to know, or only to get second-hand accounts. Geoffrey has been good, but he puts his own slant on events. You must write to both Edmund and myself. After all, if you fall, then so do we."

He gave his word that he would.

Chapter 46

1328-1329 — THE EARL OF MARCH

ON THE 29TH of December, immediately after Christmas, Roger declared war on Lancaster in the King's name. It was now imperative, for the Earls of Kent and Norfolk told Henry of Lancaster they had good reason to believe the boy's father was still alive, and accused their nephew of breaking the terms of the coronation oath and abusing Magna Carta. Lancaster was only too ready to believe them.

In addition, the Archbishop of Canterbury joined the Bishops of York and Winchester in taking the same stance, recommending that the young King be excommunicated! This could not be tolerated. Roger announced a Royal Army, under his command, would march from Gloucester to Kenilworth to confront the Earl of Lancaster. Should any man repent this outrageous slander, and their opposition to the King, by the time the Royal Army arrived at Kenilworth, they would be forgiven.

Edmund was sent a copy of this letter, which he read out to me. He was now the proud father of a son and heir, as Elizabeth had given birth at Ludlow, shortly before Christmas, much to my delight. He complied with tradition by naming him Roger. A third-generation Roger. Already, I had the sense of time advancing.

We waited anxiously for further news. Within a month it came, with the elder father true to his word. He was jubilant. When the King was refused entry to Kenilworth, he ordered the ransack and burning of Leicester on his behalf, along with other Lancastrian properties belonging to dependants close by. The destruction and robbery were wanton, though my lord emphasised he gave no orders for any killing to be carried out. Lancaster himself, still in London, marshalled his forces to move north. At the last minute, Kent and Norfolk baulked at going with him. They could not bring themselves to march against the King, and made a public declaration condemning Henry of Lancaster for doing so.

Roger moved the Royal Army on through the night and met Lancaster at Bedford at daybreak. Queen Isabella rode with him, wearing her invasion suit of armour. There was instant capitulation. Henry of Lancaster left his pavilion in the camp, and came to kneel in the mud alone and wring his hands, grovelling and weeping and begging for the King's forgiveness. He said he had been mistaken and led astray by others.

My lord announced that pardons were being openly begged from him now, rather than the King. Young Edward had agreed he should take the title of Earl of March, out of gratitude. The rebellion was utterly squashed. There would be mercy, but only at the price of installing further trustworthy (Mortimer) men in positions of power. There would also be financial punishment and the Mayor of London, who had hosted the seditious meeting between the archbishops and barons, would be sent to the Tower.

'We have won,' wrote Roger. 'We have won and shall stay in power!' Edmund and I look at each other as he finishes reading the message.

"It seems to be a royal 'we'," Edmund says. "So Lancaster is crushed but I do wonder how Kent and Norfolk can be totally restrained? The King will need Father to stand up for him when he goes to pay homage to the new French King in due course."

"Isabella will not like that. To think her son, the son of a King and a Capet has to pay homage to a mere Count of Valois! She believes her son should be the King of France in his place."

"Yes, that is true. But she will have to be pragmatic for the time being. I cannot see Father choosing to invade France for her, even if he is now to be called the Earl of the March!"

"No, he is not that stupid," I reply. "Thank goodness. I do not want my remaining sons to be pressed into such a war."

"It would certainly put Geoffrey in a difficult position with his French lands. But let's not talk of what we cannot alter and may never come to pass."

"Does he ask for you at Court?"

"No. He is extremely pleased to hear about our new son and heir, and is happy for me to stay and run the estates here."

"Now he is made Earl of the March, you will become that in time and so will the little one!"

Edmund raises his eyebrows.

"Who knows, mother? We shall see."

The young King Edward duly paid homage to the new King Philip of France, formerly the Count of Valois, in June, despite his reluctance and that of his mother. He was careful not to promise to assist him in war however, which displeased Philip. It was also the briefest of visits, lasting only sixteen days, with some of that spent at sea. Whilst he was away, my lord quietly consolidated his power.

Now he wrote to say there would be yet another double wedding this summer. Lawrence of Hastings, Aymer's nephew, was now officially endowed with the Earldom of Pembroke and would marry Agnes, as Roger had planned, whilst the Earl of Norfolk had agreed to marry his son to Beatrice. The latter arrangement was an entry into at least one half of the Royal Family! I wondered how that had been managed. Through fear and coercion? Beatrice was only ten and had never met this boy. That only left Blanche, and she was already betrothed to Piers Grandison, the son of a Marcher family, and would leave her home for his when she was old enough.

With my heart still bruised from the deaths of three of my children, I now foresaw I would lose my remaining daughters soon. Of course, I was glad they would lead a full life. It meant the keeping of my vow not to send even one of them to join my sisters in Aconbury Priory. But I had not been consulted about Beatrice and the Norfolk family. It seemed churlish to complain when she was going to marry an earl. Now Roger was an earl, too. I suppose that made me the Countess of March. Nevertheless, it had a hollow ring to it, in my ears. A Countess who was deserted? I did not see myself using the title often.

These weddings would take place in August, and would be followed, I was reliably informed, by a grand Round Table tournament at Wigmore. This would be in the style of the one held by Roger's grandfather at Kenilworth to celebrate his victory over Simon de Montfort. Roger clearly thought it fitting he should celebrate his victory over Lancaster in the same way. Yet it was hardly comparable. It would boost Wigmore's prosperity but I feared the worst. However, as a dutiful mother, I buried myself in preparations for two predictably excited young daughters.

Ludlow was grandly appointed for hospitality last year, but the sheer numbers invited to Wigmore eclipsed the previous celebrations. No expense was spared. Geoffrey told us it was all paid for by money taken by his father from the Despensers, although the King himself had granted a thousand pounds towards the event.

It was not possible to accommodate all the guests at the castle, so the valley and the fields around the town and abbey were filled with colourful pavilions belonging to knights, barons and earls. Queen Isabella stayed in the castle itself, of course, along with her son, and this time I had to give even greater precedence by moving to a lowlier room.

The food bill was enormous, for the tournament was to last three full days. I was amazed at the generosity of the King in providing gifts of jewels, and silver and gilt goblets, to be given daily to the victors. He did not even watch from the best position on the spectators' platform. Like me, he was relegated to one side of the table with Philippa of Hainault.

My lord sat in the centre, playing the part of King Arthur, and wearing, dear God, a gilt crown! The costume of Sir Lancelot might have been more appropriate as Isabella, dressed as Queen Guinevere, sat beside him. Edmund and Elizabeth were close by me. We were shocked to see our lord remain seated when the real King stood, to applaud the victors of each pitched battle.

We were not alone. A rumour was passing round the barons that Roger of Wigmore was intending to make himself King, on the strength of his Welsh ancestry, and supposed lineage being traceable back to the true King Arthur.

Edmund remained silent but it was all too much for Geoffrey. When the main party returned to feast in the Great Hall at Wigmore, with the same seating arrangements, and the same costumes worn, he rose drunkenly from his seat amongst the barons on the side tables, and marched up to the dais where the Royal family were sitting.

He sweeps his arm almost to the floor in an exaggerated bow, and raises his goblet of wine in a toast.

"Behold my Father," he announces, "Not King Arthur surely, but the King of Folly?"

There is a stunned silence as the clatter of plates, knives, and goblets is suddenly halted. Even the serving boys, carrying trays laden with food to and fro, stop in their tracks. I lay a hand on Edmund's arm. My lord looks furious but recovers some dignity with an airy wave of the hand.

"Behold my second son," he says, "who has always had a wicked and warped sense of humour."

A frightened titter runs round the Hall. Geoffrey turns on his heel and leaves the hall without consent.

"Pray eat on," my lord urges. "Do not let your fish grow cold! We have venison pies, boar, crane and swan to follow." The mention of swan occasions a murmur of surprise round the hall. This is a royal prerogative. Still, the guests fall to eating and drinking again, though their conversations are now subdued. I dart an anxious look at Edmund.

"Don't worry, mother," he tells me, "he will be forgiven. Geoffrey has always been the indulged favourite."

Had he, I wonder? I had not been aware of it. But clearly this is what Edmund feels, as least in relation to his father. I lean my head close to my eldest son's.

"I have no appetite, Edmund. And I cannot bear another day of this! Do you think it will be noticed if I return to Ludlow tomorrow?"

Edmund likewise answers in a low voice, watching his father give Isabella a peck on the cheek.

"Of course it will be noticed, mother. But I do not think there is a man or woman here who will blame you, nor who would dare make a comment on it."

By the time the swans were brought in, I had had enough. Previously, Roger had been discreet in the company of royalty. Today, he seemed to have thrown all caution away as if he knew he was untouchable. Whatever must the young King think?

I quietly excuse myself from the table and leave to look for Geoffrey. I find him pacing outside, still red in the face.

"I hope you are not come to upbraid me, mother!" he says angrily.

"No, I have not," I reply gently. "You are the only one brave enough to stand up to him and speak the truth. But, my dear, you must be more careful."

"He owes me for France, mother. For enabling him to survive there to begin with. He will not touch me."

"Let us walk a little further away from the flares and the music," I say. "The nights are already drawing in, but we would be better to remain unobserved."

We walk slowly for a few minutes into the growing dusk.

"Will you do something for me, Geoffrey?"

"Anything, mother."

"Take me back to Ludlow tomorrow. I want to leave after I have said goodbye to the girls. And I would like you to come with me. I don't feel I have the strength to arrange it myself tonight."

"Of course, I will. We will leave at first light. Whilst the guests are still busy with their ablutions."

I thank him and leave him alone – not to return to the hall, but to seek some calm in the solar block. I am about to climb the spiral staircase when I have to stop to let someone come down. It is Isabella, stepping slowly and holding up her fine skirts. No doubt she had need of the garderobe.

I do not step aside. Neither do I curtsey. This woman is no longer the Queen. That title belongs to young Philippa, even if, humiliatingly, she has yet to be crowned. It is true the Queen Mother would normally expect some deference in her own right. But this woman is also a harlot, and anger is burning inside me. She is no longer my friend, and has betrayed me. Even her bearing has changed since she appropriated my husband.

Isabella is looking at me quizzically, even insolently, with her pretty eyebrows lifted and the ghost of a smile playing round her full lips.

"I bid you goodnight and indeed goodbye," I say bluntly. "for I shall be leaving tomorrow."

"So soon? When there are still two days left of entertainment?"

"I have lost my taste for tournaments."

"Ah yes…poor little John! That was sad, though not entirely unexpected, given his nature. But it is only simple jousting tomorrow, with little danger to man or beast."

I ignore this.

"I shall be taking our son Geoffrey with me. I imagine that will please you."

"It may be as well. Roger will need time to pardon 'im."

"But he will, and, unlike you, I fully support my son in standing up to 'The Mortimer'."

Isabella flushes at these words.

"My dear, you forget yourself. I shall be gracious and put it down to an excess of wine. Now let me pass," she says, raising her upturned nose in the air.

But I do not move.

"He doesn't love you, you know. Not really. He never will. He only loves power, and his own family… "

For answer, Isabella places both hands on either side of her lower belly, pulling her loose robes tightly around what I now perceive is a neat but distinctly rounded lump, already grown halfway up to her navel.

"Maybe. Maybe not," she retorts. "Out of my way, please, Madame Joan!"

I step back, horrified, and Isabella sweeps past.

As I climb the stairs to my newly appointed chamber, every step seems a massive effort and I cannot control my breathing at the top. I sink down on the bed. The room is empty. My ladies in waiting are still enjoying themselves in the Hall; not that I could have confided this catastrophic news to them.

Once again, I miss Avice keenly, though I am glad she would never know of this. I feel utterly alone. The old woman has been replaced by a servant called Hilda. She is a sweet girl but inexperienced and naïve.

Hilda pops her head round the door, seeking to offer assistance, but I shake my head to indicate I will look after myself tonight, although I should like her to see to the removal of my belongings in the morning. I still have to go and make my farewells to Agnes and Beatrice.

That reminds me I am not in fact alone, and I repeat it to myself firmly. I have the girls, Edmund, Margaret, and their families, present and yet to come. Geoffrey too, it seems.

What a fool I had been to imagine my lord might return in time! Perhaps I should have expected this before. After all, Roger was certainly fertile, and so was the Queen Mother. Yet how dare they? How could such a child ever be acknowledged?

I remember the look on the young King's face when he watched his mother preen herself as Guinevere next to her 'Arthur' today. No matter how many goblets and jewels he gave, he was clearly not happy with his mother's behaviour. He looked very much like his father but was made of a different mettle. They continued to treat him like a boy but he was seventeen now, only a couple of years younger than Geoffrey. And, if Geoffrey could take his father to task in such a manner, what might the King not do in time?

Next morning, Hilda knocks at my door bright and early, bringing water and towels, and helps me dress. True to his word, Geoffrey has a waggon and horses outside, but I choose to ride with him rather than seek shelter. I am glad to say that Elizabeth has chosen to come too, with her baby boy, and has taken the waggon. She says Edmund has decided to stay, albeit with gritted teeth, so as not to cause too much tongue-wagging at the family's disappearance. Geoffrey's absence was only to be expected after last night.

As we pass through the gatehouse, I say a final goodbye to Wigmore, convinced I will never return. We keep up a steady trot down the hill and through the rejuvenated town, which suddenly finds itself so busy. Fires are smoking idly in the surrounding encampment, but there are few folk around other than grooms preparing their masters' horses for the day's joust.

When we have left the town behind and entered the forest, I ride ahead with Geoffrey so we can talk alone. I tackle him head-on.

"Did you know the Queen Mother is pregnant?

Geoffrey almost fell off his horse.

"No, I did not! But it would explain why Father has become even more sure of himself. How do you know?"

I tell him about my encounter with Isabella at the foot of the stairs.

Geoffrey whistles.

"By God's Holy Wounds and Stigmata! This will set the fox loose amongst the chickens!"

I tell him not to be so profane, but lack conviction.

"I wonder if young King Edward knows?" muses Geoffrey. "Of course, he is careful to keep Father on his side, but how he must hate it! Nevertheless, Father seems very confident of keeping his place."

"And will he?" I ask. "Keep his place?"

"Not if he carries on like this. Not in my opinion. I am sure there are plots, both inside and outside of court. The Earl of Kent is still very unhappy. Father may have persuaded Norfolk otherwise, but Kent still believes that Lord Edward is alive. I really shouldn't tell you this, mother, but it is actually true!"

Ah, so his father had told him then!

"With every piece of land my father and the Queen Mother appropriate, the barons despise them more and more. They say they have become worse than the Despensers. The King could use the barons' support, providing they weren't all so frightened after Lancaster."

"I am tired of all this," I say. "Roger's fate is his own doing, but he shouldn't bring you or Edmund down with him. Stay at Ludlow with us, Geoffrey."

He said he would but it was only for a short while. As his brother had predicted, he was soon forgiven and recalled to Court, where he could still prove useful to his father.

"You need not obey," I say despairingly. "Don't go, Geoffrey."

For answer, he lays a finger against the side of his nose.

"Better to be in the know, mother. Life could get very interesting. It's best that one of us knows what's going on. I will keep in touch."

Edmund agreed, and they clapped each other on the back and embraced warmly on his departure.

Chapter 47

1329 - 1330 – The Earl of Kent

THE STRANGE THING was, that despite Geoffrey's predictions, everything became very quiet for the rest of that year. We had a letter from him saying there had been a bungled attempt at an assault on Corfe Castle, and it was thought best that its guest be moved to Trim Castle secretly now. I had to explain the import of this to Edmund, who was genuinely astounded. He had not been taken into his father's confidence. But that was all.

Roger and Isabella retired to Kenilworth for the rest of the autumn, and for Christmas. I suspected this was to conceal the Queen Mother's pregnancy. By my rough calculations, based on the size I saw that night, the birth must be expected before the end of the year. Henry of Lancaster was not there but in France, attempting to placate King Philip over young Edward's lack of respect in cutting short his homage. So the lovers would have the castle to themselves.

Then, quite unexpectedly, Roger came to visit Ludlow, without Geoffrey, in the first week of December. I could hardly bear to look at him and made it clear he could stay in the new solar block, whilst I remained in the old one, as usual, feeling the new block forever tainted. He seemed subdued and did not make any comment on this. He brought presents and was especially anxious to see his new grandson and namesake, Roger, who was about to have his second birthday, proclaiming him the next-but-one Earl of March.

"And what of your other heir, my lord?" I ask him sharply.

He looks surprised but does not obfuscate.

"The Earl of Lincoln did not survive," was all he said, sadly. "I shall add his name to the list of those to be prayed for at Leintwardine."

That would confuse the chaplains, I thought. There was no Earl of Lincoln. The last baron to hold that title had been Thomas of Lancaster, through his late wife Alice, after a former Earl of Lincoln had died, but it was taken away from him, and never returned to his brother Henry; Isabella owned those lands now. So that was the title they had chosen for the child. And it had been a boy! But was no more. I did not ask whether it was stillborn, miscarried or died in infancy. I could not help but feel relieved, but it would be wrong to rejoice over the ending of such a new and innocent life.

As usual, my lord did not stay long, telling us he must get back to Kenilworth for Christmas, and then return to London in the New Year to prepare for Queen Philippa's coronation.

"Not before time," I remark, acidly.

"No," Roger agrees, "and she is heavily pregnant now."

"The continuation of the Plantagenet dynasty," I add, more brightly.

"Yes, indeed."

"God be praised."

I got up to see him leave and was glad afterwards, that I had. I did not know then that it would be the last time we saw each other, but the parting still held an air of poignancy.

"I am sorry to hear about the Earl of Lincoln," I say. "Truly I am."

There is a cold wind blowing through the outer bailey, which seems to be making his eyes smart as it whips around our cloaks.

"These things happen," he says, busying himself with his horse's girth and stirrups.

"Our grandson, Roger, is doing very well," I say to comfort him. "I think he will make a fine man. Don't you think?"

"Yes," and he does brighten at this thought.

"Young Maurice Berkeley, too."

"But he is not a Mortimer by name, and none of the girls' offspring will be."

"Perhaps that does not matter."

"Of course it matters!" he says, irritably.

"There is always Geoffrey," I point out.

"Oh, Geoffrey!" he snorts, swinging himself into the saddle. "He's always been feckless. He won't come to anything. He lacks the application, and Edmund the ambition."

"That's a little harsh."

For answer, he urges his horse to walk on. But I walk with him towards the gatehouse, past all the clutter and chaos of the outbuildings.

"Come back to us, Roger," I plead. "Now, before it's too late. Surely you can leave the court now that the new Queen is to be crowned, and Edward has almost reached his majority? Leave them! Isabella will soon find someone else."

I put my hand on the bridle, but he jerks the reins away impatiently to turn the horse's head. It whinnies, startled at this unexpectedly rough treatment.

"I cannot," he tells me abruptly. "Goodbye, Joan. You have been a good wife. Better than I deserved." He has the spirit of his uncle in him now, as he digs his spurs into the horse's flanks to make it canter through the gatehouse.

"Let the old king go!" I yell at his retreating back, regardless of who hears me. He does not look back but raises his arm once in farewell, before driving the horse on through the gates, scattering chaff and squawking chickens.

I stand there, heedless of the tears coursing down my face, until one of my ladies, following a little way behind, catches up with me and, putting her arm around me, leads me gently back to the castle.

Christmas came and went without him. Of course, he did not feel the need to make excuses anymore. I took comfort in the excitement of baby Roger, whose eyes were agog in his little round face, with its chubby cheeks, at the evergreen decorations, the great fires, the fruit and the nuts, the candied sweets and the jugglers Edmund organised. It was good to have a little child in the household again.

Thomas and Margaret came in the New Year, and brought their children with them. Even Margaret de Fiennes made the journey from France to see the new heir, and did not mention her son once. There was plenty of room, with the new solar block reserved for visitors now. The castle was full of the running steps and laughing voices of children. I have all of this, I thought. Roger may have Isabella, but has nothing else. I am the one who is blessed.

Maurice Berkeley is now almost ten, and I delight in his intelligent questions and thoughtfulness once more. I give him a beautifully illuminated Book of Hours for his present, and promise I will help him read it.

"I am not very good at Latin yet," he admits. " But I am trying and this will make me try harder. The pictures are so lovely."

Margaret has kept him at home longer than she should, but I understand perfectly why, after her separation from him when she was sent to the priory. Now Maurice tells me proudly that, in the coming year, he will be going away to learn how to become a knight. My heart sinks. He must have seen the look on my face because he pipes up straightaway.

"Don't worry, grandmother," he says. "I shan't forget you. Especially with this book to remind me. And when you are a very old lady – even older than now – you can come and live with me at Berkeley, and I will make sure you have lots of good things to eat."

I laugh at his words, but they take me aback all the same. Am I really old? But of course I am. I shall be forty-four next month! Old to a child.

The winter days pass slowly, and it is good to see the light returning at last. Queen Philippa is crowned on the 18th of February. Edmund was invited to join his brother and duly paid the visit to Westminster. When he returned, his face was grave.

"What is it?" I ask in alarm.

"Father has had the Earl of Kent arrested. I can scarce believe it. But he seeks his trial for treason, and clearly intends to have him executed."

"But why?"

"Apparently he has been trying to raise support in France and has even spoken to the Pope."

"Support for what?"

"He is still convinced the Lord Edward is not dead. He persistently tries to gain admission to Corfe to see him."

"Surely Edward must be in Ireland by now."

"We know that, but there is no reason why he should. The castellan of Corfe, John Maltravers, knows it too, but is naturally sworn to secrecy, and keeps up the pretence Edward is there. It appears that Kent arranged for his wife to write a letter to Maltravers on his behalf, and asked him to pass it on to Lord Edward. Of course, Maltravers sent it straight to Father."

"But he can't be put to death for writing his brother a letter, surely?" I ask, feeling the panic rise in my throat.

"Well yes, he could be. The letter told Lord Edward of all the support Kent has managed to raise on his behalf against the young King, to put matters right. That is treason."

I groan in despair.

"The secret is out, then?"

"No, not at all. The King cannot admit this is the truth. Neither can Father, nor the Queen Mother. The fiction must be maintained. Otherwise they could all be out on their heels."

"This is dreadful," I say. "Truly dreadful."

It was Geoffrey who wrote to tell me what happened at the trial and afterwards. Lord Roger Mortimer was the Chief Prosecutor, and accused the Earl of Kent of being the King's deadliest enemy, and of being "a common enemy unto the realm". Of course, he produced the condemnatory letter written by Margaret Wake, and read it out. The Earl could not deny it was his seal. The outcome was a foregone conclusion. Kent was found guilty and sentenced to death by execution. The crime was in attempting to free his half-brother and put him back on the throne, even though the said half-brother did not exist.

By the 16th of March, Kent had confessed fully, but threw himself on the mercy of the King, saying he had been led astray by certain Dominican friars. He did not name them, but implicated the Devil in their work instead. He promised that, if it was the King's will, he would walk barefoot in his shirt, with a rope around his neck, through the streets of Winchester and all the way to London.

'And all the while,' wrote Geoffrey, 'Father sat there with a face of stone and a cold heart, saying nothing until he finally demanded the death sentence be upheld. King Edward agreed. Kent's wife, Margaret Wake, will also be arrested, even though she is pregnant, and sent to the Tower."

"He has become Hugh Despenser! He cannot put Kent to death for merely knowing the truth. Nor imprison his cousin Margaret for doing her husband's bidding. Surely he will mitigate the sentence and put him in the Tower at the very least?" I cried to Edmund, whom I had summoned in my distress.

"I am sorry but it has happened already, mother. I am told by others that Kent has been beheaded. Apparently they had to get a latrine cleaner to do it because the official executioner refused. The Earl was a popular man. But the execution took place the very next day. It is over."

"Then it truly is over," I say with quiet fury. "Your father's soul is damned to hell. And, no doubt, he will take all of us with him."

For once, Edmund could find no words to console me.

I have been neglectful of the confessional since Father Judas left me, but now I seek out one of the younger chaplains engaged to pray in the chapel of St Peter ad Vincula, and ask him to hear me. I insist he comes alone to the round chapel of St Mary Magdalene when it is empty.

"Forgive me Father, for I have sinned…"

He must have been half my age, but the usual words spring automatically to my lips.

"How so, my lady?" He is clearly not expecting anything spectacular.

"I…misled…someone. A very important man. I hinted to him – no, I made him believe – something which affected him greatly, and has subsequently led to his death."

I sense the young priest stiffen and prick up his ears. There is a long silence whilst he gathers his wits.

"Did you tell a lie, my lady?" he asks hesitantly.

"No, it was not a lie. It was the truth but it led to harm."

The young man considers.

"Then I do not see how God can possibly blame you."

My penance is ridiculously light, and I leave the chapel feeling dissatisfied and far from absolved of my guilt.

Chapter 48

THERE WERE FORTY men on the list of supporters contained within Kent's letter. Most of them fled. They included Thomas Wake, whom Roger described – unsurprisingly and accurately – as a turncoat. He ran before Roger closed the ports.

The next step Roger took was to demand more money was raised. He was adamant this was necessary to fortify the ports, and the whole country against 'the exiles'. Geoffrey began to wonder if his father were going mad, such was his paranoia against an invasion, however unlikely that seemed. But my lord was still cogent enough to make sure the royal purse rewarded those who had been loyal to him, and also to reward himself.

The spring and summer passed quietly in Ludlow. Roger did not visit and I was glad of it. I noted, but was not impressed by, the fact he gave me the palatinate rights in Meath, along with himself of course. Geoffrey was granted most of Kent's estates, despite what his father had said about him. They appear to be reconciled then; sometimes I wonder where Geoffrey's heart really lies.

The totally inoffensive son of Uncle Roger of Chirk was declared a bastard, to make sure he would remain disinherited. I felt sickened. I had never had any love for Roger's uncle but always felt sorry for his son, afflicted with, and I was sure, caused a great deal of suffering, by his uncompromising father.

All this while, the young King was squirming and longing to cast off his chains. He sent his friend, William Montagu, in secret to the Pope at Avignon to tell him what was going on and to set up a code for letters between them so the Pope could distinguish between 'Mortimer letters' and his own.

Plots did indeed abound, as Geoffrey had warned. Richard Fitzalan attempted a rising in Shropshire and Staffordshire but was arrested. Rebels in Wales were more easily purged with my lord as the Justiciar, having succeeded his uncle there. All the Southern ports were fortified and Edmund was peremptorily summoned from Ludlow to ensure their readiness against any invasion.

Lord Mortimer himself was followed around the country by a virtual army of men. I saw him become a great spider, amidst a web of protective spies. Make to touch him and he would unfurl long tentacles of poisonous power. In the meantime, a sense of injustice and anger at the country's ingratitude surely grew within him, and bitterness never improves any character. I felt I did not know him anymore. He was no longer my lord.

It was late summer when the court moved to Nottingham and Roger installed himself and his Queen high up in the castle, on the rocky crag above the town. Geoffrey wrote to say the situation was very tense. His father's spies had uncovered a new plot. Without implicating the King, several of his young friends, including William Montagu, were holding clandestine meetings to formulate a plan on his behalf.

Roger summoned Montagu and the others for questioning, but they all remained stubbornly silent except for Montagu himself, who denied any such meetings. Reluctantly, Roger had to let them go.

The new Earl of March still remained seated in the King's presence, shared his table, let his own servants do so, and in every way acted as if he were King. This was folly indeed, as Geoffrey reminded me. There was to be a Parliament held in Nottingham in October. When the much-chastened Lancaster dutifully arrived, seeking to stay in the castle, as was his right, Roger flew into a rage. He declared Lancaster was still an enemy, and it was an insult to quarter him so close to Queen Isabella. He demanded he stay elsewhere, down below in the town.

Isabella was given the keys of the castle into her own keeping. Guards were doubled and ordered to obey only Mortimer and not the King. Only Roger's closest friends were to be trusted.

Everyone wondered what would transpire at the Parliament. Was Lancaster to be the next earl to be accused of something?

It hardly seemed credible, especially when the poor man had recently gone blind and was a mere shadow of his former self. Was the young King to be deposed? And if so, by whom? Would the old King be produced as a prisoner and put back on the throne? For now all of Mortimer's opponents were saying openly he had murdered Lord Edward, maybe he would need to do exactly that.

Is it possible to know what is in the mind of a dictator in his final days? Other than sheer panic and paranoia? Other than certainty he will rail against all those who feted him so recently, before he became such a grasping bully?

Geoffrey's letter made me feel afraid, but I knew there was nothing I could do. Edmund was still in Dover, and so I had to face this information alone. However, I had made my final plea to Roger when I saw him last, and had been firmly turned down. It was over, finished, forever.

As it was a mild October day, I took a book out into the garden to read, but could not concentrate. Thinking of Edmund in Dover made me remember that there were underground tunnels in the castle there. What an age it seemed since we were there to welcome a twelve-year-old queen into England! Did Nottingham have tunnels too? After all, it was built on a rock full of caves, but surely Roger would know all about this and have the entrances blocked up or guarded? I shivered, and not just at the chill wind which had sprung up in the arbour. No point in dwelling on such matters; he had made his choice and was not coming back. His fate was his alone.

Blanche had gone to stay with her older sister, Joan, and husband Sir James Audley, at Hellens Manor House – whilst her new husband in name, Sir Piers Grandison, was away from his seat at Ashperton. I missed her. I had been anxious about the child marrying such an older man, for Piers was thirty-four, but he seemed respectful of this and promised continuing care for the child. This settlement of her with the Audleys was reassuring. I was fond of Hellens, which was near the village of Much Marcle to the south-east of Hereford, not far away. Maybe it was time to leave Ludlow for a while and make a visit to Hellens, to take my mind off what may be happening in Nottingham.

Closing my book at the un-read page, I went back inside to call Hilda and ask her to pack some clothes. The spider must manage his own fears and paranoia; it should not concern me now.

Nottingham Castle – 19th October, 1330
The gates of the castle are firmly shut and the guards doubled. Young King Edward says he feels unwell and leaves the hall with his physician in attendance. Roger Mortimer hopes this is the case; the boy looked fine to him. But you never knew. How convenient it would be for him to die!

Philippa might not produce a living heir and, even if she did, that would mean another regency, and a long one. Roger's mind would have drifted to poisoning long ago, but for the thought of Isabella's distress. He follows her tripping little ankles up the steps to her solar as she holds her rich skirts raised above the stone.

They are not alone but followed by Richard of Monmouth, Sir Hugh Turpington, Bishop Burghersh and the knights, Sir Simon Beresford and Oliver Ingham. This is Roger's inner circle now, and he wishes to consult them over what should be done about William Montagu and his friends, all of whom left town this morning. They settle down in the Queen's solar to formulate a plan, for Roger is determined to find evidence against the conspirators, whether it is real or fabricated.

Geoffrey Mortimer is not there, because his father sent him down to the town earlier to glean any information he could from the taverns. His father does not entirely trust him anymore since the 'King of Follies' outburst. In his opinion, he spends far too much time writing to his mother and brother. But he is as popular and personable as his father is not. Roger finds this inexplicable, but is aware his son may pick up unguarded confidences because of it. In fact, young Geoffrey has not been successful and is already on his disconsolate way back to the castle.

Candles are brought, wine is poured, and the men sit down at Isabella's table before the fire. Richard of Monmouth takes up his accustomed position outside the door. Although he has felt nervous about his master's position of late, more nervous than at any time since he has known him, he does not feel especially challenged tonight. He knows the castle is bristling with extra guards at every gate, in the bailey and on the walls.

The night is black, with no moon. A handful of figures gather in the park below the castle. William Montagu is one of them, and has brought along a local man named William Eland, who grew up in the castle. Geoffrey Mortimer is not the only young man to frequent the taverns looking for information, and Montagu has got to Eland first. He knows of a tunnel leading from one of the caves at the bottom of the rock into the castle itself, emerging very close to the royal apartments. The gate is always bolted from the inside of the castle but not so tightly that a young monarch could not pull it back, especially if he were only feigning illness. A message has been sent to that effect.

So now Eland leads the way, and the young men – two dozen in all – climb the uneven sandstone steps hewn in the rock. They feel their way in the dark for the first two turns of the stairs, with their hands pressed against the walls, not daring to show a torch. When they do light them, the flares show sandstone dust on their hands and further steps rising through the winding hole. It's a long way up – at least a hundred feet – and well before the final bend, they douse the torches so an inky blackness returns. They can smell their own fear and the more cautious of them half hope the bolt will remain fast at the top, so they have to return. But the young King has played his part, as he said he would. One by one, their shadows slip through the gate. If they fail from now on in, it will be the gallows or the block for each of them and this thought serves to spur them on.

It is easier in the candlelit corridors, though they feel more exposed. There is only one man standing at the bottom of the stairs to the solar. His throat is cut swiftly, the cry silenced with a hand over his mouth, before he knows what is happening. At the top, Richard of Monmouth has returned to the room and been replaced by Hugh Turpington.

Hugh has just begun to come down the stairs to check on the sentry. He catches sight of the men and immediately yells "Traitors and evil men!" Drawing his sword, he is upon them. He wounds the first, but is felled by the second wielding a battleaxe. Montagu pushes forward past his body, a cluster of men with him, and bursts into the solar.

Isabella is screaming at the top of her voice. She is pushed back into the inner chamber, where Bishop Burghersh is already trying to climb down the latrine chute. Roger is not wearing a sword, but Richard of Monmouth, faithful to the last, shields him – until he is cut down and mortally wounded. Five men leap on Roger and pinion his arms behind his back. He is roughly bound and gagged, and held tightly. Beresford and Ingham are overpowered in the same way.

These three are bundled roughly down the stairs and back into the hole of the cave leading to the outside. By now, there will be a horse and cart waiting at the bottom for them. Montagu is taking no chances by leaving them in the castle.

The bishop is unceremoniously yanked out of his latrine shaft but is not hurt. Montagu leaves two men to detain and guard him, along with the hysterical Isabella, and take them to the King. Another three are sent to arrest Geoffrey Mortimer in his room elsewhere in the castle. They are not needed, as Geoffrey remains quiet and calm when he is told what has happened, and has no intention of putting up a fight.

He is taken to the King in the Great Hall and witnesses the unedifying sight of Queen Isabella, no longer screaming, but still wailing uncontrollably, with her arms clinging fast to the King's lower legs, attempting to stop him from walking away. Although he tries his best to break free, he is dragging her with him along the floor. She is begging for mercy and pleading for 'gentle Mortimer' to be spared. In the end, the King orders his physician to take her away and give her a sleeping draught, sending men to guard her room as a precaution.

Geoffrey bows low to the King but does not say anything.

"Ah, Geoffrey!" Edward says with considerable relief. "As you can see, my mother is distraught. But I do not intend to harm her in any way."

Geoffrey inclines his head respectfully as if to say he never for a moment imagined he would. Edward sighs. Like most people, he actually likes Geoffrey.

"I am bound to arrest you," he says.

Geoffrey inclines his head, once again, with understanding.

"But I shall not hold you responsible for the evil doings of your father, if that is any comfort to you."

"Thank you, sire. May I be granted one small request? That a message be sent to my mother to tell her what has transpired? Can they merely inform her of my whereabouts and that of my brother?"

Edward hesitates. But then, with the memory of his own mother's behaviour still fresh within him, he nods.

"I will grant your request," he said. "We must all respect our mothers. To a certain extent."

Chapter 49

I AM STILL at Ludlow when the messenger arrives. With Edmund away, I have been obliged to take on an estate matter, which delayed my departure for Hellens. I hear the news in the gravest silence. It grieves me most of all to hear that Richard of Monmouth is dead. Poor dear Richard, who was so loyal!

"Where are my sons now?"

"Geoffrey will be imprisoned in the Tower with his father, by now. The Lord Edmund is to be held under house arrest in Dover."

"Lord Roger escaped from the Tower once."

"The King is aware of that. He is to be walled up this time. There will be no escape."

"And what are they saying will happen to him?"

The messenger hesitates, but decides there is no point in prevarication.

"Queen Isabella begged her son to show mercy on 'gentle Mortimer', but they took him to Leicester that night and the King wanted to hang him then and there. However Henry of Lancaster urged caution."

"'Gentle Mortimer?' Well, he was, once. Some of the time."

"Lancaster said there must be a trial at Westminster. And that he should be accused of murdering the King's father there."

The promise of a trial gives me no false hope. I know all about show trials, and do not doubt it will end in execution. I pay the messenger handsomely and dismiss him. Then I sit alone and think for a long time. At length, I summon my knight, Sir Richard de Burgh. First I have to tell him the news. But then I say "We must go to Ireland. Immediately."

"A wise idea," Sir Richard replies. "Shall we go to Berkeley and sail from Bristol? Lord Berkeley would provide us with a vessel."

"No, I think not. The messenger told me Roger may be charged with the murder of the King's father. Thomas Berkeley may also be implicated or, at the very least, required at the trial. No, we will go north. To Chester. They will not look for us there. I am sorry to press you on this matter, Richard, but we must leave at dawn tomorrow. I have learnt from experience that a King's retribution can come swiftly."

But I am not running away, as Sir Richard assumes, and have every intention of returning. It is sensible to sail from Chester in case of apprehension, and I insist we all dress as common travellers. In view of requesting Sir Richard's protection, I did ask Lady Elizabeth de Burgh if she wanted to come, but Elizabeth declined, much to my relief. The idea of a sea voyage at this time of year was not appealing to her. So I take Hilda instead, and Sir Richard, his own squire. We break our journey at Shrewsbury and Chirk, but do not risk staying in the castles, chancing the abbey at Shrewsbury, and sending the squire on ahead to Chirk and Chester, to take rooms for us at inns and arrange a vessel.

The days are long, whether choosing to ride or be carried in the cart I have insisted upon instead of an ostentatious waggon, as I am determined to push on to reach Chester within three days. At first, I remain tight-lipped and silent. Then, on our final leg into Chester, I realise I should take Sir Richard into my confidence and tell him of my plans. He is not as surprised to hear about the survival of Lord Edward, the father of the king, as I thought he might be. He says he had not believed Lord Mortimer would commit regicide, and was previously sure Edward had died naturally, sudden though it seemed.

""Exactly so," I say. "So, if he is to be tried for the murder of the former king, we must produce that king at Westminster so everyone can see it is false for themselves. The Lord Edward is held prisoner at Trim."

Sir Richard's face is creased with doubt and worry now.

"But Madame," he says, "that could have immense consequences! And how do you know that Lord Edward would even agree to such a thing?"

"Well, he is my prisoner now. And I am sure the Cusacks would assist me in providing transport and a full guard to bring him back."

Sir Richard shakes his head in disbelief.

"But, my dear lady, have you forgotten that Lord Mortimer is also likely to be accused of the unwarranted execution of the Earl of Kent? Everyone knows he was guilty of this act, and producing Lord Edward would merely emphasise the wrong done there"

I consider this. Sir Richard has been with me many years and, unlike his wife, I do respect his quiet judgement.

"I thought," I falter, "that could be represented as a deed intended to protect the young King, by preventing the Earl from freeing his brother?"

"There are likely to be other charges, as well. After you retired last night, there was much talk of it in the inn. They say his greedy grabbing of land and money will go against him, but most of all that he has tried to rule in place of the King."

"The King's son has tried to rule in place of the King."

"Oh Madame, no! Please consider! Your assertion of that would surely lead to your own arrest and downfall. It could also lead to civil war and bloodshed if enough barons backed the King's father. I understand why you want to save your lord, but this is...well... no more than a wild dream. Let us get you to Ireland, by all means, for your own safety, but not to bring back the Lord Edward."

"I must do something."

Sir Richard shakes his head again, more violently.

"Forgive me, Madame, for speaking so plainly. But Lord Mortimer has wronged you and does not merit your sacrifice. Think of the effect it would have on your children to know that you were implicated, too."

I look at him, sadly.

"You are right, of course. But perhaps I should not be thinking merely of my own safety."

Sir Richard rubs anxiously at his grey beard before suggesting a compromise.

"If you must, perhaps you could write a letter to the King, from the safety of Ireland, telling him the truth and begging him to show mercy," he says gently.

"He knows the truth already."

Sir Richard gasps.

"Then our Lord Mortimer is truly lost, whatever you do."

I spend a sleepless night at the inn at Chester, which is not as comfortable or as clean as the one we stayed in at Chirk. I suspect bed lice and fleas and cannot rest quiet for a moment.

In my mind, I turn over the conversation with Sir Richard and come to realise he is right: the thought of the bloodshed I might provoke is powerful. My own sons would be drawn into that, against my will. Neither would my revelation be sure to save Roger. I could write to the King but knew my plea for mercy was likely to fall on deaf ears. If he had not listened to his own mother, he would not listen to Mortimer's wife. There was no hope for Roger. At least, not in this world. And maybe not in the next, without many prayers and redemption. There is only one more thing I can do.

It is not the best time of year for a crossing to Ireland, and I fear high winds might delay us. But God looks favourably on me this day as if knowing my intent, and we set sail on a calm sea with waters still as a millpond, managing the crossing within two days. I avoid Dublin Castle out of further caution, in case the King has sent out any messages to Ireland. So that means another poor inn, with its muddy, earthen courtyard, its smoking fire, and the stink of tallow candles in our nostrils, not to mention the possibility of more vermin. However, we are able to procure fresh horses for the journey to Trim there.

I feel my throat choke with emotion when those tall, white towers rise out of a low-lying mist over the marshes and pastureland. Despite the gloom of a growing dusk, I kick my horse into a final gallop toward that welcome sight and the others are forced to follow me. Sir Walter Cusack, the custodian, is there to greet us and is horrified at the news from England.

"My lady, my lady, my lady," is all he can keep on saying.

That night, I sleep the sleep of exhaustion, in comfort at last, and wake to the bells from the abbey the next day. I wash in cold water and dress quickly without disturbing Hilda, who has found the journey a challenge and is dead to the world. I put on the same brown, woollen travelling cloak, with its capacious hood that hides my features, and go down the stairs to call for a groom to bring me a mount, and ride with me through the town.

We ride to the Black Friary outside the town gate, where I break bread with the Prior. More explanations follow, although they, too, are not amazed to hear the Lord Edward is still alive. I hear Mass and pray with them for a long time. At length, I return to the castle accompanied by two of the brothers in a horse and cart. They dine with Sir Walter and myself. I am tired now, so make my request to see the prisoner kept high up in the South Tower of the keep, on the following day.

In the morning, Sir Walter takes me up the winding stairs, but I bid him stay outside the door, as I wish to see the Lord Edward alone. I do not know what to expect, but am glad to see Edward looking well and the room appointed comfortably, even though he is still under lock and key. He sits at the table reading a psalter, and is simply dressed in a plain woollen robe. His long, golden locks are streaked with grey now, and straggle onto his shoulders. His face is heavily lined and wears a serious expression, with no trace of its former arrogance or petulance. Could I dare hope that he had actually become…sensible?

He rises to his feet at my entrance and that is new too, with all his royal airs and graces disappeared.

"Lady Mortimer?"

I nod and bid him be seated.

"Is your husband here, too? 'The Mortimer'?" he asks fearfully. He has not been told then.

"No, he is not," I say. "He will never trouble you again. For your son has arrested him and he is back in the Tower. Almost certainly awaiting execution. The young Edward wants rid of him and will have him put to death."

Edward stares at me for a few moments, uncertain whether to believe me or not. Then he lets out a long, low whistle.

"How are the mighty fallen!" he says. "Me and him both."

"Yes," I answer quietly. "You and him both. You may like to know he will be charged with your murder, amongst other matters."

"Ah," he says. "So you have come to take me back to London to show myself at court."

I shake my head.

"I thought of it. But I no longer believe it would be in anyone's interest. Especially not that of your son. Or the realm, come to that. And forgive me, my Lord, but you are so changed that I do believe they would think you an imposter!"

Edward digests this slowly and then smiles.

"That may well be true. But my son would know."

"Yes, he would. But I am afraid he would not admit to it. He is very keen to rule in his own right."

Edward sighs.

"No doubt. Will he make a good King?"

I restrain myself from saying he could hardly make a worse one than his father.

"I think he will make a strong one. Already he is chafing under the yoke of France."

Edward looks at me, with his head on one side.

"You do not approve," he says shrewdly.

"It will mean war. Possibly for many years to come, with little achieved in the end."

"Hmmm. I suspect you are right. Well then, so if I am not to be taken to London, have you come to order your henchmen to finish me off?"

"No. I have come to let you go. Before any of Roger's allies – or the King's – take it upon themselves to do away with you."

He is truly astonished now.

"But why? I thought you hated me."

"I used to," I admit. "I used to rail against you in my heart for locking us up. But now you have been locked up, too – for almost the same length of time – and I find that gives me no pleasure. It would ease me better to know that you were free and content.

"There are two brothers, from the Black Friary outside Trim, who have come to the castle today. They have instructions to take you to the friary and care for you there. I remember you used to have great love and respect for their Dominican order. You will be very comfortable at the friary, as you can live in the house my grandfather, who was their patron, formerly occupied. I urge you to remain there in further contemplation, at least for a while. But you will be free to go whenever you choose."

Edward's blue eyes are misty now, but he makes an effort to sound bold.

"And what if I go to the continent and raise a great army to come back and invade England?"

"I would not advise it, my lord," I say drily. "You were never adept at military warfare."

He laughs.

"You will not accompany my army then, as my Queen did with 'The Mortimer's'?"

"No, of course not."

"I am only speaking in jest, my dear Lady Joan."

There is a short pause. Then he says "I should rather like to see the Shrine of the Three Kings in Cologne before I die."

"That should not be out of the question for a travelling friar," I reply, getting up to leave.

"And are you sure there are no Mortimer men outside waiting to overpower me?"

"Quite sure."

"Tell me, will they hang, draw and quarter him and rip his entrails out – your husband, I mean?"

I swallow hard.

"I don't know. I believe the Queen Mother has pleaded for leniency. Her son will not commute the sentence, but I hope he will avoid an excess of barbarity."

"It is what he did to my poor Hugh."

"And what your poor Hugh did to Llewellyn Bren. And so it goes on... and on, sire." I turn to leave but Edward puts out his hand to detain me.

"You are right, of course. I hope for your sake it is not done in that way. You are a good woman, Lady Joan," he says, with genuine emotion in his voice, "better than my Queen. I thank you from the depths of my heart, and will pray for you daily. I repent of having put you in prison. Can you forgive me?"

"I have already forgiven you," I say. "I hope I don't have to forgive your son on the same account."

"You will not stay out of harm's way in Ireland?"

"No, I cannot. I have children and grandchildren in England, and must work towards their exoneration from any blame."

"Then may God be with you, my lady."

When I said goodbye to Trim, I had the feeling it would be forever, even more strongly than when I left Wigmore, and I was tempted to stay a while longer under its white walls, surrounded by that alluring green land which still whispered so softly to me. Sir Richard also begged me to stay, at least 'until affairs had settled down in England', by which I knew he meant until after Roger's execution. Still I refused, feeling that at least I must be back on the same soil as my former Lord at the close of his life.

The journey back was far rougher, for the weather had grown inclement and was cold and blustery. Nevertheless, I felt as if a great weight had been lifted from my shoulders now that the Lord Edward was truly safe.

Back on shore, we heard all kinds of gossip and rumour in the taverns along the way. Roger Mortimer had been accused of his crimes at Westminster on the 26th of November. Of course, these included the murder of the former King, but this had been common knowledge for years. Some said he had ordered a red hot poker to be inserted into the King's bowels through his anus. That way, there would be no mark left on the body. You could hear his screams from ten, no twenty miles away at least...

'The Mortimer' was bound and gagged, so could say nothing in his defence. He was found guilty and his execution set for three days hence. The King had been magnanimous by letting his son Geoffrey go and merely banishing him to France.

I spent these three days on the journey back from Chester to Ludlow, riding at a more leisurely pace through the rolling hills of the Marches. It is mild but bleak, damp, misty and utterly grey. Inconsolable weather with dark days drawing in. However, I am glad I am not in London.

For I have no wish to see Roger, dressed in the black tunic he wore for Edward's sham funeral, dragged through the streets from the Tower to Tyburn behind an ox cart. No wish to hear his confession on the scaffold – that he had sinned in sending the Earl of Kent to his death. No wish to hear the howls and jeers of the people. No wish to see the rope placed around his neck, knowing he was to be hung like a common criminal, and not the nobleman he was. No wish to see his body jerking and twitching, and especially no wish to see his bruised and battered body stripped and left to swing naked on the gallows for two whole days – whilst the crows pecked at his eyes, the kites swooped down, and the crowd pelted him with rotten cabbages and other detritus.

I had barely arrived back at Ludlow and dressed myself in black when the soldiers came.

"I have been expecting you – this time," I say to their commander, with the chill of ice in my voice. "No doubt you will be taking me to Hampshire".

He has the grace to look embarrassed.

"Yes, Madame. But not to Southampton. To Odiham, where the King has ordered you be detained for a short while at his pleasure. He has, however, given express orders that you are not to be maltreated or kept in any privation."

EPILOGUE

OH LORD, WHY have I lived so long? I have even managed to survive the plague years. Is it a punishment for crimes committed? Yet my lord always said I did nothing wrong. Only he did not know the whole of it. I expect he does now.

I am a very old lady of seventy-one years, almost as old as Avice was once. Many of my children have gone before me. All but Geoffrey, whom I never see as he remains exiled in France (where he has styled himself Lord of Couhé) and Catherine, Agnes and Beatrice, the Countesses of Warwick and Pembroke and the Dowager Countess of Norfolk no less.

Edmund's death hit me especially hard. The King let him go and restored some of his estates after only a few months, because he obviously had nothing to do with his father's actions. Only he did not have long to enjoy them, as his health did not last out the year. Elizabeth married again and has sadly taken little Roger Mortimer to grow up with her new husband, the Earl of Northampton. He had all of his lands restored in time and is now the second Earl of March, Edmund never having been granted that title.

The King very soon relented and released me. So I went back to Berkeley and lived there until Margaret sadly died five years later. That was also a grievous blow. By then, I had my lands restored, but I never felt the same about them again.

Little Maurice Berkeley was true to his word though, and has always seen me well cared for. This is his manor house where I lie in bed now, but he visits me here as often as he can. He has ordered I am sent pears every day they are in season, to tempt my appetite, because he knows they are my favourite. Bless him! Of course, Hilda has to peel them and cut them up as I no longer see well, and cannot use one arm. She also has to mop the juices from my chin, and change the bedlinen all too often, for I cannot always keep my continence now. Hilda has been with me a long time and says she does not mind, and that it is only to be expected with me having borne so many lusty children. For her part, she is glad she never had any.

Naturally, Maurice is no longer little. Did I tell you he married the daughter of Hugh Despenser by Eleanor de Clare? That came as a great shock to me. But Maurice said it was all for the best – to bring peace to the warring families at last, and I suppose that is true. His wife, Eleanor, seems harmless, and they seem to be happy enough.

Maurice is great friends with young Roger Mortimer and they are both held in high regard by the King. Only they are both in France now, fighting his interminable campaigns, and I am afraid for them. Edward the Third turned out to be a strong king, just as I told his father he would. He did not leave Scotland or France in peace for long. But he is more popular than his father. There is no accounting for the taste of the populace.

The Lord Edward eventually died in a remote monastery in the north of Italy. I forget its name, but I am told he was much loved for his humility and gentle nature. That was fifteen years ago now. The King had his body brought back secretly and re-interred at Gloucester. No-one knows this, of course. But I guessed. There were great works being done on the choir at the time, so the tomb was hidden from view. Then the King began to pay his respects there, which he had never done before.

Of course *she* is still alive, so I suppose she will have the real heart now. I am referring to the Queen Mother. I never got Roger's heart, nor even his body in the end, though I asked the King for it. But I must learn to forgive her, too, as the good Lord says. Agnes tells me she is also poorly and spending all her time at Castle Rising.

We are two old crones together, then; though I seem to remember she is much younger than I. The King forgave her in time, of course, gave her an allowance of three thousand pounds a year, and allowed her back to court. I believe she had Queen Philippa to thank for that. We do not communicate. I suspect Agnes has become friendly with her, though she swears to me this is not the case and she was only invited to dinner once with her husband, the new Pembroke, so it would have been insulting not to attend.

It seems all is forgotten now. But I do not forget. It is true the King did not detain me long in Hampshire, but I shall never have any love for that county. Nevertheless, he has restored my grandson's status. He has even made him one of his most special knights in the new Order of the Garter. What a ludicrous name! Whatever was wrong with the Round Table?

The most surprising thing of all is that, a couple of years ago, the King made a public declaration that the judgement of treason made on Roger Mortimer, the First Earl of March, was made in error! He gave a cloth of gold to be laid in Roger's chantry chapel in Leintwardine, and actually visited himself to say prayers of contrition. Well, of course he always knew his father had never been murdered, and certainly not by that red-hot poker nonsense. But I was astonished.

He never punished Thomas Berkeley or John Maltravers for their failure to keep Edward safe, either. Maurice, who is also in this 'Garter', told me that the King went to Cologne to meet his father and they became reconciled. After a fashion. He still made sure his father stayed in that Italian monastery, and no doubt paid the monks to keep a close eye on him. Well, I am glad that Edward fulfilled his desire to see the Shrine of the Three Kings, and I am sure he forgave his son in the end, as I forgave him.

Not only is my grandson Roger a friend of the King, and even closer to his first son, the Black Prince, but his little boy, Edmund, is now betrothed to the King's second son's daughter, Philippa of Clarence. He is going to marry into the full Royal family! Who would have believed that, twenty years ago? I think that even my Roger would have been astounded, though extremely gratified; it is not just about Earls now, but Dukes and such like!

I doze for a while and then I wake. I do not know where Hilda is, nor the young girl she has got to help her, but it is getting dark in here. They said it was not time to light the candles, but they would for my sake, if I wished it. I do not believe the girl has done it, unless they have gone out. Mind you, I can still smell candle wax. They must be burning very dimly. I shall speak severely to Hilda about the quality of the candles. I feel a growing cold, too, when formerly I was warm. Has the fire burnt low as well? It is not like them to neglect these matters.

I open my mouth to call the girl but no sound comes out. How strange that is!

Ah, at last the door is opening. Has the girl come back? But no…it is not a girl standing in the doorway. It is a young man, with hair and eyebrows black as a raven, and eyes that are deep brown, like pools I might drown in. Surely it cannot be? Roger? My Lord Roger, and not my grandson who is still in France with the army – for I do occasionally mistake them. The handsome figure smiles at me and nods, just as he used to once – before all those terrible events occurred.

"How are you here?" I ask. I still make no coherent sound, but he seems to understand me.

"Well, you did ask me to come back," he says, "and in the end, I have. But oh, dear Joan, you have kept me waiting so long. Twenty-six years!"

"Serves you right!" I mutter crossly.

"You never remarried."

"Not for want of being asked! They were all after my wealth. I sent them all packing."

"Then will you come now? Remember, you used to say we should go on a pilgrimage to Santiago de Compostela for St James? I promised we would, but we never did. I can do it now. Will you come too?"

"Perhaps," I say.

But I know full well what is happening now, and why he looks so young. I have to go. He has come for me and he is my fate, in eternity.

When Hilda returns a few minutes later with a pitcher of fresh water, she is brought up short by the silence in the room. Previously, her mistress's breathing was long and harsh, though interrupted. She stands at the foot of the bed, listening. There is nothing. She tiptoes softly up to the still figure. Putting down the water, she stretches over and gently closes Lady Joan's tired eyelids and open mouth, before crossing herself reverently. The young girl opens the door to join her when she calls, and looks questioningly at Hilda, who nods.

"The Lady Mortimer has gone to a better place," she says.

*****

But still the years come and go, rolling ever onwards. Joan's favourite grandson, Maurice, is severely wounded at Poitiers but survives to succeed his father as Baron Berkeley. Her other grandson, Roger, is not as fortunate, and dies on campaign at Rouvray in France, though not in battle. His son does marry Philippa of Clarence, however, and therefore enters the royal family.

Catherine Beauchamp, neé Mortimer, has a long and happy marriage and bears fifteen healthy children. She is eventually buried alongside her much-beloved husband, the Earl of Warwick.

King Edward the Third is not spared personal grief when his son, the Black Prince, dies after a long illness leaving only a young boy, Richard, to inherit the throne. He is supported loyally by Edmund Mortimer, the husband of the said Philippa of Clarence, but Richard is eventually forced to relinquish the throne and is starved to death in Pontefract Castle on the orders of a usurping Lancastrian king.

Two generations later, the male line of the Mortimers dies out. However, Anne Mortimer marries Richard, Earl of Cambridge, and is consequently mother to Richard, Duke of York, who fathers two kings – Edward IV and Richard III. And so the Mortimer genes do carry on into royalty, nurtured in the end by their womenfolk.

Scholars have found different versions of the Wigmore Chronicle, which are now housed safely in various academic libraries on both sides of the Atlantic. But they are all copies. The original manuscript, written by a canon of Wigmore Abbey, has never been found. Perhaps someone burnt it?

END

HISTORICAL NOTES

THIS IS A novel based on the premise that Edward II did not die in Berkeley Castle in 1327 but escaped, or was taken elsewhere.

There are now a number of eminent mediaeval historians who contest the long accepted version of events surrounding this unfortunate king's death. Their arguments are based on the lack of any sound evidence for murder, and its unlikelihood (especially regarding the method said to be used) plus a document known as the Fieschi letter, narrating Edward's escape and subsequent arrival in an Italian monastery.

I must acknowledge the arguments and scholarly work of Dr Ian Mortimer and Dr Kathryn Warner respectively here, whose factual knowledge has been invaluable in writing this novel. I would recommend their books in the list below for those readers who wish to find out more. I would not have been able to write this without first reading Ian's biography of Roger Mortimer and I must also thank him for supplying the family trees. Any mistakes or misconstruement of the facts are entirely mine.

I have tried to keep faithful to historical events and timelines, although I have taken some liberties. We do not know where Roger Mortimer went for his training in knighthood, for instance. I have chosen this as being to his uncle, Roger of Chirk, thinking about their closeness in later years. The two of them paid their homage to the new Prince of Wales in Kenilworth, rather than Conwy, but the selection of Conwy enabled me to insert some Welsh history.

The quoted rebuff to Edward when he thought the Scots were kneeling to ask for his mercy, before the battle at Bannockburn, is authentic, but was not said by either Roger Mortimer, although they were at the battle and likely to have been by the King's side. The younger Mortimer was indeed captured and tasked with returning the Royal seal and the shield.

It may also be that Roger visited Joan in Pembridge at an earlier date after her release, but the meeting is unlikely to have been a happy reunion. Likewise, we do not know that Lady Joan Mortimer ever kept a journal, although we do know she definitely could read and therefore probably write. She was probably arrested at Wigmore Abbey, rather than the castle, as an inventory of their goods was found there. Initially imprisoned in Hampshire, though the exact location is unknown, she was moved to Skipton Castle after her husband's escape from the Tower, and this is well documented.

Her daughter Margaret was married to Thomas Berkeley, and it did not seem to me beyond the realms of possibility that she may have visited her daughter there, and even been present when Edward is said to have died. Avice is a fictional character of course, but the corpse was embalmed by an unknown old woman, his body never viewed, and it was never displayed after leaving Berkeley. Neither did the young Edward III make any visitation to his father's magnificent tomb in Gloucester until 1341, a full fifteen years after the supposed death, though he did visit the chantry at Leintwardine much earlier with his gift of a cloth of gold when he restored the family fortunes of the Mortimers.

The poor Earl of Kent was beheaded as described in the novel, though Lady Joan is unlikely to have 'tipped him off' about Edward's survival, but who knows? Roger Mortimer did regret his treatment of Kent and confessed the Earl had been a victim of conspiracy. This was on the scaffold at Tyburn. No doubt Mortimer did this in an attempt to save his soul, as everyone in these times firmly believed in a God. Interestingly, he did not confess to ordering the murder of the king, at the same time.

Avice, Hywel, Brothers Benedict and Jerome are fictional characters, but all the others were actual historical people, including Father Richard Judas, despite his unlikely name. My apologies if I have not done their characters justice.

BIBLIOGRAPHY and ACKNOWLEDGEMENTS

Ian Mortimer: *The Greatest Traitor – The Life of Sir Roger Mortimer.* Jonathan Cape 2003. ISBN0-224-06249-2

Mediaeval Intrigue -Decoding Royal Conspiracies. Bloomsbury 2010. ISBN 978-1-4411-0269 0

The Times Traveller's Guide to Mediaeval England. Vintage Books 2008. ISBN9781-8459-5099-6

Kathryn Warner: *Edward II – The Unconventional King.* Amberley 2014. ISBN 978-1-4456-4120-1 hardback ISBN 978-1-4456-4132-4 e-book.
I would also highly recommend Dr Warner's blog on Edward II and her other books on the period.

Michael Potterton & Matthew Seaver (Editors): *Uncovering Mediaeval Trim -Archaeological excavations in and around Trim, Co. Meath.* Four Courts Press 2009. ISBN 978-1-84682-169-1

Margaret Wade Labarge: *Gascony -England's First Colony 1204-1453.* Hamish Hamilton 1980. ISBN0-241-1030-6

Gwen Seaborne: *Imprisoning Mediaeval Women -The Non-Judicial Confinement and abduction of Women in England c.1170-1509.* Ashgate 2011. ISBN 978-1-4094-1788-0 hardback ISBN 978-1-4094—1789-7 e-book

Kevin Goodman: *Ouch!-A History of Arrow Wound Treatment From Prehistory to the Nineteenth Century.* Bows, Blades & Battles Press 2012. ISBN 978-0-9571377-0-7

Thanks are also due to Barbara Wright for information on Joan's incarceration in Skipton. Also to Dr Paul Dryburgh, Fran

Norton and Margaret Woolmer for their feedback. Finally, I am indebted to Bob Fowke of You Caxton publications and to Shirley Mclellan, my diligent editor.

BV - #0022 - 240820 - C0 - 216/140/21 - PB - 9781913425241